Praise for Carolina

Canto

Winner of the Stonewall Book Award
Winner of the Reading Women Award

"A lyrical, richly sensory novel. . . . Pointedly relevant to our own dangerous age, Carolina De Robertis has gifted us a majestic work of song and imagination, a handbook to survival for us all."
— Cristina García, author of *Here in Berlin*

"A gripping, lush, and ultimately hopeful story of five queer women fighting for their lives under a dictatorship. It was the type of good that when I finished I thought: I am going to read everything [De Robertis] writes forever." — Madeline Miller, *PBS NewsHour*

"Rich and luscious, De Robertis' writing feels like a living thing, lapping over the reader like the ocean. Carefully crafted and expertly observed, each sentence is an elegant gift. . . . A stunning novel about queer love, womanhood, and personal and political revolution."
— *Kirkus Reviews* (starred review)

"*Cantoras* is a wise, brilliantly compassionate, wide-ranging novel about women in Uruguay and about the power and realities of love. Carolina De Robertis is a force: prepare to be astonished."
— R. O. Kwon, author of *The Incendiaries*

"It's impossible not to fall in love with these fierce 'girlwomen'— queer, courageous, and adventurous—as they find freedom in their relationships with each other while living under a ruthless dictatorship." — Angie Cruz, *Vanity Fair*

CAROLINA DE ROBERTIS

Cantoras

Carolina De Robertis, a writer of Uruguayan origins, is the author of *The Gods of Tango*, *Perla*, and the international bestseller *The Invisible Mountain*. Her novels have been translated into seventeen languages and have garnered a Stonewall Book Award, Italy's Rhegium Julii Prize, and numerous other honors. A recipient of a National Endowment for the Arts Fellowship, she is also a translator of Latin American and Spanish literature and editor of the anthology *Radical Hope: Letters of Love and Dissent in Dangerous Times*. In 2017, the Yerba Buena Center for the Arts named De Robertis to its 100 List of "people, organizations, and movements that are shaping the future of culture." She teaches at San Francisco State University and lives in Oakland, California, with her wife and two children.

www.carolinaderobertis.com

Cantoras

Cantoras

CAROLINA DE ROBERTIS

VINTAGE BOOKS
A Division of Penguin Random House LLC
New York

FIRST VINTAGE BOOKS EDITION, JUNE 2020

Copyright © 2019 by Carolina De Robertis

All rights reserved. Published in the United States by Vintage Books, a division
of Penguin Random House LLC, New York, and distributed in Canada by
Penguin Random House Canada Limited, Toronto. Originally published in
hardcover in the United States by Alfred A. Knopf, a division of
Penguin Random House LLC, New York, in 2019.

Vintage and colophon are registered trademarks of Penguin Random House LLC.

The Library of Congress has cataloged the Knopf edition as follows:
Name: De Robertis, Carolina, author.
Title: Cantoras / Carolina De Robertis.
Description: First edition. | New York : Alfred A. Knopf, 2019.
Identifiers: LCCN 2018051196
Classification: LCC PS3604.E129 C36 2019 | DDC 813/.6—dc23
LC record available at https://lccn.loc.gov/2018051196

Vintage Books Trade Paperback ISBN: 978-0-525-56343-3
eBook ISBN: 978-0-525-52170-9

Book design by M. Kristen Bearse

www.vintagebooks.com

Printed in the United States of America
6th Printing

*Para las chicas
and to all queers and women
who have lived
outside*

I was determined at all costs to become a person who would love without boundaries.

—Qiu Miaojin, *Notes of a Crocodile*

Have you never carried inside a dormant star
That burned you wholly without shining?

—Delmira Agustini, "The Ineffable"

Contents

Part One

1977–1979

I

Escape

THE FIRST TIME—which would become legend among them—
they entered in darkness. Night enfolded the sand dunes. Stars clamored around a meager slice of moon.

They would find nothing in Cabo Polonio, the cart driver said: no
electricity, and no running water. The cart driver lived in a nearby village but made that trip twice a week to supply the little grocery store
that served the lighthouse keeper and a few scattered fishermen. There
was no road in; you had to know your way. It was lonely out there, he
remarked, glancing at them sideways, smiling to bare his remaining
teeth, hinting, though he stopped short of asking any questions about
what they were doing, why they were traveling to this of all places,
just the five of them, without a man, and it was just as well because
they wouldn't have had a decent answer. The trees gradually receded,
but clumps of brush still reared their tousled heads from the smooth
slopes as if just being born. The horse-drawn cart moved slowly,
methodically, creaking with the weight of them, hoofs muffled in the
loose sand. They were stunned by the sand dunes, the vast life of them.
Each traveler became lost in her own thoughts. Their five-hour bus
ride down the highway already seemed a distant memory, dislodged
from this place, like a dream from which they'd now awakened. The
dunes rippled out around them, a spare landscape, the landscape of

another planet, as if in leaving Montevideo they'd also managed to leave Earth, like that rocket that some years ago had taken men to the moon, only they were not men, and this was not the moon, it was something else, they were something else, uncharted by astronomers. The lighthouse rose before them, with its slowly circling light. They approached the cape along a beach, the ocean to their right, shimmering in the dark, in constant conversation with the sand. The cart passed a few small, boxlike huts, fishermen's huts, black against the black sky. They descended from the cart, paid the driver, and carried their packs stuffed with food and clothes and blankets as they wandered around, staring into the night. The ocean surrounded them on three sides of this cape, this almost-island, a thumb extending off the hand of the known world. At last they found the right place, or the closest thing to it, an abandoned house that could act as windbreak for their camp. It was half-built, with walls only partially constructed and no roof. Four unfinished walls and open sky. Inside, there was plenty of space for them; it would have been an ample house if it hadn't been left to be eaten by the elements. After they set up their things, they went outside and built a fire. A breeze rose. It cooled their skin as whiskey warmed it, flask moving from hand to hand. Cheese sandwiches and salami for dinner around the campfire. The thrill of lighting the wood, keeping it burning. Laughter spiked their conversation, and when it lulled, the silence had a glow to it, crackled by flames. They were happy. They were not used to being happy. The strange feeling kept them up too late together, giddy with victory and amazement. They had done it. They were out. They had shed the city like a hazardous garment and come to the edge of the world.

Finally they drifted to their blanket piles and slept to the gentle pulse of waves.

But deep in the night, Paz startled awake. The sky glittered. The moon was low, about to set. The ocean filled her ears and she took it as an invitation, impossible to resist. She slid out of her covers and walked down over the rocks, toward the shore. The ocean roared like a hunger, reaching for her feet.

She was the youngest in the group, sixteen years old. She'd lived under the dictatorship since she was twelve. She hadn't known air could taste like this, so wide, so open. Her body a welcome. Skin awake. The world was more than she had known, even if only for this instant, even if only in this place. She let her lips part and the breeze glided into her mouth, fresh on her tongue, full of stars. How did so much brightness fit in the night sky? How could so much ocean fit inside her? Who was she in this place? Standing on that shore, staring out at the Atlantic, with those women who were not like other women sleeping a few meters away, she felt a sensation so foreign that she almost collapsed under its spell. She felt free.

*

Flaca was the first to wake up the next morning. She walked to the bare window of the abandoned house and looked out at the landscape around her, so different by day, the great blue ocean visible on all three sides as if they were on a small island, unbound from the rest of Uruguay. Rocks and dry grass, the water beyond, a lighthouse and a smattering of huts in the distance, homes of fishermen and a box of a store somewhere among them. She'd look for it today. She'd go exploring.

Curiosity flared up in her, a rare feeling she'd grown used to suppressing, automatically, without thought. The city, Montevideo, was not a place to be curious, but a place to shrink into yourself and mind your own business, to be careful, to keep your curtains drawn, to keep your mouth shut with strangers because any one of them could report you to the government and then you could disappear, and you could see it in passersby on the street, the flattened gazes, the postures of fear so familiar that they'd become ordinary. She barely noticed, anymore, the constant tightness across her back, which sharpened whenever an army truck lumbered by or a police officer stopped someone in her peripheral vision, then receded back to its low-level presence. Here, now, she became aware of it only as an absence, like the hum of a refrigerator that you only hear when it stops.

To go exploring.

With the others, if they'd come.

She turned to look at them: four sleeping women. Girls. Girl-women. Was it possible. Were they here. She stared for a long time. Malena lay faceup, mouth slightly agape, eyebrows raised as if her dreams surprised her. About a meter away, Romina curled into herself, like a soldier protecting something—a jewel, a missive—hidden under her shirt. Even asleep, she managed to look tense. Would she ever relax, or would she stay tight as a spring throughout their week here on the beach? There was something comforting about her tension, guilty as this made Flaca feel, considering everything her friend had been through. Romina had always looked out for Flaca, and her vigorous friendship had helped Flaca take risks, take leaps, set out on adventures like this one. Adventures like Anita, who lay just a meter or so away, her luxurious hair pulled into a long, loose braid for sleep. Hair that, if unwound from its braid, fanned out like a lush brown world that could be plunged into, inhaled, a scent to get drunk on. But not now. They weren't alone. Beyond them, at the outer edge of their small group, lay Paz, a *chiquilina,* almost a child. Perhaps they shouldn't have brought her. Perhaps Romina had been right (as she often was). And yet, Flaca hadn't seen any other choice. When she'd first seen Paz at the butcher shop, she'd seemed so out of her element in the ordinary world that Flaca had felt a stab of recognition. Girls like her had to be saved from themselves. They had to be saved from the horrors of normalcy, the cage of not-being. Which was the cage of this whole country and all the more so for people like them. Paz had reminded Flaca of her own early adolescence. She'd struck up friendly conversation. At first, the girl had shown little outer reaction to the friendliness, answering questions laconically and refusing Flaca's first invitation to come behind the counter for a round of yerba mate. But even then, her eyes had spoken everything.

Flaca walked beyond the half-built walls to gather kindling for a fire. First order of business: heat the water for yerba mate. That was breakfast. She'd kept just enough water aside last night for a good long round of *mate* for everyone. They'd have to go find more water later today. As she arranged the kindling in the ring of stones she'd assembled yesterday, she gave thanks, again, to her father for having taught her how to light a fire, all those *parrilla* Sundays, even though, almost every time, he bemoaned the fact that he had no son to share his skills with. "Three children and no boys," he'd say, shrugging, "ah well, what can you do about fate?" She, Flaca, was the only one who showed any interest in learning to get the flames going for long enough to turn the logs to embers over which the meat could roast all afternoon. Flames up, embers down and glowing. She wasn't his ideal student, but still, she knew that some fathers would never teach a daughter, that she was lucky, that she wouldn't be able to build this fire now if her father had been a lesser man.

Romina stirred just as the water was approaching a boil.

"Good morning," Flaca said. "How did you know the *mate* was ready? You have sensors in your brain?"

"*Mate* antennae. I'm an alien."

"Of course you are. From Planet Yerba."

"Sounds like home to me." Romina squinted out at the ocean. "This place is so damn beautiful."

"I was hoping you'd say that." Flaca beamed. "How did you sleep?"

"Like a rock. Actually, on the rocks. They probably slept better than I did—the rocks, I mean."

"Maybe you'll sleep better tonight."

"Oh, that's all right. I've slept in worse places."

That shut them both up for a few moments. Flaca filled the gourd and passed it to Romina, who drank the *mate* down until the leaves gurgled. Then she passed the gourd back to Flaca, who filled it again and took her turn drinking through the *bombilla,* the metal straw. The grassy, bitter taste soothed her, woke her mind. This was the first time that Romina had referred to her recent arrest of her own volition, and it was a relief to see the ease in her posture, to hear her make a wry remark about it only two weeks after the fact. Flaca hadn't known how to broach the subject, trying out the varied approaches of affectionate words, righteous rage, and careful silence since Romina had returned to the land of the living, but no matter what she said or did, she was always met with the same blank eyes. The truth was that, when Romina was arrested, two weeks ago—on the Day of the Dead, no less—Flaca had been terrified. Most people who were arrested didn't return. There was a neighbor whom she hadn't seen in years whose daily existence she fought hard not to think about. And there was Romina's brother, of course, and others—regular customers from the butcher shop, a cousin of her sister's longtime friend—but none of the other people she knew who'd been taken were as close to her as Romina, who had been her best friend since they first met at a Communist Party meeting in early 1973, when Flaca was seventeen years old and the whole world still felt like a long story waiting to unfurl before her, largely because she didn't read the newspaper or follow politics, so that even with the occasional evening curfews and the sudden presence of soldiers on the streets, she'd been able to see the world as more or less normal, the country's problems as possible to fix in the long run. These had been the benefits of not paying attention. In those days she didn't see politics as having anything to do with her, or with her hopes for the future, which, at that point, involved finding a way to stay alive while also being herself. She'd only gone to the Communist Party meeting out of boredom and because the flyer had been handed to her by a pretty university student with glossy, intoxicating hair, and Flaca had wanted to see her again. The pretty university student was not at the meeting, which was interminable and chaotic, full of passionate monologues from young and old men who took pastries from trays without saying thank you to the women and girls who brought them. Communism, Flaca thought, must not be for me. The best part of the meeting was Romina, one of the enthused purveyors of pastries, eighteen years old. Romina's hair was not glossy—it was, in fact, just the opposite, a dark riot of curls. Also good to drown in. There was something about her, a kind of billowing intensity to her gaze that made Flaca want to stare at her all night and then some. Toward the end of the meeting, Romina finally had a chance to speak, and she did

so with such a passion that Flaca became officially obsessed. She buried that obsession under a mantle of friendship—best friendship, fast
friendship, tell-each-other-all friendship—for a month, until finally,
one night, they kissed in the bathroom of a nightclub in Ciudad Vieja
after dancing with a string of hapless young men. She was stupefied to
discover that this could happen, that a girl could kiss her back. It was
as good as in her dreaming. Better. The world turned inside out to fit
her dreams. Between the world of boy and the world of girl, they'd
found a chasm no one spoke of. They fell into it together. They met in
their homes when their fathers were at work and their mothers out at
a card game or the hair salon, the sex furtive, sharp with the danger of
being discovered. On three glorious occasions, they saved up pesos for
a cheap motel room where the bored clerks assumed them to be sisters
when they checked in and where they never wasted a single hour on
sleep. They took delight in each other in absolute secret. Then the coup
happened, and Romina disappeared. Her parents disclosed nothing;
when Flaca called, they hung up as soon as they heard Romina's name.
Flaca didn't dare knock on their door. Romina, arrested: her dreams
filled with images of Romina's body twisted or bruised beyond recognition. To distract herself, and to drown out the despair that droned
through every waking minute, she took advantage of her after-school
work at her parents' butcher shop to seduce a restless young housewife with acrobatic thighs and a full-lipped librarian who worked at
the Biblioteca Nacional and demanded to be spanked with her gold-
embossed edition of Dante's *Inferno*. It seemed to Flaca that both of
them were gripped by a furious erotic charge unleashed by those days
of chaos and danger, though neither lover ever referred directly to the
coup. She had never seduced a woman who was so much older than
her before; the thrill of it helped her survive the terror of her days.
She was only seventeen years old but she'd been watching men for a
long time, the way they acted as if they knew the answers to questions
before they were asked, as if they carried the answers in their mouths
and trousers. Her lovers seemed to forget how young she was, perhaps because they wanted to, hungry as they were for distraction and

pleasure as the world spun out of control. For the rest of her life, Flaca would wonder whether this period shaped her into a Don Juan, or simply uncovered what was already inside. She would never settle on an answer. When Romina surfaced again—she hadn't been arrested, she'd been hiding at her aunt's home in far-flung Tacuarembó, where no one would have thought to look for her, she was in one piece—she quickly discovered these two dalliances, as Flaca made no attempt to lie. Romina exploded. She did not speak to Flaca for a year. Finally, one day, she came to the butcher shop, and Flaca's heart pounded in her chest. By then, the housewife had shrunk back into her marriage in a panic, while the librarian had expanded her repertoire of ways to mix books with sex. And Flaca had missed Romina every day.

"Don't get your hopes up," Romina said. "I love you, and you're my friend, but there'll be no more *chucu-chucu* for us, not ever."

It was enough for Flaca. She didn't press the question. From then on, their bond was sure and unconditional. They told each other their secrets and turned to each other whenever they needed help.

With the passing of years, Romina had seemed safe. But then, just two weeks ago now, Romina had disappeared for the second time, and Flaca had been possessed by fear that she'd never see her again, that she'd been caught up in the great hidden machine. She was wrong about the first fear, but she was right about the second. After three nights gone, Romina reappeared again at the side of a road at the outskirts of the city, almost but not quite naked, and more or less in one piece, with just a few cigarette burns and a new glassy look in her eyes to separate her from the woman she was before. Flaca was flooded with gratitude to have her back, a gratitude shot through with rage and pain at the cigarettes, at whatever had given rise to the glassy look. She wanted to offer something, a way to forget, a way out, a way through. Something special, she thought. A reprieve, an escape.

"We're going to celebrate," she told Romina over *mate* at the butcher shop.

Romina stared at her as though she were crazy; it was the first time she'd made eye contact that afternoon. "What the hell is there to celebrate?"

"The fact that you're alive."

Romina didn't answer.

Flaca pulled out a map of the Uruguayan coast and spread it on the counter where she usually wrapped meat for customers. "There's this place I've heard about, from my tía, this beach. A beautiful beach."

"I've been to Punta del Este. I'm never going back."

"Bah! I'm not talking about Punta del Este. This is the opposite. No glitzy nightclubs, no expensive bikinis, no luxury apartments. Actually, there's no luxury at all in the place I'm talking about."

"None?" Romina couldn't keep her curiosity from showing.

Flaca smiled, thinking, it's working, this project is going to take her out of the sinkhole in her mind, keep her busy with something else. "None at all. There's a lighthouse, a few fishermen's shacks—that's about it. There isn't even electricity out there, or running water. It's all candles and oil lamps—"

"What about flashlights? Do people use flashlights, or are there no batteries out there either?"

"I don't know. We could take flashlights. Look, don't worry. The real thing is that we'll be far away from the city, from the noise of—all of this. It'll be fun, a kind of a party. In the wilderness."

"With no running water? What are we going to do, shit behind trees?"

"I don't know yet. But there are fishermen there, I'm sure they shit somewhere! Anyway, what makes it a celebration is that we're out there together. And—there's a woman I'd like to bring with me, too."

"Aha! So that's what this is about!"

Flaca put her hands up in an exaggerated gesture of innocence. "I have no idea what you mean."

"You just want to have a romantic escapade, seducer that you are, and you're dragging me out on some lovers' escape—"

"If I wanted it to be like that, do you think I'd be inviting you out there with me?"

Romina stopped, and registered the hurt on Flaca's face. "I'm sorry, Flaca. I was joking."

"This is *our* trip, Romina. Actually, to tell you the truth, I'm terrified of going. I've never lived without running water or electricity for a single day of my life. I have no idea how we're going to shit or what will happen to us. Maybe we'll starve, maybe we'll freeze, maybe we'll hate each other by the end, I don't know. It's not really a vacation at all."

"Then what is it?"

"I don't know. An adventure. No. More than that. A test."

"A test of what?"

"Of—staying alive. Of coming back to life. Because—"

She stopped and stared at Romina. The words caught in her throat.

"Say it," Romina whispered. "Just say it, Flaca."

"I'm dead here in the city. Everybody is, we're all walking corpses. I have to get out of here to find out whether I can still be alive. Montevideo is a fucking prison, a huge open-air prison, and I'm sorry if that sounds like I'm reducing what you've been through but—"

"Shut up for a moment," Romina said. She reached for Flaca's pack of cigarettes on the counter. Flaca struck a match and gave her a light. Her hands were shaking and so, she realized, were Romina's. They both pretended not to notice. Romina inhaled.

"Romina, I'm sorry, I—"

"I said shut up."

Flaca nodded. She lit a cigarette of her own. A good deep scratching of her lungs.

"I understand," Romina said, eyes on the smoke. "I'll come."

And so the trip had come together. In the evenings, they met in Flaca's bedroom to plan, as her parents watched television just down the hall. Flaca spread three different maps open on her bed, trying to get the lay of the land, and started various haphazard lists of the things they'd need to survive out in nature. On their last night of planning, the night before their departure, as Flaca was packing and organizing her rucksack, Romina brought a friend over: Malena, a woman whom Romina had met in a plaza near the university, during the lunch hour, each of them eating empanadas from the nearby bakery. They had a parallel ritual of buying one ham and cheese and one creamed corn empanada and saving a bit of crust for the pigeons; this had led, naturally, to conversation. Malena was an office worker and looked the part: she was efficient, prim, tidy. Pretty, yes, with a sensuous mouth and almond eyes, but her bun was as tight as her smile. She was three years older than Romina, twenty-five, and dressed like someone twice her age. That matron's cardigan. Flaca would not have guessed that this woman was one of them.

"Malena's never seen a sea lion," Romina declared, as if that settled everything.

Flaca didn't contest this until Malena went down the hall to use the bathroom. "Are you sure about this?"

"It's fine. She's fine. She's one of us—"

"Have you asked her?"

"Do you ask women what they are before you bed them?"

"You're going to *bed* with her?"

"No—not that it's any of your business."

Flaca sighed. She couldn't fight Romina and win; her friend knew her too well.

"Anyway," Romina went on, "you're bringing what's-her-name, your latest housewife, so it's only fair."

"She's more than just the latest housewife. She's—"

"Aha! So she *is* a housewife! I knew it."

"—she's different."

Romina looked skeptical. "Different, how?"

"I don't know. She just is." Flaca fidgeted. She'd waited as long as she could to break this last bit of news. "Also, eh, I've invited one more person."

"Who?"

"A girl I met at the butcher shop."

Romina laughed. "And what's your what's-her-name going to have to say about *that*?"

"No—it's not like that. With this girl, I mean. She's—don't get angry, Romina? She's young."

"How young?"

Flaca looked down.

"Flaca. How old is she?"

She'd meant to lie to Romina, to keep this detail out of sight, but what was the use of lying to someone who could see right into you? It always caught up with her in the end. And, with all the lies and silence Flaca relied on to keep her life intact, it was this very being-seen-into that made her bond with Romina as essential as breath. "Sixteen."

"Flaca."

"But she's definitely one of us. And she seems to be alone."

"Did you ask her? Whether she's one of us?"

Flaca stared at a stain on the wall as if it might suddenly reveal secret hieroglyphs. "Checkmate," she finally said.

"This is crazy," Romina said. "Absolutely reckless. Five of—you know—of us? Have you ever done such a thing before?"

Flaca considered this. *Us.* The word glided through her mind like a leaf, or a stone, troubling the waters. Over the years, she'd encountered a range of women who could be seen as part of this *us,* whether they'd admit to it or not. She and Romina trusted each other, had forged a bond, a miraculous secret society of two. But five. Five? All in one place, all of them admitting to what they were? Not that everyone on this trip was doing so yet, but wasn't joining the trip a kind of incrimination? Five, together. She'd never heard of such a thing. Here, now, in this Uruguay, you could be arrested for holding gatherings of five or more people in your home without a permit. As for homosexuality, it was a crime that could land you in the same prisons as the guerrillas and the journalists, prison with torture, prison without trial. There was no law against homosexuality, but that didn't matter because the regime did whatever it wanted, laws or no, and also because there was a law against *affronts to decency* and since long before the coup few things had been more of an affront, more repugnant. No worse insult for a man than *puto.* The men were more reviled. And more visible. "No."

"You amaze me, Flaca."

"We'll be all right," she said, uncertainly. "It's not like the city out there. There's no one to snitch, to know what we're doing or—what we are."

"How do you know?"

"From what my aunt told me."

Romina stared at her as if making a furious calculation. "This beach of yours. It's either going to be Ithaca, or Scylla."

There she goes again with her literary references, Flaca thought. It was from the *Odyssey,* wasn't it? She'd had to read it in school. One of those was the site of a shipwreck, the other one was home, but which was which? She couldn't remember; unlike Romina, she'd been a poor student, hadn't really cared.

Malena was back, scanning their faces as if sensing that she'd missed something. Had she been listening in the hall? How long ago had the toilet flushed?

"What do you think, Malena," Romina said, glancing wryly at each of them in turn. "Are we headed to Ithaca or Scylla?"

"I don't know," Malena said, with a gravity that surprised them both.

The three women stared at each other in silence for several seconds, which stretched and ached around them.

"I suppose," Malena went on, "the real question is, which one are we looking for?"

*

Where in God's name am I? Anita thought the second she opened her eyes. Confusion spilled through her as she stared at the sky above her, blue and already growing hard with sun. She sat up and looked around. An incomplete house. Rocks, ocean. Flaca and Romina were a few paces away, sitting, drinking *mate* together in an easy silence. Anita had been nervous to meet Romina, her lover's best friend, who, it seemed, was also her lover's ex-lover; to meet her lover's ex-lover seemed a combustible thing, something no woman should ever voluntarily walk into, a murder waiting to happen, but here, the rules seemed different, distorted, as if left to melt in the sun. The way Flaca had talked about Romina made her sound less like a jealous ex-lover and more like a trusted sister, one whose approval would be necessary if this thing was to last.

Do I want it to last?

The question seared her. It had been an insanity, to strike this up with Flaca, to return her gaze. It had never once occurred to her to think of a woman the way one thinks of a man—not consciously, not with the serious part of her mind—until she saw that look in Flaca's eyes as she handed over the skillfully wrapped package of raw meat. That linger. That message of hunger, a declaration of wanting, all in a look. She hadn't known that women were capable of it. She expected it from men, saw it in them every time she walked down a city street, but—from a woman? It caught her off-balance. She pretended not to notice and quickly tucked the meat into her shopping bag. All night, as she cooked and nodded at her husband's long complaints about work and washed the dishes while he watched the television news anchors tell their same dull lies, she thought about that gaze. What it might mean, what it could possibly mean, for a woman to look at another woman that way. Perhaps she'd made it up, misunderstood, she thought as she dried wineglasses. It was nothing. She was being stupid. No reason to keep thinking of that butcher with her lean grace and muscular arms. She heard a splintering sound, and only then did she notice that the wineglass had burst under the pressure of her hands.

She went back to the same butcher shop the following afternoon, even though it was out of her way, not her usual spot, a place she'd ducked into spontaneously on the way home from tea at a friend's house. She was returning just to be sure, she told herself. Just to understand.

Flaca had been there and ready and now Anita's days were filled with Flaca or with thoughts of her when they were apart.

The horror on her friends' faces if they should ever find out. If she could still call them friends, those childhood classmates she'd played with because they grew up on the same block in the sleepy neighborhood of La Blanqueada. Each of them had grown up to become a good wife, a mother, with carefully done hair and too much floral perfume. She saw them sometimes on Sundays, when they all went back to their parents' homes for family luncheons, and found each other in the neighborhood plaza afterward. They were dolled up, but in a dutiful and tidy way, like old ladies in training. *What's new with you?* they'd ask, eager for gossip in which other people could be cast as the villains. Once, when Flaca was making love to her, Anita had imagined these childhood friends gathered against the far wall, awash in horror, and she'd come with a ferocity that had astounded them both.

There were parts of her own self she hadn't known existed, that were locked up tight until Flaca came along with her glinting key.

Do I want it to last?

She didn't know the answer, didn't want to know, not yet. She knew only that she wanted to have the choice to go on. She wanted to win. She'd always loved to win. She'd picked her husband out of a flock of men who would have married her in a heartbeat. She was the prize, back then. Now, five years later, she felt old, used up at twenty-seven, her life already shrunken and defined until she died. She wanted to escape that. Wanted to follow Flaca into a reality where more was possible: joy, for example. Expansion. And she wanted something else, too, something nebulous, something aching: to understand this secret club she'd stumbled into, this strange new labyrinth of women. To know what, if anything, it had to do with her own life. Was she one of them? Would they accept her as such? Who will I be, she thought, after seven days alone with these strange women? The question frightened her; she pushed the fear aside, and stood up.

She stretched, and peered out of the window. The landscape stretched before her, green land rolling out to rocks and sandy beaches, languorous against the blue. There was so much blue. The ocean glistened, vast, majestic. Something about it hurt her. *"Por Dios,"* she said.

"Good morning," Flaca said.

They looked at each other. That burn in her eyes. Anita couldn't look away.

"Oh, for God's sake, you two," Romina said, though not without good humor. "Isn't it a bit early for that?"

"It's never too early," Flaca said, "to say good morning. Which is all I said."

"Oh!" Romina crowed. "Flaca the innocent."

"Why not?" Flaca grinned, poured another *mate,* and handed it to Anita.

Romina snorted, but she smiled at Anita.

Anita sipped the *mate,* relieved and bewildered by Romina's ease. "I didn't know it would be this beautiful here."

"That's exactly how I feel," Romina said.

"What," Flaca said. "Neither of you believed me?"

"Oh, calm down." Romina smacked Flaca's arm. "In any case, you hadn't been here before either, right?"

"True."

"So you didn't really know."

"No," Flaca admitted. "I didn't. But my aunt described it so vividly that I had an idea." Enough of one to drag you all out here like a mad-woman, she thought.

"I'd never heard of Cabo Polonio." Anita finished her gourd and handed it back. "All my life, I thought I knew about the beaches of Rocha, or at least knew their names. But this?"

"The best part," Romina said, "is how many other people haven't heard of it either. It's like we've traveled into a zone where nobody can find us."

They were silent for a moment. Anita fidgeted, unsure of what to say. She knew of Romina's recent arrest and had sat with Flaca two weeks ago as Flaca fought back tears and panic over what could be happening, where her friend was, whether she'd ever see her again. Romina's quick return had been the most profound relief—but, still, this didn't mean that horrors hadn't happened. Like everyone else she knew, Anita had learned, in recent years, to avoid the subjects of arrests, torture, terror, censorship. Was Romina making a direct reference here, or an accidental one? She didn't know her well enough to tell.

"That," Flaca said, cradling the gourd as she took her turn drinking, "is exactly the point."

After a few more rounds of *mate,* Malena woke up and joined their circle. Flaca took out remnants of cheese, bread, and salami, sliced them into pieces, and passed them around. They chatted easily, about their sleep, the ride in over the sand dunes, the astonishing landscape around them, its oddness, its beauty, its absolute lack of a toilet, were they really going to dig holes to shit in? We are, Flaca said, and the shovel is ready, who wants to start? Nobody wanted to start. Everyone's bowels were tied up. In endless knots, Romina said, like my mother's macramé. They laughed over their macramé bowels. They laughed at Paz, the girl, still sleeping through all of it, even as the sun rose up over her.

"How can she sleep with the sun on her face?" Anita said. "And it's already so hot."

"Especially for November," Flaca said. "Our first heat wave of summer."

"It's not summer yet!" Anita said.

Flaca smiled. "Close enough."

"Close enough for what?"

"Heat," Flaca said.

"Oh, stop it, you two!" Romina picked up a few pebbles and threw them at Flaca, but she was laughing. "You are the worst. Both of you."

Anita felt her face flush. She glanced at Flaca, hoping she'd say something to dispel the mood. But Flaca didn't seem awkward at all; she was grinning at Romina, full of ease and mischief. So this was how they were together. Now that they weren't surrounded by strangers—in the city, on the bus down the coast—this was their language. She looked at Malena, who'd watched the exchange in silence, her hair already pinned back in a tidy bun, when had she done that? And why bother with uptight hairstyles in a place like this? It made no sense, unless the pinning of hair was a kind of armor that Malena was loathe to let go. She seemed guarded that way, this Malena; the kind of woman who thought far more than she said aloud.

"I am just saying," Flaca said, "that it's going to be a hot day."

"Oho, and aren't you glad of it," Romina said.

"Well, I was hoping to go for a swim."

"Me too," Anita said.

"Then go." Romina took the *mate* and drank.

"Now?"

"Why not? Nothing's stopping you. We can do what we want, isn't that why we came?"

Anita considered this. She glanced up at the sun—a thing her mother had always told her not to do—then out at the southern beach. "I think we should go in search of supplies first. It looks like a fishing boat is coming in—over there, look, toward the beach."

They all looked. A dark red speck on the water, gliding slowly toward the shore.

"Maybe they'll sell us some of their catch." Anita looked at Flaca. "Isn't that what you said we were going to do? Buy fish from the fishermen? You had a whole plan."

"To make fish appear," Romina said.

"Like Jesus Christ," Malena said.

Romina laughed, and Anita joined her. Malena stared at them in surprise for a moment, as if she hadn't seen the humor in her own words, then tentatively smiled. Flaca felt at once flustered at being the butt of the joke, and also proud at having built a circle of women that was getting along so well. She'd hoped they would, but she hadn't expected this, for them to gang up in their teasing, and on the first day. It had to be a good sign.

"Or like a pilot. *Nuestra pilota,*" Romina said, mock-saluting like a sailor.

"We'll find fish," Flaca said, uncertainly. "And there's that grocery. But we should start with the boats."

Anita stood. The other women watched her legs unfold languorously under her long, diaphanous skirt; Anita felt their eyes, warm, keen, like the eyes of men only coming from women and so made new. The hot sharp pleasure of it. "I'll go talk to them."

"I'll go too," Flaca said quickly. "We need water, and if they can supply us, I can carry it."

"I'll come too, Pilota," Romina said, pleased with the new nickname that teased and paid tribute to her friend at the same time. "We certainly wouldn't want this beautiful woman to go unaccompanied."

Flaca looked down sheepishly, then up at Anita, smiling.

Something lurched inside Anita then, the wild part of herself that kept getting wilder—the thing that Flaca had unlocked with her glinting key and her swagger, *oh, what's this over here inside you, let's open it, shall we, and have a look.* That impish smile of Flaca's. The things that followed that smile when they were alone. Who she herself became under Flaca's hands: the radiance and savagery of it. How it spooled out, ravenous, seeming infinite, until time put up its borders and she rolled it all back into a corner of herself so she could make room for the good girl, the good wife, every picture the good wife—only now, today, for the first time, things were different, as she didn't have to make even a centimeter of space for the good wife for seven days, seven blisteringly sweet beach days where there were no toilets and no telephones and no husbands.

"Come with me, then," Anita said.

And so they went: Flaca, Anita, and Romina, leaving Malena to watch over the fire and the sleeping girl.

Romina felt buoyant as she walked across the grass. Perhaps, she thought, this is all that life can give us, all it can give me, the most voluptuous gift it will ever offer. A day. A day in which the boundaries of you can expand to fit the sky, to fit the sky inside yourself, and no city streets no kidnap fears no familial duties can hem you in, shrink you down, curl you tight inside. She was walking over grass, toward a sloping path. She was draped in sunlight. She was free, breathing, stripped of pretense, untethered from the lies of everyday survival. She was walking with a friend and her lover. Their lust crackled in the air, made it shimmer, and even though it wasn't hers, it flushed her with a kind of happiness. They too were untethered. They too were real. How long had she had it in her, this hunger to expand, this need for space? This need to breathe all the way into the bottom of her lungs. The city was a fist that grasped you tightly; there was always something sitting against your chest, hard as lead, pushing you closed. She closed. She shut down. She had learned to live inside a shell covering, tender parts hidden inside. Fear had become so familiar that she could no longer see it, couldn't sense its borders, couldn't tell how deeply it had seeped into her conscious mind. In Montevideo, the air itself was a hostile creature, lying in wait around you, breathing, invisible, a threat. People didn't speak to each other anymore. The grocer didn't smile or meet her eye as he wrapped her lettuce and measured out her rice. When the sun shone, outside, she barely felt it on her skin. There was no such thing as safe. Deeply, she knew this, understood this, in her skin, the not-safe of her body, of her days.

Romina had known, all these four years, that she could be taken at any time, so that, when it finally happened, it was almost a relief—*all right then, here it is, the slide down, the falling, it's begun*—even though another part of her mind had resisted the possibility at the same time: *no, that wouldn't happen, not to me, of course not, I won't get caught, I'm not a Tupamara guerrilla, I'm not even that committed as a Communist, not like my brother, Felipe, or Graciela or Walter or Manuelito or Pablo or Alma or the rest of them, the real subversives, I'm not one of them, and anyway the worst of the round-ups is over now,* and this was true, the government had slowed down its exhausted machine, but that did not explain why the next-door neighbor had been taken just last year, in '76, why his wife now stood at her kitchen window with her arms plunged into a tub of dirty water and plates, not washing, just standing, stock still, staring out the window with blank eyes. As if she'd been removed from her own body.

When the coup happened, in '73, Romina had just begun her first year at the university. It was June, and she was preparing for exams, studying at the linoleum kitchen table as the first cold winds of winter blew against the window. She was studious, a goodgirl to her exacting parents, in love with Flaca, from whom she'd recoiled when she'd first seen her at the Communist Party meeting, because she knew immediately what Flaca was, she wore her masculinity like a cologne, she even wore cologne, men's cologne, so brazen was she. Hair pulled briskly back into a rubber band, broad shoulders, the tang of masculine scent.

A steady gaze. Girl. As dangerous as a snake, coiled and hungry, ready to bite. And there was Romina, serving coffee and shuffling papers because she was helping change the world, there would be justice for the workers and a new day for Uruguay, a revolution that would shine as brightly as the one in Cuba, Workers of the World, Unite! She believed in it all. She had no boyfriend. It had been so easy to be a goodgirl, to linger in books and ignore the attentions of boys, who cared about boys? Then came Flaca with her naked allure. She felt the coldness of her comrades toward Flaca, the disapproval for her short ponytail and plain blue T-shirt. Her own brother, Felipe, the one who'd brought her to the meeting, twenty-one years old and a student of law, looked at Flaca with a mix of disdain and fear. Romina found it hard to look away from her. Snake in waiting. What kind of snake? Majestic anaconda? A boa with its power to wrap you in its long muscular body until you can't breathe? Flaca wrapped around her, Flaca strong and lean, coil, flick, bite. That was how it began. With the invasion of her imagination. Their months together hurtled along, bursting with discoveries. Sex, first sex, at eighteen. Aching flames unleashed, spilled out into another body. The vigor of desire. The heave and stab of it. Like eating the ocean and still wanting more. Dissolving into ash, and then, when your body returns, when the room returns, she is still there, woman, girl, gazing at you with animal eyes. All of it shrouded in a shawl of quiet. They were perfect together, or, more accurately, together they shaped perfection out of nothing and cradled it in their arms. Romina was happy. Even as the situation around them grew more chaotic and the government increased its crackdown, she held out the beacon of the better world around the corner, Workers of the World, Unite!, and what if in that new world—breathless thought, rabid thought—there could be more room for women like her and Flaca? Would the Communists fight for that too? There was no evidence whatsoever that they would. She dared dream it only in the glow after sex, lying naked and limb-woven with her lover.

Like so many others, like her own Communist brother, she didn't see the dictatorship coming, as their country was supposed to be immune to such collapse. Uruguay was special. A tiny oasis of calm. Their neighbors throughout South America were one thing, with their shaky democracies, their sordid political legacies, poverty, repression, Peronism, corruption: but Uruguay, drab little Uruguay, was the stable little sister, the goodgirl one, the safe one, the Switzerland of South America; they had arrived at social advances—the abolition of slavery, votes for women, separation of Church and State, eight-hour workdays, the right to divorce—before the giant nations around them. Her high school history class told the story of a progressive democracy, a role model, a Latin American jewel, using that very word, *jewel,* making her imagine a tiny yet exquisitely polished Uruguay-shaped gem among big plain stones. She'd never left Uruguay, so what did she know, really, except what she could see with her own eyes, and hear with her own ears? She heard little in the conversations around her to prepare her for the coup.

That morning, the morning of June 27, 1973, the headline was gigantic and in thicker black letters than she'd ever seen. PARLIA-MENT DISSOLVED. President Bordaberry had turned over his powers to the generals of the military, an institution to which Uruguayans had rarely given much thought until the recent years, when troops had been called out to quell the workers' strikes and round up the Tupamaro guerrillas. There had been unrest for some time now, and curfews for civilians, searches of private homes without warning, rumors of torture in the prisons where the subversives were kept—but even so, this? A coup? They were not calling it a coup. *Transfer of power,* they called it. Like handing over a cluster of keys. Here, take this. Look after it for a while, while I go down the road, to the sea, to the abyss. The President was in the photographs on the front page of the newspaper, and he didn't look chained or wounded or even afraid, just grim as he signed a paper on his desk with the generals towering over him, gathered in a ring. She wondered what was happening in his mind, whether he secretly feared for his life or whether he felt safe in that ring of generals, safer than everybody else, whether he'd be able to sleep soundly in the nights to come and what he'd dream. After that her brother had disappeared. He went to the store and never came home. Her terrified parents cornered her and learned the truth about their children's attendance of Communist Party meetings. Were you Tupamaros too? her parents asked. Can it be? You? Her mother scouring under Romina's mattress and in her closet for hidden guns. No, of course not, Mamá, we were never Tupas, Romina said, thinking that the very idea was ridiculous considering that the Tupamaro guerrilla movement and the Communist Party had never gotten along even for a minute, with Communists accusing Tupamaros of rashness and Tupamaros calling Communists all talk and no action. But her parents, of course, knew nothing of that, they knew only that their children were in danger, not so different from the danger that Mamá's family had been running from when they fled the Ukraine, and Russia before that. Her parents withdrew her from school and sent her up north to Tacuarembó to hide out with her aunt, and, sure enough, it was just in time, because soldiers came and swept their house at 3:15 a.m. one night, though they found neither Romina nor any of her Communist pamphlets or books. She had evaded them, and when she returned to Montevideo (and to Flaca's infidelities, which had crushed her then but which she now saw as Flaca being Flaca), she returned to her university studies with her head down.

Four years passed.

Four years and no arrest.

An almost obscene amount of luck, considering the fate of so many of her comrades and of her brother, whose name was no longer spoken in her home. Romina carried the weight of all parental expectation, the burden of easing her brother's absence with her own perfect performance as a daughter. It was never enough. The dinnertime silences ached and stung, the three of them at the square table that had always had one side for each member of the family. When her own arrest finally happened, just two weeks ago, the great relief was that it hadn't happened at home, with her parents watching; that had always been her worst fear, that she'd be taken in front of her parents, that they'd have to watch, unable to stop what they saw. She'd already given them enough suffering and disappointment, with her Communist past and her plain appearance and no boyfriend in sight, never as pretty as her own mother had been though they would never say that directly and that wasn't the issue anyway, you have such nice eyes, if you wore a little more makeup and smiled more often, they'd say, though these days with a tone of resignation. In any case, they had not seen the arrest, had not sullied their eyes or ears; mercifully, it had taken place on her walk home from the Biblioteca Nacional after a long afternoon of study. Two men on the sidewalk, flanking her suddenly, a waiting car, a push. Hood over her head. Long drive. Circles, she knew, to keep her from knowing where they were going, and though she tried to keep track of the grid her steady sense of direction failed her, dissolving after a particularly sharp turn. No beating until they arrived in the cell. They wanted names. It seemed that someone else, a prisoner, had given them her name. Who. Who. It doesn't matter, don't think about that, don't think. Don't give them names. You have no names. Say it aloud: I have no names, I don't know anyone. I don't know. I am not. Cold. The floor is cold. Waiting for the rape. It doesn't come. Not coming makes it terror more. Second day, the machine. Electric. No. Knew it would be. Knew it. No not that not there. Will leave no marks, she knows. There is knowing but the knowing it does not protect. Have nothing, have no names. Sorry. Sorry sorry. Cannot help you. Act stupid, like a stupid woman, useless. Useless good. They talk. They ask. Demand. You are not. But in the end they stop and she is back in the room from before and on the second night the rape is only one. Only one. Where are the others. Why this luck. Some luck. A halfhearted arrest. Why is that. Is the whole damn country tired. And what is next, is this forever, will she ever see the sky. The next day, no machine. No rape. No beating. Ignored. At night, the rape returns and the same one is back, she recognizes does not want to but she does, she knows him, she will know him always for better or for worse, and, it is worse, he is not alone this time, she counts them, one, two, three. Only. Three. The stories are of numbers much larger than three. How do the others do it, she thinks, survive the numbers larger than this counting, and tell me someone are they true, the stories, is this story true, the story she is trapped in, is it her forever, is it her world now to be one, two, three, every night and on and on. At last they are gone. Ignored again. What is this. What is this. And then dragged out, no explanation, pushed into a car and pushed back out of it somewhere on the edge of town. Alone. Alive. Luck. Luck. Sky.

It is less, what happened to her. She tells herself this when she wakes in the night.

And now, here, Polonio, sunshine. Copious. Flagrant. Ocean everywhere.

Celebrate, Flaca had said.

She would not tell Flaca about the cell, the machine, the Only Three. Not because she didn't want to, but because language could not hold it. Her tongue failed her. There was no speaking what those days had been, those nights, nor how their terror spilled into the days that followed, into the now even here on this beach, and into the future, which would not be the same because those days had taken place and all the more so if her period never came—and this was the thought she must not think, the thought that tore her. She kept searching her body for signs of menstruation, a leak, a soreness, anything. Bleed, body. Bleed and set me free. Bleed! The happiness of this moment stained by that ferocious prayer. This too she could not speak of. This too she could not say. The wide-flung joy of being here was a liquor she could drink from, to drown out, to forget.

But what if liquor made it harder to shut herself back down?

What if so much living made you dangerous?

*

They arrived on the beach before the fishing boat reached the shore, and stood to greet it like long-lost relatives. The fishermen were not surprised to see them, or at least showed no outward signs of curiosity or wonder. There were three of them, with weathered faces and muscled arms, and they welcomed the women with the gentle silence developed over years of hard labor, or so Flaca thought of it, having come from a long line of such men herself. She'd been bracing herself for too-long stares, for prurient interest in them as women visitors unaccompanied by men, sidelong comments like those made by the cart driver the night before, about where their husbands were, why they were alone, what they were looking for in such an isolated place. But none of that came.

"We're visitors," she said to them. "Would you sell us some fish?"

The man at the stern nodded. He seemed to be the youngest, perhaps in his twenties. He tipped the nearest basket forward so they could see the fish inside. Heaps of silvery cool flesh.

Flaca waded to the boat and leaned over the edge to look at the wares, choosing fish for their lunch, standing ankle-deep in the waves. Foam engulfed her calves, licked at her legs. She struck up a conversation with the young man. His name was Óscar. His father-in-law, El Lobo, owned the little grocery of Cabo Polonio, which could be found over there, he said, pointing. Flaca was used to men tensing up around her, and his calm, unsmiling ease was refreshing. She placed the fish in a bucket she'd brought for that purpose.

Anita, back onshore, marveled at how competent and prepared Flaca was, how she seemed to have thought of everything. I could trust that girl with my life, she thought. So young and yet so capable. Those hands, so sure of themselves on the slippery fish. Lifting their bodies to right where she wanted them. Making them bend and flash in the sun.

"How much?" Flaca asked, pointing at the full bucket.

The fisherman shrugged. "Whatever you think."

Flaca counted out pesos and handed them to the man, a generous amount, and they started back toward their makeshift camp. She was elated. They could procure food, and the fishermen would leave them to their haven. Now they were here—more than ever.

"Let's leave these at our camp, and go for a swim," Flaca said.

"Good idea, it's getting hot," said Romina.

Hands, Anita thought. Flaca's hands. Underwater, in the ocean, nobody else would see. "Yes," she said. "It is."

Paz was finally awake—groggy and smiling—so the five of them changed into their bathing suits and took the path down to the shore. The water called to them, blanketing the sand with its low roar. Come, come. Down the slope, to the shore, to the waves. To the long blue. Feet bare, leaping, sinking into wet sand, dark sand, into the wet darkness. Feet into foam.

Flaca strode in first, Romina close behind her.

"Cold!" Romina cried out.

"Don't worry, you get used to it. Here—" Flaca cupped up water, threw it toward her.

"*¡Ay!*"

"It'll help!"

"Oh, some help!" Romina splashed her back, in mock outrage.

Malena was just behind her, submerged to the neck, giving herself immediately to the ocean.

Paz took courage from the sight of Malena, gliding through the water, eyes closed as if in an indestructible state of prayer. She wanted that, too. The cold pricked at her calves; she hadn't been in the ocean since she was eleven, since before the dictatorship, when her mother still took her down the coast to a cousin's beach house for a couple of summer weeks. Now she sometimes bathed in the Río de la Plata, down at Playa Pocitos, a city beach always sure to draw a crowd in the summer, just a short bus ride or long walk from home, and the river there was like the sea, so wide you couldn't see the other shore, wide enough that she'd come to think of it as the same thing, as almost the same thing. But it was not the same. This water had a different force, a majesty. The Atlantic. Roaring. Reaching all the way to Africa. These waves just the beginning, connected to the wider world. Paz stepped out further and plunged her chest, her neck, her head in until the whole of her was captured by a presence even hungrier than her own.

"Look at that!" Flaca said. "Paz and Malena did it. You see, Romina? Nothing to be afraid of."

Anita had sidled up beside Flaca. "Nothing?"

Before Flaca could respond, Anita doused her with water.

"Ha!" Romina said. "See now, Pilota, you have to be careful—I've got allies!"

Flaca, dripping, turned to Anita in surprise. Anita in her blue polka-dot bikini. Reducing the world to curves and lust. She had never seen her lover's body—or any of her lovers' bodies—in the sun. Lovers were for secret places only. Dark places. Now this, so much sky, so much light, and a body catching all that light into its skin.

Anita took her hand and pulled her down into the cold water.

"Swim out with me," she whispered into Flaca's ear.

Romina watched them go with a pang of envy, not because she wanted either one of them the way they wanted each other—she hadn't been with anyone since Flaca, having decided to focus on her studies and keep her head down after the coup, which was easy given that women didn't make advances under a dictatorship (except Flaca, of course, who'd made it her specialty) and she found boys' and men's advances easy to tune out. No. What she envied was their ease and freedom, the flow of their own lust. To come to a place where you could do that, in broad daylight. Look at Flaca: loving a woman so openly, under a broad blue sky. The high of it. She'd watched it play across Flaca's face. She wondered whether she, Romina, would ever know what that felt like. To love so openly even for a minute of her life. And if the chance did come, would she be able to take it? Even if the other two miracles fell into place—a woman who would love her, and a place where she could love—would she have it in her to love back? What if it never left her, this clench against the Three the Only Three, their stink in her nostrils, their memory scarred into her skin? She could not think too far ahead. She still didn't know how much they'd done. What was dead inside her or was living. If they'd done it, if they'd started a life—but no. Ocean, no. Are you listening. You can't I can't so please. She sank deeper, down to her neck, are you listening. Deeper. Face underwater and the tears mix into waves. Salt to salt. Pain to ocean. Take me. Save me. Hold me, water. And the water did.

*

Flaca and Anita swam out toward a rock that protruded from the waves, and, when they arrived there, Anita grasped it and kissed Flaca on the mouth. Flaca kissed back, thinking, kissing in the middle of the ocean, well now, there's a first time for everything. Anita pushed her barely covered breasts against her, her tongue insistent, skin demanding, and soon Flaca stopped thinking, her hands were greedy on Anita's body, amazed by it, ever amazed, Anita filling her hands like joy and it was all so close, right there, under that skimpy little bikini bottom, which was nothing really, just the flimsiest little ribbon of cloth that you can swoop under like this. She had no foothold, the waves pressed at them, calm waves today and thank God for that because Anita was writhing furiously enough to drown her—"don't stop," she murmured, but Flaca thought, What? How to go on? Ridiculous, we can't go on, one slip and we both drown or crack our skulls against the rocks. But then Anita said it again, "don't stop." What will this woman do to me, she thought, wildly, drunk on the question, knowing that she should stop, but she did not, she turned Anita around so that she was facing the rock and could hold on for them both, and she did so roughly, with that way of taking charge that she knew Anita liked. The position itself was awkward, and unstable, but no matter. Flaca could not deny a woman like Anita. "Hold on tight," she whispered into Anita's ear as she slid into her from behind, and then, keeping balance with her free hand on Anita's waist, she did her lover's bidding, pretending at power when in fact her life was at the mercy of Anita's steady grip.

*

The three other women heard the cries, faintly, gliding in over the water. They could have been the call of a faraway exotic bird, or, perhaps, the song of salt in water, rising from the ocean itself. Romina glanced at Malena, who either hadn't heard or was pretending so effectively that it amounted to the same thing, that calm collected look she often wore when gathering up her things after lunch to return to the office, everything in order, everything in its place. Then she looked at Paz, who seemed to be trying, and failing, to hide her reaction. Her mouth was open, eyes wide. They should have been more careful, Flaca and Anita, especially with Paz around. And yet, Romina couldn't wholly fault them. In the city, Flaca lived with her parents, Anita with her husband. They were always fighting for the smallest shreds of privacy. She knew what that was like. Still, Paz was terribly young. It was a situation with no road map.

"You all right?" Romina asked Paz.

"What?" Paz stared at her. "Oh. I—yes." Her face was solemn. "I mean, I've never been better."

This caught Romina by surprise. She took a good long look at the girl. Who was she? What was going through her mind? She had a recklessness or disregard for normalcy that amazed Romina, a brazenness she could never have imagined at that age. Maybe Flaca was right about her. How had she known?

"I'm glad you're here," she said.

Paz blinked furiously. She flashed a quick smile that disappeared as quickly as it had come. Then she pushed off to float on her back in the shallows, leaving Romina to her silent conversation with the ocean.

The couple took a long time to return. When they finally did, Anita arrived first, rising from the waves, dripping, tall, voluptuous, her long hair slick against her shoulders and chest, her knees scraped from the rocks. Glistening Anita, triumphant in the foam. She had the figure, Romina thought, of the women in the superhero comic books her boy-cousins were so obsessed with and surely jerked off with at night, two of which she'd stolen from them and used as a teenager to do the same. Romina could not rip her eyes away, not even when Flaca rose from the water a few paces behind her.

Flaca saw Romina staring. She saw Paz staring, too, closer to the shore. She moved toward Anita, on legs still shaky from sex, moving as if to save her—how? from what?—but then Anita's posture stopped her. Her lover didn't need saving. She was beaming. Basking. As if the other women's stares were rays of sun.

Paz was staring as if the last oxygen in the world were packed into those curves.

She wants her, Flaca thought, she wants my woman. And why wouldn't she. A stab of surprise and pride and just the tiniest prick of fear.

Though what Paz really longed for, what she couldn't stop consuming with her eyes, was something else. Something larger than Anita, that spread around her in the sunlight. Happiness. Wholeness. A secret way to be a woman. A way that blasted things apart, that melted the map of reality. Two women in love. That a woman like Flaca should exist, should know what to do with a woman like Anita, have the power to draw out from her those sounds that glided in over the waves. They were the sounds of the world tearing open, into a wider form than it could ever have had before. She felt hot and damp and dwarfed by her own ignorance. She longed to know what Flaca knew. What had happened over by the rocks? How did you get a woman like Anita to look at you that way? She had no idea. She burned to find out. The things that happened in a basement years ago gave her no answers, only questions. The kid, they'd called her on the walk down to the beach, and she'd laughed along with them, but the truth was that she didn't feel like a kid. At sixteen, she felt old already in a gray trap of a world. All the adults around her were shut down tight, as if they had no inner life, as if no such thing as an inner life existed anymore. You shut down and mind your business and you never make waves, since the slightest ripple could kill you. She had no friends her age because the girls at school were too silly for her, with their chatter about makeup and ways to straighten their hair, nor did they want to be friends with a gangly weird girl like her. As for the boys, they wanted nothing to do with her either as she'd already made it clear that she would never under any circumstances accompany them into the dark janitorial closet at the end of the basement hall, and they had no other use for her. She had no use for them either. She belonged nowhere. Or, more accurately, she had belonged nowhere until this woman, this Flaca, had lifted her out of oblivion with a look, a round of *mate,* an invitation to the beach. *What do you want to be when you grow up?* she was asked, all her life, by all the adults around her, though in recent years they asked the question with a new layer of dullness that suggested she should answer with a dream of modest size, a word like *secretary* or at most *teacher,* and certainly never *social worker* or *journalist,* jobs that made you disappear. She'd never had an answer for the dull adults; the future had seemed too bleak to consider. But now it seemed to her, as she stood knee-deep in waves, that there was no greater life achievement than this, than learning the secrets of how to melt a woman open, and she thought yes, why not, that's what I want to be when I grow up, a woman like Flaca, and to hell with the danger, to hell with prison cells, to hell with my mother's disapproval, I don't even care if they kill me for it. At least I'll have lived along the way.

Flaca splashed water at Romina, breaking the spell. *"¡Epa!"*

Romina yelped as the water struck her, and threw water back. "You devil."

"Look who's talking."

"I have no idea what you mean."

"Oh! How prim of you!"

Anita cupped her hands, dipped them, and poured foam over herself. She should probably feel guilty for enjoying this moment, this little tussle over her, but instead she felt radiant and alive. "Speaking of prim," she said, "where's Malena?"

The others looked at each other. They hadn't realized Malena was gone. Neither Paz nor Romina knew how long she'd been away from their part of the shore. They scanned the horizon, the sand, the rocks at the edges of the beach, and then, finally, they spied her, a dark speck against the water. She'd swum out farther than any of them. They'd missed her at first, because she'd blended in with the waves.

They called out to her once, then louder, and finally, the third time, she turned and waved.

Years later, after the shattering, they would all think back on that moment: the shock of distance, and the rise of Malena's arm, its gesture resolute and tiny against the infinite blue.

2

Night Fires

IN CABO POLONIO, night fell like a shroud: softly at first, then decisively and with subsuming power. Nothing escaped the darkness. That second night, Flaca lit a fire in the ring of stones she'd made, and the friends set about preparing dinner. They'd been too hungry after their swim to bother cooking the fish for lunch, and instead had devoured the bread, salami, cheese, and apples they'd brought from the capital. So now, in the dark, at eleven o'clock according to Malena, who was the only one to have brought a watch, they set about preparing the fish for the grill.

"Ugh, don't make me gut those," Anita said.

"I shall do it, fair damsel." Flaca bowed dramatically.

Romina was at her side, chopping carrots. "And what, good *caballero,* are you going to get in return?"

"A true gentleman, a true *caballero,* asks nothing in return."

"Maybe you're not a *caballero* at all," Anita said, "but a *caballera.*"

"Oho!" Romina raised her knife to the air. "An invented word! What would the Real Academia Española say about that?"

"Forget them," Anita said. "They don't own the Spanish language."

"Actually," Romina said, "they do. As a high school teacher–in–training, it's my sad duty to report that if they don't put it into their dictionary, it's not part of our great mother tongue."

"Well, as a high school student," Paz leapt in, "I'm with Anita." She was sitting in the dark, legs crossed, watching them in the flickering light of the fire.

Romina glanced up at her wryly. "Of *course* you're with Anita."

Anita beamed over at Paz, who flustered and looked away, then back, smiling.

Flaca, hand inside a cold fish, felt a stab of possessiveness and quickly brushed it aside. She was overreacting. Yes, she'd learned this afternoon that her lover enjoyed the attentions of other women. And so? It didn't mean anything, did it? She was only teasing Paz, who, after all, was no more than a child. A child Flaca had brought here to take under her wing. She'd been confident that she'd read the girl right; now, there was no question. She was one of them, and how. She couldn't blame the girl for having eyes in her head, and she herself would have thought the same way in her shoes. What would it be like to be in those shoes, sixteen years old with a group like this, sixteen years old and the nation shut down around you like a cage? Hard to imagine. She hoped they could help Paz, somehow. That they could all help each other. Never in the history of Uruguay had there been a night like this. She sliced another slick belly open. Fish were so much softer than the beef she handled at the shop every day, you had to be careful to keep your knife strokes supple as well as strong. How she loved knives, their smooth power, their simple logic, their opening and opening of flesh. Not to hurt but to feed. Opening flesh could be a gift. Butchers could be kind, loving, spurred by generosity. Her father was like that and her abuelo had been the same.

"No, but really, I mean it," Paz went on. "Why should those stuffy old people in Madrid decide whether we can or can't say *caballera*?"

"Or *cantora*?" Romina said.

"Cantora?" Anita looked confused. "You mean, a singer?"

"Oh, my sweet innocent dove," Flaca said, and her chest ached warmly as she said it.

"Don't you 'sweet innocent' me," Anita said. "I have a lot to learn, but I'm learning fast."

"Oh, nobody doubts that," Romina said.

Laughter rose and wrapped around them.

"So yes, a cantora is a singer," Romina said, "for the Real Academia Española. But it has another meaning for us."

"A cantora," Flaca said, flopping another fish into the clean pile, "is a woman *who sings*."

"A woman like us," Malena said, with such a clear steady voice that they all turned to her in surprise. She'd been so quiet throughout this conversation that they'd forgotten she was there. Her job had been to gather bricks from the abandoned house to hold up the flat grill top Flaca had brought from home; they sat in orderly piles beside her.

Romina stared at Malena. "So you are, then? A cantora?"

Malena looked at her, eyes wide. "I suppose that's what I just said."

"You did," Anita said.

They all waited for Malena to say more, but she just stared into the fire, and the silence filled with the low roar of waves.

Anita rolled the word across her mind. Cantora. Its connotations were beautiful, but also obscene, depending on how you approached it.

They became aware of the lighthouse beam, swirling slowly across them in a slow bright pulse.

Romina put a pot of water on the fire, to boil the carrots, and the women gathered round.

"All right, Romina," Anita said, "how about you tell us how you met Flaca?"

To Anita's surprise, Romina did as she requested, detailing the story of the Communist Party meeting, how good Flaca smelled in her men's cologne—"the daring, can you imagine?" "Yes I can," answered Anita—and the month of friendship that culminated in a dance club bathroom. This brought shouts of delight from the other three women; even Malena seemed to brighten with curiosity. Romina went on to summarize their months together and her months of hiding in Tacuarembó when waves of kidnappings took hold of the city. To Flaca's relief, Romina left out the part about the other lovers Flaca had taken up with when Romina was away, ending instead with her arrival back into the city, intact but shaken, her brother gone, Flaca still there.

"That's quite a story," Anita said.

"It's not a story," Romina said tightly. "It's what happened to me." She took the carrots off the fire and stepped away from the flames.

"I'm sorry, I—"

"She didn't mean it like that," Flaca said, gently.

Romina shrugged and poured the carrot water out, right onto dark earth. Water, hot, streaming into the dirt. Do not fall back into the cell where the Three the Only Three, not that, not now, get away get out there is no out—

"Romina," Flaca said.

"What."

"Don't be angry."

"Fine," Romina said. "It's fine. They're all stories. We all have a story. And I want to hear the story of La Venus over here," she added, jerking her head toward Anita.

Anita straightened and tried to dissemble her pleasure at the name. "Is that me?"

"Who else?" Romina glanced around the circle at the others. "No offense to those present—you're all beautiful *muchachas,* of course."

"None taken," Malena said amiably. "I have eyes in my head."

"None taken," said Paz, recalling that afternoon, the bikini, foam, the stab of sunshine on bare flesh.

Anita flushed. "What do you want to know?"

"Whatever you'll tell us. How you got here, for example."

She took a deep breath. "The same way as you."

"You're cheating."

"All right, all right." Anita pulled her knees to her chest and wrapped her arms around her legs. She watched as Flaca put the grill over the fire, for the fish. "All right, fine. Look, I'm married. You probably all know that."

Silence. Ocean song.

"I didn't know that," Paz said.

Anita scanned Paz's face for judgment, but found none. She's just a child, she thought, what will she understand? And should she even hear this? But the air around her was so open. She pressed on. "Well. We're not happy. At least, I don't think he is, but—what I should say is, I'm not happy. I mean, I loved him. I thought I loved him. But now—" She spread her hands open before her, empty.

"There's a reason you married him," Romina said.

"I suppose so."

"It wasn't his cock."

"No! No. Of course it wasn't. I mean, I'd never seen his cock when we got married, what do you take me for?"

Romina raised her eyebrows. "Can I assume that's a rhetorical question?"

"Maybe." Anita smiled.

"And when you did see it?" Flaca asked before she could stop herself. She'd always avoided the topic of her lover's husband, a strategy she'd learned a long time ago. Stay in the moment, keep the peace, don't remind women of the cluttered duties waiting for them outside the dim room where you can be together. That's what husbands were, clutter and duties, or so it seemed to Flaca. But this was different; they were not in a dim room, but in a vast expanding night, getting drunk on starlight and each other's company. And this lover, she was now beginning to see, this particular woman, had a different effect on Flaca than anyone else had since Romina. She wanted to know Anita's story, to see inside her life, to know everything about her, including what she thought of her own husband. The realization was unnerving.

Anita shrugged and rolled her eyes.

Romina laughed, and Flaca beamed in triumph, having won a tiny shred of space over her rival—and alarmed, at the same time, that she was starting to see the husband as a rival at all.

"So you didn't marry him for that," Malena said, amused. "Why, then?"

The embers glowed. Three fish lay on the grill, rubbed down with salt and parsley, their bodies inert, their scent wild, lush, rising. Paz's belly rumbled, but she didn't want dinner to be ready, didn't want this atmosphere of bold talk around the fire to ever stop.

"I don't know," Anita said. "I had to marry someone, and he seemed better than the rest. My parents wanted me to get married, they wouldn't have stood for anything else." She stopped abruptly, as though she'd just remembered where she was.

A low flame licked the air, crackled. Receded back to its nest of wood.

"My parents wanted me to marry too," Romina said. "They still do. They're always asking me whether I've met any new men."

"What do you tell them?" Anita asked.

"Different things each time. Generalities. No, or maybe, or a shrug that they can interpret however they want to. Whatever gets them to drop the subject."

"How long do you think that'll work?" Paz said. Her mother never asked these things, and of course she was still too young to marry, but then again her mother never asked much about her life at all.

"As long as I can make it work."

"My parents used to ask." Flaca stirred the embers with a stick. "They've given up now."

"Do you think they know?" Romina asked.

"No. Yes. I really don't know." Flaca looked across the fire at Malena. "What about you? How is it with your family?"

Silence fell. Malena stared at them like a startled animal.

They waited.

"We weren't talking about me," Malena said steadily. "We were talking about La Venus."

"La Venus," Flaca said slowly. A naming. Once is a witticism, twice a baptism, as she well knew, having been Flaca for so long that no one ever called her by her birth name. She elbowed her lover lightly in the ribs.

"It's who she is," Romina said.

La Venus smiled slightly in the firelight, and didn't protest, though, of course, it would have made no difference if she had; nicknames, as everyone knew, could never be chosen or turned away once they had settled on your skin.

"But anyway," Flaca said, turning back to Malena, "we *can* talk about you. This circle we're sitting in, the fire we're gathered around, it's not for any one of us. It's for everyone here."

"And the stars, O poet?" Romina sang. "Are they shining for the five of us too?"

"Why not?" Flaca kept her eyes on Malena.

Malena wrapped her arms around her chest as if to shield it and she looked so vulnerable that La Venus longed to gather her up in her arms. She'd been right about this woman's armor. So much roiled underneath. She was moved to see it, moved by what could open among women around a fire. She touched Malena's arm. "It's all right—"

"No," Malena said.

The lighthouse beam swept over them and disappeared.

Paz wondered what Malena's story could be, what kept her so tightly shut around it. There had to be something there, a radioactive core—perhaps involving brothels or murder or torrid sex or more ordinary realities like secret prisons—to make her act this way. She had to be hiding something. Paz thought of her own story, the basement story, and wondered whether she'd be asked to tell it, and, if she was, whether she'd dare—and if she did, if she told, giving voice to it for the first time, would these women understand? Was this circle of women, this fire sparking into the night, the only place in all of Uruguay where such a telling could be heard and understood?

"Your fish are going to burn, Flaca," Romina said.

"They're fine," Flaca said, but she stood to check them, and soon they were on plates and a new set of fish were on the grill. They began to eat the first round, three fish between the five of them.

"All right," Romina said, "back to La Venus. You married the man. And then?"

"And then things changed," La Venus went on between bites. "We were fighting all the time. He wanted me to have dinner ready when he got home from work, the house spotless, and be all made up and perfect-looking, just pining to hear about his day. That sort of thing. And you know how it is, how these years have been. There's never any good news from his day. He was going to be a famous musician, before the coup. I believed him. He was good enough, and bold enough, that it seemed possible. Now we can barely even listen to music; we destroyed most of our records, back during the searches, just like everyone else. He's trapped in a job he hates. He can't talk to his colleagues. He doesn't know whom he can trust."

"No one does," Romina said.

"Well, sure," said Anita who was also La Venus. "Fine. Everyone's in that boat. But then, as a wife, I'm supposed to carry that load? I have to pretend to be interested in everything he says? Feel sorry for him, spread my legs for the poor baby? He never asks about me, about how my day went, about how I seasoned the damn meat, nothing." She struggled for more words, for ways to articulate the blunt knife buried in her days. "He's a perfect husband, everybody says so."

"Who's everybody?" said Malena.

"My mother, my sister, my sister-in-law. Friends. And I suppose they're right. I suppose I'm just allergic to perfect husbands."

Paz opened her mouth to laugh, but caught herself just in time, when she saw that no one else was laughing. The women had become suddenly serious. They were quiet, then, the five of them, the fire rustling, stabbing at the air.

The ocean moaned.

"Where does he think you are?" Romina asked.

"With my cousin, in Piriápolis."

"Hm," Romina said. "Piriápolis. There are certainly better toilets in Piriápolis."

Laughter.

"That's true," La Venus said, "but I'd rather be here, with you, shitting in a hole."

"I still can't shit here," Romina said. "Have you done it yet?"

"Well, yes," La Venus said, "since you asked. And it wasn't so bad."

"La Venus! Our first shitter!"

"Long live La Venus!"

The last fish came off the grill. They ate. Bread and carrots and the catch of the day. The stars sang voicelessly above them. When they were done, they put the dirty dishes aside in a stack and brought out the whiskey and the *mate* gourd. Romina put water on the fire, to boil for the *mate* thermos.

Flaca handed Paz the whiskey bottle and watched her take what looked like an expert swig, with more self-assurance than the night before. It was normal, of course, for whiskey to emerge after dinner, a Uruguayan tradition, and Flaca herself had tried her first sips as a teen at Sunday *parrillas* with her family. Those first whiskeys. A copper blooming in your chest. "*¡Opa!*" she said. "Like a pro!"

Paz smiled and wiped her face with the back of her hand.

"It must be strange for you," La Venus said, "to hear all these older women speaking so frankly about their lives."

"Wait a second!" said Romina. "Some of us aren't that much older."

"What are you? Twenty?"

"Twenty-two."

"You see?" La Venus said. "That's worlds away from sixteen."

"Does that mean your age is worlds away from mine?" Flaca asked, impishly.

"Tsk—the scandal!" Romina crowed. "Flaca the innocent!"

"No it does *not,* and we weren't talking about that," La Venus said. The whiskey had flung something open inside her. "We were talking about Paz."

"Talking *to* Paz," Romina said.

"Right. *To* Paz."

"About whether she's shocked," La Venus said. "I'm really curious."

"Shocked by what?" said Romina.

"By—us!" La Venus spread her palms open. "By the things we talk about. By what we are." She looked directly at Paz. "I mean, it has to be the first time you've heard women talk like this. When I was your age, I didn't even know it was possible. I mean—that two women could—" She broke off, and felt her face grow hot, though thanks to the darkness no one seemed to notice.

"That two women could *chucu-chucu,*" Flaca finished off.

"I just didn't know," La Venus said, a bit defensively. "No one speaks of it. And if they do, it's to say that two women together would be like—" She gestured, patting her flat palms together, turning them back and forth.

"Like a *tortillera*," said Romina.

La Venus nodded.

"I hope you've been disabused of that notion now," Romina said, glancing meaningfully at Flaca.

Flaca stifled a smile and glanced at La Venus.

"About a thousand times!" La Venus said.

The women hollered in delight.

"But anyway," La Venus said, "calm *down*, ladies—anyway, Paz, for you this must all be very new."

"Actually," Paz said, "I've known for a while."

"What do you mean?" Romina asked. "Known what?"

"That two women can be—together."

A stunned quiet fell over the group.

"Someone told you about it?" Venus said.

Paz gazed into the fire. It flicked and coiled, licking the night air, inviting her to hurtle forward. "More than that."

She watched their faces as they wrestled with what seemed to be a thick tangle of reactions: confusion, astonishment, disturbance, fear, a slash of envy.

"Who was she?" Flaca asked.

The question hung over the fire. Everyone waited.

"A Tupa," Paz finally said.

"A Tupamara," Flaca said more than asked.

"Oh, for God's sake, Flaca," Romina said, "what other kind of Tupa is there?"

"All right, fine," Flaca said. "Will you let the girl talk?"

They waited. The fire sang. The lighthouse beam swished over them three times, like breaths of light in the darkness. Once. Again. Again.

Paz stared at the heart of the fire. "My mother—" she said, and stopped.

"It's all right," Romina said gently. "This may be the one place in the entire country where you can talk about Tupamaros without endangering your mother."

Paz wrestled with herself, and with the mantle of inner silence, which draped over everything, which kept you alive.

The women waited.

"My mother hid a few of them over the years," Paz finally said. "The first time was right after the coup, two young women. We have a basement you can't see from the street, that you get to through a trapdoor my mother covers with a rug."

She paused. All these things she was to never say. Romina nodded encouragingly, La Venus had an indecipherable expression on her face, and Flaca was stirring the fire, which she'd rekindled now that the embers didn't need to be low for cooking, with a stick that kept her attention rapt. Malena was looking at her calmly. She was the only one who didn't seem shocked; her eyes were kind.

"So anyway, the fourth time, it was just one woman." Paz felt her chest fill with heat at the memory of those days, the dawning realization that a new person was hiding downstairs, her mother's whispered conversations with friends close to the blaring radio so the neighbors couldn't hear, in case they were spies, anyone could be a spy or become one by reporting you on a whim, and she could only catch the whispers in scraps and shards, *she got here last* and *did you know the baker's wife they say was also* and *nowhere left to go, they want them all dead, no, all gone, not even bothering with a grave.* "I never learned her real name. We called her Puma. She stayed in the basement. My mother would send me down there with plates of food. I cleared her plates too, and her—you know, her bucket. She couldn't come upstairs to use the bathroom."

The women nodded. Tales of hiding were not unfamiliar.

La Venus thought fleetingly of the hole she'd shit in earlier that day. The dirt she'd used to cover her feces. Suddenly seen in the light of luxury.

"We started talking a little, when I came down. She was easy to talk to." Paz remembered the way Puma had asked questions, keenly, with a gaze so unblinking that Paz had the bizarre sensation that there was nothing she could not tell her. That no matter what her soul dredged up and no matter how ugly her revelations might seem to her own ears, Puma would simply take them, easily, eagerly, with an unwavering welcome. It made her want to spill everything. When Puma first arrived, she was trembling, and Paz brought her blankets and sweaters because she assumed it must be from the cold. But the trembling kept on until one day Paz instinctively put her hand on Puma's. That's when the woman stopped, grew suddenly still, and looked her in the eyes. Her body was warm. The revolution. The warmth of revolution in her hand. The war had been lost, so her mother had said; repression had won, it sat in the Government Palace now and that was the end of that. Love had lost, fear had won. Revolution, dead. And yet. Here was this woman, this Puma, still warm and breathing, like the last survivor of a shipwreck. And there was death in her eyes, pain in her eyes, but something else, too. That night, Paz waited until her mother was asleep and tiptoed back down to the dark basement and curled up beside Puma. She would never know exactly why she did it. The basement was stone cold but Puma's body was warm. She didn't dare fall asleep, as she had to be back upstairs before her mother woke. She just lay beside Puma and listened to her breathing, slow with sleep. It wasn't until the third night that Puma's hand reached out through the darkness and sought hers, gently, and when they held hands the cold melted away.

She couldn't put this into words for the women around the fire. They were waiting. She struggled against the silence for another minute, then shrugged. "She was my friend."

"And more than a friend?"

Paz looked away, into the fire.

"When was this?"

"The summer after the coup."

They were silent. Doing the math in their heads, repeatedly, as though there had to be an error in the arithmetic.

"You were twelve."

"I was almost thirteen." She picked at her nails. "I've always looked older." Always felt older, she thought.

"And she—" Romina began, but could not finish.

La Venus wore a face of disgust. "She had no right! A child!"

Paz shrank back.

"Go easy," Flaca said. "Look, Anita, when I first—with Romina—we were young, too."

"First of all, you were both the same age—weren't you? That's completely different. And secondly, you told me you were eighteen!"

"Seventeen," Flaca said, "yes."

"That," La Venus said fiercely, "is a world away from twelve."

Almost thirteen, Paz thought, but did not say.

"You must have been so scared," Romina said.

"You don't know that," said Malena.

Romina stared at her, surprised. There was more inside that woman than she'd understood.

Malena leaned forward, and her face caught the firelight. "Paz is the one who knows. Whether she was scared. What it was like. She's the one we should listen to and believe."

Romina opened her mouth, made a sound. The fire crackled. She looked at La Venus, who looked startled, then at Flaca, whose brow furrowed. Neither spoke.

Malena turned to Paz. Her eyes were gentle, and she seemed, in that moment, older than any of them, as old, Romina thought, as the very earth. "Do you want to tell us?"

Paz swallowed, hard. "I wasn't scared. It wasn't like that! She was—" Again the wordlessness rose up around her and she couldn't speak. There was no way to speak it. How to ever say. The way that Puma stroked her hair, as if it dazzled her, as if it contained the mysteries of the night sky and so she said it, *your hair is more beautiful than the night sky. You're a miracle, Paz, you are everything.* Puma, as gentle as water in a pool, shaping and reshaping around you. Broken, whole. Awakening. Silence, haunting, full of the unsaid. *Only if you want* was her refrain and then her breathing was a song. *Only if.* Deep in the silence. Revolution. *You want.* "She was kind. She showed me what I am."

For a long time, no one spoke. The fire sparked and hummed; Flaca added another log—the cart driver had been right that firewood was scarce here, and she was glad now that she'd bought as much as she could from him. She hoped that tomorrow the grocer would have more to sell. She was spending down a year's worth of savings on this trip. And who cared. To be here with these stars and these women, surrounded by an oceanic song, a *wssssshhhh* that undergirded every word and thought. Beauty draped in blackness. Night and fire. The whiskey bottle started going around again. When it reached Paz, she took another sip and nobody teased her about it this time.

The silence shifted, thickened, a lush thing between them.

Romina stole glances at Paz, trying to take her story in. Angry at Puma for using a child—even though Paz said she'd wanted to. The revolutionary in the basement, a hero. An opener of worlds. But twelve. *Twelve.* Her mind stopped over and over at that, at the thought of a Paz even more vulnerable than the girl she saw before her, all thorns and spikes and hunger, a restless, wandering kid. She had to sit on her hands to keep herself from going to Paz and wrapping her arms around her because Paz clearly didn't want that and would take it as condescension when in fact it was something else, a need to protect so ferocious it almost knocked the breath from Romina. She'd never felt this kind of urge before. The tenderness of a lion for her cubs. Strong enough to kill. Maternal love—was it like this? Could it be the secret thing inside her giving her this feeling? No. Not that, turn away from that—free me of that nightmare, black sky and stars and fire and rocks, and I will give my never-be-a-mother love to this girl Paz.

The fire danced and sank in gleaming tongues.

La Venus nestled into Flaca, her comforting body. Flaca was lean and strong, as strong as her husband, perhaps even more so as Arnaldo sat at an office desk all day, while Flaca heaved and cut and carried. La Venus felt as though she'd never stop wanting this woman, and the depth of her hunger frightened her. The rest of her life stretched before her, uncharted, full now of this secret self that would always breathe beneath the surface of her days, no matter what she did or didn't do. It wasn't so simple, to return to your life the way it was, after you've torn it open. She would always have sat on this beach with a ring of women who saw her secret become an ordinary thing, a woman leaning on a body she was not supposed to love, yet loved. She ached. But for what? For Flaca? For the future she would not have? And which future was that? Perhaps she was aching for Paz, this girl, and that Tupamara, who had done something terribly wrong and no amount of Paz explaining could convince her otherwise. Two women was one thing, a woman and a child was another. And yet. Paz. Here on this beach, at sixteen years old. To know so much at such a young age about what's possible. About women. How would her own life have been different if she'd known? Who would she be today? Would that other version of her be more free or less free than she was now?

*

A new day, drenched in sunshine. The women woke slowly and dispersed after their *mate,* to the sea, to the dunes. They went for swims, walks, explorations of the rocks around the lighthouse. Malena sat on the beach, sifting sand through her fingers, looking out at the water. Romina dove out past the waves to where she could float with her eyes closed. Flaca and La Venus found a hollow between sand dunes— "cleavage," La Venus called it, laughing—where they made love on the burning sand, then ran to the ocean for relief and did it again in the water.

Paz struck out alone, roaming, unsure of what she was looking for. She needed time to think. After last night's confessions, she felt embarrassed, exposed, as if these women were her sisters and her aunties all at once. The first thrill of arriving here was settling into a strange unease, just under the surface of her skin. She wanted to escape—but escape what? And why? Escape her own skin? Escape into a basement and hide in the dark, as she'd done over the years since Puma left—the dark hollow under the trapdoor had become her secret refuge—but that wasn't possible here, there was no basement anywhere on this damn cape, there was barely a tree to hide behind, everything had a raw quality to it, bared to the open wind. She walked. The motion soothed her. Again she was alone. Just like at home, where she was alone with a mother who did not want her around and for whom she was a not-right girl, an annoyance, in the way. She shouldn't have told her new friends about Puma. Now she was torn open with no way to close the seam. *Sola,* she thought, alone, *so - la,* a syllable for each step, left foot *so,* right foot *la,* step *so,* step *la, so, la,* on and forward. Surprised to find herself at El Lobo's grocery store. A box of a hut with the curtain tied back in the open doorway. They'd been meaning to come here for supplies, but hadn't yet; the plan had been to go together later in the day.

She stepped inside.

The air was dim, thick. A long table served as a counter, behind which an old man presided over shelves painted a chipped and hopeful light blue, lined with scattered provisions.

"Good morning," he said. He was white-haired, surprisingly hardy, as if years of outdoor labor had at once shriveled and toned him, made him belong entirely to the sun. He stood with the majestic ease of a ship captain, the old kind of ship, Paz thought, all sails and masts and salted rope. In his hands, the man held a piece of wood and a carving knife; curls of wood lay in a small pile on the counter. She wondered what he was shaping.

"Good morning," she replied.

"You're new."

"Yes."

"You came in with that group of ladies?"

Ladies. She fought the urge to contradict him. "Yes." She hovered uncertainly, realizing only then that she'd brought neither money nor a shopping list. "Are you El Lobo?"

He nodded slowly, staring at her as if she could be deciphered, like the wind. Then he turned back to his carving.

Paz scanned the shelves, with their careful wares. Paint, glue, rice in a burlap sack, spices in unlabeled jars, packets of yerba mate, toilet paper, tanks that looked like they might contain water, two sleeves of vanilla cookies cloaked in dust, a huddle of scrawny apples, a single head of lettuce already browning at the edges. She wondered what it would be like to live here, so far from civilization. In the presence of this man, she felt transported to another era, a time before telephones and televisions and airplanes that took exiles from the country, a time of timelessness, where life was bound to the rhythms of the ocean.

He looked at her, amused.

"What?" she asked, immediately feeling rude.

"You seem lost."

"I know where I am."

He shrugged. "Are they your sisters? Aunts?"

Paz hesitated. She opened her mouth to explain that they were friends, but it occurred to her that she might then have to explain why friends like these were traveling together without men. "We're cousins."

He carved without responding.

She hovered, lingered, trying not to seem lost. Flies congregated around the apples and anemic bell peppers. A beam of light from the door caught motes of dust. On the far wall, behind the counter, hung a strange mask with a long metal snout, suspended on a matrix of pale yellow bones.

El Lobo followed her gaze. "That's an oxygen mask. For sailors. My wife mounted it on those bones years ago. She's dead now," he added, and raised his eyebrows as if this news surprised him.

"What kind of bones are they?"

"Human."

She shrank back.

He laughed, revealing the holes where some of his teeth had been. "Oh, child. No. They're from a sea lion. I used to hunt them, and seals, but I don't have the strength anymore."

"And the mask?"

"It's from the *Tacuarí*."

She stared at him blankly. It sounded like an indigenous word, a Guaraní or Charrúa word—there were places that bore indigenous names, like the town of Tacuarembó, or that street down in Montevideo's Old City, Ituzaingó—but what did any of that have to do with oxygen masks that looked hoisted from photos of the Second World War?

"You don't know about the *Tacuarí*?"

"No."

"Ah. You just got here."

"Yes."

"How much longer do you have?"

"Four more days."

"Well, come back and I'll tell you the story, all right?"

She nodded.

"Do you want to buy anything?"

"I'm sorry. I forgot to bring money," she said, though she hadn't so much forgotten as not planned to be here at all.

"That's no problem. Take what you want and you can pay me when you come back."

"Thank you."

"Here, wait."

He ducked through the door behind the counter, into the back room, which she now realized must be his home. He returned with two fried dumplings on a piece of white butcher paper. "*Buñuelos*. My daughter Alicia made them this morning. A welcome gift for you."

She took the packet. When she was a child, buñuelos were her favorite food; she'd sometimes helped her mother mix the dough, and blend in the spinach or corn before watching her dollop the mixture into hot oil on the stove.

"They're made from seaweed."

"Seaweed?" She'd never heard of such a thing, had never imagined seaweed could be food. "You mean, you harvested it? From the ocean right here?"

El Lobo gave her a look, as if to say, *crazy city girl, what other ocean would it be?*

A few minutes later, she was heading back to camp with the buñue-los, a few apples, and a sleeve of cookies bundled into her arms, wondering what seaweed tasted like, whether her friends would be disgusted by the idea, whether they'd try such a thing, whether the buñuelos would be fishy or soggy or gritted with sand. The camp was empty, no one yet back from wherever they'd gone. She put down her things and went to the beach they'd all swum at the day before, where she took off her shoes and walked in the waves, calf-deep, her toes sinking into wet sand below. Then she stopped. They were out there in the distance, just two of them, Flaca and La Venus—it had to be them—heads bobbing close together, were they yes they were they must be, or they could be, swaying, staying close, don't look, don't look, don't listen for them turn around Paz *turn around,* and she did, though not immediately, and not without a stab of disappointment that she hadn't heard a thing.

At the camp, she unwrapped the greasy paper and ate a seaweed buñuelo, then another. They didn't taste like fish at all, but like ordinary spinach buñuelos, only with a streak of salty ocean about them, the aftertaste of a long swim through the waves, though even that was light, subtle, a hint you had to listen for with your tongue.

*

"Do you ever feel bad that we're the only ones having sex?" La Venus said, hands curling into Flaca's hair.

"Why should I?"

"Well, I mean, the others aren't having the same—you know, the same kind of time. And we disappear a lot, don't we?"

"We're having sex on behalf of the whole. Doing our part."

"Ha."

Flaca continued her slow, tongued descent.

La Venus gripped her lover's hair tighter, clamped her thighs around her waist where they lay in the dunes. It always amazed her, the way Flaca could talk as if sex—the things they did—were good, even virtu-ous. "Do it, then."

It was dusk, the light softening all around them. The third day. The third jewel on a necklace of seven. Only four days left, she thought sadly—and here they were, with lust showing no signs of letting up. It was just the opposite: the more time they spent in this unworldly place, the more clearly their desire rang out, as if it were a radio signal sent from the heart of the wild.

Afterward, they lay heaving, sweating on the sand dunes. A thought poured into La Venus, blindingly bright: *this must be love.* But what did that mean? Not love for Flaca, exactly, though it was a feeling sparked by her—this woman of the bandit hands, lithe Flaca, steady Flaca, muscular Flaca who made your body roar—but that wasn't all of what had her reeling. It was something else. Being here with Flaca, in the sand, in the waves, blending bodies and crushing against each other, she sought her own annihilation, sought to set herself free. Flaca *was* freedom—she'd never seen a person so free, or not, at least, in the years since the coup. She'd started thinking that freedom was an idea that belonged to another time, the era of bohemian dreams wherever you turned, when everyone, or at least people as young as she, really thought that revolution was coming for Uruguay. Was rising among Uruguayans. But now even the musician-husbands were hunchbacked bureaucrats, small-minded and bitter and riddled with fear. Good wife. No room for freedom. A smaller and smaller world. And now this. This blasting open, this ragged breathing. This enormous self.

This delicious self, larger than life, a goddess: La Venus. Venus of the foam. Venus of the dunes. Venus of the legs that open for a woman's tongue.

The sand was cooling with the fading of the day. Flaca was stroking her, murmuring syllables that made no sense, *ta—tatatatata—bue—la—lililila,* a stupid happiness that mirrored her own.

What if she could be La Venus all the time? What if she could walk down the streets of her own city as the impossible, sparkling woman she was right now? She didn't want to return to being Anita—not ever. Even though she had to. There was an old life out there waiting

for her to be Anita, people expecting her to live inside that name, people who would look into her face and see the old Anita and nothing
more—her husband, her mother, her sister, the grocer, acquaintances,
and so-called friends. But no matter what they saw, no matter what
they thought, that Anita was a shell now, a broken shell like that of
a hatched egg. It was too late to go back. She would never again be a
woman who didn't long to open for women. She had to be Anita, but
Anita was a lie. So how to survive, then? she thought furiously. She
raised her back so that her breasts filled Flaca's hands, so the stroking
wouldn't stop. How to survive?

"My god," Flaca said, "still hungry?"

"Always. For you always."

"Say that and we'll be here forever."

"Good."

"You want to be here forever?"

"Yes."

"Or you want—me, forever?"

"Oh God, that's so good."

"Answer the question."

"Shut up, don't stop—"

"I'm not stopping." The world tipped, blew open. Flaca inside, Flaca
everywhere. "See?"

"More."

"More fingers?"

"Yes."

"First answer the question."

"Oh fuck you I can't remember the fucking question—"

"What were you thinking about?"

She couldn't remember the original question but she knew it hadn't
been that. She wanted to ram her hips against Flaca's hand, to demol-
ish herself against this woman's solidity. She was wide open, her body
a burst seam. These delays of Flaca's could lead to orgasms so ferocious
that she almost felt afraid. "That your hands on me are like food. And
I didn't know I was starving."

"Ah." The movement returned. "No need, my Venus, to go hungry now."

*

On the fourth day, Paz returned to El Lobo's store and he finally started telling stories. It happened as he was drinking *mate* and she was taking an unreasonably long time to pore over the produce, ignoring its itinerant flies. She thought he'd forgotten his promise to tell her about the *Tacuarí*. She'd held on to that word, rolling the syllables though her mind as she looked out at the ocean or drifted off under the stars, so as not to forget them, *Ta-cua-rí, Ta-cua-rí.* She'd started to wonder whether she should ask directly, but wasn't sure how to go about it without intruding on the nebulous feeling she had of the shop as a place of quiet, of immersion in the rhythms of the sea. And then, just as she was reaching for a skinny bell pepper, El Lobo said, "We're known, you know, as a land of shipwrecks."

"Who?"

"Us, here. Cabo Polonio. This little thumb of land poking into the ocean."

He extended the gourd toward her.

She sipped the *mate.* It tasted as though he'd added a few *yuyos,* as she'd heard that country people did. Some said the extra herbs were there for flavor, some for medicine or witchcraft. She wondered which of these it might be for El Lobo.

"We earned that name long ago, in colonial times, because the waters here are shallow. Treacherous. Sinking many ships. Sit, sit." He pointed at a stool.

Paz sat. She waited. He didn't go on immediately. Time was slower here. Time, slow and wide, unrushed, time a calm in which it was possible to float.

"Treasure, merchandise, sailors' bones: it's all there, in the belly of the ocean you can see from this door. It gathered there over many generations. In fact, some people think that the very name Polonio came from the wrecked ship of Capitán Polloni of Spain, in 1753—oh, don't look so surprised that I know the dates. We keep true to our histories around here. And yes, there are other versions of how the cape got its name, but those aren't the true ones, because you know how it is, the truest story is always the one that endures over time and speaks the most deeply to the people."

His daughter Alicia poked her head in from the back room, which Paz now understood was their living room and kitchen. She was round-faced, with a long braid down her back and a small child on her hip. "Papá's subjecting you to his stories?"

"She wanted to hear them, you know."

Alicia smiled broadly at Paz. "The truth is, he wants to tell them. And actually, he knows all the stories of this place—he's holding them for everyone." She kissed El Lobo's forehead with a casual tenderness that made Paz go hollow inside. "*Chica,* I'm making buñuelos, do you want some?"

Paz nodded, mouth watering. "Thank you. They're delicious. I have money."

"Oh, how interesting for you! Absolutely not. You're our guest."

It shamed her, the thought of taking from the little this family had—they all lived in those cramped back quarters, El Lobo; Alicia; her husband, Óscar; and three or four children—but she feared that if she pressed on about paying, she'd offend.

"So, then," El Lobo said, filling the gourd again as Alicia disappeared behind the curtain, "Capitán Polloni of Spain. He arrived here with a ship full of over three hundred passengers. Some of them were priests coming to America to convert the heathens, to tame a land they thought needed taming." He paused to sip through the bombilla. "They had merchandise on board. Unlabeled. It wasn't part of what they'd been commissioned to bring over. Booze, tobacco, playing cards, all of which, you understand, were strictly forbidden. Well. The crew broke into the secret cargo and got so drunk that their songs could be heard by the very stars and there were many stars, it was a clear black night, there could be no excuse for their wrecking that ship against the rocks. There were only two possible reasons for the crash. Either it was the curse of the heathens, who hadn't wanted anybody coming to convert them; or, the crew was drunk."

"Or both?"

He stared at her, slowly, carefully. "Well, sure. Or both."

She was listening with her ears and all her pores open. She was on the deck of the ship, under the stars, surrounded by drunken sailors and their loud, slurred songs. She was beside them, climbing over a shattered prow, into the water, onto the rocks, scrambling for life. Reaching the shore bedraggled and raw or maybe drowning along the way. And meanwhile, the heathens—the Charrúa Indians or out here would it have been the Guaraní? she didn't know—waiting in the sand dunes, possibly having cursed the priests who cursed them, because wasn't that also true, that the arrival of the priests was itself a curse depending on the angle at which you looked? She'd never liked church, the stiff dresses, the kneel and up and sit and pray and sorry for my sins. She could never win the sin game, and so she'd stopped trying, only took communion to avoid a fight with Mamá, who luckily only took her to church a few times a year anyway. In this moment, absorbing the story of Polloni, Paz thought of her own home as a kind of ship with a lonely crew, just her and Mamá. Her father had left her and her mother when she was two, gone to São Paulo for a job and never called, and though he sent money, he never answered the letters she'd written back when she was still too young to know better. When she and her mother were home together, their house bucked and leaned with the captain's changing moods, as if the thing might capsize or collapse at any moment and drown them in the suffocating night. And there was no destination, no map to elsewhere, just a terrible emptiness that threatened to drift on forever. Maybe it was better to crash, to break against the rocks, so that you could at least arrive somewhere, however broken. She wanted space for herself, a larger life. The kind of life people in Uruguay didn't have anymore—and not only didn't have but no longer dared imagine. She would set sail and sweep across the sea until she landed in Brazil, Venezuela, Canada,

France. China. Australia. With nothing but tobacco and playing cards in her hold.

"Did they die?" she asked.

El Lobo shook his head. "The whole crew survived. That's the crazy part. The only casualty was a priest who was said to have died from the shock of having crashed right in the middle of a self-flagellation, which was known only because he was found dead on his bunk with lash in hand."

Paz laughed. "Is that true?"

"Why wouldn't it be?"

Why would it be? she thought, but didn't say. Histories tend to grow richer with time, gathering details as they pour down generations.

"That, of course, was all a long time ago. Since then, there have been many other shipwrecks. Understand: this is a rocky place. Sharp edges everywhere, once you dive down to look. The most recent shipwreck was the *Tacuarí*. That just happened, in 1971, so that would be, let's see"—El Lobo raised his gaze to the ceiling—"six years ago, yes, that's right, six years. Two sailors died. The rest swam out to the shore or rowed in emergency boats, and by the next morning they were all gone to the nearby town of Valizas, leaving the ship and its treasures behind. The ship is still there, out in the water, off the Playa de las Calaveras. It's sinking, though. Slowly. A little more each year. Things keep floating out from the shipwreck, washing up on the shore."

"Like that oxygen mask?" Paz asked.

"Like the mask."

She waited for him to go on, but he picked up the wooden carving on the counter and whittled in silence. The stories were over. Paz thought of his wife, the dead wife, who'd turned the mask into the core of a work of art. The piece of wood was becoming a doll, with surprisingly delicate features. She felt awkward, standing in the center of the little store, and yet she didn't want to leave. The smell of frying oil, of buñuelos cooking, wafted from the other room. El Lobo's presence enveloped her; it made her feel alive. She wanted to swim in his company for as long as she could. So she started cleaning up the wood shavings from the counter, under his hands. He let her do it, not looking up from his work, as if they'd been doing this together for years, as if it were the most normal thing in the world. When she dared steal a glance at the oxygen mask, it looked different somehow, less like an object and more like a face, hovering on its pale nest of bones.

*

They scattered in the day, did as they pleased, and gathered around the fire at night. There, they cooked, drank, ate, lingered, cleaved to each other as if to long-lost relatives from whom they'd soon be torn away. They confessed secrets, retold the forays of their days, and dreamed up wild, absurd adventures that, in the crackling glow of the flames, they could almost pretend were possible.

On the sixth night, as Flaca and Romina were bickering warmly over who would be the pourer of the *mate,* La Venus said, "Tonight, I'm going to insist on it, Malena: your turn to tell us more about yourself."

Malena looked startled. She was sitting at the fire, casting fish bones from her plate to the flames. "Me?"

"You."

Silence fell over the women. Flaca gave the thermos to Romina with a shrug, *you win.*

"I don't have much to tell," Malena said.

"Bullshit." La Venus's voice was gentle. "Look, I don't mean to upset you. It's just that, well, we all talk so much—why are you all laughing? we do!—we talk so much that we should remember to make space for quiet people."

"I'm a quiet person?"

"Aren't you?"

Malena didn't answer. The fire licked and sang. Romina poured water into the *mate* and handed it first to Malena. Inside, Romina was drunk on happiness, because she'd felt the blood arrive that afternoon as she was walking to the beach for a swim. No baby. No new life.

No yoke to the Only Three. She'd walked into the water and, once immersed, took off her bikini bottom so she could look at the stain, see it with her own eyes, such a glorious red smear, she could frame it and put it on her wall and admire it for all her days, and then without thinking she opened her legs wide underwater and bled into the ocean, an offering, a thank-you, a sealing of some indecipherable pact. And now, here she was, with these women, browner from five days of sun, so easy with each other that they could almost forget that some of them had recently been strangers and that soon they'd all return to their other, pinched lives. "We don't have much longer," she said now.

"I don't know what kind of person I am," Malena finally said. She curled her hands around the gourd and looked up at the rampant stars. "Well, all right. Are you going to twist my arm on this?"

"Possibly." La Venus grinned.

"I can tell you this one thing, I suppose. I used to live in a convent."

Romina thought she must have heard wrong. All the women were staring. "What?"

"I was a novice."

"You mean," La Venus said, "preparing to be a nun?"

"Yes."

Silence.

"You're joking," Flaca finally said.

"Shut up, Flaca, for God's sake," Romina said. "Can't you see that she's not joking?"

Flaca had a thousand questions, but she held back and busied herself poking at the fire with a stick.

"And—why did you go?" La Venus said. "You loved God?"

"No. I mean, I wanted to love Him." Malena drank from the *mate,* slowly, intently, as if the brew were the antidote for a long-swallowed poison. "It's a long—it's a long story."

Silence rasped between them again, flecked with the murmur of the flames.

"What—" Flaca began, but La Venus held her back with a hand on her knee.

"We have time for a long story," Romina said quietly. "There's plenty of time."

Malena seemed to shrink into herself. The fire flicked and danced. "I had to get away," she said, and then a blankness fell across her face like a curtain.

"What was it like?" Romina asked. "Being there, I mean." She'd always been curious about convents, having grown up in a Jewish household and only seen nuns from a distance.

Malena squinted at the flames as if seeking a familiar face in a crowd of strangers. "It was quiet. Rigorous. Everyone thinks life in a convent is about retiring from things, but, in fact, you're kept busy with all the prayers and work. Then under the surface of all of that, you're alone, and so, on the inside, it's quiet. You start to hear yourself inside the quiet. So it was comforting. But also terrible. To hear yourself so much."

"Is that why you left?" La Venus asked.

"No. I left because I couldn't do it. I just couldn't."

"Do what? Believe in God?"

"No, not that."

"The Church hates people like us," Flaca said. She'd never spoken those words aloud before, and they scalded her tongue. "Was that the problem?"

"Maybe. I don't know," Malena said. She'd grasped a fistful of her skirt and started worrying at the hem, as if trying to iron it out with her bare fingers. "I just couldn't. It was too late."

"What do you mean, too late?" La Venus leaned forward. "You must have been very young, no?"

"Even young people can break," Malena said.

Paz felt these words in the pit of her body. No wonder this woman had understood her, been willing to see.

Romina poured another *mate,* and passed it to Flaca, and she couldn't stop her hand from trembling. She tried to imagine Malena as a young novice, hurting inside for who knew what reason—but it couldn't have been too late, could it? The young could break, but couldn't they also heal?

They waited for Malena to continue, but the gourd made its slow rounds and she didn't speak again.

*

The sixth day. Their last full day at Polonio. Paz was on her way to El Lobo's to pick up bell peppers and bread for that night's *asado*— they'd be grilling fish and making a special feast for their last night fire. Romina had lain down for a siesta, while Flaca and La Venus had disappeared into the dunes. Paz hoped that El Lobo would be in the mood for stories. On her way, she saw a lone figure down past the lighthouse, perched on the rocks. It looked like a woman. She walked closer. Malena. How long had she been there? How long had she been gone from the group? She had taken to wandering away without warning in the afternoons. Her figure cut a human hole in the blue sky. Her hair hung in a ponytail down her back, a more relaxed style than the bun she'd arrived with, and yet Paz realized at that moment that she'd never seen Malena's hair loose in the wind.

"Can I sit with you?"

Malena started and glanced up. "Fine." Then she seemed to soften, remember something about herself or the young woman before her. "I mean, of course."

Paz folded her legs beneath her on the rocks. The ocean was calmer today than yesterday, luxuriously blanketing the rocks below them, then pulling away, returning.

She didn't know what to say. She strained for something, then blurted, "Do you ever miss the convent?"

"Why would you ask that?"

"I don't know. It seems a different world, a different universe."

"I don't want to talk about the convent."

"Sorry."

"No, it's not your fault. I'm prickly and I know it. I'm sure you're all sick of me by now and wish you hadn't invited me."

"No! That's ridiculous," Paz said, though she was also thinking that it wasn't she who'd invited anyone to this place.

Malena shook her head, eyes out on the horizon.

"Really." Paz moved closer, so that their shoulders touched. "The others feel the same, I'm sure of it. You're needed here."

"Where did you get *that* idea?"

"I don't know. We need everyone." She wondered where those words had come from. Whether they could apply to her. "There's room for everyone." Unlike in the city. Too soon, tomorrow night, they'd all have to face all that again: streets, tightness, thin walls, pretense. People who couldn't see them. Even at home.

"But I'm different. Not like the rest of you."

"You think I don't feel different?"

Malena turned and finally looked at Paz. "Yes. I suppose you must."

"I'm like a kid to them, that's what they all call me, even you. La Venus is married, Flaca is, well, Flaca—we're all different. That's why we came."

"Is it?"

"Isn't that why you came?"

Malena turned away and faced the horizon again, jaw clenched. When she faced Paz again, her eyes were wet, and she seemed on the brink of breaking open.

Paz leaned in and kissed her on the lips.

First kiss since Puma.

Time distilled.

Plush lips, surprisingly warm.

There was pull in Malena, a deepsea whirlpool, drawing her in for one beat, two, and then Malena drew back. "No." She wiped her mouth.

Paz couldn't move. Shame poured through her. "Oh God," she said, and then, "I'm sorry," even though she wasn't, or if she was, she didn't know what for.

"This isn't right."

What isn't right? her mind shouted back. Kissing you, or my age, or two women's mouths together at all—but her mouth wouldn't open to say a thing. She sprang to her feet and ran up the rocks toward El Lobo's.

"Tell me about the sea lions," Paz said.

She was sweeping the floor with a broom made by hand from bundled sticks. El Lobo no longer protested when she reached for the broom or a rag to dust the shelves with, a victory that pleased her.

He watched her from the counter. "You're not really leaving tomorrow."

"I am."

"What a shame."

"That's why you should tell me about the sea lions."

"What do you want to know?"

"You used to hunt them, right?"

"Every day."

"And seals?"

"Yes."

She nosed the broom into a corner. She didn't know how to pull stories out of this man. The best way, it seemed, was to wait, to sit inside the silence until he broke it, only now she had no time left, and this man was so comfortable saying nothing that it sometimes seemed he'd never break it at all, as though silence were a precious thing to be kept whole. It was new to her, this sort of silence, not corrosive at all, but warm and solid, like a quilt shared on a winter night.

"It was hard work," he finally said. "They are powerful creatures. I hunted until I didn't have the strength to be out there anymore. They thrash, you know, fight for their lives, and slaughtering them takes strength. It's not for the old—or for the faint of heart. You know, city people don't come out here much, but when they do, they don't want to hear about this sort of thing. They want to look at the beautiful waves but they don't want to know what it really means to live out here, what it takes to survive. They don't want to see the blood in the foam."

Her mind filled with foam, red foam, bristling on the surface of the sea.

"But you're not like that."

"I hope not."

"And so I talk to you. And it's strange, *hija.*" He looked at her tenderly. "I've never talked to a city person so much before."

Paz gathered the broom around a tidy pile of dust. She didn't know what to say. She thought fleetingly of her own father. "Do you have a dustpan?"

"We just sweep it all out the door. Look, like this."

He came out from behind the counter and took the broom from her hands. She watched him sweep her little pile out and into the surrounding grass. Malena was out there, somewhere, likely laughing at her, maybe telling the others about the kiss so they could all laugh. She waited inside for El Lobo to return. *El Lobo,* she thought. Of course. Not *lobo,* wolf. *Lobo marino,* sea lion, seal. Named for the creatures he'd hunted.

"I'd want to see the blood in the foam," she said when he returned.

He made a grunting sound.

"I mean it," she said, trying to keep the hurt out of her voice. "I want to stay here."

"Hmm. For how long?"

"Don't know. Maybe forever."

"Forever! What would you do here?"

"What do *you* do here?"

"You know the answer. I used to kill sea lions, and now I run a store."

"I'll do that too."

He put the broom in its corner, and returned to his counter. "Polonio doesn't need another store. There's barely anyone to sell to."

"I'll open a restaurant."

"Hah!"

"What?"

"This isn't big old Montevideo."

"There's nothing for me in Montevideo."

He stopped and looked at her intently. "Why do you say that? Don't you have a family?"

She shrugged. "There's my mother."

"School?"

"To hell with school!"

He laughed. Again she was startled by the gaps where teeth had been. She laughed along with him this time, surprised that he hadn't lectured her on the importance of school, as adults almost always did. "You haven't seen Polonio's winter storms," he said.

"I love storms."

"Listen, *hija,* I'm glad you like it here. But you'd go crazy if you stayed."

"I don't think I would."

They looked at each other for a long time. His expression shifted, grew thoughtful. He searched her face as if probing for the answer to an unformed question.

"Well," he said, "I might have something for you."

"What kind of something?"

"A place you could call home."

*

The women prepared a feast for that final night, with the luxury of extra wood that Flaca and La Venus had spent all afternoon gathering, so they could have fire for a long time, really celebrate, which seemed questionable to La Venus and she said as much: what was there to celebrate about having to leave?

"The fact," Flaca said, "of having made it here at all."

Romina had bought a full bucket of fish from Óscar, the fisherman who lived behind El Lobo's grocery with his wife, Alicia; her father, El Lobo; and the children, Lili, Ester, and Javier. As darkness gathered, they lit candles and held flashlights for each other while the fish opened their bellies to knife and hand and salt. Everyone seemed happy, sated after their day outdoors, salt in their hair, dirt under their fingernails, even though Flaca thought she detected a streak of sadness below it all, at everything ending, at this being their last night. Leaving was painful. But this was what she'd wanted, wasn't it? A deepening of connections, a week of joy? The trip had been more successful than she'd dreamed possible. She'd thought they might get relief from the city, perhaps make friends, but she hadn't known they could come to feel like something more than friends, something larger, a kind of alternative family stitched together by the very fact that they'd been torn from the fabric of the accepted world. She pushed her fingers deeper into the slick body of a fish. Yes, they had to go back to the city, to the dullness of it and the fear, the smallness of the sky, but she didn't want to think about the city right now. It would all be there for them tomorrow. Stay here, in the moment, on these rocks, under this indigo sky, in this holy unholy communion that had no name and yet meant more to her than anything else in her life.

They roasted the fish over embers, along with whole bell peppers and a couple of eggplants, all of which they served with olive oil and Alicia's freshly baked bread. It was almost midnight when they finally gathered to eat, the moon high above them in a drove of stars.

A quiet fell over them.

"I don't want to go back," Romina finally said.

No one dared respond. The ocean spun its rhythmic song out in the distance.

"I can't stand it anymore," Romina went on. "And yet I have to stand it. We all have to."

"The city?" Flaca asked.

"The dictatorship," Romina said, louder than she'd meant to.

The word *dictatorship* hovered between them, over the fire, slinking around it, dark and weightless. No one ever used that word in the city. Many people didn't even think it anymore, or so it appeared from the outside. Even here, out in Polonio, far from civilization and its spies, no one had uttered the word or heard it.

"You mean *El Proceso*," La Venus ventured. The Process. The regime's term for the curfews, kidnappings, censorship, searches, surveillance, interrogations, rules, decrees, all the changes they'd imposed on the nation, as if a word could sanitize the horrors away.

"I mean the dictatorship," Romina said. The bleeding between her legs emboldened her. *They took so much,* the blood crooned, *but not your womb and not your voice.* "Why can't we call a thing by its name? You think it's some kind of 'Process,' like the steps involved in fixing cars or curing leather? The disappearing of my brother, the—what happened to me? The fact that I can't ever get a job as a teacher if I'm categorized as a B or C citizen, a threat to the nation—and I probably am categorized that way—or if I'm ever overheard criticizing the State or even accused of it? My brother and I have both been arrested, that's enough to threaten my career. And if the government got wind of everything I've just said—forget it, I can't say any of this in the city, it's impossible, you all know that, that's why you're all staring at me right now like I'm crazy but you know what? I'm saying it because tomorrow night I won't be able to, we'll all be back in our cages."

She fell silent. Flaca moved to stoke the embers into flames. She added kindling, a log. Now that the food was all roasted, the fire could spark up again for their warmth and pleasure.

"I often wonder how long it'll last," La Venus said. "I'm always looking for clues that the regime is crumbling, that next month or next year things will be back to normal."

"There is no normal to go back to," Romina said.

"Now now, Romina," Flaca said, "no need to be unkind. La Venus is just holding out hope, is that so wrong? We all need hope, don't we?"

"We need to survive, Flaca. If hope is what gets you there, fine. But I can't rely on holding my breath until it's over."

"Why not?" Malena asked.

Romina stared at her, and softened. She was a kind soul, Malena, for all her layers of hiding and her deflections; she bristled when you got too close, and yet, when she sensed need in someone, she gave without a thought. "Look, I'm sorry if I've upset you—any of you. I don't mean to be negative. This is our goodbye party, our celebration. It's easy to see why we avoided the topic until now."

"It's fine," La Venus said, reaching out a hand to Romina's knee. "I'm the one who's sorry. I'm rather dumb about these things, it's true."

"You're not dumb, Venus!" Flaca said.

"My husband calls me stupid all the time."

"Your husband's an idiot!"

"Enough, you two," Romina said, though in truth she loved the tender look they exchanged, as if a gaze between women could wrestle a man's insults to the ground.

"But look, Romina—I really do want to know your answer to Malena's question," La Venus said. "And I bet everyone else does, too."

"Really?" Romina scanned the circle.

"Oh, sure," Flaca said. "Of course I want to know. But I'm going to need a hell of a lot more whiskey."

A freshly opened bottle started making the rounds, and when it reached Romina she swigged and wiped her mouth with her sleeve. "All right. Two reasons. First of all, because some nightmares last a lifetime and that's it. Look at what Trujillo did to the Dominican Republic. Look at Paraguay. Some dictators hold the reins forever. I know we Uruguayans think that couldn't happen to us, that we're a different kind of country, but guess what? That's exactly why we didn't see the coup coming! Secondly: even if this does end before we're, say, fifty years old, we can't just push a button and miraculously rewind to 'seventy-three. Even if all the political prisoners are freed, even if all the exiles come back, what do we do with them? What do they do with themselves? We'd have to start taking stock of the ruins, of what's broken in our country, and it won't all be sun and rainbows—it's when our work will begin."

She fell silent.

Flaca whistled. "So speaks the prophet."

"Shut up," Romina said.

"No, I mean it—you're like John the whoever it was."

"Or like Cassandra," Malena said. "She really saw all of it."

"And the Trojans didn't believe her," Romina said.

Malena gave her a look so intense it was almost hungry. "Well, there you go."

"One thing is clear," La Venus said. "When all of that happens, however old and gray we are, we'll make you president."

Laughter erupted.

"You're already drunk," Romina said.

"I am! But it's true! You're what we'll need! Come on, you have to at least become a senator, won't you?"

"Oh, all right," Romina said. "And I'll also fly unicorns to the moon."

"I could use a unicorn to ride," La Venus said.

"I'll find you one, my angel," Flaca declared.

La Venus flashed a radiant smile. "I knew you would."

"I tell you what," Flaca said, "let's get so drunk that tomorrow doesn't even exist anymore, that all of reality is right here on this beach."

"So we never go back?"

"So we never go back."

"I don't want to die," said Romina. Pleasure spread across her chest as she realized that, in that moment, it was true. She was here, on this rock near the beach, reddening the cloth between her legs, the cigarette burns almost faded from her limbs, her ears full of ocean and women, and she wanted to live.

"Neither do I," said Malena, with a note in her voice that resembled surprise.

"I'm not talking about dying." Flaca lit a cigarette. "I'm talking about living forever inside this moment."

"And how do we do that?" Romina reached into Flaca's pack for a smoke of her own. "Witchcraft?"

Flaca smiled. "I'm game."

"Me too," Paz said.

"The witches of Cabo Polonio!" said Romina.

"I already feel like a part of me will be here forever," La Venus mused. "I've never felt so alive in my life."

"We all know why that's true!" Romina raised the whiskey flask.

"No, really—"

"I feel that way too," Malena said, reaching her palms toward the embers. "As if part of me won't ever leave."

"Actually," Paz said, "I have some news. About some witchcraft that could keep a part of us here."

Flaca exhaled smoke and stared at Paz. "*Chica,* what? Out with it."

Once she started, it all spilled out, each word cascading over the ones before it. "I went to see El Lobo today, and you won't believe it, his nephew has an empty house—a hut, really, you know, for fishermen—right here in Cabo Polonio, just a short walk from the store and he used to live there, the nephew, with his wife and daughter, but the daughter has asthma and it's not good for her to live out in the elements, she was suffering, her health was I mean, so they moved to Castillos, that nearby town we saw on the map, remember?—where there's an apothecary and roads to get to the hospital if they have to go and they want to sell the place but they haven't advertised or anything, they want to sell it by word of mouth."

She fell silent and the women savored the thoughts that poured through their minds.

"How are we supposed to buy a house?" Romina said. "My family can barely afford meat these days."

"Calm down, Romina, we're just talking," Flaca said. "Here, have another swig of whiskey, relax."

"Go to hell." Romina took the flask cheerfully, and drank.

"How big is the hut?" La Venus asked.

"Tiny," Paz said. "But who cares?" She took the flask as it came around and relished the liquid burning down her throat. "It's one room for everything, beds, kitchen, you know how it goes. And god knows about the toilet. But El Lobo said he'd recommend us."

"It sounds perfect," said Flaca.

"Except we can't have it," Romina said.

"Why do you have to ruin the fun?"

"I'm just saying—"

"I've always wanted to see inside one of those fishermen's huts," La Venus said. "Haven't you?"

"Sure," Romina said. "But I can't buy one."

"Why not?" said La Venus.

"You're drunk!" Romina pointed a finger to the sky, as if to emphasize her case.

"Not drunk enough—pass the whiskey."

"Fine, fine. But the house—"

"What about it?" La Venus leaned in seductively. "Don't you want it?"

"Hey, hey," Flaca said, pulling her back, "easy there."

"My love, I'm just asking our friend whether she wants a house."

"Put it like that and she'd want any house."

"I haven't even seen the house!" Romina said.

"Yes, you have," Paz said. "It's the one with dark brown walls before that lone tree on the way to El Lobo's—"

"How am I supposed to know which one that is?"

"I think I know the one," Malena said thoughtfully.

"The real question," La Venus said, "is why buy a house at the edge of the world?"

"Because it would be ours," Paz said. "Don't you see? We'd always have a place to be free."

That shut everyone up for a while. The fire sparked, sang. The lighthouse beam brushed over them, left, brushed again. The women looked at the flames, at each other.

"Let's go see it," Flaca said.

"Let's go!" said La Venus.

"Why not?" said Malena. "Maybe it'll have something to tell us."

The others looked at her in surprise. Malena, the sensible one, the reserved one, the ex-nun, suggesting they listen to a house?

"Now?" Romina said.

"Now, *¡boluda!* When else?"

They took a single flashlight. They stumbled through the dark, drunk, full of fish and bread and starlight and each other's excitement. The dirt shimmered darkly beneath their feet. Malena walked close to Paz. "Can we talk?"

Paz shrugged, but let herself lag back to walk with Malena.

"Listen. About today."

"Forget it," said Paz.

"I just want to say—you're not the problem. I'm the problem. I'm terrified and I don't know what any of this means for me."

It surprised Paz, the spilling rawness of the confession, perhaps propelled by the whiskey. "It means whatever we want it to. That's the point."

"Oh really? So we have a few days of fresh air and swims at the beach, declaring the sort of women we are, and then what? We have to go back to the city. We have to be good and proper."

"I thought you were always good and proper."

Malena snorted. "There's a lot you don't know about me."

"I'm sure that's true."

A quiet step, another, another.

"And if we can't act the same anymore in the city," Malena went on, "what do you think will happen to us?"

"We'll be safe."

"How do you know?"

"We have each other."

Malena made a barking sound that might have been a laugh. "You're something else, Paz."

"I mean it."

"I know. But I'll never be safe."

"You don't know that."

"The way you talk, I forget sometimes how young you are."

Paz gritted her teeth. "I'm not a child."

"I didn't say you were a child. I know very well you're not. When I was your age—" Malena broke off, fixed her gaze on the backs of their friends in the darkness ahead.

"What? When you were my age what?" Paz was desperately curious and seemed on the brink of revelation. Malena at sixteen. A novice at the convent? Or?

"Never mind."

She'd closed up again. It was shocking, how good Malena was at closing up, at shuttering her mind to others. It seemed a useful skill; Paz couldn't exactly blame her. As they walked on, she spooled Malena's words out in her mind: *I'll never be safe, never be safe, be safe.*

"I admire you, Paz."

A glow of pleasure, surprise.

"I want to be friends."

A slap. Rejection. It stung, because what she'd done with Malena had been a first, an attempt at being bold like Flaca, though when she stopped to think about it she wasn't sure whether she had a crush on Malena because of who she was, or simply because she was there. Not that Malena wasn't pretty: she had delicate features and eyes you could get lost in. But she was so tightly wound, with her bun and her knees together, that Paz would not have noticed her if she hadn't been out on this beach, with these women, signaling connection to this tribe. Maybe the primness wasn't her real self at all. Maybe she was finding her way to her real self, just like Paz was. She felt a deep yearning, though she didn't know for what. "Of course, Malena. We'll always be friends."

The hut loomed, appearing black in the night.

"Is this the one?"

"I think it is."

It was long and narrow, with a pitched roof that seemed to catch shards of the moon. The door stood at the center of a long wall, a window to one side, bereft of glass. An awning hung over the front door to form a small front patio.

"Quaint," La Venus said.

"A dream," Flaca said.

It seemed that way to Paz, too, reminding her of the humble huts in fairy tales where fishermen's wives had wishes granted by mythical fish who longed for another day of life.

"A wreck," Romina said.

"It'll need some work," La Venus admitted. "That roof looks like it would let the rain right in."

"Nothing we can't handle," Flaca said.

"What's this *we*?"

"You, my queen, my Venus, won't have to lift a finger."

La Venus smiled, and approached the door.

Romina moved toward her, whether to stop her or to follow, she wasn't sure. "What are you doing?"

"Well, no one's home, right?"

The door was not locked.

One by one, they stepped through.

There was no furniture save a narrow table in the area that must have been the kitchen, judging by the stacked metal pails and the cooking pit dug in the old peasant way. A packed dirt floor. Three windows, none of them paned. Gaps in the walls wide enough to let the wind through. A hole-pocked roof stretched over a bare rectangle of space.

They stood together in that empty space. The lighthouse beam slashed in through a window and swept over them, a cloth of light, followed by the deeper cloth of dark.

*

The next day, hungover, dizzy with the exhilaration of their seven days, they packed up their things and left Polonio on foot. First they stopped at El Lobo's shop to say goodbye. Alicia and the children came out, too, and the women accepted a *mate* and lingered, talking and playing with the children—Javier, the youngest at four years old, brought out the seal bones he used as toy soldiers and sparked a little war in the dirt with Flaca, which her army promptly lost—until Alicia finally pointed out that they should go if they wanted to catch the last bus to the city from the bus stop on the highway. They left with promises to return—*and we'll be ready for you,* El Lobo said, with a tender look at Paz, which she pocketed away in the deep recesses of her mind—and then they struck out along the long, sprawling northern beach, the Playa de las Calaveras, named for skulls because, once upon a time, that beach had been riddled with them. The women were silent as they walked, each harboring her own roiling thoughts, the sand a damp thud under their feet. To their left, the ocean waves sang out rich music, beckoning for them to stay, but they walked on. At the end of the long beach, before the sand dunes began, they turned to look back one last time. There, behind them, the low slope of Polonio, and the majestic curve of the ocean. There, the lighthouse, its tall body like a finger held, *ssshhhhh,* to the closed lips of the horizon.

3

Into Madness

AT FIRST SHE couldn't bear to shower. For four days, La Venus wiped her armpits with a washcloth but kept the rest of her body soiled with Cabo Polonio, its film still on her, gilding her, humming against her skin. She couldn't stand the thought of losing the last grains of sand from between her toes, between her legs. Her mother called, *why won't you come for tea,* and her sisters and sisters-in-law, *come on, where are you?,* but she couldn't see them until she bathed, so she held them at bay. Pretending that she could slow down time. As if the smell of her own sweat could keep the dream intact.

None of it worked. Her body clamored to be clean. It was no use trying to hold on to the traces of beach, of freedom; the scent of the ocean was soon overpowered by her own odor; sweat gilded her skin and gradually made it smooth again, slipping sand grains away to oblivion. Arnaldo hadn't noticed—or, if he had, he hadn't said a word. He said so little these days. How small their lives had become, how confined by fears no one spoke aloud.

The question was how to live here in the city without letting it crush you.

The question was how to live in the city at all.

She was ungrateful, and she knew it. They were alive. Neither of them had been arrested even once since the coup. Arnaldo had work.

He hated it, but he had it. He processed paperwork at the Ministry of Education and Culture, a job he'd had since they got married five years before. Back then, he'd been excited about the possibilities: he, a musician with big dreams—*the John Lennon of Uruguay, that's what they'll call me, just you wait*—was going to get paid to work in the government offices of culture, helping decide the destinies of artists. Those were heady days, long-haired, bell-bottomed. Arnaldo her bohemian man. She'd had her pick of men, all sorts of them lined up to gladly lick the floor she walked on: middle-aged businessmen with deep pockets, young doctors launching their careers, sons of former senators with glitzy beach apartments in Punta del Este, fervent poets, brilliant philosophers, law students with tongues of gold. She chose Arnaldo because he had seemed to embody a bohemian life. He looked a bit like Mick Jagger and spoke as if all his dreams were already true. He made you want to repeat his words because they tasted so damn good, because he rolled them like honey in his mouth. When she was with him the world was wide. She became a rock star's girlfriend and then, very soon, a rock star's wife. But after the coup, it didn't take long for the rock star to become the Incredible Shrinking Bureaucrat, smaller and smaller with each passing week. He swallowed all his rage and disappointment, brought it home in tight packages that splayed out their unhappiness behind closed doors. He stopped playing music. He stopped laughing without malice. Sex was his only consolation, his expected reward for a long day of dullness, fear, and doing the will of the regime. She was his medicine, the shot of whiskey meant to drown his sorrows. He drank her bitterly. Afterward, he'd fall asleep and she'd lie in the sour aftertaste, his bitterness lodged under her skin.

Now she'd been ruined by Cabo Polonio, by those big gulping breaths of ocean air. Her lungs had expanded. Their apartment gave her no room to breathe. There was no room here for La Venus, for the damp woman in possession of every inch of her own body, desired and bursting with desire. Glowing. Seen. What had that thought been, in the sand dunes? That Anita was a lie, a broken shell. How could she fit herself back into that lie, that old self in which she no

longer believed? And yet she had to. So she got up and—as if she'd
never been to the sand dunes, as if no dunes existed on this earth—she
brewed the *mate,* toasted bread for her husband's breakfast, smiled at
him when he stumbled into the kitchen, brightly, automatically, as if
she were a machine programmed to stretch its mouth at the sight of
him. When had that begun? Was it new, or had she simply not noticed
it before? It disgusted her. She disgusted herself. A broken shell. She
had to leave. She couldn't leave. Ridiculous! She would lose everything: her parents' respect, her old friends—all married, women who
would never in a thousand years be caught pressed up against a Cabo
Polonio rock—her home, her ability to buy new clothes and keep a
tab with the grocer, the baker, the butcher—perhaps not the butcher.
She could go further down the road, to Flaca's. Flaca would surely give
her meat. Flaca would give her a lot of things. She certainly would. But
Flaca lived with her parents, she was so young, all that swagger made
it easy to forget that she was only twenty-one, too young to burden
with this question of how a married woman might survive without
her husband.

There was one more thing, too, that she would lose: her chance to
have a child. She'd miscarried once and it was the most intense sorrow of her life. Leaving her husband to go be La Venus, goddess of an
underworld where women made love to women, would mean leaving
the chance to be a mother. All her life she'd longed for the sensation of
pregnancy, the fullness of it, and every baby she'd ever held had made
her ache to hold her own. Could she walk away from that? Only barrenness awaited La Venus: barrenness and sex and a true life.

Scared to leave. Scared to stay.

She hovered in the space between fears.

On the fifth day, she showered and scrubbed her skin until it was red
and raw, then put on meticulous makeup and a clean, elegant blouse
that revealed no cleavage. No distractions. When her husband came
home, she was waiting for him at the kitchen table with a ready *mate.*
She watched him drink and waited for the watery dregs to gurgle in
the gourd before she spoke.

"I don't want to have sex with you anymore."

He stared at her for a moment as if she'd suddenly started speaking Czech. "What's the matter with you?"

"Nothing's the matter."

"What have I done? If I've done something, you have to tell me."

"It's nothing like that."

"Something I haven't done?" His voice grew sly. "Something you . . . want?"

"No."

His jaw clenched. "There's another man, then."

"Arnaldo, calm down—"

"Who is he?"

"There is no other man."

"Liar."

"It's the truth."

"Then why would you—"

"Please," she said gently. "Don't make this difficult."

"Difficult?" he said. "Me?"

She reached for his hand. He drew back, sprang up from the table, and left the room.

That night, he reached for her in the darkness and she pushed his hand away. He turned from her and went to sleep. She thought she'd won her space. But on the following night, he reached for her again, and when she brushed his hand away, he returned, more forcefully this time. She pressed at his chest with the flat of her palm, but he didn't yield.

"Don't be stupid, Anita."

"We've been through this."

"Oh for fuck's sake. Either you tell me his name or you stop being childish."

I'm not being childish, she wanted to say, *just the opposite,* but his hand was back and so was the rest of him, on her now, and suddenly exhaustion overcame her and she wondered whether it was worth the scope of the fight since her attempts to push him off weren't working anyway, he was stronger than she, it was no use, he had her pinned and was doing what he liked, and maybe he was right and she was stupid, he was her husband after all, she belonged to him, and hadn't he had another terrible day in a string of grim and terrible days, what was her problem, tell me that, what is your problem, stupid Anita.

*

The streets were hostile zones, pocked with reminders of torture. Romina flinched at almost nothing, and this shamed her: all the people who'd been tortured for months on end, and she quakes like this after only three days? And yet it rose in her, insistent. Sometimes it seemed that people were seeing into her, could read what had happened in her face or in the way she held her shoulders. At other times she thought she read torture in those around her: was that why the kiosk vendor never met anyone's eyes anymore, or why the neighbor at the end of the block swept her porch steps brutally, as if they'd crossed a line and had to be punished? It could be anyone who passed her on the street, really. How to know who else bore those same wounds? Certainly those who'd never met *la máquina* still lived in fear of it, didn't they? Who hadn't heard of it? Maybe everyone bore the wounds, no matter what had or hadn't happened to them; maybe they were all part of the same vast, bruised body in the shape of a nation. A body groping for the slightest illusions of safety.

She never would have thought this way before Polonio. Where had her pragmatism gone? She'd spent seven days in dreamtime, in a landscape of beauty, of refuge, of the impossible, and she'd relaxed too much, she'd bled gleefully into the ocean, and she'd even been so reckless as to talk about the dictatorship—using that very word, no less—out loud, in the open air! Now she feared herself. She feared she might have lost the restraint she needed for the city.

She kept her head down in her studies. History. The colonial era. The heroic tracts and battles of Artigas. Artigas was a liberator, yet the generals allowed him into their censored history books, still lauded

him as a hero, hadn't toppled a single statue of the man. How could
that be? To them he was a military general, like them, their predeces-
sor, who'd made this country they now got to run at the expense of its
own people. Liars. Their histories were a lie. But she studied them. She
memorized them. Why? Because she was a traitor? That's what she'd
thought at first, in the first years of university, that she was betraying
her Communist brother who'd disappeared into those very generals'
prisons, that she was betraying her neighbors and the people of her
country and her very own ideals, and she'd been ashamed of spew-
ing their lies back out in essays and exams. She'd thought of herself as
small-minded, like a rat, running through the junta's maze, reduced to
following their orders. But now, she saw things differently. Was it her
arrest that had done it, or her days on the beach? The arrest showed her
that no matter how much she kept her head down and obeyed, they
could lock her up or assault her whenever they wanted. The beach,
meanwhile, had shown her that another kind of air still existed in the
world. You had to get to the far edges of reality to breathe that air; it
wasn't easy to find; but if you found it, breathing was still possible.

"You seem quiet lately," her mother said as she gathered the dirty
dinner plates, though she stopped short of asking what was on her
daughter's mind.

"All these exams." It was the first thing she could think of. She'd
been bending close to her textbook at the kitchen table, jotting notes
occasionally in hopes that this would fool her mother into thinking
she was focusing. But her mother was no fool. "Here, Mamá, I'll help
you with the dishes."

"No, study—otherwise you'll be up too late, and you need your
rest."

It was the greatest gift she could give her daughter, Romina knew:
her blessing to not wash the pots and dishes, to occupy herself with
bookish pursuits after dinner as if she were a husband or a son. Over
the years, they'd grown accustomed to sharing the small kitchen in
silence, one studies, one cooks. It was generous of her, though sometimes Romina wondered whether Mamá only did this because Felipe

was gone and there was no son to coddle, and then she felt guilty for her own cynicism. "No, Mamá, you're the one who should rest."

"I'm fine," Mamá said, but she let Romina take over the sink without further protest. They began working quietly, side by side, Romina washing, Mamá drying, an ancient mother-daughter ritual that surely harkened back to the days of Exodus, the plates washed in slavery under the Pharaoh until that famous night the Jewish people left in haste and probably left stacks of dirty pots and pans for the Egyptians to handle on their own. Passover was Romina's favorite holiday, embedded as it was with a liberation story, one that held more fascination now than ever, and standing here, washing beside Mamá, with the Polonio waves still fresh in her mind, Romina thought about that great escape that was her inheritance and thought, what if—

Come on, finish the thought.

She thought it furiously, again, what if—?

Soapsuds foaming, circling, seeping into the skin of her hands.

What if she shed her fear?

What if she could be brave?

Arrests like the one she'd recently been through were meant to immobilize, to terrify people into obeying the government so it never happened again. But now she saw how what they did—their punishments, in her case, for no known or stated crime—could have the opposite effect.

Because if it can happen to you when you keep your head down like a good little rat, then she'd cracked open their secret: *obedience did not protect you.*

In which case, why bother obeying?

Why not resist?

She scrubbed hard at a pot with stubborn grime.

There was one reason.

Her parents.

Romina glanced over at her mother, who was carefully drying a pan. She was a small, compact woman who wore a kerchief over her hair while doing housework—which was most of her day—in the fashion of the Old Country. She had a gentle soul and a deep reserve that made Romina wonder whether she simply didn't want anything, or hid her wants so well, subsumed them so successfully for her family, that they became invisible to the naked eye. She suffered without complaint, her mother, which only made Romina feel worse about wanting things for herself. Especially now. With Felipe gone, everything depended on Romina. On her building a life. On her making them proud. On her making up for the hole he left. Her life was not solely her own: it belonged to her parents, who'd given her everything, and in fact it had begun before she was born, when her parents had fled the Ukraine, or else before that when her grandparents had fled pogroms in Russia. Romina's grandmother had been the sole survivor of a family of six when, one Easter Sunday, a Christian mob had celebrated the resurrection of their Savior by terrorizing the Jewish Quarter. They had burned down her family's home, though nobody knew exactly how the deaths had happened, whether Abuela's parents and brothers and sisters had been stabbed or shot or burned alive, as Abuela never spoke of the details. She, Romina, only knew that their survival had resulted in their arrival here, in Uruguay, where she and Felipe were born as a new generation of hope, the pinnacle of all that suffering and sacrifice. And this had always been enough of a reason for her to stay locked up in her maze. Until now. Until Polonio.

"Mamá," she said, and the sound of her voice startled them both.

"*¿Sí, Romina?*" Her mother's back stiffened, but she did not turn or stop drying the dish in her hands. "What is it?"

I can't stand it anymore. Why not resist. Also I will never love a man. Zero chance she'd be understood. And she had zero right.

"Never mind," Romina said. "It's nothing."

*

Paz returned to Montevideo with a flush of courage. Her mother seemed not to notice any difference, caught up as she was with her boyfriend, a widower twenty years her senior with a sixth-floor apart-

ment in a gleaming building with a doorman and balconies that over-
looked the river. The boyfriend worked for the government, doing
what, Paz didn't know, though she guessed that he knew nothing of
Mamá's past sympathies for and assistance of guerrilla fighters. Mamá
was rarely home. It was still summer; school was weeks away. Paz slept
all morning, lolled around the house all afternoon, then went out to
walk the neighborhood, gripped by sexual fantasies about the young
women—and some of the not-so-young women—she passed. She'd
been sparked. Her body was a knotted bundle of flames. Only walking
eased the ache of it, and so she walked: on the Rambla, the promenade
that sinewed along the shore; down the main artery of Avenida 18 de
Julio, crowded with shops and kiosks and café tables crammed onto
the sidewalks; into the Old City with its ornate, exhausted buildings
and narrow streets tucked into each other like cobbled secrets; through
plazas whose statues of various heroes wore their pigeon shit with an
air of resignation. She walked until darkness pushed her back indoors
because, though there was no longer a legal curfew, the nights were
not safe, police and soldiers prowled the streets, and if they stopped
you they'd ask for your papers and where you were going and why and
anything else they chose to do was covered in night. Inside, at home,
she read all night, pulling down books from her mother's shelves,
Jules Verne, Cervantes, Shakespeare, Homer, Juan Carlos Onetti,
Juana de Ibarbourou, Sor Juana Inés de la Cruz, Dante Alighieri, the
books she'd been able to keep under military rule. She sorely missed
the other books her mother had burned in the *parrilla* the night after
the coup: Benedetti, Galeano, Cristina Peri Rossi, Cortázar, and even
Dostoevsky and Tolstoy, all the Russians emphatically had to go, since
any Russian name smacked of Communism. Orange flames had licked
the pages, made them curl and blacken and disappear. How quickly
flames consume things. How her mother had wept as her books shriveled and went up in smoke. It was a silent weeping, completely still, a
stony face streaked with tears.

"It's so quick," Mamá finally said.

Paz, twelve years old, had been watching, not daring to say a word.

"Fire," Mamá added, as if that explained everything.

She looked beautiful in the flickering light. And sad. A sad and pretty woman, and, for the first time in her life, Paz looked at her mother's face and saw her as young. *I was so young when I had you,* she always told Paz, *with my future still ahead of me until you came along.*

"Before you know it," Mamá said to the flames, or into them, "everything is gone."

Mamá went to bed that night without cooking, and Paz ate María cookies with dulce de leche for dinner, in the kitchen, alone.

Ever since then, she'd felt as though the fires lit in that grill still held, somehow, the ghosts of those books, that the embers they used to slow-roast meat glowed with the light of vanished words. Mamá didn't barbecue often, but when she did, Paz would chew her chorizo or bell peppers very slowly, imagining that she was taking in lost sentences along with her food.

Now the books in their house were fewer, more limited. To compensate, Paz had developed a habit of turning back to the beginning of a book the moment she finished it. As if a story were a circle, its ending secretly embedded in its opening line. As if a book were a long and unclasped belt, with the first chapter at the buckle and the last page the end tip, an extended supple thing she could bend and wrap around the waist of her mind, curved, fastened, solid enough to stay. Endings morphed into beginnings and new meanings were revealed. King Lear, raised from the dead, was haughty again, gathering his three daughters, responding to betrayals by returning for more. Dante, after seeing everything, returns to the lip of the Inferno and still feels its pull. Don Quixote dies and then promptly becomes—what else?—his own self in that library where he fell into books and was first inspired to make his absurd helmet, as if his madness were also a kind of arrival into heaven. Time was a loop and people were caught inside of it, trapped by inevitable destinies, their futures fastened to their pasts. But was this true? And what was *her* inevitable destiny? *You'd go crazy if you stayed,* El Lobo had said. *You haven't seen the winter storms.* He might be right. But the heroes of books never heeded such warnings.

That reckless Dante, he just kept walking to the lip of the underworld, didn't he? Determined to follow his soul, to see what was there, and to hell with the price of the journey.

Her walks grew longer. She was never sure what she dreaded more, finding Mamá with her widower boyfriend, being alone with Mamá, or being the only one in the house. Each possibility held its own thorns. Her walks started landing her at Flaca's butcher shop, at first with the excuse of buying some meat, later just to dawdle and be with her. It was comforting to be around Flaca. It made her feel more herself, as if there were room for who she was in her own skin.

"Give me something to do," she said one day.

"I'm sorry." Flaca pulled out a tray of cuts of beef to tidy them. "We can't afford to hire anyone."

"I don't want money. I just want to help."

"Ha!"

"I mean it. I'm bored, I want to do something."

"Don't you have homework?"

"It's boring and I could do it in my sleep."

And so she started working, a few afternoons a week at Flaca's side, making herself useful in whatever way she could. She sorted money, ran errands, learned to cube beef just right for stews, grind certain cuts for sauces, slice the fat off other cuts so they could be sold as lean steaks. When March rolled around, with its end of summer and new school year, she continued to come twice a week and help, donning a blood-streaked apron over her school uniform. Over time, as they worked side by side, she heard the story of how Flaca came to run the butcher shop four days a week. She'd started helping out behind the counter when she was five, watching her father closely, and playing butcher, fashioning both her knives and her pretend meat out of cardboard and paper. Her father had only had daughters, and it grieved him not to be able to one day pass his store on to a son, as his own father had done. Flaca's older sisters had married men who showed no interest in becoming butchers for the worthy neighbors of Parque Rodó. Flaca's father had tried to change their minds, but to no avail. And so he'd taught his youngest daughter the arts of butchery, an apprenticeship she'd always wanted. She'd already been working the cash register and carrying things for him when his back ached, which was more and more often, and now, for the past three years, she'd been doing all the jobs that he did and giving him days of rest.

All of this fascinated Paz, the idea of having a father who taught you his bloody and noble trade, the idea of having a father at all. Flaca's parents, who sometimes came through the shop, were always warm with her. They were stout, with kind and tired faces, and older than Paz had expected them to be, in their early sixties. Flaca had been the last child, conceived when her mother thought her childbearing years were done; the opposite, Paz thought, of her own mother, who'd had a baby before she'd had a chance to see herself as a woman.

She didn't ask about La Venus, not wanting to pry, but she saw the way Flaca lit up when talking about her, and how, on other days, she grew rigid at the mention of her lover. There were clearly ups and downs between them. Paz listened for the smallest scraps, wanting to memorize this way of being. Even the most mundane detail of their relationship screamed itself up to the status of miracle, *two women!*

Autumn gave way to the cold winds of winter, biting Paz at the neck.

"How's Romina?" she asked one day, as an August storm pelted the windows of the shop. She saw the others less often than she did Flaca, and still felt shy about calling them too often out of the blue. They'd all slid back into their own city lives, in which they were grown women with serious things going on and she was a teenager with little in common with them, at least on the surface, where the world could see. The butcher shop was her tether to Polonio, her mundane proof that it had not all been a dream.

"She's all right, I think. I just talked to her last night and, you know what? You won't believe this, she asked me about the hut."

"What hut?"

"You joking? *The* hut! *Our* hut. The one you told us about, the one we saw on the last night. She was all excited, saying she had a dream about it the other night, that we were all in there. She thinks we should buy it. All of us together. It's odd, because Romina is one of the most prudent people I've ever met, but here she is stuck on that crazy idea."

"What's so crazy about it?"

Flaca laughed.

"Don't laugh at me."

"I'm sorry, Paz. I take you seriously. I do."

She seemed about to say more, but a customer entered and they quickly broke off conversation. Paz wrapped the requested meat for the lady while Flaca rang her up and counted out change. *That crazy idea.* That very one. She had no money to her name, none at all. Would they leave her out? Would they have their home at the edge of the world without her?

When the customer was gone, Flaca took out a cigarette, and Paz boldly reached for the pack on the counter.

"You shouldn't smoke," Flaca said, halfheartedly.

"I shouldn't do a lot of things."

Flaca focused on the flame of her match until her cigarette was lit. "Good point." She lit Paz's cigarette from the same flame. They stood quietly for a few moments, blowing out smoke, watching it disappear.

"I still have the number El Lobo gave me," Paz said. "For the grocer in Castillos who can send him messages. I could call and get the message to him that we want to know whether the house is still available, at what price."

"So you don't think it's crazy."

It wasn't a question.

"Do you?"

Flaca gazed up at the ceiling. "I don't know. But maybe that's not the right question." She lowered her voice, as if the censors could be listening, as if government surveillance might bother to spy on two young women in a butcher shop. "Maybe crazy and impossible are two different things."

*

It took almost two weeks for Paz to confirm with the grocer, who sent messages into Polonio when the cart driver took supplies, that the house was still available. Once they knew, Flaca summoned the four friends to her house. They gathered in the early evening so there would be plenty of time to talk and disperse before night fell completely, before walkers became more vulnerable to men in uniform. Flaca urged them each to arrive exactly on time, at staggered intervals—5:30, 5:38, 5:48, 5:55—to avoid giving the appearance of a gathering of five or more, which, as they had no permit, could incite a skittish or vindictive neighbor to report them. Before the coup, life in Uruguay had never clung to clock time; you arrived when you arrived, and the best time to join the party was whenever you wound your way through timelessness to the door. Not so, now. Martial law breeds martial time. You become precise to stay within the lines of safety or, rather, what you pretend are lines of safety, since those parameters could stop working at any moment.

When they'd all arrived, Flaca grabbed the fresh *mate* she'd prepared, along with a thermos of hot water, and she led the way into her bedroom. Her parents waved good-naturedly from the armchair and rocking chair where they sat watching the news, which was as grim and bland as always, harping on about the heroic regime, the evil Soviets, evil Cuba, heroic soccer, country people gathered in the province of Durazno to thank the government for the great generosity and architectural brilliance of a new bridge in their region.

Flaca's bedroom was sparsely decorated. Nothing hung on the graying walls except a single old photograph of the Plaza Matriz, at the heart of the Old City of Montevideo, with turn-of-the-century men walking past the cathedral in their tails and black top hats. It was a sepia-toned image, in a rustic wooden frame that Flaca had made herself.

Paz thought that there was nothing in the room to suggest that Flaca was the kind of woman she was, not a wisp, not a trace.

Romina wondered whether she would ever be able to set foot in this room without the old days rushing back to her, the afternoons of quiet lust and animal pleasure, even though she no longer lusted for Flaca herself.

La Venus felt slightly suffocated by the small room with so many women in it; it felt wrong somehow, obscene, to share this space that had become her intimate secret.

Malena entered last and stood against the wall, fidgeting with the strap of her purse.

Flaca closed the bedroom door, and the television sounds receded. Her four friends stared at her expectantly. She gestured to the bed, as grandly as she could, as if she were offering them some kind of collective throne.

Romina, La Venus, and Malena sat at the edge of the bed, while Paz sank cross-legged to the floor. Flaca remained on her feet, facing them, and at that moment she realized that they hadn't all been together since their trip to Polonio. This gathering was a kind of return, and it made her feel complete somehow, fired up, a hum of electricity circling between them.

"All right," Flaca said. "You all know why we're here."

They stared at her.

"We want a house in Polonio. That is to say, a house in paradise."

The women nodded.

"A house that we can't afford and yet seems destined to be ours."

She waited for someone to chime in, to protest, to crack a joke, but no one did; instead, the silence gathered around her like a rising tide.

"It seems irrational to spend money we don't have on a shack full of holes a day's journey from here. Not only that, it also seems impossible. And perhaps it is. But none of that means we shouldn't try. Break the mold. Break the reins. That's the only way great things have ever happened."

They stared at her, rapt, as if a female, beef-carving Che Guevara had just appeared in their midst. She felt elated, as if she could say anything next and they would follow her, into the jungle, into the revolution, into madness. The sensation rushed through her and then vanished, leaving her feeling hollow and exposed. *That crazy idea.* What would they think of her? What if she failed them, and lost the only friends she had? She couldn't bear the thought. She pushed forward.

"All right, so here's my vision. Each of us puts in what we have—

whatever we can. We add all that up and see how far we've gotten. But here's the catch, and this part I insist on: no matter how much each woman puts in, we all hold an equal share. We all own this place equally or we don't own it at all."

Something wrung at Paz's heart, her heart was a wet rag, she couldn't breathe. She had no money. And this. To be included. To be carried. To be held.

"*Mirá vos,*" Romina said. "Those Communist meetings did you some good, after all."

Flaca bowed solemnly, accepting the compliment. "So who agrees to these terms?"

"I do," Romina said.

"I do," Malena said.

"Why on earth not?" La Venus beamed.

"I do." Paz could barely hear her own voice.

"All right, me too, so that's it, then. Next question: how much does each of us have?"

They took turns answering the question. La Venus had a bit of cash she could put in—"not much," she said, "I'm sorry, it's the most I can take out without him noticing"—and Romina had an old pasta sauce jar full of bills and coins from tutoring jobs she'd done for local kids. She'd counted the money before coming over, and told them its amount. Flaca had a little saved from her work at the butcher shop; Paz had nothing, absolutely nothing, but she knew that she could ask her mother for movie theater money and would get enough for the ticket plus pizza with *fainá* afterward, and, also, she could forgo her monthly bus pass and walk to school, for as long as necessary.

"Let's say for four weeks," Flaca said. "Just to get a number."

Paz did a furious mental calculation and told them her paltry little sum, cheeks burning with embarrassment.

It was Malena who, to everyone's surprise, offered the largest sum, without an explanation.

Flaca wrote all the numbers studiously on a piece of paper, then added them up in pencil, carrying ones, checking her work. They had two-thirds of the funds they needed to buy the house, a sum much smaller than the cost of a house in Montevideo, but still, for them, out of reach. After she announced this, they sat in silence for a while. Muffled television voices beat their dull insistence at the door.

"It was such a lovely idea," Romina said quietly.

"Shut up," said Flaca.

Romina looked at her tenderly. Flaca, her Flaca, who dreamed up new ways of being and pursued them, who'd first turned the world inside out for her. It was one of the things she loved about Flaca, this infinite ability to see a place for herself in the world, and to hell with the world's failure to return the favor. Romina chided her for it, but at this moment she saw that it also stirred other things in her: envy, and the need to protect.

"It's not over," Flaca insisted. "It has to work."

Nothing has to work, Romina thought but did not say. Everything and anything can be broken.

"*Mi amor*," La Venus said gently, "we've all done what we can."

"I'll get the rest," Malena said.

They all turned to stare at her. She was perched at the edge of the bed, back straight, knees together under the pencil skirt she'd worn to work that day. Her hair was pulled into its bun, tamed and glistening with pomade.

"How?" Romina said.

"Let me guess," La Venus said, relieved to think that one of them had hidden means. "You'll ask your parents?"

"No," Malena snapped, and her vehemence took everyone by surprise. "I don't have parents."

Muffled television sounds throbbed through the bedroom door.

"I mean, I do," Malena said, "but we haven't been in contact for years. They're not in my life and they never will be."

How can you know that? Romina wanted to say, but Malena's face was so raw that she kept her mouth shut.

"I'm sorry," La Venus said. "My mother doesn't understand me either."

Malena studied the picture of Plaza Matriz as if the top hat men had stolen something from her, held it hidden in a pocket she was determined to find.

Flaca couldn't imagine a life without her parents. Her soul hurt for Malena. But it seemed like the wrong thing to say. "What's your plan, then?"

"That doesn't matter." Malena glanced at her, then back at the picture. "I can do it. And I really want to. The only thing is, it'll take me some time."

"How much time?" Flaca said.

"I don't know. Let's say two months."

"I can skip another bus pass," Paz said.

"And I can ramp up the tutoring," Romina said.

La Venus shrugged. "A few pesos here and there out of my husband's pockets—he won't notice."

"All right," Flaca said. "We have a plan, then. We'll pool what we have and all save and gather pesos where we can. And we'll hope that the house waits for us."

*

The house did wait. Malena came up with a significant additional sum, and the rest of the women brought their harvests from marital pockets, extra students, buses not taken, meals occasionally skipped. Three months and thirteen days after their meeting, in the warm December sun, Flaca traveled up the coast to Castillos and exchanged a box of pesos for the deed to the house. All five of their names went on the new paperwork, in alphabetical order.

They celebrated over beers in a corner café, a soccer game blaring on the overhead television. They'd never gathered in a public place in the city before, and at first they were tense and coded, referring to the house as *church* because it was the first thing that leapt to Flaca's mind, *we'll go to church soon, last time we went to church.* Middle-aged and old men hunched over their drinks and grilled sandwiches at nearby tables, and at first they ogled and seemed about to come over and try to start a conversation, but they were tamed with a few severe looks, they weren't threats after all, it seemed, just sad men with the air punched out of them by life, by the years, by the Process. The women toasted and took turns staring with exhilaration at the paper Flaca passed around surreptitiously like a guerrilla's communiqué. It was a thing they'd never seen or even heard of before: a deed for a house, full of women's names and only names of women.

The sight of the paper thrilled Romina, though it also hurt her, knowing that the victory meant nothing to her parents. *You spent your savings on a fisherman's shack,* her mother had said, more bewildered than angry, *and you have to share it with people you barely know?* Romina had tried to explain that she knew these women, that they were in fact good friends, but she found herself stopping short of too much detail as that could raise suspicion, either of subversive organizing or of the truth, and which of those would be worse? She didn't know. *Hija,* her father had said sadly, *when are you going to think about your future?* And by *future* he of course meant husband and children, since her studies were going well and she was almost a fully trained teacher. She'd failed them. The knowledge of her failure cut her open. But here she was anyway, holding this deed, this piece of paper with her name on it, and, though it seemed foolish to her parents, it meant more to her than any marriage certificate or future baby or even teaching job ever could.

La Venus was restless as she nursed her beer. In the winter, with its heavy rains, her apartment had felt like a prison. The very thought of her marriage bed repulsed her. It had become a place where she disappeared from herself, and this hut on the beach was well and good and yes, she'd gotten excited about it along with the others, but she couldn't live there all the time, now could she? What would she eat, where would the pesos come from? How was this deed to a faraway shack supposed to save her from her life?

"What's on your mind?" Flaca said. "Where are you? Aren't you happy?"

"Sure. Of course I am." La Venus made her best effort at a smile. "I just need to get out of the city."

"Well," Romina said, "that can happen soon enough."

"When shall we go?" said Malena.

They compared their schedules. Christmas was coming, with its family dinners in the sweltering night, its neighborhood fireworks. Better to wait until all that was done. January, Flaca said, and the others agreed. School would be out for Romina and Paz, the butcher shop and Malena's office would close for a summer break, and they could all go together. It would also allow them to stay for longer—a week, maybe more—and they could start repairing the walls and making lists of what else they'd do to turn the house into a home.

"It might take years to get it into shape," Romina said.

"Who cares?" Flaca said. "We have years."

This thrilled Romina, and she was about to answer when she felt a prickle in the air. She turned. One of the men from a nearby table stood over them, too close, a sneer on his face that she supposed was intended to be friendly.

"What are you ladies talking about?"

"Nothing," Romina said quickly.

"Nothing that concerns you," Flaca said.

The man looked at Flaca and his expression became hostile. He was a tall, balding man with heavy jowls. "You're no lady."

All the men were watching now, the ones slouched over tables and the one in waiter's uniform behind the bar. No one spoke. The man pulled up a nearby chair and sat down between Malena and Paz.

Romina felt Flaca tense beside her. If she lost her cool it would not make anyone safer. "Sir," she said, as evenly as possible, "this is our table."

"It's a public place, isn't it? And you're missing something at this table. No sausage." He laughed, then scanned the room for appreciation of his joke. The waiter chuckled as he wiped the counter with a rag.

Flaca sprang from her seat.

Romina pulled pesos from her purse and put them on the table. "Let's go."

The women fumbled for bills, began to rise. Paz felt a pang of sadness at leaving her beer behind—after these months of saving, a drink in a café was a great luxury and she'd hoped to enjoy it down to the dregs. She took a long, greedy swig as she put coins on the table with her other hand.

Romina was holding Flaca's arm, to calm her or restrain her, or maybe both.

The man was looking closely at Malena now. His hand landed on her shoulder. "I know you from somewhere, don't I?"

Malena went rigid. "No."

"You look familiar." His fingers fondled her shoulder, moved slowly up her neck. "You do. Ha! How many of you are *putas*?"

Panic spread across Malena's face. Flaca had never seen her so afraid. She curled her hands into fists. "You get your hands off her—"

"Not that one." He sneered at Flaca. "Can't be. She'd never make a centavo."

"We're leaving." Romina steered Flaca toward the door, relieved to feel the others moving with her. Outside, the sun bore down on them. They walked in a cluster, fast-paced, hearts pounding loudly in every chest. The café had released them with no more than a low wave of laughter in their wake. They reached a plaza with empty benches, but did not stop walking. Flaca turned in the direction of the river, and they followed.

"Damn them," Flaca said.

"You didn't do anything," Romina said as reassuringly as she could.

"I know damn well that I didn't do anything!"

"Malena," La Venus said, "are you all right?"

"I'm fine."

"He had no right to—"

"I said I'm fine."

She didn't seem fine; she was shaking; but it was clear that Malena had retreated into herself, a hunted animal, prepared to bite any hand that approached.

They walked in silence for one block, two.

In a panic, Romina thought of the deed to the house—she'd held it in her hands, and then what? time itself had blurred—but then she saw that Flaca held the large manila envelope she'd brought it in. "The deed?"

"It's in here," Flaca said.

"Thank god."

They fell silent again until they reached the river, the Rambla, the paved promenade that hugged the city's coast. There, they allowed themselves to sit on the low wall overlooking the water. If anyone bothered them, it would be easy to get up and keep walking.

The Río de la Plata offered up its tiny shards of light.

It had been a mistake, Flaca thought, to meet in a café. She was an idiot. She'd been so flush with excitement at their victory that she'd lost her good sense, had forgotten where she lived, where they lived, what they were.

"Does anyone remember," Romina said, "what we were talking about before we were interrupted?"

"I do," Paz said. "We were talking about how it might take years to fix up our house. And how we could do it." She remembered the exact words, as in the moment they had made her hands itch with excitement. In just a few days, she'd be finishing high school, and that milestone seemed like nothing, a stupidity, compared to this. "Flaca, you said, 'We have years.'"

Flaca made a snorting sound. Her throat felt dry. She wanted to say something with brio, to restore their mood of exuberance, but she couldn't muster it. He'd gotten under her skin, that man, and she hated herself for it.

"Meanwhile," Romina said, "we can go no matter what shape it's in. We can get out of this city."

"I'll gladly sleep on the floor," Paz said.

"Me too," Malena said, with a force that surprised everyone. Strands had escaped her bun, and for once she'd made no effort to force them back. It was almost, Paz thought, as if the man had unlocked something inside her, untamed rage. How long had it been in there, biding its time? "We'll bring blankets, the way we did last time, and make our own nests that we'll add on to little by little until they're what we want them to be."

Flaca felt herself expand inside, spark up again. It was the talk of the years ahead that fed her, not so much the blankets and chairs they'd find for the hut but the very fact of having a square of space to love and the will to love it.

Romina was looking wryly at Malena. "You're not becoming optimistic, now, are you?"

"Maybe."

Romina was struck by Malena's large dark eyes, their beauty, the wildness in them after all. "Ithaca."

"What?"

"It's definitely Ithaca."

Malena seemed perplexed, then smiled as she remembered.

"What are you two going on about?" La Venus said.

"One of Romina's literary things," Flaca said.

"I love literary things," Paz said, in hopes that Romina would explain.

But Romina just poked Malena's arm playfully, and Malena's eyes widened in what could have been surprise or pleasure or alarm.

*

They arrived in Polonio late on a Friday, after the New Year, when it was already 1979. They walked in over the dunes, through the growing twilight, anxious to arrive before they lost all light and risked losing their way. By the time they arrived at their hut, their legs ached and their heads spun with exhaustion, but the thrill of being in their hut—their hut!—made it impossible at first to sleep. Flaca lit five candles and placed them at the center of the bare, empty floor. The five of them sat cross-legged in a circle around the flames and watched each other's shadows leap and curl along the dark walls. Outside, the waves glowed with song. Already the city was shedding from them. Home, they thought, in wonder, amazement, doubt, delight. Home. A whiskey bottle made a few rounds, and then they blew the candles out, spread their blankets across the floor, and went to sleep in a haphazard circle, pulsed over by the lighthouse beam.

The next morning, over *mate,* they took more careful stock of their surroundings. The walls were scuffed, and pocked with holes where rain would enter in the winter—and in summer, too, Flaca pointed out, let's remember that this coastal area sees all kinds of storms—so those should be fixed, and the privy was no more than a bucket in a small stall behind a reed door, but it was a decent start, a solid hut, theirs.

"It's a palace," Romina said.

Malena laughed, but stopped when she saw the hurt on Romina's face.

"I thought you were joking," Malena said.

"I wasn't." Romina had meant it. It was a palace, because every inch of it belonged to them, and within those four walls they could be anyone or anything they wanted. Be themselves. She'd never lived in such a place before; the freedom dizzied her. It was strange, she thought, how you could live all your life in a home defined by people who loved you and took care of you and shared ancestors with you and yet did not entirely see you, people whom you protected by hiding yourself. Much as she loved her parents, home had always been a place for hiding, until right now. She opened her mouth to try to say this to Malena, but then stopped short, lacking the words.

Malena touched Romina's arm. Communication enough.

Each of them had brought one plate to start their kitchen, as well as one fork, a knife or two, a cup. It was all they needed for now—that and the earth and the ocean. They settled these items onto the two shelves in the corner that was the kitchen, and then they gently scattered for the morning. Flaca investigated the holes in the walls and began to patch them with plaster she'd brought from the city. Malena, Romina, and La Venus went for a walk in search of seashells with which to decorate the windowsills, driftwood from which to fashion shelves. They would douse themselves in the ocean along the way. Paz, meanwhile, headed off to El Lobo's for bread and conversation. He was unabashedly happy to see her. "I told you I'd come back," she said, then set about dusting the merchandise. Javier came running in, his face leaner and hair longer than last time, excited to show her an Indian arrowhead he'd found out in the dunes. There used to be many of them, El Lobo said, when he first arrived in El Polonio as a little boy, about Javier's age, with his parents, who were desperately seeking work and found need for laborers in the local sea lion and seal trade. They'd arrived in a horse cart with all their possessions tied into blankets; he still remembered the tremble and rattle of the cart, the bundles under his back, the heat, his mother's warm damp hand around his. In those first years, he'd often found arrowheads scattered on the land, until, when he was in his early teens, a group of men came from the city and gathered them all up for a museum in Montevideo, perhaps Paz had seen them?

Paz had not.

"Well then, where did they put them, if schoolgirls like you don't learn about it?"

"I don't know. We don't learn anything at school." It was all lies, stupid government-approved lies, and she'd come to detest school days.

"I would have liked to go to school." El Lobo glanced at his grandson, who'd settled into a corner. "At your age, I was out on the hunting boats with my father."

She felt like an idiot. Ungrateful. "I'm sorry."

"Don't be. Alicia's great with the little ones, they'll learn more than I did. And anyway, I loved hunting. It was hard work, but there's nothing like the power of those bodies, the thing that happens inside you when you're wrestling a great creature like that at the end of its life."

Blood in the foam, she thought.

"I want to wrestle creatures!" said Javier.

"One thing at a time," El Lobo said, which seemed to satisfy the boy.

"I told you I'd live in Polonio one day," Paz blurted out.

El Lobo smiled. "And here you are."

She waited for him to say *not living here, not really,* but he didn't. "What do people say about us?"

He looked up at her thoughtfully. He was whittling again, and it amazed her that he could keep carving with precision with his gaze turned elsewhere. "It's unusual, of course, a group of female cousins in a fishermen's hut."

She did not breathe.

"But, of course, it is no problem."

She felt her muscles relax. Maybe no one knew. Maybe all was well. She listened to the sound of El Lobo's knife, the soft scrape of it against wood, and realized that his strokes kept time with the low, constant sound of ocean waves, a single rhythm, sand and water, blade and wood. Did he do that on purpose? Or did he do it without thinking, having lived so long in this ocean-place that the song of it seeped into everything? He seemed to live as if military rhythms couldn't reach him. As if they didn't exist, or, at least, were drowned out by the everywhere of waves.

"You know, I have an idea for connecting you more deeply to this place."

"Another one?"

"Yes."

She felt a prickle of hope. "The first one worked out well."

"We could start a business. Together."

"What!" Paz laughed. "After saying that you can't imagine me living here."

"Well, I can't. That's true. But that's not what I'm talking about. You would still live in the city, but you'd sell seal skins there, to make those coats the fancy city ladies love to wear. I'd gather the skins here, you'd get them to Montevideo, where there are plenty of buyers."

"Isn't there already a skin trade?"

"Bah, the government runs it—the hunters barely earn a peso. This would be"—he leaned forward, squinted—"under the table. We'd share the profits. You'd get thirty percent of everything."

Why not fifty percent? Paz wondered, though the thought was fleeting and she didn't dare speak it. The whole idea was ludicrous anyway. She'd just finished high school the month before, with little fanfare, and at the end of the summer she'd be starting at the university, studying literature, which she'd chosen because it was her only passion that had anything to do with school. It was what she was supposed to do: keep studying. Where it would lead, she couldn't say. Still—her? A smuggler? The last thing she needed was an illegal job. She wondered how risky it would be. El Lobo didn't seem worried. But still, even if it were safe, how would she transport those skins—as mounds on the bus? The bulk, the weight, the smell—it all disgusted her already. Her fantasies of freedom had never looked or smelled like animal corpses. Then again, what had her fantasies looked like? Open. Nebulous. No sign of earning a living, that impossible, essential thing. She wasn't like her classmates, with their dreams of becoming a doctor or teacher or rich man's wife. Her only ambitions were to live and to be free. Making a living wasn't a clear part of the dream, while marrying money—the ambition of many smooth-haired girls—was out of the question (she'd rather die). Her life goal was the same as the first time she'd come here: to follow Flaca's example. But Flaca had parents who seemed to like her even though they saw at least flickers of who she really was, and, what's more, they had a store she could run, work she could step into. Paz had none of that. Not the family-that-likes-you or the family store. "I don't know," she said.

"It's not for you, then forget it." El Lobo waved, as if swatting the idea away. "In any case. Tell me, are you and the girls going to celebrate your new home? Old Carlitos has some lambs, you know, he could slaughter one for you."

He started talking about Carlitos's lambs, the best meat on the coast of Rocha, and Paz let the question of the skin trade fall away, though it would keep snaking through her mind, slow, sinuous, curling at the dark edge of thought.

*

The friends were excited about the lamb and the idea of celebrating their new home, all of them except La Venus, who said that it was too much meat, a whole lamb or even half a lamb, they couldn't afford it, what would they do with so much food? Flaca suggested that they invite the locals to partake of their abundance. "They're our new neighbors, after all. And that'll really make it a party."

"But we don't want the neighbors around," La Venus said.

"They'll be around no matter what we do," said Romina.

"Exactly," said Flaca. "It would be a show of goodwill."

"It's an excellent price, that Old Carlitos will give us," Paz said.

Romina nodded, but La Venus said, "The whole point of coming here is to have space to ourselves."

"Venus, *querida,*" Flaca said. "They were here first. This is their home."

"So?"

Flaca flinched at the harshness of her tone. This was a side of her lover that irritated her, the side that could so easily discount men who were laborers, honest people who worked from dawn to dusk. *So?* as if humble men with rugged faces were not worthy of niceties. Humble men with rugged faces like her own father's. She was a butcher's daughter; sharing meat was a language of community, a way to sink your roots into a place. "So, we should be neighborly."

"I don't want to be neighborly." La Venus had been counting the hours until she could get away from her husband, from the constant proximity of men who always wanted something from her and flicked from praise to rage with dizzying speed if they didn't get what they were looking for or did get it but still felt shitty inside, because that's all it was, wasn't it, this male preying and prowling, an attempt to relieve their own shitty feelings, a project with no damn end. *Not on your life,* Arnaldo had said when she told him she was leaving for a few days, refusing permission though she hadn't asked for it. She'd dropped the subject and slipped out while he was at work. She'd left a note on the kitchen table, but there was no phone number to give. She already dreaded what awaited her when she got back home. All she wanted was a few damn days in which she didn't have to cater to men, and now here was Flaca trying to invite male strangers to their fire.

"Venus," Flaca said, "don't be so selfish."

La Venus stared at her in open anger and Paz took a step back toward the wall.

"Listen," Malena said. "Let's all calm down. There might be a way for each of us to get what we want."

"How's that?" Romina asked. She couldn't imagine a way through.

"We could buy the meat, throw the party, but hold it somewhere other than our home." Malena looked steadily around the room at each of them. "Paz, didn't you say there's a fisherman who runs a bar?"

Paz nodded. "Benito." She'd heard stories about Benito, a survivor of the *Tacuarí* shipwreck who'd decided to stay on where destiny had hurled him and now fished by day and ran his bar by night, and his dreams of storms before they came and of twisted metal washing up to shore had given him a local reputation as a weather prophet. It didn't seem like the moment, though, for all these details. "The bar is called the Rusty Anchor."

"Well then," Malena said, "what if we ask Benito if we could host a *parrilla* at the Rusty Anchor?" She looked at Flaca. "Would this satisfy your need for hospitality?"

Flaca shrugged. "Sure. I suppose." It wasn't the same but she just wanted the problem to go away.

Malena turned to La Venus. "And you? Would this satisfy your need to feel safe?"

La Venus blinked to fight back tears.

Safe? Flaca thought. This fight was about safe? And if so, how did Malena know? How deeply she saw, Malena. Suddenly it seemed to Flaca that Malena hid an ocean inside her, depths never spoken, full of slippery wakeful things.

"Yes," La Venus said.

An hour later, everything was settled, and that night they gathered at the Rusty Anchor, which turned out to be no more than a small room built against the side of the owner's hut with extra space outside dotted with stools and low tables fashioned out of driftwood and scavenged parts from the *Tacuarí* shipwreck. Word had spread among the residents of Cabo Polonio, and they'd arrived, seven or eight men and two women, among them Alicia, children in tow, playing underfoot as Flaca tended the *parrilla* and amiably fended off men's attempts to take over the grill. The drinking began well before dinner, and continued deep into the night. One fisherman brought a guitar, and another turned a crate upside down for a drum, sambas filled the air because they were not so far from the Brazilian border after all, and soon the songs inspired dancing, and the new women of Polonio danced with the fishermen and with each other under the stars, women dancing together, an innocent thing, common enough to slide by without suspicion, and nobody disrespected anyone and La Venus seemed happy and relaxed and unperturbed, she danced, everyone danced, everyone seemed happy, full of tender meat roasted to perfection over embers in the Uruguayan style and wine and locally distilled grappa and the welcome seemed easy and complete until Flaca, finally, at two in the morning, realized what was missing. The lighthouse keeper hadn't come. She hadn't met him before, but had hoped he'd consider himself invited; he was part of this land too. Was he ill? Too much of a recluse? She went to ask Benito.

"He's gone," Benito said.

"Gone? What do you mean?" How could there be a lighthouse without a keeper?

"The government replaced him." Benito scowled.

"You don't like the new keeper?"

"New keepers—a whole troop is coming."

"A troop—you mean—" She looked out at the lighthouse. Its slow light suddenly seemed to pulse with menace. "You don't mean soldiers."

Benito nodded with an air of indifference, or perhaps resignation. Storms, soldiers, they go, they come, what can you do but weather what you must and have a grappa or two along the way.

"How many of them?"

"How would we know?"

"They're not here yet?"

"Just one for now. More are on their way."

"When do they arrive?"

He shrugged.

Flaca went and sat down on a stool at the edge of the gathering. She watched her friends dancing, still smiling, scanned the whole gathering. Their refuge. Invaded already. All their savings and scrounged money poured into a hut, a dream of sanctuary, and meanwhile the regime was moving in just up the path. Suddenly she felt exhausted, emptier than she'd ever been in her life.

"What the hell is the matter with you?"

It was Paz, hand on her shoulder.

"Nothing."

"Bullshit."

"Not here. I'll tell you later."

And so Paz waited as the party wound down, as fishermen ebbed toward their homes well before dawn because they only had a bit of time before their boats had to launch out onto the sea, there were fish to catch and mouths to feed, and the women followed their flashlight beams to find their way home. When they were back inside their hut, the second the door closed behind them, Paz said, "Out with it, Flaca."

"Out with what?" said Romina.

"Something's wrong."

Romina stared at Flaca, searching her face for a denial.

"For God's sake," La Venus said, "what's going on?"

"We should sit," said Flaca.

They settled down onto the sheepskins they'd just bought that day from Old Carlitos, their mattress and blankets and seating all in one.

And Flaca told them.

As she talked, the others became very still. Malena stared at a spot on the wall as if it held secret hieroglyphs. Romina's eyes closed against the world. Paz felt her jaw clench the way it did at school when she saw boys approaching and readied for a fight.

"I can't believe it," La Venus said. "We came so close."

"What do you mean, close?" Flaca said. "We're here."

"Yes, well, so are the soldiers," Romina said. "Or they will be any moment now."

La Venus rose, went to her bag, and pulled out a nightgown. She turned her back on the group and changed. Her hands trembled as she pulled off her clothes. "We just bought this place, and now it's lost to us."

"No! It's not. How can you say that?"

"Because it's true, Flaca. It's not safe here anymore."

"She's right," Malena said sadly. "The soldiers will be just up the way."

"So? Isn't that something we're used to by now?"

This silenced the group. The ocean sang, unchanged. Suddenly, the hut seemed shabby to Romina, nothing like a palace at all, just a battered shack in the middle of nowhere, vulnerable to storms.

"I thought—I thought this was our refuge." La Venus was back in the circle now, brushing her long hair. Her nipples were visible through her silk nightgown. "Our escape." She could hear her husband's voice, *stupid Anita.*

Paz had been feeling her world collapse around her—their refuge, gone already, the whole dream of a secret tribe on the verge of dying—but the sight of La Venus's nipples distracted her, shifted her mind, and made space for something else. A wave of delight. A wave of hope. "It's still our escape," she said. "I don't like the soldiers either, but Flaca's right, we all know a thing or two about how to handle them."

Flaca glanced at her gratefully.

Paz made two fists against the sheepskin. "We can fight them if we have to."

"We won't have to fight them," Flaca said. "Listen, all of you. This is still our damn refuge. You know why? Because it's our home. And those motherfuckers, they don't get to take that away from us."

"I hope you're right," Romina said.

And then Flaca did something that surprised them all: she crawled over to Romina, right over the sheepskins, and gathered her into her arms. Paz, watching from across the circle, expected Romina to stiffen, to resist—for when was Romina not resisting? when did she ever loosen her grip?—but instead Romina seemed to melt against Flaca like a scared child, cradled, emitting a small sound between a hum and a moan.

"You'll see, *querida*," Flaca said. "You'll see."

4

The Woman's Dream

THEY RETURNED THREE MONTHS LATER, during the fall holiday, in that last stretch of reliable sun before the days slowly shrank their way to cold. This time, they splurged on a cart to take them over the dunes, and the breeze filled their hair and thrilled their skin as they traveled across the sand.

"Let's agree," Flaca had said just before they boarded their bus in the city, "not to talk about the lighthouse for at least the first day."

They'd all agreed to this, though Romina was reluctant and mustered no more than a shrug. *Lighthouse,* in this case, as code for *soldiers.* They could very well not talk about them, she thought, but soldiers weren't ghosts: they didn't disappear just because you put them out of mind.

Still, on the ride in, she was glad of the pact they'd made, and saw the logic—classic Flaca logic—of changing the subject so as to immerse yourself in the moment, in your actual surroundings, so as to let the dunes become as real as distant looming troops, the sand palpable, shifting, shaped by the wind, heavy as hills, larger and older than your thoughts or problems, a balm to the mind.

As soon as they'd unloaded their rucksacks and bags from the cart, Paz ran ahead, determined to be the first through the door. Back. Alive again. Surrounded by their small dim room, she felt large inside, able to face the world.

La Venus came in close behind her and took a deep breath. "Mmmmhm. Nothing like the smell of mold to make you feel at home."

Paz hadn't noticed the smell. "It's not so bad."

La Venus wrinkled her nose in disbelief.

"In any case," Romina said, close behind them, "it's nothing a little wipe-down can't fix."

"What's this?" Flaca was in the doorway, cigarette dangling from her lips. "We've just arrived in paradise, and already talk of house-work?"

"It's *our* paradise, you nitwit," Romina said, crossing into the kitchen corner and running a finger along the narrow table they'd been using as a counter. "It's up to us to keep it beautiful. Or, what, did you think we had bought a palace full of servants?"

"I wouldn't mind servants," La Venus said, thinking of Olga, who came twice a week to her Montevideo apartment and would surely make this place gleam in a matter of hours if she got her hands on it. Of course, if La Venus left her husband, there would be no Olga and no groceries or the rest of it.

"Spoken like a true bourgeois lady," Flaca snapped.

Everyone froze. No one said a word. Malena had been lowering her heavy bag, and lifted it back to her shoulder as if it suddenly feared the ground.

Romina felt the impulse to say something—*ouch*, perhaps—but she held her tongue. The tension had been palpable between those two since leaving the city. Flaca seemed out of line, but it was best not to intervene. She started to unpack a few rags for cleaning, then remembered that there was no running water. Flaca was the one who knew the pump.

"Excuse me?" La Venus said. "Who's the bourgeois one?"

Flaca crushed her cigarette butt against the doorway. "What the hell are you talking about?"

"You're a prude, as bad as any of them."

Prude? Paz thought. Flaca, a prude? She couldn't imagine such a thing. She shouldn't be staring—Romina was fussing with her bag, Malena had slipped outside—but she couldn't help it. They'd been forming a kind of family, woven from castoffs, like a quilt made from strips of leftover fabric no one wanted. They wanted each other. They had to stay woven. They could not fray.

"Goddamnit, Venus, that's not what I—"

"Isn't it, though?" La Venus's voice was rising steadily. "What else, then?"

"We need drinking water," Romina announced, theatrically. "And bread, if Alicia has baked any today. Paz, will you come with me?"

Paz wanted to hear the argument, every word of it, but she knew that there was only one right answer. "Sure."

Outside, Malena joined them, and the three of them left the couple in the hut and headed toward El Lobo's. At a fork in the dirt path, Romina turned toward the ocean.

"El Lobo's is this way," Paz said.

"I know," Romina said, "but aren't you dying to see the ocean?"

"I know I am," Malena said.

Romina glanced at Malena. She hadn't spoken since they'd arrived. The longing in her voice was palpable. She always seemed so serene, Malena, following the flow of the group, holding back quietly until suddenly something burst from her. In this case, desire. For the shore. What else did Malena long for? What else was she not saying? "Well, there you have it. And in any case, it's probably good to give those two some time to fight."

"And maybe start cooling off," Malena said.

"Who knows about that," said Romina.

"What's the matter with them?" Paz asked.

"You don't know?"

Paz shook her head, chafing at the thought that others had known before her, that she was being treated like the little sister, the baby of the family, kept in the dark.

"La Venus has a crush on someone. Not just anyone, but a famous singer." Romina grinned. "And Flaca is going mad with jealousy."

"She did that to Flaca?"

"First of all, we don't know how much La Venus has done yet." Romina laughed. "Secondly, if she *has* done it, she didn't do it to Flaca."

"Which is exactly the problem," Malena added, laughing too.

Their amusement stung Paz. She wasn't a child. "That's not what I meant."

"I know what you meant," Romina said. "But here's the thing: Flaca's never had this happen to her before. I suppose I shouldn't enjoy it so much. There's nobody in the world I love more than Flaca."

Paz listened for the silent sentences beneath that one. *Not even my parents. Not even my brother in prison.*

"But to see her get a taste of her own medicine—well, that's something."

"She cheated on you," Malena said thoughtfully.

Romina shrugged. "I won't deny it. Not that I care. It's ancient history. But it might do her good to know the other side of the story."

"But they'll make it through this, won't they? They'll last?" Paz imagined Flaca and La Venus still swooning over each other as wrinkled old ladies with canes. Side by side on a park bench. Themselves. Manless. Holding hands like aging sisters. Hiding in plain sight.

"What does that mean, 'last'?" Romina was walking briskly now. "There's no thinking that way for people like us."

"Why not?"

"We don't have lasting things. We get no forevers, no futures, no bride in a veil and all that bullshit."

"I know all that," Paz said defensively. "Obviously. But can't we—couldn't we—" She struggled to form the thought. She didn't want to sound like an idiot. It had something to do with forming their own path of forevers, outside the bride-and-veil world and maybe outside the real world altogether, but what sense did that make when, these days, even the sweetest most upstanding old ladies in her neighborhood lived in fear? She didn't want to think anymore. She craved the ocean, its salt and heaving, the break from gravity. Perhaps Romina was right; perhaps it cheapened the present moment to burden it with thoughts of a future that didn't and couldn't exist. She glanced over at Malena, who hadn't said a word. Sometimes, in conversation, she grew so quiet you could almost forget that she was there. But she was listening, wasn't she? "What do you think, Malena?"

Malena took so long to answer that Paz thought perhaps she hadn't heard. "I think the future doesn't belong to us. I think *forever* is a strange word. It can't be trusted. I do know that Flaca and La Venus love each other deeply and it's something I've been privileged to see."

This raised a thousand questions for Paz, but she didn't know where to begin, so she said nothing. They reached the shore. Feet in sand, approaching the waves, which were low today, almost languorous, reaching toward them and pulling back into a body of endless blue. Paz thought of all the creatures below that calm surface, their slick bodies, the way they must slip and glide through corals, currents, shipwrecks long barnacled by the years. She tried to imagine the sea lions, the seals, their great majestic bulk as they swam and coupled and fed their young. Marine mammals; of the ocean, yet not. Could the babies suckle underwater?

"Ssshp," Romina whispered. "They're here."

Paz had no idea what she was talking about. She began to turn.

"Don't look." Romina kept her voice low. "Not at the same time. You first, Paz, then Malena."

Paz slowed her gaze, turned to the left, and saw empty beach. To the right. Three figures, no, four, out at the rocky outcropping where the beach curved away, sitting on the last of the sand. Men. She could tell from their postures, the boastful sprawl of them. And the uniforms. Splotchy green and beige. She turned back to the water. Soldiers. "You can look now, Malena."

"I don't want to." Malena's voice was tight. "We should go."

"We have to go?" Paz said. "Just because they're here? It's our beach too!"

"It's not our beach. It's always their beach. Every grain of sand in the damn country is theirs, *punto*." Romina pushed back a wisp of hair that had escaped its rubber band to writhe in the wind. "But still, that doesn't mean we have to leave."

"I'm just saying," Malena said, "that we can go if you want."

It struck Paz that Malena wasn't suggesting they leave for herself, but for Romina, to protect their friend. Their once-captured friend. Romina seemed to think of the same thing. She looked over at Malena, then down at the sand.

"I don't know what I want," she said.

They stood uncertainly, listening to the waves.

"I want to break them all into pieces."

The rise of a wave. Ebbing. Another rise, more powerful than the last.

"What are they doing now?" Romina's voice was very quiet.

Paz glanced back at the men. One of them seemed to be looking in the women's direction and pointing, but he hadn't stood. His companions broke into laughter, then passed something around between them, a bottle, a book—no, they were putting it to their mouths and what's your problem, Paz, you really think these guys would share a book? Burning. All those pages burning beneath the grill, among hot coals.

"They're not coming over here," she said. "I don't think they will."

"Let's walk," Romina said.

They headed in the opposite direction of the soldiers. Sand slipped and sank around their feet.

"It's not that I want to kill them," Romina said, then stopped.

"It's all right," Malena said, "if you do."

Romina took a deep breath. What a thing, to open your mouth with soldiers right there in the distance and *want to break them into pieces*. How many of them were there, in the Polonio barracks? Would the beach always be infested with them? She'd had her doubts about coming back, had assumed that the soldiers' presence would shut her down in fear. And yet, she felt strangely expanded, seeing them there on the beach, human-size, visible yet out of earshot as she said the forbidden things out loud. "I mean, I would kill them. If I had to, to protect us—to set the country free. But that's not what I want. What I want is to take our power back. What I really want to break is the—" She stopped, took one step, two; even here, even now, with the wind at her back and waves at her side, she couldn't say the word *dictatorship* aloud with them so close at hand—"the Process."

"Yes," Malena said gently. "I understand."

Does she? Can she? Romina thought, but she didn't ask those questions, distracted as she was by the hunger to speak. "I want to get involved again. You know, with the resistance. I've been thinking about it for some time." Her brother rose in her mind, behind bars six years now, and if she ever saw him again would he be whole or broken? proud of her or ashamed?

"So why haven't you?" Malena said.

"My parents. With my brother gone—for now, perhaps forever—I'm the only one left. They couldn't stand to lose me and it seems unfair to do that to them."

They had almost reached the end of the beach. They walked in silence for a while.

"What do you think?" Romina said, embarrassed by the nakedness in her own voice. She knew that Paz was likely to encourage her to do whatever she wanted—she was young and hadn't yet learned to fully weigh the risks of things. But it was Malena, solid and reliable Malena, who surprised her by answering first.

"What I think?" Malena's voice was tinged with steel. "You do not owe your parents your life."

"They've had it very hard, you know," Romina said. "My grandmother survived pogroms and she—"

"Your life doesn't belong to them," Malena said. "No matter what."

Romina stared at her. There it was again, the bright burst of passion in Malena's voice. Here was a woman capable of great calm, and also fire. A woman who did not speak to her own parents, a circumstance that she, Romina, found difficult to imagine. She started to form a thought about how you couldn't flatten the pogroms with a *no matter what,* there was no escaping those histories or the way they pushed up inside your skin, she didn't understand, couldn't understand—but she was stopped by Malena's eyes. They were wide open, liquid, full of the unspoken, full of mystery and she could stare into them all day, she realized, plunge into that darkness and be wrapped in it, enfolded, remade. She was fond of Malena, but had never seen her as sexy—mainly because it hadn't occurred to her to consider it; she hadn't been attracted to anyone since the time of the Only Three, the thought of having a lover made her gut clench—and certainly she'd never wondered how Malena might look in pleasure, in her naked pleasure, whether her lips would part, her back arch, her eyelids flutter closed, or would she stare with her eyes wide open, what a thought, for Malena was still staring at her now.

Paz coughed.

They both turned, away from each other, toward the girl who stood a few paces away, looking a little sullen. "I'm going to El Lobo's."

"I'll come," Romina said quickly.

Paz shrugged.

"Me too," Malena said. "We'll need as many arms as possible."

*

When the others left, Flaca began by striding back and forth in the hut, searching for words that would not come.

"Will you stop?" La Venus said. "You're making me nervous with all that pacing. You're like an animal at the zoo."

"You want to tell *me* what to do?" Flaca said. "With *my* body?"

La Venus flung up her hands. "I'm sorry, my tiger—pace away."

Flaca knew that she'd meant it lightly, as a way of cutting the tension, and *my tiger* sank into her skin like honey. But she wasn't about to admit it. Not to this new Venus, the one caught in Ariella Ocampo's spell. What a mistake, to have taken her to the concert at Teatro Solís, what had she been thinking? That a night out would revive the spark between them? For too long now they'd been meeting furtively, always behind closed doors, and she could feel La Venus's interest waning, see the faraway look in her eyes as she put her clothes back on, ready to go home. *I have to leave him,* she'd told Flaca. *I can't take it anymore. I flinch when he touches me, I can't hide it, and he doesn't even care.* Rage at the thought. Hands curled into fists. Flaca wanted to punch this husband she'd never seen, beat him to a pulp. *Don't let him touch you. He has no right.* But La Venus would only gulp in broken air and say, *That's not true, Flaca. You don't know a thing about marriage.* And then Flaca would be angry. Of course she knew. She'd seen her mother, her sisters, watched the way they wrapped their days around their men, the way it worked, a code she'd always known she'd avoid for her own life, who wanted it? what was the point? It wasn't worth having a man no matter how much people mocked you for lacking one. She'd never understood the appeal of marriage, her sisters' flushed delight as they approached their wedding days and had the seamstress tuck and nip their mother's wedding dress to fit their own bodies, and one day we'll do this for you, Flaca, her sister Clara had said, we'll have to pull it in furthest for those nothing hips of yours—kindly, laughing—but that was years ago, when her family still seemed to believe there might be a husband anywhere in her future. Husbands. People crazy enough to think that washing their boxers and cooking their food and listening to their boring rants for the rest of your life would make you happy. And yet, she had to admit that her sister Clara seemed happy with Ernesto, and Flaca's own mother had always seemed happy at home; she was a shy woman outside the family, but with Papá she flowered open, laughing at his jokes and teasing him back with the giddy joy of a schoolgirl. Flaca could never imagine Papá pushing his touch on Mamá. They flirted, she batted his hand back in the kitchen when he came up behind her at the sink, but she was obviously pleased, playing out a dance of two bodies happy to be aging by each other's side. This Arnaldo, this husband of Venus, was another sort of man. Flaca couldn't stand the thought of him near La Venus. He had no right. Didn't deserve. Unable to stop the source of her lover's pain, she searched for a balm to ease it, if nothing else through a distraction. This concert, a night of tango and opera brashly mixed together, seemed as good an antidote as any. It was the talk of the town, the concert, or so it seemed from the posters outside the grand Teatro Solís, which was the only measure of culture Flaca knew about. This was her first time buying tickets for a show at Solís. Their nation's opera house. Her parents had only gone there once, when they were first married, and her mother still talked about it as the most romantic thing her man had ever done. The butcher and the butcher's wife, at Teatro Solís, surrounded by the voluptuous curtains and elaborate frescoes; Flaca could just see them, dressed in their wedding best, dazzled and a little cowed. Now it was her turn. The butcher's daughter. She could be cultured. She could be a gentleman, a *caballero*. Or a *caballera* (what a word, what a not-word!). If anyone saw them out together and reported back to La Venus's husband, she could say she went out to see music with a friend. Nothing outlandish, nothing forbidden. The only problem was that Flaca would have to wear a dress. She hadn't worn a dress in seven years. She borrowed one from her sister Clara—the middle child, four years older than Flaca, always the most understanding—who laughed gleefully as she rummaged through her closet, *what, Flaca, you're going cultured now? I'm going to drown you in ruffles,* chica—and then, after finally settling on a more sedate gown, simple lines and a lime green that had been in fashion ten years ago, back when fashions used to reach this city: *whom are you trying to impress?* Spoken gently. Clara knew. Not everything, but enough. Flaca had always sensed it; here was proof. Still, she put no words to the matter. She only answered the question with her eyes. She had a dress, she had tickets, they were going to pretend for a single damn night that nothing was wrong with this country or their homes, and yes, she knew what Romina would say, *sure why not go listen to opera while political prisoners waste away* but what else was there to do? weren't the prisoners going to suffer whether there was opera or not? La Venus looked gorgeous that night, shimmering in an electric blue gown. It was her color. Every color was her color. Flaca walked into Teatro Solís feeling like the king of the universe, beside this woman who stole the gaze of every single man they passed. *And me. She dis-*

robes for me. The one she wants is me. Their seats were only four rows
from the front. The concert began, and Ariella Ocampo took the
stage. She was not what Flaca had expected, although she'd seen the
posters outside of an elegant woman with red lips, and the woman on
the stage before her had the same elegance and the same red lips. Now
she wore a glittering green dress that made Flaca think of mermaids.
She looked younger than in the photograph, almost vulnerable, and
for a moment Flaca feared for her, though she couldn't have said why.
But then Ariella sang. Time stopped. Time stretched open, pulled
apart by music. Pulled apart by Ariella's voice. She was singing an aria
that glided into a classic tango, then back to opera in a single melodic
line. The orchestra followed her like a flock of sheep, as if her voice
were a staff, pointing the way, cutting it open. Flaca had never heard
anything like it, not that she knew the first thing about music, but she
could feel that the more cultured audience around her was equally riv-
eted and amazed. They were not, in that moment, trapped in a small
cage of a country; they were transcendent, aloft, made aerial by sound.
Sound that was theirs and not theirs, close and foreign, high and low,
opera and tango, slipping into each other, made one. And then, in
the fourth song, Ariella's gaze had settled on La Venus. It stayed there
for a minute that seemed eternal. She glided across her melody as if
caressing La Venus's curves. Flaca felt her lover's body light up beside
her. The whole great hall seemed to fall away, leaving only the two of
them, the singer and the beauty, suspended in space. The song lifted
them up together onto a melodic stratum only they could reach,
together, quivering, aloft on a taut ribbon of sound, and then Ariella
stopped in the middle of the song and flicked her gaze across Flaca,
one, two, as if to size up the kind of company the Electric Blue Woman
kept and what it meant about her—as if to say *so she's one of us too*—
but Ariella? This Ariella Ocampo? A woman like *that*? It couldn't be.
But there it was, the subtlest glance, over in an instant, recognizable
only to those who know. The singer was a cantora—the cantora, a
cantora!—and the pun was so ridiculous that Flaca almost laughed
aloud. She bit her tongue to hold it back. Ariella's eyes were elsewhere,

and did not return. Flaca breathed a sigh of relief that only lasted until the intermission, when an usher brought a note to La Venus. *What is it?* Flaca asked. *What does it say?* La Venus refused to show her and they spent the rest of the concert tense. Flaca kept waiting for the singer to look at La Venus again, as if daring her, ready with a blazing defense, but it didn't happen. Ariella Ocampo, regal in her mantle of music, a queen. On the bus ride home, La Venus had finally relented and laid the note bare. Nothing but numbers. A phone number. No words. *But you won't call it, will you?* Flaca blurted out, immediately embarrassed at her own petulance. *Of course not,* La Venus said, not looking at her.

But then she did.

"It's just not fair," Flaca said now, staring out the window at the ocean. "That you won't tell me what happened when you went to her house."

La Venus looked at her with something resembling pity. "I thought we were free women. No ownership. Wasn't that how you put it? Choosing to be together because we wanted to, not because anyone told us to. Free love, like the hippies, only better because we're free of men. Defying the fetters of marriage—your words, Flaca."

"I know what I said. And we're not married." Obviously. What a stupid thing to say. "But—" She searched for the right words. What right did she have to be jealous? How many times had she let her attention and even her hands roam when she was supposed to be with another woman, when the woman she was supposed to be with was devoted to her? She'd always thought it one of the good things about being an *invertida*, a breach of nature, a woman made for women: that she could live beyond marriage. Not be owned by anyone. Follow her own urges, the truths that sprang from her body.

The problem was that her body wanted La Venus: hungrily and truthfully and without end.

"You could have told me you were going to her house."

"I have to tell you everywhere I go?"

"This is different."

"Why? It was a party. I can't go to a party without telling you? For God's sake, now you sound like Arnaldo."

Flaca stared at her. *You didn't invite me,* she thought, but held back from saying. When La Venus had first told her that she'd gone to a party at Ariella Ocampo's house, she hadn't believed it. Though parties were no longer against the law, the permitting process for gatherings of more than five was so onerous and people were so wary that large gatherings were rare, and she ached for the loosening of an apartment full of bodies, drinks, music, laughter, the way birthdays used to be, for everyone's birthdays: her parents, her sisters, her little nieces and nephews, great-aunts, great-grandfathers, all occasions for cake and *pebetes* and whiskey and tangos and guitars. But it only took a bit of investigation to learn that it was true: Ariella Ocampo held parties, at her old mansion in El Prado, where she could blithely make her art and not worry her pretty brow over how to pay the goddamn bills every goddamn week because she was rich, not from her art but from the family into which she was born. Must be nice, the parties were nice, or so it was said. Incredibly, the regime seemed to turn a blind eye. The catch with those parties was that unless you lived right there in the neighborhood it was best to stay until morning to avoid the night patrols. Which led Flaca to the question with the obvious answer that she had not yet dared ask. "You stayed all night?"

"Flaca. Can you hear yourself?"

"Why won't you answer?"

La Venus turned away. "Most people stay. It's a long party and it's safer to disperse after sunrise."

"So what did you do, then, until sunrise?"

"You want to know all the details, Flaca? What I ate, what I drank, what time I took a piss?"

Flaca felt something in her crumble. She looked out the window, at the dirt path to the beach and the strip of blue beyond it, and struggled for breath.

"Flaca?"

"Just tell me you don't want to see her again."

The silence grew vast between them, draped over the distant chant of waves.

Flaca thought of those waves, the way they kissed the sand, over and over, always returning to the same caress. But was that really true? Wasn't each wave composed of different water, or the same water arranged in infinite combinations? Were two kisses ever alike? She'd never wanted so intensely for a thing to stay the same. She'd been so stupid. Thinking that La Venus was her discovery, a housewife she'd brought over to the Other Side, the invisible side, where women took their hidden joys. She compared herself to her lover's husband, and delighted in her triumph. She was better than him, gave his wife more pleasure, she was winning. She'd been so self-satisfied that she hadn't seen a thing like this coming, a rival right here on the Other Side, a rich and glamorous rival, with a house of her own, money, fame, forbidden parties, all these things that Flaca lacked. And beauty. Of the feminine kind that enraptured onstage. Flaca had abandoned femininity years ago, striding away from it, all relief and motion, no looking back. She had no urge whatsoever to return. There were always women who'd be drawn to her the way she was, angular, lean, brash. She got the nickname Flaca in early adolescence, when the other girls grew hips and breasts and she stayed flat and reedy, and she'd embraced it with good humor and a kind of pride. And yet. And yet thinking of La Venus with that damn opera star made Flaca suddenly feel ugly, misshapen, and small again, rained on by the stones of older boys on the walk home. She could feel the thump of the stones on her skin, hear their cruel, coppery voices in her ears.

"I can't," La Venus said.

*

Paz, Romina, and Malena returned from El Lobo's with the supplies they'd gone for, plus three large pieces of cardboard and a bucket of green paint.

"What on earth are you going to do with those?" La Venus asked, amused, and also relieved at her friends' return, the change of subject.

"We're going to make signs," Paz said. "They're from El Lobo, a housewarming gift. The paint is left over from the shelves in his store—which look lovely now, by the way, wait till you see."

La Venus smiled at Paz. That girl, able to take such fierce joy in cardboard and a bucket of paint. How long would that last in her? In times like these? She was so young. But not carefree—no one had that anymore. "What kind of signs?"

"Paz hasn't told us yet," Romina said. "It's all very mysterious."

"No, it's not," Paz said. "We're going to make a sign for our home, announcing its name, the way fancy people do in the fancy beach towns." She looked up at the others for a reaction, at Flaca, who was in the back doorway, smoking a cigarette and picking at her nails. She didn't seem to be listening.

"But what *is* its name?" Malena said.

"That's what we'll have to figure out," Paz said. She hesitated for a moment; she'd imagined this differently, all five women in a circle, the way they sat at night, only this time around a green-dipped brush, making this thing together. She looked at Flaca again, but Flaca wouldn't look at her.

"How about Paradise?" Malena said.

"Shanty," Romina said.

Malena shot her a look of mock outrage. "What!"

Romina grinned.

Paz reached for the brush, dipped it in green, and started writing. "Go on."

"The Seashell," La Venus said.

"The Hovel."

"The Palace."

"The Church."

"The Temple."

"The Cave."

"The Ship."

"The Prow."

"Freedom."

"The Edge of the World."

"The Fireplace."

"The Fire."

"The Voice."

"The Song."

"The Dream."

Paz was painting furiously, words all over the cardboard, straining to keep up with the names.

"The Fisherman's Dream."

"The Woman's Dream."

"Yes!"

"The Tongue's Dream."

"Now you're talking," Flaca said from the far wall, and Paz felt a jolt of happiness that she'd returned to them, the ring of them complete again.

"The Two Fingers of Your Right Hand's Dream—"

"Come now, why not three?"

"You're blushing!"

"*You're* blushing!"

"The Five Fingers of—"

"The Right Hand's Dream."

"The Left Hand's Dream."

"Left?"

"I'm a lefty!"

"The Cunt. The Hips."

"The Happy Hips—"

"The Happy Cunt—"

"*¡Chicas, chicas!*"

"That's it! *Chicas, Chicas* is a perfect name."

"Oh, of course. *That* won't attract any attention."

La Venus gestured toward the brush. "Can I take a turn?"

Paz handed her the brush. "It's yours."

La Venus painted around the words for a while. The others watched. Names in cursive, names in block letters, shouts and whispers, arrows, swirls. Riotous vines of green.

"Wow," Paz said. "You never told us you could paint like that."

La Venus scratched the back of her neck. "I'm not sure I knew."

"But you know we can't hang that," Romina said. "Ever."

"We have to!" Paz said. "This is our house."

Romina just looked at her. "That's beside the point."

"Actually," Malena said, "that *is* the point. Because it's our house, we have to be more careful than anyone."

"We could put it inside," Paz said, doubtfully.

"I have an idea," La Venus said, and she picked up the paintbrush again. She painted over the clustered words, brushing green sweeps over them, drowning them in whorls of color.

Paz made a whinnying, disappointed sound.

"Wait," La Venus said. "I'm not done."

As the paint dried, she set to cutting letters out of the remaining cardboard. She set those letters in over the green, swirled surface. L-A-P-R-O-A. La Proa. The Prow.

La Venus looked at Paz, who was still sulking. "All the other words are still under there, Paz. Remember that."

Flaca had brought a hammer and nails from the city, and they used these to hang the sign to the right of their front door. In the hours that followed, Paz stole looks at it whenever she could, watching the way the green shifted in the changing sunlight, first brightening, then sinking into deep shades that made her think of witches and their thick, ancient brews.

That was the sign's color that evening when the military trucks drove by.

New arrivals from the civilized world.

One, two, three, in a line, right past their home even though there was no road there, no road anywhere in Polonio, only open sand and dirt that these trucks pressed long continuous tracks into as they churned past.

Romina had been sitting outside to escape the heat trapped in their home. She didn't look directly at the trucks and tried to pretend they weren't slicing her mind in half, weren't pressing at her body as the wheels pressed at the land, the sound of their engines like the low growl of the car in which she was taken to the cell where—don't be stupid, Romina, come back to the moment, that's not where you are, look at the ocean down the way there, they don't own it, see how blue and endless, fill your eyes.

Paz was doing a handstand for no good reason except that she liked doing handstands and nobody stopped her here. She watched the trucks pass, upside down. Their upturned wheels made her think of beetles stuck on their backs, waving their stumpy legs in the air.

La Venus had ducked inside as soon as she saw the trucks coming— she was wearing a bikini and a long skirt and nothing else—and she watched through the kitchen window. She saw soldiers in the covered wagons, soldiers with eyes in their heads, scanning for female bodies. Finding them.

The trucks drove through the twilight, over the rolling field toward the lighthouse, until they finally disappeared around a bend.

"Paz," La Venus called through the window.

"What?"

"You should come inside."

"I don't want to. It's too hot."

"It's safer in here."

"Oh, for God's sake. They're gone now!"

"We should all go in," Malena said.

"And what?" Paz said. "Stay in our traps for as long as there are soldiers?"

Flaca arrived, carrying the paltry twigs she'd gathered for a fire. There wouldn't be much of one tonight, but at least they had their candles. The others told her about the trucks, but Flaca already knew from the tracks crushed into the open space in front of their hut. They debated what to do about their fire that night, and dinner. They shouldn't attract attention. They shouldn't give up their rights. There were no rights. That shouldn't be true. It didn't matter what should or should not be true. They couldn't go on like this forever. It wasn't forever, this night of new trucks, a time for extra precaution. They'd been planning to grill. It didn't matter. It mattered. They didn't have fire-wood anyway. They could cook inside, in the cooking pit. They could light candles and sit around them indoors. They would be together. They would be fine.

With the dinner plan changed, Flaca and La Venus went to El Lobo's for a few additional ingredients. They seemed to be taking a long time, Romina thought. Perhaps they were patching things up. This gave her hope, then scared her. What if, in patching things up, they'd tried to steal a bit of private time out on the rocks? There was no knowing where those soldiers might wander after hours or what they'd do if they discovered two women entwined. *Goddamnit,* she thought, *Flaca, get the fuck back here.*

Paz slunk outside. She'd been cooped up long enough. What could happen to her? She'd stay right here on this stool, her back to the hut that she owned, that she co-owned, her name on the deed and thank you very much. Here she was, two weeks away from her eighteenth birthday, sitting at the door of her own house like a queen. Nobody in her university classes would ever imagine it, not the professors or the classmates who looked past her at the shiny lipstick girls. She looked out at the landscape, now cloaked in the last dregs of twilight. A beauty she could never get used to, never wanted to get used to, though she longed to know it in every light and mood.

A figure was approaching from the direction of the lighthouse. A wide figure, not Flaca or La Venus, but not a soldier either. It was hard to make things out in the diminished light, so it wasn't until the figure was almost upon her that Paz saw it was a woman, a lady, an old lady, dressed in pearls and garish makeup and a fur coat that was ridicu-lous on this warm autumn night. Immediately, Paz decided that this woman was rich and foolish, the kind of woman who would bring an expensive fur coat to a far-flung rugged beach and then insist on wear-ing it just to show off that she could, heat be damned. The Fur Woman was looking at her now, at Paz, on her stool wearing a bathing suit and a short skirt. She seemed to expect a greeting, or something more, a show of deference, as if she, Paz, were part of the rabble and the Fur

Woman a passing queen. I'm not the rabble, Paz thought, and then it crossed her mind that perhaps she was. The proletariat, with its shabby huts. Well, she thought, it's *my* shabbiness and no one else's. The Fur Woman was still staring. Paz stared back and did not smile.

"Sit properly," the Fur Woman snapped.

"Excuse me?"

"Close your legs and sit like a lady."

Paz felt her spine tense. She hadn't realized that her knees weren't together, that she was sitting with her legs relaxed and spread apart, open in a manner for which her mother had scolded her since before she could remember.

The Fur Woman glared at Paz as if she were a poorly trained dog. "Didn't you hear me?"

"There is no law against sitting."

The Fur Woman's face changed, now, and Paz felt her first slash of fear. She should pull her knees together and apologize, she thought. This was still Uruguay. But her body would not move.

"Where is your mother?" the Fur Woman asked.

Romina was in the doorway now. How long had she been there? "Señora. I am very sorry. The child is very sorry."

"You?" The Fur Woman looked doubtful. "You're her mother?"

"No, I'm her cousin. This girl is under my care, and she's sorry— aren't you, María?"

The fear cut deeper. Romina saw fit to hide her name. She would only do that if she sensed danger. But maybe Romina, with her past, her arrest, her imprisoned brother, was prone to reading danger when it wasn't there. All these grown-ups with their fear responses to every- thing, to everyone, they were part of the cage, weren't they? It made Paz want to scream.

She didn't answer and the silence grew deafening.

The Fur Woman's face had settled into hardness.

"She's very sorry," Romina said.

The Fur Woman looked pointedly at Paz's legs, then at her face, and then she turned around and walked down the path without another word. She vanished into the quickly gathering darkness.

Paz felt a rush of triumph.

"What the hell were you thinking!" Romina hissed.

"Oh, for God's sake, will you calm down?"

"Paz, that woman came in with the soldiers."

"You saw her?"

"No, but—"

"Then you don't know."

"Think, girl. Who else would she be with? El Lobo?"

"There is no *way* that woman is a soldier."

"She doesn't have to be a soldier to destroy you."

"Will you please stop worrying? You're not my mother!"

The look on Paz's face was so fierce, then, that Romina dropped the subject.

Paz stormed inside, and when Romina followed, she saw her in the sleeping corner, curled around a book.

"Are you all right?" It was Malena, by Romina's side.

"Yes. No. I don't know." Romina leaned against the counter. What were they doing out at this beach? Escaping? Some escape! At least in the city you could fear soldiers and shit comfortably at the same time. There wasn't even a decent kitchen here, the knives weren't clean, there was no phone, not even a bugged one over which you could speak in code, only the ocean to run to and whose side was the ocean on?

What kind of question was that?

A sob rose up inside Romina. She stifled it. No. If she started, she might not stop. "Let's clean up around here."

Cleaning always calmed her, and by the time Flaca and La Venus returned, she was breathing normally again, able to turn the Fur Woman incident into a good story. She coaxed Paz into telling it with her, a kind of peacemaking between them, and as they interjected details over each other—inside, with the door closed, Romina made sure of that—the others burst out laughing.

"I wish I could have seen the look on her face!" La Venus cried.

Paz looked pleased, and proud, the evening's hero.

Romina felt a wash of relief at La Venus and Flaca's delight, their utter lack of concern. Perhaps she'd been overreacting after all. Then again, perhaps those two had found their moment on the rocks and were too full of afterglow to remember the need for fear. Sex could do that to you—sex, and Polonio; both of them could fill you up with beautiful, get you drunk on it, unhinge you from the ugliness that pervaded the world and lift you out of it to soaring heights where you forgot that you were in fact still mortal in a broken world.

"'Sit like a lady!'" Flaca crowed. "Oh, if only the poor woman knew."

*

It was two and a half hours later, as the friends were chopping onions and potatoes for dinner, that a knock came on the door. Persistent. Hard.

They all looked at each other.

"Yes?" Flaca said, rising to her feet, but before she could get to the door the soldiers crashed through it without any effort because it wasn't even locked, what's the matter with us, Flaca thought, that we ever dreamed we didn't need a lock?

The tall one at the center scanned the room, then settled his gaze on Paz. "Her."

It happened too fast for anyone to stop it. Three soldiers around Paz, grasping her arms, and dragging her to the door, ignoring her shouts of protest. Flaca was on the back of one of the soldiers, trying to pry him from her friend because they could not could not take her. Paz was shouting. The room was red.

"Stop it," Romina hissed from somewhere worlds away. "Stop it, Flaca."

Me? Flaca thought. She's trying to stop *me*? "They can't. You can't!"

Another soldier came up to Flaca and punched her in the face. Red, more red, pierced by bursts of white.

"Sirs, please, where are you taking her?" Romina again, louder now, and pleading.

The men didn't answer.

And then they were gone, just as swiftly as they'd come, leaving a single soldier keeping watch outside the door.

Paz, gone.

The world spun.

The four women stared at each other.

Flaca reached up to feel her face. Wet. Swelling. In that moment, she understood that her love for Paz had become a ferocious force—as ferocious as her love for Romina, as ferocious as anything she'd ever felt in her life—and that she'd do anything to save the girl from harm.

But if it was too late.

It could not be too late.

"The songs," Malena whispered.

What was she talking about? Flaca stared at her blankly.

"These." Malena reached for the pile of papers that lay under a heap of shells Paz had gathered on the beach that day. Old songs, from the 1960s, from the time before. Paz had found them among her mother's papers and brought them for the women to see, perhaps even to sing them, curious relics from an era now long past, rare survivors of the fires and raids that followed the coup. Liberation songs. Bohemian songs. Songs that could get you killed.

Romina moved to help Malena gather the lyrics sheets from the various corners and rucksacks where they were stashed, wondering how she did it, how Malena could think so steadily at a time like this. Steady Malena. Calm Malena. Reserved-but-in-control-of-things Malena. Of course, the first thing to do after an arrest was to scan the space for any evidence of subversion, or anything soldiers could construe as evidence of subversion, and to destroy it. How could she herself not have leapt there immediately? What was wrong with her?

They didn't dare wait for the time it would take to kindle a fire in the cooking pit, so they dipped the pages into a candle flame and watched them burn in a metal pail.

Words turned to flame, then ash.

It was Malena who picked up the knife first, returned to chopping. La Venus soon joined her, though her hands shook. No one spoke. Flaca started the fire in the cooking pit and Romina folded and unfolded her clothes, thinking furiously, a plan, a plan, they had to have a plan.

The stew came out fine, but no one had an appetite. They tried to eat. They still had bowls on their laps when a knock came on the door.

Another soldier entered, holding a clipboard. "Identification cards," he said.

The women went to their rucksacks to get them. Romina's mind raced. They hadn't asked for ID cards immediately—it had taken them an hour to do what would have taken seconds in the city. They were disorganized, unprepared. A weak spot. How to use it. There had to be a way.

"Sir," Flaca said, when the soldier had finished recording their names and ID numbers, "if you could tell me where our friend is."

"So she's *not* your cousin?"

"I—"

"She's my cousin," Romina said, stepping forward. They had to get their stories straight, or else. "The rest are our friends."

"And what are you doing out here?"

"Taking a vacation."

The soldier glanced at Romina, let his gaze travel up and down her body.

She forced herself to let him look, to seem pliant, to seem like nothing.

"She didn't mean it," Flaca said. "She's just a girl."

"A girl who insulted the Minister of the Interior's wife."

Romina went cold, remembering the Fur Woman's rigid face. The wife of the Minister of the Interior. It was worse than she'd thought. "My cousin would be glad to apologize."

The soldier's gaze drifted over to Malena, then to La Venus, where it landed, raw, hungry. "Where are your husbands?"

Flaca dug her fingernails into her palms to keep from punching him.

"In Montevideo, sir," La Venus purred in a seductive voice, the voice she'd used for years to bring men to their knees, a voice that belied the fear shooting through her spine and that she hoped could help save

Paz by taming this man, though it could also backfire if he took it as a reason to come back and rape her. But it was worth the risk. If he wanted to rape her, after all, he'd find a reason no matter what.

Romina marveled at the genius of La Venus's grammatical construction. She'd told the truth: her husband was in Montevideo. And yet, she'd given the impression that every one of them had a husband, caring about their whereabouts, making them more respectable.

"We'll be conducting a thorough investigation," the soldier finally said, eyes still on La Venus. "You stay inside."

He walked out, but his steps didn't take him away from the doorway, so Flaca shushed her friends and took a glass to the door, to hear him speak to the soldier posted outside the door.

"Got a smoke?"

Shuffling. A sigh.

"Thanks." A pause. "Crazy girls. They're either drug addicts or Tupamaros. We just need to find out which."

Two hours later, just past one in the morning, the interviews began.

*

"She's the niece of an important general," Romina said.

She was sitting across from two soldiers, the tall one who'd come in before, and another one with pretty green eyes. He must hate his eyes, she thought. Pretty is no help at all for a soldier.

They were in a fishing hut that had been emptied for these interviews. Just her and them. Separate your suspects. See if their stories match, see if one of them will break.

The soldiers kept their faces blank, and glanced at each other. The tall one hesitated before he spoke again. "What's this general's name?"

"She won't tell me his name."

"But you're cousins."

"Yes. It's on her father's side, not the same side of the family as I'm on, and, you know, she's very modest, an innocent girl. Once, in fact, when we were—"

"You'll limit yourself to answering my questions."

"Yes, sir." She'd overplayed her hand. She should pull back. But still, her strategy could work; if they looked into the claim and discovered it to be false, there could be reprisals, but if she kept the story vague she might succeed in planting a seed of doubt. A seed was a seed, however tiny. And this wasn't Montevideo, where the well-oiled machines of torture waited for new bodies to consume. They had no clear plan. They'd sent some poor man stumbling out of his bedclothes to use this hut—the sheets were whorled and tangled on the single narrow pallet—because, for some reason, they didn't want to bring their suspects to the barracks. They probably hadn't even known where to hold Paz. Who was she with? The soldiers? The lighthouse troops? The local police? There was no way to find out—asking would only anger them—but either way, they wouldn't be expecting a prisoner like her, and if they were less prepared they might be less cruel.

Or more cruel.

"So you don't know her uncle's name?"

"No, sir. But she spoke of him with great admiration. In passing. She loves him. He's of great service to our country."

The officer took another good long stare at her, scanning, she thought, for sincerity or sarcasm. *Act like you mean it*. Her throat was dry, her chest hollow and cold.

"Your ID."

How stupid. He'd already seen it. Was he stalling? She handed it over again, trembling.

It was Pretty Eyes who walked her back to her hut afterward, and on the way he put his hand on the small of her back, as if to steer her, as if she didn't know the way to her own damn house, as if she wouldn't notice when the hand traveled down to her ass and that's exactly what she pretended, that she hadn't noticed, that it wasn't happening, that she was simply walking beneath the starry sky to a place she loved without a hand on her ass and the memories of the cell and the *Three the Only Three* surging up inside for her to push back down.

She was still pushing at them when she walked back through her door.

"You next." Pretty Eyes gestured toward La Venus, who rose and followed him out. She'd done her best to cover her body with a shawl. And yet she walked regally, Flaca thought; she couldn't help it. She was queenly all the time. For a second she flashed on an image of La Venus walking away, not with a soldier, but with Ariella, with glittering Ariella just as regal by her side, and then shame flooded her for having such a petty thought at a time like this.

She turned to Romina, tried to read her face. "Well? How did it go?"

Romina shrugged. All of a sudden she felt sick. She dropped her voice to a whisper. "I told them about Paz's uncle."

"Wh—"

"The one who's a general, a powerful general, whose name we can't remember."

It took Flaca a second to understand. "You're a genius."

"Ssshhhh."

"What else did they—"

"I can't, Flaca. Leave me alone."

Romina went out to the back of the hut, where the soldiers had not posted a guard. She couldn't deal with Flaca now, her invasions, her eagerness, she meant well but what did she know? What did any of them know? They'd never been inside the machine. Her stomach clenched. She sat down on the ground, her back against the wall, and let the sound of the ocean reach up and enfold her. They'd surrounded her, the men, the Only Three, especially the one who'd come the first night, he'd encased her completely in the smell of his sweat, and he'd been so heavy on her body that she'd thought her ribs might break, she was almost breaking under him and he didn't care, it didn't matter, she didn't matter to the man surrounding her, she could drown in his flesh and he'd just keep on going, no, it could not happen to Paz, the thought made her want to tear her skin off. She flinched at movement just behind her. A figure joined her on the ground. Malena. Breathing deeply, and only then did Romina realize how ragged her own breathing had become. Her breath steadied, slowing to the rhythm of Malena's breath. To her intense relief, Malena made no attempt to speak. She only sat. Her presence a thing you could lean on. A quiet. A comfort. A calm.

Flaca saw them from the window. Two figures in the night, unmoving, not turned to each other, yet somehow linked in silence. Two figures at home in a shared silence. Why hadn't she seen it before? That the two of them could be? It seemed obvious now, and yet the thought had never crossed her mind. Perhaps because they both seemed so tightly shut, each in her own way, Romina skirting away from her arrest and what had happened in those days, as well as anything else (her brother's imprisonment, her parents' disappointment) that pointed toward pain, while Malena was so quiet that one could almost forget she was there. She was a listener. A woman who kept things tidy, tucked into their place. But maybe it wasn't that simple. Maybe she too bit back the stories of her life and pushed them down, pushed them out of view, to survive, and maybe that was why they saw so little of her inner world, which could in fact be as vast as anyone's. How could two such women ever form a bond? And how would they ever—? Who would stoke the fire, rip the panties off or sidle past them? It seemed unlikely, almost laughable. Yet here they were. After it had come to seem certain that Romina had renounced passion forever, left it behind in whatever bleak cell they'd kept her in—after all that, here they were. And in the rich air between those two, the way their bodies seemed to tune in to each other without touching, the peaceful yet alert way they sat and sat—in all of that Flaca could see that the thing between them, unlike the affair she herself was in, had the power to last.

*

The cell was small and rank. Rat shit crusted the pallet on the floor. Paz stood at the bars for a long time, for an endless stretch of time, before sitting down on the pallet, eyes open in the dark. She could not sleep. Sleep was a thing buried in the impossible. Night stretched long and dead around her. There was one more cell beside hers, empty. She was alone save for the guard whose snores occasionally ebbed down the dark hall.

She'd been driven out of Polonio, blindfolded, hands cuffed behind her back, as if she stood a chance of getting away from three armed soldiers in a truck—and now she was somewhere else, back on the grid, that much she knew from the single dim electric bulb outside her cell.

She'd been told nothing.

She had to pee but there was no toilet in the cell and she didn't dare wake the guard. She hadn't been beaten yet, hadn't been raped, didn't want to give them a reason. Hold it. Hold the pee, hold it in, hold in everything.

Morning came and with it a visit from the guard, with a plate of stale bread and a cup of water. He pushed these through the bars without a word.

"Excuse me, sir."

He turned to her.

"May I please use a bathroom?"

He handcuffed her before he led her down the hall, as though she had anywhere to run, as though she were the dangerous person in this jail rather than he, and she wiped herself as best she could, at once relieved by the release and mortified by the watching guard, and yet, she thought as he led her back and locked her up again, and yet he hasn't raped me. Why not? Wasn't that how these things went? Were they waiting for something—and if so, what? Every muscle in her body tensed, vigilant, waiting for a sign. She would fight like a beast. She would not fight. She would let them do what they wanted but refuse to make a sound. She would kill them. She would beg them to go easy. She would give them anything as long as they didn't cut her, would there be knives? She couldn't stand the thought of knives. Couldn't stand the thought of—

Stop it. Try to eat.

She tried a bite of bread, couldn't swallow it, spat it out. Water. Tepid, but good, a coming back to life as it went down. She didn't dare more than three sips, intent as she was on putting off further trips to the toilet.

The hours passed.

Around and around her thoughts spun, a wheel unhinged. She herself was unhinged, she thought, more than once, as she struggled to rein herself in. The guard listened to the radio down the hall, shuffling to the door every once in a while. Voices outside, their words indecipherable. She would keep her head down and ask no questions, not tempt fate. She'd be lucky if she got out. She might never get out. Thousands of people had not gotten out. The shape of her future twisted horrifically, beyond recognition.

She tried not to think.

She thought of the ocean.

Its roar, its welcome. El Lobo's keen eyes.

She longed for El Lobo's oxygen mask, imagined tearing it down from its nest of bones and holding it to her face. Just the thought of this steadied her breathing.

It was almost dusk when the guard came and took her from the cell to a bare little office with a single brown desk, behind which sat a man with an air of authority.

"Sit," the man said.

She sat.

The man nodded to the guard, and the guard stepped out and closed the door behind him.

"So," the man said. "You're Paz."

She nodded.

"And you're eighteen, huh?"

She was not quite yet eighteen, but knew better than to correct him.

"Young and stupid."

She could not argue with this man. She bit her tongue to keep herself from speaking.

"What the hell were you doing out on a deserted beach with those women?"

"Just—trying to—" *have fun,* she'd almost said, but those words seemed dangerous. She shunted them aside. "Trying to appreciate nature."

He looked at her. "Aha. Nature, is it."

He stared as if he could bore a hole through her by looking. He wasn't very tall, but he was burly, broad-shouldered; she could wrestle him back for a few seconds, perhaps, but not much longer. He had a paunch and the pinched face of a surly corner grocer. He seemed to be assessing her and she tried, with all her strength, to look ugly. All those nights in the bathroom at home, staring in the mirror, feeling ugly, her face wrong, too angular and wide-jawed for a girl; she tried to summon those times, summon all that ugly up into her skin like a shield.

"You shouldn't be away from your family," he said. "Much less with the likes of them."

"Yes, sir," she said, and immediately was flooded with shame at the disavowal.

"You could get into trouble." He studied her again. "You don't want that, of course."

"No, sir." She was disgusting. Pathetic. Groveling for her life.

He looked at her silently for a long time, and his expression grew strange, almost bewildered, though she couldn't imagine why. Finally, he said, "Is there anything you want to tell me?"

He hadn't told her why she was here, though she guessed it had to do with the Fur Woman, the talking back, the refusal of a teenage girl to sit with her legs closed. Nor had he told her where they were, in what town, how long they were planning to keep her, nor even his own name. She could ask, but he hadn't invited questions and every single thing it crossed her mind to say seemed spiked with danger. "No, sir."

He knocked on his desk, and the guard returned and took her back to the cell. He opened the door and, as she stepped through, he brushed against her breast with his hand and she went rigid *it begins* but then the door slammed and he was gone.

The rest of the night she waited for him to come, hands in fists, but he did not, and the next morning it was another guard who brought stale bread and stared as she fumbled to wipe herself at the toilet. This guard limited himself to stroking her ass and, the next day, pushing his erection against her, but she pretended not to notice and almost wanted to laugh at these country people, they clearly weren't trained, weren't used to political prisoners, didn't they know what went on in the city? and then the almost-laugh caught in her throat, the saddest poison on earth.

*

On the fourth morning, the guard from the first day was back, and, to her surprise, after breakfast and the toilet he took her, handcuffed, to the front door. Two men stood outside. They were in ordinary clothes, and yet she knew them from their faces. They were two of the men who'd taken her from the Prow. Soldiers. Panic poured through her.

"You'll come with us," one of the soldiers said.

"Where are you taking me?"

"Where do you think?" the second soldier said.

She didn't know what to think, but soon the handcuffs were removed and she was walking away from the little jail which she now knew, from the sign outside, was the tiny police station for the town of Castillos. They walked to the highway and out of the town, walked for what seemed like hours, until they reached an isolated bus station and stopped. She didn't dare ask what they were waiting for, a bus or the arrival of some nightmare. There was a single bench and no one on it but the soldiers stayed on their feet, smoking cigarettes and saying nothing, so she didn't sit, not that she wanted to anyway, her body ached from nights on the pallet and lack of food and the vaulting blue above her head was enough to get drunk on, the sky, the sky, had it always been so relentlessly beautiful?

A bus arrived, and the soldiers led her onto it and to the back, where they sat in the long row of seats and flanked her on each side. They rode in silence. Through the window, she watched the landscape blur and shake. Fields and trees and squat little huts with naked children and laundry hung like desperate flags. It seemed like the road to

Montevideo, which stirred hope in her, even though it also stabbed her not to return to Polonio, to let her friends know she was all right.

When a woman boarded in a town to sell empanadas from a basket, the soldiers bought eight and gave her two. They were fresh, manna compared to what she'd eaten in jail.

"Thank you," she said, and then she felt humiliated by the act, thanking her captors!

But they could have chosen not to feed her.

These soldiers whose superiors couldn't spare a car for a prisoner transport.

Backwoods, pathetic—but she was grateful. She was safer on a bus than in a car.

She'd been right about heading into the city. Gradually, over the hours of riding, the bus began to fill. By the time it reached the outskirts of Montevideo it was crowded, every seat near her was taken, and though at first she'd feared repulsing others with her smell—she hadn't bathed in four days—she soon realized that nobody noticed. Nobody saw. There she was, a prisoner flanked by soldiers in plain clothes, and yet she looked as free and normal as anyone else. The essence of dictatorship, she thought. On the bus, on the street, at home, no matter where you are or how ordinary you seem, you're in a cage.

*

The soldiers got off the bus downtown and walked her into the city jail, where they deposited her unceremoniously in a cell with one other woman and left without a word.

Paz watched them through the bars as they walked away. Fear clawed at her.

"What did you do?"

It was her cellmate, who was more of a girl than a woman, and a prostitute, judging from her low-cut blouse and heavy makeup. She sat with her head cocked, waiting for an answer.

Paz hesitated for a moment. "I talked back to a rich lady."

The girl laughed. It was a sharp laugh. "That's it? Just talked?"

Paz shrugged.

"She wasn't paying you?"

"No," Paz said before she fully understood the question. When she did understand, her mind roared. Paid? By a woman? That's what she thought? Had this girl actually done that before? So she knew what to do, she was willing to—and did she—what if—

"What did you say?" The girl was open-faced now, curious. "When you talked back?"

"Not much." Paz took a closer look at the girl. She had a narrow face and rich black hair. They were about the same height and age. She was pretty, Paz realized, and suddenly their looking at each other acquired another layer, something thick about it. The girl staring at her so frankly. Paz looked away, then back at her. The girl seemed to be searching her for something. There was something keen in her eyes, what was it? Paz couldn't breathe. And then it ended, the girl's face closed, became a wall of exhaustion. Without another word, she lay down on her pallet and closed her eyes.

Fitful sleep that night, on the ground.

The next morning, a guard arrived at the cell door and motioned at her to come out.

He pushed her down a hall toward the front entrance.

There, in the lobby, stood her mother.

The look on her face worse than all the soldiers put together.

*

The bus ride home was dead silent. Inside, her mother went straight to the kitchen and put on the kettle, then stood over it, rigid. Paz hovered in the doorway. She had to speak, but didn't know where to begin.

Silence spread its dark, wide wings. She couldn't bear it. She longed for a shower, fresh clothes, a real bed. These things would clear her mind. She turned to leave.

"You'll stay right there," her mother said in a voice Paz didn't recognize.

Paz waited.

"How could you? Don't you know better? Haven't I taught you anything?"

An icy ache spread up her body. In the days of hiding guerrilla fighters, Mamá had always fretted over the guerrillas' well-being, what they must have suffered behind bars, were they hurt, they deserved a doctor and what a crime that they couldn't safely be taken to see one. Now she didn't seem to care what had happened to Paz. She hadn't so much as checked her daughter's arms for bruises. "I didn't know this would happen. We were just—"

"You were acting stupid. *In times like these.*"

"You're the one who hid subversives in the house!"

"Will you lower! Your! Voice!" Each word spat out in a low hiss.

The neighbors. "Sorry." A slash of guilt. What if that outburst had cost her mother her safety? Paz felt hot with shame, but then the shame bled back into rage, because even now she was the problem, it was she, Paz, who was always the problem, as if she were not a girl but a barrier keeping her mother from her life and even now it was her loud voice that was the problem and not the roaming soldiers everywhere, the Fur Woman and her spite, the hands and more hands and cold jail floor and fear and Puma, what about Puma, what about—tangled thought, she could barely trace it—what about the way her mother had protected Puma without seeing the child?

Her mother was staring at her just as brutally as before, though her jaw had softened slightly. She took a breath and put her hand on the counter, as if to steady herself. "Resistance is one thing. Acting stupid is another. Haven't I taught you anything?"

"Obviously you haven't."

"How dare you—"

"Well you haven't!"

"You're an ungrateful—"

"Not that again."

"How dare you?"

"You already said that."

"You're a disaster."

"*You're* the disaster!"

Mamá slapped her across the cheek.

They stared at each other in fury and surprise. It took a few moments for Paz's face to begin to sting.

"Why did you have me," she said, "if you never wanted me?"

Even then, as her mother clapped a hand over her mouth and blinked back tears, the answer knifed into her mind.

Mamá was young when she married Paz's father, eighteen years old, and Paz was born six and a half months later, this temporal discrepancy always glossed over in the official version. But sometimes, the silent story is the real one. Abortion could kill you, pregnancy trapped you but at least you had a better chance at staying alive. She'd had Paz because she had to. And now here she was, still young, still beautiful, her husband gone, trying to live her life with a difficult daughter in the way.

Mamá turned from her, hand still over her mouth. Paz tried to summon something to say, but Mamá marched out of the kitchen, and Paz could not move, could only listen to the footsteps and the bedroom door as it slammed shut.

Steam shot from the abandoned kettle for a long time before Paz removed it from the fire.

*

The following afternoon, before her mother came home from work, Paz packed a bag and walked to Flaca's house. When Flaca saw her in the doorway she made a keening sound unlike anything Paz had heard before, and then she was crushed in her friend's arms.

"You're back."

Her eyes stung. The ferocity of Flaca's embrace woke the emptiness inside her and filled it, made her feel small in a manner that she sank into, relieved to be small, relieved to cling, for all her constant protests that she was not a *chiquilina,* not a child. "Can I stay with you?"

"Whatever you need. Come in."

Within the hour, Flaca had set up bedding on the floor of her room, insisting that she'd be the one to sleep there while Paz took the bed, waving off Paz's attempts at protest, saying, "It's no problem, really, you can stay as long as you want," and these words flooded Paz with gratitude even though it seemed crystal clear to her that she most certainly could not stay as long as she wanted, which in that instant was forever. Flaca's parents were kind and generous, smiling at her over dinner as if she'd always been at their table helping herself to mila- nesas, encouraging her to eat more, eat more, there is plenty, fussing over her yet asking no questions about why she was sleeping in their home. They were the polar opposite of Mamá, older and more settled, thick of waist and large of heart, already grandparents, with the air of a humble old couple made happy just by seeing their family alive and well, which, given the times, was a lot to ask of fate. And they loved Flaca. She took care of them, washed the dishes while they drifted off to the television, reminded her mother to take her medications. She takes care of them, Paz thought, just like, in Polonio, Flaca takes care of us.

That night, after dinner, and after a call with Romina during which both she and Paz wept more than they spoke, Paz and Flaca settled down to sleep and turned off the light.

"So," Flaca said, rustling in her sheets. "You're all right?"

"I suppose so."

More rustling.

"I mean, yes. Nothing happened to me." It didn't quite feel accu- rate, to call those days *nothing*—it was the terror of the next that had torn her most—and yet she knew that alongside most arrests that was exactly what they were.

Flaca exhaled long and slow. "Good. And your mother?"

"I don't want to talk about her. Not yet."

"All right."

"Tell me what happened in Polonio."

And so Flaca recounted how things had gone at the Prow after Paz was taken, the long vigil, the interviews, and Romina's gamble to protect Paz, the yarn she'd told the officers about the arrested girl's powerful uncle, counting on poor communication with the capital to keep the story afloat. And it had worked, Paz thought, remembering the guards, the man in the office, their restraint. Romina's strategy had kept her safe. They'd stayed two more days, Flaca said, during which it became clear that Paz was no longer in Polonio and that their best bet to find her was to head back to the city. Romina had been making calls to secret networks that she wouldn't name in hopes of finding her. Now she can rest, Flaca said. She'll come see you tomorrow. Meanwhile, the day after they returned from Polonio, La Venus had knocked on the majestic oak door of the singer Ariella Ocampo's house in El Prado, and there she had been welcomed in with open arms, not that Flaca had seen the open arms or what the arms had done next as soon as the door was closed but she could imagine it, she certainly could, not that she wanted to, she spent most of her waking moments trying to do the opposite. She had lost La Venus. They were over. But there was good news too. Romina and Malena. They were going to be something. They might not have acknowledged it directly yet, but Flaca had seen it.

"I saw it too," Paz said, thinking of the afternoon on the beach.

"I think they'll be very good for each other."

"But what about this situation with La Venus?"

"What do you mean?"

"What does it mean for the rest of us?"

"It's our breakup, not yours."

"But still—" Paz tried to gather her thoughts. In so many ways the world now slid and shifted beneath her feet. She couldn't bear the thought of this makeshift tribe breaking apart so soon after it had formed. It was everything to her. She had no one, nothing else.

"Still what?" Flaca sounded annoyed.

"Well, we're a group, aren't we?" She'd wanted to say *a family,* but hadn't dared. "We have the house now."

"So you think she's going to leave the group? Or that I'm going to kick her out?"

"I hope not." Although they'd bought the house together, in equal parts, it seemed to her that if anyone had the power to determine who stayed and who was cast out, it was Flaca. It was Flaca, after all, who'd led them to this, Flaca la Pilota, who'd rounded them up and realized the dream.

"I don't know, Paz, I really don't. I don't know how we can all be together there again."

"Ever?"

"I can't think about 'ever.' I can barely think about today. I mean— if she were to bring Ariella—what a nightmare!" Flaca tried to laugh, but the sound came out strangled. "We never made any rules about who could bring whom. It's all of our house, I see that. But we didn't plan for something like this."

"We didn't plan at all."

"Now, Paz, that's not fair, what about—"

"That's what makes the Prow so wonderful. It wasn't a plan. It was a dream we brought to Earth."

Flaca laughed. "I didn't know you were a poet."

"I'm not."

"Don't be so sure. It could come in handy one day, you know—with the ladies."

"Noted."

"No, really!"

"Yes, really—I'm keeping notes on all your advice for the ladies, Flaca."

"You're going to be *tremenda*."

They laughed, and Paz felt a flush of joy for the first time since the arrest.

"Look," Flaca said, her tone serious again, "about La Venus. It's still her house, and I know it. I hope that's enough for you."

Paz stared into the dark. "Why not."

"Now, what about you? You're going to class tomorrow?"

"Shit, I don't know. Do I have to?"

"I'm not your mother."

"And thank God for that."

"What are you implying?"

"Sorry. You'd be a great mother."

Flaca snorted.

"No, really." The thought of a mother who was anything like Flaca made Paz ache all over. To be seen, mirrored, from the very beginning of life? By the person who birthed you? It was more than she could even imagine. "It's just that I'm sick of mothers right now."

"Does she know where you are?"

"No."

"Paz."

"She doesn't care."

"Of course she cares. She's your *mother.*"

"Not all mothers care."

"Give it time, Paz."

"I've given it time. I can't live with her, Flaca. I can't, not now, not ever again."

"Then what will you do?"

For this Paz had no answer.

*

What to do: she had no idea.

For days she burned like a lit thing, determined, aching.

She would not go home.

She would not.

She would rather walk the streets with the ladies of the night than go back home. Even though the thought of that work, unzipping men, made her stomach churn. Not to mention that, with the night patrols, such work had become more dangerous than ever.

Still, this much was clear: leaving home meant no more studying. Not if there were bills to be paid.

She called her mother, from Flaca's living room, with Flaca sitting in a rocking chair beside her, holding her hand. She told her that she was safe, and her mother sounded indifferent, or perhaps still angry, or else afraid of talking on a surveilled call, but in any case she said little and asked for no more information than Paz gave. The call was brief, curt. She didn't go to class, instead roaming the city, walking the unkempt parks, the gray streets, the Rambla with its breeze coming in over the water like the breath of an enormous lonely soul. She walked until evening, then ducked into Flaca's house and helped Flaca's mother hang laundry and make dinner. Flaca's mother was a small woman, surprisingly spry, full of chatter warm enough to soothe your aches and pains. She would let me stay, Paz realized. She wouldn't throw me out. She probably even knew, by now, what Flaca was, though they'd never exchanged a single word about it, and even so she kept clattering away with her pots and pans and gossip, while Paz's own mother had gone cold without even knowing the core of her daughter's crime.

At night, she slept fitfully, gathering pieces of her future in her mind like shattered glass.

On the tenth morning, she got up and packed her rucksack, and by seven o'clock she was at the bus station, waiting for the 7:15 bus down the coast.

*

When she reached Polonio, before doing what she'd come to do, Paz went to their hut alone for the first time. The painted sign still hung over the door, reading THE PROW, with all those other names buried in swirls of paint. She opened the door and was relieved to see that the inside still looked the same. Almost as if the soldiers had never come.

But they had come.

She sat down at the center of the floor. Took a breath. The scent of mold a comfort. Anything can be a comfort if it smells like home. It was her eighteenth birthday and all she wanted was to be here. The air was thick with afternoon light. Sweat clung to her from the long hike over the sand dunes, on which every step had been an incantation, *I will, I will.* She would what. Live. Survive. Do whatever she had to do. Belong. What did that mean? How to belong? How can you be of a place and also unsafe there? How can you be of a place when soldiers could pull you from it at any time? Stupid thoughts. She should know better. There was no other kind of place, not in this damn country. No inch of it was beyond the reach of soldiers. And so. She tried to think. And so. And so she had two choices: either she could belong nowhere—nowhere in the whole world, because leaving Uruguay, if it were possible, meant being a foreigner forever—or she could claim a space and demand it be her home, the way one demands water from the desert, juice from a stone—and why not here. In this wild place. This room. Where Flaca and La Venus had fought, where Romina and Malena had quietly entwined their minds—she'd felt them do it—where she herself had laid out cardboard and painted dozens of names, flamboyant, silly, towering. Where her friends had known what she was and loved her for it. Where Flaca had taken a punch for her. Where the five of them had laughed and whispered as the candles burned down and the whiskey bottle slowly lightened its load. This room. And also, the land below this room. Land older than the soldiers, the generals, their wives. Older even than the country's name and borders. She tried to reach down with her consciousness, under the packed dirt floor, to the layers of sand and bedrock beneath. If she could reach the land directly, would its own mind rise to meet her? Could they tangle roots and claim each other? The soldiers had not taken this place from her. She'd been torn from this room, bruised and dragged, and yet, returning, she felt no fear. Only a rising up inside her, a stubborn stalk pushing toward growth. *Here,* she thought fiercely. *Here.* She sat still for a long time.

*

When she walked into the grocery, El Lobo looked up at her with pleasure but no evidence of surprise. "Welcome back." And then, scanning her with probing eyes, "I knew you'd return to us."

She waited for him to say more, to mention her arrest directly or ask whether she was all right, but to her relief he did neither. His gaze was warm but he did not smile.

The shipwreck stories he had told her swirled in the air, invisible gusts, holding specks of dust aloft.

She stood in the doorway, trying to make herself tall. "Tell me more about the skin trade."

Part Two

1980–1987

5

Flights

FREEDOM. TO GLOW WITH IT. Ariella in the morning, draped in sun. Ariella at night, radiant, laughing loud, as if nothing mattered, as if the police couldn't do a thing to her or if they could she didn't care, to hell with it, she was alive and would laugh when she wanted. Even now, nine months into their relationship, La Venus felt her world expand in Ariella's presence. She wanted to expand the way this woman did, to crack the code, the secret. To be this impossible thing: a woman in times like these who said and did what she liked.

A living miracle.

And an artist. A true one. Not like Arnaldo, who used to talk of future stages and fame, but an actual artist who lived to create. To live in her orbit was to live inside of art.

Enough to get drunk on.

And, in the past nine months, she had.

*

The first night she saw Ariella, at the opera, she'd come home and lain awake beside Arnaldo with the note crumpled in her hand. She already had the numbers memorized, and yet she could not put the note down. It curled and grew warm and damp against her palm. She would call. She would never call. In the morning, Arnaldo reached for her without opening his eyes and fucked her before getting out of bed, as he sometimes liked to do. Better than coffee, he used to say back when they got along, when he still checked for her mood before taking what he wanted. It was a stalemate now, her refusal to show signs of pleasure false or true, his bitter insistence made all the more acute by her refusal. For God's sake, it's like having sex with a limp rag, he'd said to her one recent morning, and she'd felt a thrill of victory, followed by shame: this was what her life had been reduced to? The triumph of becoming a bad fuck? She thought of Flaca, patient, eager to please, a joy to be with though there was also a growing weight to their time together; Flaca was young and poor, dependent on her humble working parents; she could hold La Venus's pleasure, but not her growing despair. Now, on this morning, the morning after the opera, she lay in bed listening to the hiss of Arnaldo's shower and staring at the crumpled note on the nightstand. Ariella radiated. She surged with poise and mystery. She'd held that whole grand hall of people in thrall *and fixed her beam on me.*

She forced herself to wait three days to call. She was accustomed to being the pursued, couldn't let her hunger show. Ariella answered after the third ring. The call was short, so short that Ariella never even asked her name.

"I'm having a party on Saturday," she said. "Come."

A party. Had she misheard? The invitation had been less of a question than a statement, an assumption. This ruffled La Venus—that this woman would command her to attend, that the invitation was not just for her but for who knew how many others too, and what did that mean, in any case, a party? who had parties anymore?—and she thought of not going. But in the end, Saturday found her appearing at the door of that mansion in El Prado, combed and glittering. A woman in a black evening gown opened the door when she knocked, then walked away down the hall without introducing herself. She followed the black-gowned woman to a large room lit by an old-fashioned chandelier, of the kind the wealthy had purchased at the turn of the century, heady with the thrill of electricity's arrival. There were maybe two dozen people, milling and laughing, and at the center stood Ariella, luminous in a yellow dress and—La Venus couldn't breathe—a red tie slung around her neck. Nobody seemed to react to this transgression, the mixing of male and female. The tie hung long and thin, like a flame. La Venus hung back by the drinks, determined not to chase this strange woman, this luminous, maddening singer. Why had she come? She would leave. Any second she would leave.

But she did not leave, and two hours later she was following Ariella up the stairs. The party's warm clamor faded when the bedroom door closed behind them. Ariella did not turn on the light. La Venus stood, waited, and when the singer's hands reached her body she was startled by their sureness, how clearly they wanted, how much they seemed to know.

Ariella was nothing like Flaca. She was all curves and woman. But she was not shy. La Venus felt her knees shake as the zipper down her back split open under Ariella's hands. Ariella peeled both dresses off, and her manner was both solemn and efficient, like a high priestess preparing the temple for an ancient ritual. Gowns draped carefully on chairs, she returned, and their bodies pressed together. La Venus felt the familiar sensation of melting, of her body losing its boundaries and definition, of pleasure turning her to liquid that could pour into the liquid of a woman, but she also felt something else, the raw vertigo of starting life anew, of trembling just before you raze your house to the ground.

Afterward, they lay in candlelight—when had the wicks been lit?—and Ariella said, "I still don't know your name."

"They call me La Venus."

"My Venus." Ariella stroked her skin. "Sent from the gods. You are going to be my Muse."

This stayed with La Venus throughout that last trip to Polonio, where she'd fought with Flaca, where they'd lost Paz, almost lost her completely. She thought of it the whole bus ride back to the city and throughout her first night home, which she spent still shaky with fear for her disappeared friend, hands trembling as she cooked dinner for a husband who did not ask her about her trip but who later, in bed, pressed her head down to his groin, payment for her days of absence. *Sent from the gods,* she thought as he bucked against her face. The next day, she got up and repacked her rucksack with clean clothes and a few beloved books and photographs.

She might not let me in, she thought on the bus to Ariella's house. She might laugh at me. Or she might take me inside for a few hours and then send me back to my husband.

She arrived and knocked. Her hands shook.

Ariella opened the door and looked at her for a long minute with an unreadable expression on her face.

La Venus held her breath. The rucksack dug its strap into her shoulder. She didn't feel like a Muse at all, but like a beggar, her hunger laid bare. It shamed her. It thrilled her.

Ariella let a subtle smile break over her, the smile of a genius, the smile of a thief.

She opened the door wide and stepped back to let La Venus in.

The rest of it was easy. She knew Arnaldo's work schedule like the pulse in her own veins. While he was out of the apartment, she returned and took as much as she could carry, paring back to her most treasured things, leaving the furniture, much of which had come from her parents' and in-laws' homes anyway so who wanted it? They could keep their dainty lamps and submissive coffee tables. She left a note on the kitchen counter that explained the situation in elliptical sentences, which, after roving through the metaphysical limitations of a marriage like theirs, eventually landed on the core point, *and I'm not coming back.*

Later, she fielded her mother's horror on the phone, her sister's and brother's incomprehension, her sister-in-law's spurning.

"But why, Anita?" Her mother moaned, drawing out the vowels in her words as if to wring them dry. "What did Arnaldo do—did he beat you?"

"Mamá, no, he didn't beat me."

"Then what's the problem?"

"It's not about what he did, but about what I want."

"What you want! You married him! You insisted on him over Beto, Miguel, that other boy with the big *estancia* in the north, Artigas or wherever it was—"

"It was in Durazno."

"Fine, wherever. The point is, you already did what you wanted."

"It changed."

"What changed?"

"What I wanted."

Her mother sighed, a heavy, burdened sound. "Anita. You want to be alone all of your life? This is what you want, to be living with some spinster?"

"She happens to be a very successful artist."

"But why there? Why not come here?"

Because of this exactly, La Venus thought but did not say.

"Tell me your phone number."

La Venus was silent.

Her mother's voice, now cold with suspicion. "And your address?"

Arnaldo. Mamá might give the information to Arnaldo.

"Hija."

She couldn't have her mother calling at odd hours, any hours. Or showing up at her doorstep. "I'm sorry, Mamá. Don't worry, I'll call you."

"What kind of place is this? What did you do, move into a brothel?"

"No." *Something worse, by your standards.* "Really, Mamá, I'm fine."

The line spat static into her ear.

"You'll at least come over for Sunday lunch?"

"Of course I will, Mamá. Soon."

"When soon? Next weekend! I'll be expecting you."

She'd meant to go, but she woke up that Sunday with a heavy sense of foreboding weighing on her chest. She wasn't sure she could bear her smug sister and sister-in-law, their lectures and their pity. What would she tell them? There was nothing she could say. And yet they'd be demanding answers.

"Just call and tell them you have a headache," Ariella said. "It's what I do."

She called, and was bumbling through her apology when she heard an all-too-familiar voice in the background.

"Mamá. Who's that?"

"Who's what?"

"Arnaldo's there? You invited him, knowing I was coming?"

"Ay, Anita, you two need to talk. It's not right that you won't even give us your phone number, I mean you're crazy, really crazy and we're worried about y—"

She hung up. Heat rushed through her. She felt the urge to run. It was strange: she'd lived with Arnaldo all that time, even put up with him when things soured, but now that she had some distance and had started sleeping in a bed free of his weight the very thought of him sent panic through her body. It made no sense. *You're crazy.* And perhaps she was.

From then on she only called her mother at random times, sporadically, and never on Sundays, hanging up at the first sign of harangue.

No matter. She wasn't alone. She had her Polonio friends (all but Flaca). And she had Ariella; she was sailing Ariella's high seas.

She was an artist in every way, that woman. She created herself anew each day and each languorous night. It seemed that she'd found a way to live beyond the masculine-feminine divide, not so much crossing it as flouting it entirely. She peppered men's clothing into her attire, wearing a necktie over a ruffled blouse, a men's suit jacket with silver bracelets that clamored brashly as she talked, a fedora with a sequined dress and feather boa. She only did this at home, never outside, and not just for parties; often, on days when no one else came over, Ariella changed her outfit two or three times in the course of a day, feverishly adding and removing pieces that pushed and merged the edges of gender, her clothes an expression of her restlessness, her frenetic creative mind. Her moods changed more often than her clothing. She sparked, shot, brooded, blazed. She lived outside the rules of the world. She received La Venus's presence as if she'd always been in the house, always been part of her sphere. In those early days, they spent many nights awake by candlelight (Ariella believed that no light held as much power as natural flame), making love and talking. Ariella told her of her travels, how trapped she felt in Uruguay, her longing to leave the country, to breathe foreign air again and fill it with her song. She had first gone abroad at the age of nineteen, with a scholarship to a school called Juilliard, in New York City. The land of the *Yanquis* had enchanted her: people there acted as though they were all born for big lives. The city had hummed and roared around her, a living music. She befriended musicians, dancers, painters, poets, actors; she attended parties where talk and art and drugs and seduction blended into a single, glittering whole. It was in New York that she first went to bed with a woman, a jazz singer born in the southern state of Alabama who played the clubs up in Harlem and took her home for a single radiant night that would for the rest of Ariella's life be the measure of passion. Harriet was her name. She sang to put the stars to shame. Her voice could have melted walls of stone. Ariella had gone up to Harlem with a small group of fellow students, among them a baritone who'd been trying to bed her for weeks, in vain. In Harlem, she felt she'd crossed into another realm, like the Barrio Sur and Palermo of her native city, only not like those neighborhoods at all, not like any other place in the world. Harriet shimmered on the stage, her poise regal, surrounded by a band that held her sound aloft as if to say, our song, our beat, our voice, and even the most cocky of the Juilliard white boys were reduced to grudging silence at the power of the music. Harriet spotted Ariella from the stage and met her eyes for one long breath of song. Ariella knew that she'd been claimed, that she'd do anything to stay inside that gaze. When her fellow students left the club, Ariella stayed, against their protests. Harriet's rented room turned out to be eight blocks away. Afterward, they smoked cigarettes and Ariella answered questions in her tenuous English: she sang opera, she was a student, her country was called Uruguay.

"You have your own music? In Uruguay?"

"Yes. Of course."

"What kind of music?"

"We have the murga. Tango. Candombe. The candombe, it is of black people, like you."

Harriet raised her eyebrows and said nothing for a long time.

"And these black people, from your country," she finally said. "They don't ever come to Juilliard."

"I don't know," Ariella said, immediately feeling stupid because it probably hadn't been a question, and also because what she'd just said wasn't true; she did know. The black people she'd known personally back home were maids in her parents' house. They had less of a chance of reaching Juilliard than of reaching the moon.

"And you. You don't sing Uruguayan music."

"No."

"Why not? Wait, let me guess—you don't know the answer to that either."

I said nothing then, because, Venus, I was too foolish, I didn't yet understand anything, but the conversation would swim inside me for years and later give birth to my most important work. It started there, right there with a woman who burned forever into my mind, don't be jealous now, Venus, I'm just telling you the real story so you have it, a woman who redefined the world for me but who closed herself off to me while I was still lying beside her, naked. I snuck out from her room in the cover of dark. I never went back to Harlem. She hadn't given me a number, hadn't asked me to call or come around. There was something hard in her eyes after I said *Juilliard,* something aching, pain flung up between us like a wall, and it was too big to cross. There would never have been a place for her, or for her music, up at Juilliard, as we both knew. Here I'd seen all the *Yanquis* as the ones on top, the ones with power, and me from my poor little Latin American country, but with Harriet the pieces all seemed rearranged. Well. After that, there were lovers, but not so many, I was busy with my lessons and classes and performances, working long hours, you know, the artist's life. I got very little news from home, sporadic references to the growing unrest from my mother on long-distance phone calls, but Uruguay was never in the newspapers, except in 1970, when the Tupamaros kidnapped that *Yanqui,* Dan Mitrione, you should have seen how they made him sound, like a hero and a martyr and not a word about how he came to Montevideo to train torturers. Oh don't look at me like that, I can say it here, the neighbors can't hear us and anyway they're all asleep. So when I finished my studies, in 'seventy-two, I had to leave because my visa ran out. I found a job in Chile, at the National Opera there, and I wanted to keep seeing the world, so off I went to Santiago. It was there that I began performing, in my spare time, with a local tango troupe—the seed of Harriet's question started taking its first flower—and together we embarked on experiments with fusion. Opera and tango, blending their bodies, like two women having sex. You know. Like we do. As if centuries of rules didn't exist. As if sex were new—as if sound were new. That's how exciting it was. Everything was exciting, back then, in Chile. Allende was president, the socialists had won, and sure, the economy was a mess, the right wing furious, getting more violent every day, but still it seemed like we were on a glorious ship headed into the sunrise or some shit like that, though of course we all know what really happened. 'Seventy-three, that's what happened. First Uruguay fell, then Chile three months later. Pinochet rose up, and that was it. Half my tango band disappeared. I was lucky I got out; they could have taken me too. I tried to get on a plane to Argentina, since it wasn't a dictatorship yet—my God, those poor Chileans and Uruguayans who fled to Buenos Aires for refuge! how many of them are gone now without a trace! And I could have been one of them—but I was only permitted to go back to my own nation. And now I'm stuck here, forced to make my art in this jail of a country, where you can't have a performance without filling out several forms and submitting them for approval to the police, where you can't walk through the streets at night, where you have to watch your mouth and everybody looks like they're on their way back from a funeral all the time.

La Venus shifted in the bedclothes. It seemed to her that freedoms were much greater on this side of town. The people she knew, the people she'd known before Ariella, all lived in apartments or small, squat houses that shared kitchen walls and night sounds, you always knew when the neighbors were fighting or laughing (rarely) or, sometimes, succumbing to the pleasures of the body. In quarters like those, people watched what they said and kept their voices down, the curtains closed. Here, in the majestic neighborhood of El Prado, with its clean streets and ample trees, it seemed that the Process didn't reach as deeply into people's lives. Neighbors were far-flung and kept to themselves, nestled in their large houses. In the land of the rich, there was more privacy, less surveillance. Fewer landings on which neighbors could spy on your apartment door, listen for stray footsteps, hear forbidden music or conversations through thin walls.

Though even here, there were precautions. Guests stayed until the sun was up and the night patrols were done. So Ariella served dinner and breakfast, with plenty of drinks in between. In the middle of the night, the artists came together in a haze of cigarette smoke and talked, argued, burst into song, made sounds with their voices that wove strangely into musical fabrics La Venus had not thought possible. Meandering sounds, sharp sounds, lazy, biting, aching, sensuous. Sometimes they seemed to make it up as they went along, while at other times classic melodies—Puccini, Piazzolla, tangos from the Old Guard, folk songs from the border towns of Salto and Paysandú—threaded through the smoky room. Couples vanished into corners of the house, into bedrooms on the second floor, bathrooms with the lights out, the dark garage that used to be a stable in the old days, when horses still pulled the world. The house was like a grand old lady, her dress full of folds, pockets, secrets both sticky and smooth.

It surprised La Venus to hear Ariella speak of Uruguay as a constraining place, as causing her suffering. Ariella's parents owned the mansion and paid for its upkeep as well as for the live-in maid, Sonia, a young black woman whom Ariella gave instructions without looking in the eye and without saying *please* or *thank you,* which unsettled La Venus every time and made her think of Harriet, sending Ariella out of her bed into the New York cold. Sonia was sweet-mannered and either never was annoyed or never showed it, even managed to be graceful in her movements as she cooked meals and made beds and washed clothes and looked after the little boy.

Because there was a little boy. Another surprise. La Venus stumbled into him on her second day, playing with a toy train in the living room. His name was Mario, and he was three years old. He smiled up at her with a friendliness and open warmth that caught her off guard. None of her nieces or nephews had ever beamed at her that way. She felt an old ache rise up in the pit of her belly, a dull hunger for what she could not have, and she could see the bloody mess in the toilet bowl again, the rivulets down her leg, her failure to keep life inside. But what if she had succeeded in staying pregnant years ago? Where would she be now? Later, she learned that Mario was conceived accidentally, with a certain unnamed "hippie guitarist," in Ariella's words, who'd been passing through town, on tour from a European country she refused to identify. She had found the guitarist amusing and pretty, and she'd let him keep her warm for a couple of sleepless nights, even though she liked women better than men. This too fascinated La Venus, that a woman who loved women could also take pleasure in a man. So it wasn't all or nothing. She hadn't been sure. Her Polonio friends all seemed to have sworn off men entirely, and even, when they were out at the beach drunk on whiskey and stars, scoffed at the very idea. She stayed quiet when they did. That wasn't how things were for her, and she'd ended up feeling as though she were somehow lacking because she'd enjoyed being with her husband, at least in the early days, when things were still good between them.

Mario was an energetic boy, sweet-tempered and curious. La Venus had her days stretching out before her, with nothing to do. She started playing with Mario, during the day, at first to amuse herself, and, soon, to contribute to the household. Ariella had her rehearsals and performances, very little time for the boy, and Sonia had her hands full with the cooking, washing, and cleaning. Although she never complained aloud, it was clearly a relief to her to have La Venus's help with the child. Meanwhile, caring for the boy gave La Venus a way to be of use, to fill her days. She learned to wipe his bottom, make snacks, tell stories silly enough to keep Mario's attention. She came to crave the boy. His limbs were plump and softer than petals; once, when he raced into her arms, she saw wings spread out from his delicate shoulders, white wings like those of an angel, the angel she'd lost years ago to the toilet bowl, what if this was him, if a spirit once inside her had returned as this boy? She caught him in her arms and dared to think it true. For his fourth birthday, she made him a boat out of fruit crates, painted it blue and white, with a sail made out of an old sheet strung on a chipped broomstick. It was large enough for the two of them to huddle inside of and sail away, she thought, into his dreams, into wherever they wanted to go.

"Venu!" he'd cry out—"Venu! Come see!"—and his high pure voice would not exactly break her heart, but melt it, make it a soft, expanded thing, threatening to pour out of her body.

*

She invited her Polonio friends to their parties, all except for Flaca of course—she'd never come, it would take time, wouldn't it? for them to be friends again? *don't worry about her,* Ariella would croon in the pale wash of first dawn light after the last guests had finally left, *she's just jealous, she'll get over it*—but the others. They all came together once: Romina, Malena, and Paz. Romina and Malena never left each other's side, hewing to the periphery of things. La Venus approached them just as Romina was listening to a bearded man, a painter, passionately reminiscing about the Paris of his youth. "None of us go to Paris anymore," he bemoaned.

Romina's face was tight. "There are plenty of Uruguayans in Paris," she said. "Right now. More than ever."

The man coughed. "Oh. Sure there are. But I didn't mean exiles." He placed the word in the air carefully, as if proud of his daring. "I meant artists. Les Deux Magots and all that."

"Many of our exiles are artists. Writers. They've been publi—"

"Certainly, of course. Yes. Well, in any case, if you could see the Louvre, the Notre Dame, you'd never be the same, I'm sure you'd agree." His eyes were glazed now, roaming. "Ah! Venus! The goddess herself!"

La Venus smiled. "There's more sangría in the kitchen."

"Aha! I'm off to find it. If you'll excuse me, ladies." He bowed deeply, and was gone.

La Venus turned to her friends. "Are you having a good time?"

Romina glanced at Malena, and they shared a look. On becoming a couple, they seemed to have forged an intimacy that sustained them both. "That man. So ignorant."

La Venus nodded. Romina had become involved with a secret circle of dissidents who smuggled written words into the country: letters, essays, and newspaper clippings from Uruguayan exiles speaking out abroad about the human rights abuses back home. Apparently, out beyond the nation's borders, there were publishers who listened, readers who cared. It all seemed insanely dangerous to La Venus. Why risk yourself for the impossible? How could those words change anything here, where the authorities held all the reins? And then there was Romina's direct political work, here on the ground; she wasn't sure of the details, but she'd heard the rumors of new networks of subversives, sprouting up and organizing acts against the regime. But what would it change, all this meeting and word smuggling? Only the safety of those who did it. She wished her friend would come to her senses, but didn't dare say this to her, as she knew it was the last thing Romina wanted to hear.

"I'm sorry," she said. "But at least you can talk about these things here."

"I suppose so."

"I mean, these parties are a kind of oasis, no? Like our Polonio."

Romina gulped down the rest of her wine. "No. Not like our Polonio at all."

La Venus tried to hide her irritation. What was it in her that angled so sharply for these friends' approval? They went to Polonio without her, were going soon. She should go sometime. It was her house too. She didn't dare take Ariella—it seemed an invasion, and in any case Ariella would be horrified by the cramped space, dirt floor, bucket for a shower—but she could go by herself. And yet she did not go. She missed Polonio but could not find, inside herself, the will to go alone.

Malena reached her hand out to Romina and rubbed her back. No words, just touch, but Romina seemed to calm and flower open under her lover's hand. They were good for each other, La Venus couldn't deny it. They seemed to have a secret language that ran under the surface of things, always connecting, always hearing each other. For all that being with Ariella lit her up inside, La Venus knew that her lover would never in her life spend an entire party close at La Venus's side, the way these two women kept to each other. Ariella flitted around the room, absorbing everyone's attention. She gloried in it. Romina and Malena didn't cling to each other, exactly, but they kept close, as if absorbed in an invisible and constant conversation that no one else could hear.

Paz, though, was a different story. She dove into the party with abandon. There she was now, talking with a couple of young women La Venus had never met. Since she'd moved out of her mother's house, Paz had blossomed. She smuggled seal skins from Polonio to the city, and seemed to have become adept at managing all the business relationships with men. She was renting a room from a couple in Cordón whose only child was twenty-four and long imprisoned. For Paz, these parties, locked in all night with drunk artists steadily getting drunker, were a golden opportunity. La Venus saw it in the way she scanned the room. She looked older than she was, twenty at least, though in truth she was only eighteen, unmoored in the world. For now, it seemed to suit her. Paz was going to end up in some corner with one of those young women before the night was through, that much was clear from the way they angled themselves toward her, like sunflowers poised to catch the sun.

Months into their relationship, La Venus still felt a thrill at being with Ariella, at entering a room with her. Each of them turned heads on her own; together, they took a room's attention and wound it around them, claimed it. In bed, Ariella was demanding, precise. There were nights when she'd whisper into La Venus's ear the number of orgasms she wanted to give her that night. "Six," she'd purr, and her word was law, even if La Venus was sated after the fourth, or even worn out, longing only for a nest of sleep. And she couldn't fake it, the way she had sometimes with Arnaldo for reasons of convenience or diplomacy. Here, there were no substitutes. On other nights, Ariella demanded to be serviced. It was she who wanted the orgasms, and they had to be vast, vigorous, nothing counted but the blaze. Thrilling. Thrilling, except that in the early morning, La Venus was the one who rose when Mario cried, who made his breakfast, started his day, no matter how late his Mami had kept her up the night before, because she was that person now, Mario's main person, the one he sought out when he woke up, the one he reached for when he scraped his knee. Sometimes, in the morning, as Mario played and Ariella slept and La Venus stumbled through preparing the *mate,* she thought that her lover's lust might kill her. And then she'd light a cigarette and say to herself, there are worse ways to go. She was being ridiculous. She was, after all, living the dream.

"And how long do you expect to be able to live off this rich lady?" her mother asked on the phone one day.

"I'm not living off of her. I contribute. I help take care of her boy." She tried to keep the impatience out of her voice. They'd been over this before, and yet her mother insisted on the question, as if repetition could squeeze out a different answer.

"Whom she had out of wedlock. I mean really, Anita. *What* are you doing with your life? Babysitting? As if you were some teenage girl, or servant—you think I raised you for that?"

"Mamá. That is *not* what I am."

"Then what are you?"

She couldn't answer.

"Ay, *hija*. Where on earth is your life headed?"

She had no idea. She wasn't thinking of the future. There was no future in the godforsaken country, much less for women like her. She'd settle for living in the now.

*

"Look at this," Ariella said over lunch one day, placing a letter on the table. "I'm getting out."

La Venus read the letter, once, then twice. It was an invitation to

Brazil, embossed with the name of a university in Rio de Janeiro. A fellowship. Visiting artists. Two years long. The start date was three months away.

Ariella was watching her closely. "You're not happy for me?"

"Of course I'm happy." La Venus tried to sound as if she meant it. She made her voice light, pushed food around her plate. "You've earned it. You're brilliant—the greatest genius in all of Uruguay."

Ariella snorted. "That's not saying much."

La Venus felt stung; her country might be small, and *provincial,* as Ariella sometimes put it, but it was still her country and she had no other.

"I mean, all the great minds are gone now, aren't they? Off in exile. I've been so alone here." She stared out of the window.

La Venus felt a knot rise up inside her, hard as a fist.

Ariella looked at her. "Oh, not like that—you've been wonderful, of course. Delicious company." She smiled, stroked La Venus's hand. "But I still need more. Things are open in Rio de Janeiro, for artists. There's more embrace of mixing genres. Fusion is the future. Not just for art, but for all of culture, all of life. Art is the place where changes begin, and then, before you know it, they're everywhere."

La Venus nodded, though she had no clue what Ariella meant.

"Of course that only works if the artists can survive. Look at all the exiles, all the *desaparecidos*—look at Victor Jara. You know I sang with him in Chile, a few times, before the coup? A good man. A brilliant man. They killed him just like that."

In moments like this one, Ariella seemed a different kind of being, larger than life, shimmering right there at the kitchen table with the superhuman glow of fame, of history, an aura that anointed any mortal permitted to approach.

Ariella was looking off into the distance, and La Venus thought that she was lost in her memories of Chile, of the coup. But then she said, "Come with me."

"Where?"

"To Brazil."

"Me?"

"Who else? Is there anyone else here?"

Victor Jara, La Venus thought, but she said nothing. Ariella didn't believe in ghosts.

"I want you with me."

She gulped those words into her mind, tried to savor them as they went down. "I can't leave the country. I'd only get a tourist visa. I'm not the one with the fellowship."

"We'll figure something out." Ariella thought for a moment, then smiled. "I'll put you on the application. You can come as my nanny."

She bristled. Which word was the sharper thorn? *Nanny,* or *my*? She didn't feel like Mario's nanny. He'd started calling her Mamá. She never corrected him. It hadn't happened yet in front of Ariella, and there was no saying how she'd react.

"Come on. The world is so much larger than Uruguay. Don't you want to live? Dream? See more of the world?"

La Venus reached for the pack of cigarettes on the table, took two out, and lit them. She handed one to Ariella, not meeting her eyes. Of course she wanted to live, to dream. But whose life? Whose dream? She was being too touchy. Ariella was freedom, adventure. But even so, something inside La Venus galloped and flashed, untamed, resisting the harness of someone else's plan. Brazil. Rio. A sprawling city, spiked with mountains, shouting with light. Beaches swallowing the sun. She thought of Polonio, the way the ocean there enfolded her, made her feel for dizzying instants that the world could one day be whole. It was the same Atlantic, kissing Rio. It was violent there, or so she'd heard; there was poverty; the Brazilian dictatorship was older, more established, than the one in Uruguay. But perhaps, in a bigger city, there was also more space to get lost, to breathe. She would have to learn Portuguese. She'd have to hurl herself into new currents. The world seemed to open before her, unfurling like a tightly wrapped flag, and she knew that there was only one possible answer.

*

The Río de la Plata stretched out before them, long brown water all the way to the horizon. The flagstones of the Rambla spooled out beneath their feet, a sinuous promenade along the shore. Romina and Malena took this stroll every Saturday afternoon, with their *mate,* their one concession to leisure. They'd invited La Venus to join them before, but she was always busy with Mario. Saturdays were rehearsal days for Ariella. Today, though, she'd left Mario with Sonia. He'd protested and raised his arms up toward her, and for a second she'd thought of bringing him, but she wanted to have a few moments to herself with her friends. She didn't have a lot of time left. She hadn't yet told them.

"I always forget how pretty the Rambla is," La Venus said. "How it feels like looking at the sea."

"It calms me," Romina said.

"Though it's a shame that we can't see Buenos Aires from here. Such a beautiful city."

"Not all of it," Malena said sharply. "It's ugly, too."

"I didn't know you'd been there," La Venus said. There was a great deal that she still didn't know about Malena. She supported, she soothed, generous acts that gave so much to others yet at the same time might serve another purpose, La Venus thought, a kind of emotional sleight of hand to keep people from noticing what she didn't share about herself. In the early days, La Venus had tried to draw Malena out, with little success. Even now she felt that there were undertows inside her friend that she would never see or understand. "When was that?"

"A long time ago."

They kept walking. Romina stole a glance at Malena, passed the gourd to her as if it held a secret only they would taste. She was coming to know Malena's body language—it was ripe for the reading, if you knew how to look—and she saw the struggle now to keep memories at bay. Bad things had happened to Malena in Buenos Aires. Romina didn't know all of it, just part of the story. It had begun to spill out one night as they lay naked together, having just made love after arguing all night about the idea of moving in together, a thing Malena wanted to do and Romina knew she couldn't do, not when her parents needed her, when her brother was still in prison for God knew how long and she, Romina, was all they had, *but you don't owe them that,* Malena had said, to which Romina had responded *I owe them everything.* Malena had gone quiet and that might have been the end of it, but then Romina blurted out, "You almost never talk about your parents."

"So what?" Malena said.

Romina groped for the right words. It seemed bizarre to her, incomprehensible, that Malena lived in the same city as her parents but had not spoken to them in years. It couldn't be good for her; she had to be suffering. She'd tried to broach the subject before, tried to hint at the idea of reconciliation, but was always met with a wall of silence. If she knew more about what had happened, perhaps she could find the opening, however small, through which to help her lover reconnect to her own people. "How can I know you fully if I don't know about your family?"

"I am not my family."

Romina meant to protest this—her parents had years ago learned the Italian proverb *he who doesn't know where he comes from doesn't know where he's going* and repeated it so often it felt to her like law—but then she saw the gleaming hurt in Malena's eyes, and she reached out to stroke her face and back and hips and any part that would have her, which, that night, was all of them.

Afterward, naked in bed, Malena turned to Romina and started talking. Head on Romina's chest, face hidden. Her parents had sent her away when she was fourteen, she said. To fix her, she said. To a nightmare of a place. To this day she wondered how they'd learned of its existence. It happened after her parents found her with the neighbor girl, *touching her,* Malena said, and at this Romina had a thousand questions but voiced none of them, amazed. All this time she'd thought that Malena, when they met, had been the repressed one, the one who didn't know herself, who was scared to look inside and see what she was. That was how they'd all seen her. As a reserved, straitlaced woman to be brought out of her shell. But maybe she'd broken from that shell long before. She'd done something at fourteen that Romina herself would never have dreamed of at that age. Touched a neighbor girl. How? Where? Did the neighbor girl like it? Was Malena—could it be—the one who started it? How far did they get before they were discovered? Was she, Romina, Malena's first, or wasn't she? This Malena, who had told her friends on the beach about the convent but not about the neighbor girl. This living enigma. She shut up and listened. Malena went on. The neighbor girl fled, buttoning her blouse as she ran. Her name was Belén. Malena had been terrified that her mother would call Belén's mother. There was a tenderness in her voice when she said that name, *Belén,* that Romina had never heard before. Mamá didn't call Belén's mother, and at this Malena breathed a sigh of relief, thinking her worst fear had been averted. But it turned out that she still had a lot to learn about fear. Three nights later, she was on a boat to Buenos Aires with her mother, who didn't tell her where they were going or what awaited them on the other side of the river, who said almost nothing to her for the whole eleven-hour glide across the water. She'd thought that perhaps they were going to visit her uncle, go to the theater, start pretending nothing had happened, because her mother was an expert at pretending. But that wasn't what happened. Instead, Malena said, I was locked up for four months.

"In a prison?"

"In a clinic."

"Oh," Romina said, and relief washed through her. The word *clinic,* coupled with the name *Buenos Aires,* evoked the farthest thing from a prison: polished brass, crisp lab coats, nurses waiting on your every need, fancy doctors attending to your every hangnail, crystal cups of water just a bell's ring away. Things her own family could never afford. "A clinic. I see."

"No." Malena pulled away. "You don't see. You don't understand anything."

What was the matter with her? What had she, Romina, done wrong? "But I want to understand."

Malena said nothing.

Romina reached out for her.

"Stop it." Malena batted her away, a new sharpness in her voice. "Forget it."

"Malena, please. Tell me the rest of the story."

"There is no rest of the story. I'm tired, I want to go to sleep."

And that was it. Romina decided not to bring the matter up again, to wait until Malena brought it up herself, but she never did. She hadn't liked the clinic. She hadn't wanted to be there. The doctors must have looked down on her for what she'd done with the neighbor girl, been less than understanding. What was a luxury to some was a nightmare to others. No two prisons are alike, not all of them have bars, she should have been more open-minded, she'd do better next time. Now, here they were at a next time, strolling on the Rambla with the name *Buenos Aires* hanging in the air. She put her hand on Malena's back, as if to let touch speak for her, and Malena paused and leaned into Romina for a moment before passing back the gourd.

La Venus, watching them, felt a sting of envy. It was so palpable, the bond between those two, that it almost felt solid, a thing you could grip and tug. She wanted that. She had that. She thought she might possibly have that. Do I? And if I don't, what in God's name am I about to do? She pushed the thought away.

"I went to Buenos Aires once," La Venus said. "As a child. I thought it was wondrous. It expanded my horizons, getting out of the country." She paused, drew in breath. "Which is what I'm going to do now."

"You're leaving the country?" Romina looked at her with raw surprise.

"Yes."

"For where?"

"Brazil."

Romina dropped her voice. "How?"

"I'm getting a work visa, through Ariella. She has a fellowship and she's including me on her application, as a nanny."

Romina stared at her for a long time. "Her nanny."

La Venus fought back a slash of irritation. She'd said *a*, not *her*.

"You can't be serious."

"Well, what else is she supposed to call me, her husband?"

Romina and Malena both laughed.

La Venus felt her face grow hot. "So, then? What else are we supposed to do?"

"Is she going to pay you?"

"Technically, yes. I mean, she wrote some salary down on the application. But of course that money will really go to groceries for all of us—you know, to living."

"Hmm."

La Venus fidgeted. She wasn't sure what she'd expected. She'd imagined her friends barraging her with questions, but instead they were quiet, and she found that all she wanted to do was change the subject. "And you? How are you?"

Romina stared out at the water. "All right."

"Tell her," Malena said. "About Felipe."

"Felipe? Your brother?"

Romina nodded, eyes still on the river. "I went to see him."

"You got in?"

"Yes. Our requests were finally accepted, who knows why—nothing's changed about us but we've been denied so many times that the last thing we're going to do now is complain."

La Venus nodded. The authorities were like that: fickle, random. Ariella had stories of musicians who'd submitted paperwork for concert permits and had them approved, only to have the approval revoked ten minutes before the show, with no reason given, as if the giving and removing were itself a kind of whip. You took what you got, you didn't protest, didn't trust you'd still have it tomorrow. "How was it?"

Romina had no answer. She didn't know whether she'd ever be able to describe the experience in words. She and her parents had all been stunned when they received the news. Mamá had read the official letter aloud three times in a single evening, then handed it to Papá, who didn't even glance at it, just let it hang limp from his hand for a moment before dropping it to the floor. To Papá, Felipe was still the wayward son, who'd betrayed the family by joining the Communist Party without a thought of what such a choice might do to those who loved him. As if the ruin of Felipe's life had been by his own hand. Was Papá really so anti-Communist, or did he believe this because it was somehow easier to think that Felipe had sabotaged his own life than that all of this had been done *to* them? Felipe. Delicate, bespectacled Felipe of the big dreams and lanky gait, who stayed up too late reading and never went to the bakery without bringing home a pastry for his sister. Romina had counted the days, the hours, until the first visit day, then took the bus into the neighborhood of Punta Carretas, her mother beside her, gazing straight ahead. Her father had decided not to come just the night before. Her parents had fought about it in their bedroom, into the night, and he had not emerged for breakfast. Now Mamá clutched her purse on her lap as if it were a life raft. Romina had dressed conservatively in case this helped placate the guards, but in fact there were no problems when they arrived, only a long tense wait in a dull little room with a glass wall down the middle that contained a single round hole. Felipe entered, handcuffed, and the guard pushed him toward a bench in front of the glass. He leaned toward the hole in the glass, the place through which they could speak. She stared at him. He was unrecognizable, a ghost of his past self, a tired old man long before his time—what had she expected? It had been seven years. Brutalities beyond name. *How are you?* her mother had asked, a stupid question that had hung in the air between them, impossible to take back or erase. Felipe had looked at them both for a long time, unsmiling, raw sadness in his eyes. *Happy to see you,* he replied. The rest of the visit was filled with empty words, about the weather, the neighborhood, careful words, all calculated to raise zero alarms among the guards. It wasn't the words that mattered. It was the drinking each other with their eyes. The glass barrier between them seemed to melt away with all their looking. He was still here. He existed in an alternate dimension, one hidden from the ordinary world, but he was here. The scars of torture were not visible on his skin, but could not be kept from his eyes. Romina left the Penal de Libertad that day more deter-mined than ever to fight the current government, to work for human rights. She couldn't stop, not for her own safety or even for the safety of her parents. Who was she to give up when Felipe was still there, inside?

"It was horrible," she told La Venus now. "It was a relief. A good and awful waking. I can't put it into words."

La Venus nodded, took the *mate*, drank.

The next time Romina had gone to visit Felipe, they'd both been a little more prepared. *I have an itch on my forehead,* he'd said, and then he'd repeated the words more slowly, eyes darting at the guards to make sure they weren't paying attention. She'd wanted to reach over to scratch his forehead for him, her handcuffed brother, and would have done so if it hadn't meant putting any future visits at risk. Only later, on the bus back home, had it occurred to her that he could have been speaking in code. Forehead. *Frente.* Frente. The Frente Amplio, the leftist party formed out of a coalition of Communists, Tupamaro guerrillas, socialists, and many others—if the Frente was the itch, what did it mean? Either it was bothering him or it was on his mind and he supported its efforts, wanted her to know. Which was it? That night, as she washed the dinner dishes, her parents murmuring in the other room, she convinced herself that the word *itch* meant that Felipe was bothered by the Frente, didn't support its growing resistance efforts or its imprisoned leader, was suspicious of blending so many factions into one. But then, the next day, she woke up sure that the opposite was true. He was pro-Frente. He was with them. *Itch* meant that he'd been giving them thought. He was following the unfolding of under-ground organizing through secret information channels, and he wanted to support it as he could. Was it possible that he'd even heard of her involvement? Was he saying that he was proud of her (a flicker of warmth)? Or was he trying to ask her, obliquely, whether she was involved? She was deeply involved. Every day she plunged deeper. She smuggled articles from other countries into Montevideo so the resis-tance here could know what exiles were publishing overseas, how the human rights abuses here were being decried. She waited for hours at the port for ships on which a single sailor carried the contraband, the secret stash of words, which he then handed off to her in a packet of peanuts or stinking fish, between the newspaper layers. And now, there was the plebiscite, coming up in November, when the Uruguayan population was being asked to vote on a new authoritarian constitution for their nation, making law the persecution of "subversives" and giving the National Security Council power over any future civilian government—all the same old things the regime had been doing, seeking the legitimacy of law. The foreign human rights report had been part of pushing them, she was sure of it. Of course it hadn't been covered in the news here, but it was all over the bulletin articles and international newspaper clippings the exiles sent, that she helped smuggle into the country: a group called Amnesty International had named Uruguay as the nation with the most political prisoners per capita anywhere in the world. And so the generals wanted to get out of their spotlight, by demonstrating a mandate from the people. In Chile, Pinochet was attempting the same thing. Terror breeds submission. Voters were afraid. If the measure passed, the horrors would only deepen. But what if they could win this vote? What if they could beat the regime? This was what kept her up all night, and risking herself to deliver communications from exiles to local leftist leaders. If they could succeed where Chile had failed, take this vote and turn it around to throw back in the generals' faces, flex the muscle of the people in a way heard by the world—then what?

She looked up at La Venus, who was waiting, listening, taking in her silence without asking for more.

"I don't know where this all ends," Romina said.

"Where what ends?"

"All of it. The nightmare. We might never have our country back, but even if we do, then what? How do we restore what's been broken? If you shatter a plate, it's never whole again."

"A country isn't a plate," La Venus said.

"Maybe not. But it can break. It can go from being one large thing to many broken pieces."

"It's not the same. They can come back together."

"How do you know they can? Will all the exiles come back? Will the tortured become untortured?"

"No," La Venus said, "but torture ends. Or it *can* end. And when it does, people can heal."

"How do we know that's true? Have you asked the tortured?"

"Romina," La Venus said, "I'm on your side."

Romina sighed. "I know. But. All this time we've been living in our own corners, wondering about the people on the other side of the bars, fearing the worst for them. Going inside was like seeing a tiny crack in the dam. Just the smallest leak. But it's enough to drown in. It's worse than I feared, but also more ordinary in a way I couldn't fathom. I don't think I'm making sense."

"You're making sense," Malena said, and La Venus marveled at the tenderness in her voice.

Romina took the gourd back from La Venus, filled it. "God knows what'll happen when the dam comes down—if it ever does."

"It will," La Venus said.

"But how do you know that?" Romina said, surprised by the heat in her own voice. "It won't happen on its own. Only with enough people pushing and pushing and pushing."

La Venus looked her in the eyes, then looked away.

"I hope it does, of course," Romina said, more quietly, so her words would be draped by the wind. "That's the dream, right? For prisoners to be free, for exiles to come home. It's just that, now that I've seen Felipe, I've realized that the story won't end there."

La Venus let her gaze rove out to the horizon. It was a blue day, deceptively calm. "I hope you're not angry at me. For leaving."

"You know what, to hell with that. We've all got to figure out our own way through."

La Venus scratched at the stones of the promenade's low wall. All the people who'd sat here before her. All the ones who'd now flung themselves across the world and might never come home.

"We missed you last month, though. In Polonio."

"How's La Proa?"

"The same," Romina said.

"Better," Malena said. "Paz keeps going in and making repairs. She's stopped up the holes in the walls and roof. Says she wants to be able to visit in the winter."

La Venus smiled, tightly. She longed for the Polonio house, and it was hers, too—but she didn't dare go, even now. She couldn't take Ariella as she'd never understand, couldn't go while Flaca was there, and she balked at going alone, telling herself it was the rustic discomforts that put her off though it was really something else, what she might hear inside herself while alone at La Proa, what La Proa might do to her solitary mind. In any case, she was of another world now, Ariella's world. She wondered which world she belonged to. Wondered why the question made her ache. "I'd love to see Polonio in the winter. Those legendary storms."

"We're planning to go, this July," Malena said.

"Maybe one day I'll see it, when I come back," La Venus said, thinking as she spoke that she had no idea when that would be.

"You'll have plenty of beach, anyway, where you're going," Romina said. "Copacabana. Ipanema. And it's never cold there, I hear you can swim all year long."

She'd said it as a kindness. To ease her friend's flight. But La Venus knew in that moment that there would be no Polonio in Brazil. There was no Polonio anywhere but Uruguay. Suddenly she ached for her small, drab country. Sullen country. Broken country. Land of the tired. Land of cold ocean, of hidden shores, of a flat muddy river stretching to the lip of the sky.

They lingered quietly over their *mate* after that, gazing out at the water, each watching her own ghost on the horizon.

6

The Seeing

OVER THE NEXT TWO YEARS, La Proa blossomed.

New cracks appeared in the walls, let in the wind, then burrowed under layers of plaster. A bucket, rope, and pulley appeared in the bathroom, a homemade shower, with holes along the bottom of the bucket through which water could drip, sprinkle, pour.

The kitchen bristled with knives, spoons, pots and pans from the city, gathered chaotically along the shelves, like refugees.

Bedding piled higher with every passing season.

Shelves sprouted along the inside walls, hammered slats of wood bearing books, matches, candles, seashells caught up from the beach, crumpled pesos, painted stones, painted sticks, more books.

Grime thickened in the corners and along the floor by the stove. Deep cleaning peeled the layers back so they could gently accumulate again.

Furniture gave slow birth to itself: a table started as a plank on four stacks of bricks, then became a slab of swirled driftwood, found on the beach and dragged back home, cut, placed over the bricks at first until the attempt began to hammer on legs and to sand the knots and whorls on the top into a more even surface. It never became a completely even surface. Instead, everyone learned how to balance cups and plates along the rugged landscape of the Polonio table, and though there were spills, though bowls teetered, the table stayed, always stayed, the right table for them, hunched low on all fours, alive with patterns, as strange as it was beautiful.

Paz came the most often. Business brought her to Polonio at least once a month—to check on supplies, organize a transport, discuss the season's seal counts and calculate skins with El Lobo and pull a few old stories out of him if he was in the mood to get talking, if possible one of the old shipwreck stories that seemed to glimmer with new details each time—and she always tried to come earlier than needed so she could spend time at the house. Work brought her, but she didn't only go to Polonio for work. She went to be alone. She went to listen. She went to unclasp herself. She'd hike in over the sand dunes and arrive sweaty or cold or wet from rain, depending on the season, and then she'd sit inside the house in silence for a long time. She walked on the beach for hours, long enough for the burning inside her to subside to a bearable level, long enough for the city and highway to fade from her mind and the ocean to fill it, wash it clean. There were no more visits from the Minister of the Interior and his wife, and as for the lighthouse soldiers, they left her alone now. They knew who she was, she kept to herself, they didn't care. They changed guard constantly, it seemed, or perhaps they just seemed faceless to her, interchangeable, as that was the thing about soldiers, wasn't it, they were like the sun: not to be looked at directly for too long. It was a relief to be away from the city, and from her mother, whom she now spoke to on the phone about once a week and met occasionally for tea in one of the cafés downtown on Avenida 18 de Julio, for tight exchanges that set her teeth on edge and made her chest ache at the same time. Mamá was dutiful about these teas, and mainly seemed relieved that Paz had forged a life for herself that didn't require much from her mother anymore.

And, on these solo trips, it was even a relief for Paz to be away from her friends; they loved her and she loved them back, but sometimes they were too much like aunties, fussing over her as if by doing so they could fix the holes and rips in their own pasts, gaping at her through the prism of their prudery. Even Flaca had chided her once, for having two girlfriends at the same time—Flaca! She was one to talk! Sometimes she thought that it had been a mistake to tell them about Puma, years ago, when she first came to Polonio. They'd never understood it (though, to be fair, she sometimes felt that she didn't fully understand it herself). There were things about her they'd never fully see. That's how it was. How the world was. Even when loved, you were never fully seen.

Only the ocean—the Atlantic, the wild unfettered waves of El Polonio—could see all of her. Or at least enfold her. A wholeness beyond compare.

And so she came, repaired things, fixed the roof, made a shower out of rope and bucket, hammered wood, built the house and loved it with her hands as best she could, always thinking of the way they'd bought this house, her pathetic contribution, the smallest of the five. Now that she had an income of her own, she'd tried to pay them back, but her friends would have none of it. *It's what we agreed to,* Flaca would say, and that was that. And so there was this: her repairs, her work, the sweat and muscles of her hands improving the house. Her way of paying in.

She would always be the younger one to her friends, the *chiquilina*, even though she was now a grown woman of twenty-one. Sometimes it shocked her to look in the mirror. She felt at once younger and older than she was, a strange creature, outside of time. Not like any other woman of twenty she'd known. A university dropout who knew passages of Cervantes by heart. An avid reader with a laborer's muscled arms. A woman who often smelled like slaughtered seal, even though she spent hours scrubbing in the bathtub after her hauls, determined to leave the stench behind, but it wasn't so easy, she now knew, the smell of your work had a way of settling into your skin. Like Flaca's father, who always had a whiff of raw meat about him, as if the butcher shop had seeped into his body—that's how it was for workingmen, factory men, laborers, men of the land, like her, woman of the land, of the sea, smelling like men's work.

She'd been supporting herself for almost three years now, with a man's job, paying for a room of her own in the apartment of a couple whose only son was locked up at the Penal de Libertad; she slept in the son's room, the prisoner's room, and gathered her pesos as if each bill were a ticket to freedom. She worked hard for every bit of it, shepherding those skins from the edge of the world to the capital. At each stage of the journey—the gathering at El Lobo's, the horse-drawn cart across the dunes, the hired truck from a farm outside Castillos, the garment factory in the Jewish Quarter of Montevideo—there was a man to interface with. She stripped the femininity from her appearance as much as possible, so they would take her seriously. Hair slicked back into a ponytail, like a male rock star or soccer player. Trousers, baggy sweater. Grim face—not unfriendly, for that too had its hazards, but just the right amount of set jaw for men to resign themselves to her rate and rules and silently thank their lucky stars that their own daughter had not turned out like *that*. She couldn't enter the men's world—not that she wanted to be a man; what she wanted was their power—but she could, she realized, skirt its edges as a kind of nongirl, as a failed girl, an in-between, and this role had a better chance at grudging respect than pretty girls ever would and she had never been a pretty girl anyway, not even close, so she took it. She ran with it. She channeled her ferocity into math, the brisk unrolling of bills. This much for you, this much for you, and no that's enough or do you want me to call another driver next time? And all the swagger she'd learned on the job was what got her up the skirts of women too. You had to carry yourself as if you knew all sorts of things and didn't need a damn soul. It had taken her months of practice, of thinking, of rehearsing alone in front of a mirror, to approach a woman for the first time. It had been at a bar in the Jewish Quarter, after delivering a load of skins. It was in her first year of trading. She'd had a pocket full of damp bills and had felt euphoric, loathe to go home to her quiet little room with the old couple's television sounds pulsing through the walls. And so she'd ducked into a bar, the kind of neighborhood spot where you could get a beer and a sausage fresh off the grill, with couples at tables, a few bigger groups, no children, no women alone. She'd sat at a table in the corner and curled around her beer, thinking that, anytime now, she'd go home, and then she felt eyes on her. A woman. She seemed to be in her early thirties, heavily made up, in a red dress that looked home-sewn. The man she was with was much older, and he was talking with the other men at his table, arguing uproariously, ignoring her. The woman's eyes were a deep brown, she was plump and had a sensuous air and a frank hunger on her face that made her, surely, the most beautiful woman in Montevideo. Paz looked back at her and willed herself to hold the woman's gaze as if she'd done this a hundred times. The men were laughing now, still not paying attention. To them, Paz was just a sorry girl in the corner. But the woman was still looking at her. Paz got up and headed to the bathroom. On the way she brushed past the woman's table and glanced down rapidly, meaningfully, *come.* When she arrived in the back, she was flummoxed to find that the bathroom was no more than a single tiny room off the kitchen. No privacy to speak of—though neither the waiter nor the cook seemed to have noticed that she'd slipped through the door. She was sweating, hot with nerves. She'd wait five minutes and then go. What was she doing. What had she been thinking, what—and then the woman appeared in the small bathroom and without a word turned off the light and locked the door. Dark. Limbs. Heat, body. She so close, waiting, and Paz for a single instant terrified that she would lose this chance because she was too awed to move, but then she did move and the woman's mouth was everything, was joy in her own mouth, her skin a balm to fingertips, her breathing sharp as they kept on in absolute silence, there could be no sound, no words, only touch and rhythm and as there was little time Paz lifted the woman to the small sink as if it were a throne, and there, right there, thighs opened like the thighs of a queen, demanding worship with a gesture to which Paz complied, thinking and breathing *worship,* pouring that word into her hands.

It was over fast. The woman came hard against Paz's palm. Paz would have liked to do more, much more, fingers still enclosed in heat, but there was no time and they both knew it. The woman clung to

Paz's neck for a few beats as the kitchen clanged and rattled on just outside the door, and then she pulled away, flipped the light on, and briskly smoothed her hair in front of the mirror.

"What's your name?" Paz whispered, but the woman only smiled, not at Paz, but at her own reflection, then was gone.

Since then, she'd had much more practice. She'd learned how to reel in a woman, learned that you could do it anywhere. At bakeries, on the bus, on the street. It was all a matter of the eyes. The gaze couldn't waver, it had to hold everything, both questions and answers. Make promises women longed for you to keep. But the gaze had to be balanced, tempered, just long enough to make its point, but brief enough that if you'd misread a woman she could tell herself that of course it wasn't what she'd thought, that she'd made it up, that you were a perfectly nice girl who perhaps mistook her for someone else. Without speaking, everything could be asked and known, and you could stay safe from authorities because there would be nothing for spies to report, no reason for the government to recategorize you from A to B class of danger to society, or B to C. Keep your mouth shut and your eyes alive. Keep your body awake and you will know.

Finding women wasn't the trouble.

The trouble was, they never stayed.

She remembered what Romina said, years ago, when Flaca and La Venus were still together, about how there was no such thing as lasting, no future, no forever for people like them. Romina of all people, who'd now been holding steady with Malena for almost three years. They almost seemed like a married couple, so fused were they. What would she have to say now?

Not that Paz always wanted women to stick around. Some connections were fine for a night, a week, a few adventures. There had been women whose depression or frenetic need had overwhelmed her, women who expected Paz to not only give them pleasure but also save them from a wretched marriage or an overbearing father, more than she could do. Then there were the women who didn't want to leave their misery, for whom Paz was like a bottle of whiskey that could help you warm up for a while and forget. There were women whose names she never learned, whom she loved in park bushes and café bathrooms and cheap hotel rooms when cash was flush. There were women whom she got to know, who spilled confessions as they lay naked in their husbands' beds (Paz didn't dare use her own room in the old couple's house, they were always home and knew nothing, they'd gone through enough by losing a son to the regime, so she kept her sex life separate from their home). No matter who the woman was, and no matter the place or circumstances, Paz always loved the sex. She was at home between the legs of women. Alive there. As if she were the sole member of some occult, forgotten sect, a persecuted devotee with no church in which to pray, the women's bodies were the church, the site of consecration. Or was it desecration? What was this rite in which she plunged into women until they begged for mercy or wept with savage joy? Some of the women—not all of them—reciprocated, but nowhere was the pleasure more intense than in the giving. Strange rite. Lone believer. Cosmically alone, except when she reminded herself of Flaca and the others, her Polonio tribe, the five of them a circle of the possible.

Many of the women had men in their lives, husbands or boyfriends or lovers. "You're the perfect cheat," a housewife told her once, naked, stroking her hair. "You can't get me pregnant or give me syphilis. It's a dream." Paz was left wondering how many of the women felt that way about her. The perfect cheat. Safe. Safer than a man—not as serious. Was it possible that some of them weren't really cantoras? (And what made a cantora real?) Or could it be that they chose to bury what they were, so as to keep their lives intact? She didn't care. She told herself she didn't care. For a while, she believed it.

Then, last year, when she was twenty years old, she'd met Mónica. Wild Mónica, brass-laughing Mónica, single and tied to no man, cheerful secretary at a downtown office by day, good daughter by night, except when she was out with Paz demolishing her virtue. Sex with Mónica was like hurling herself into a volcano. Mónica was the first girl Paz brought to Polonio, once with the group, who welcomed her, and before that just the two of them for three days of naked light.

"I love this place," Mónica had said, tangling her fingers in Paz's pubic hair. "It's magical."

Paz laughed. "You've barely seen it."

"I have too seen it."

"We've barely left the Prow."

"We'll leave soon enough."

"You keep saying that."

"You keep making it impossible."

"Oh, so it's my fault?"

"Obviously."

"You innocent flower."

Mónica widened her eyes in that mocking I-am-so-pure manner that always made Paz ache with lust, even now, hours into sex. "Secondly: the Prow *is* Polonio. Why do I have to go outside?"

"Well, there is the small matter of the ocean—"

"—which I can hear from this corner. And even taste."

"Oh?"

"Right here."

"Mmmmmm."

"I'll show you."

"Do."

Five months, they'd lasted, and Paz had not been with any other women, had begun to imagine Mónica as her last woman, her forever. How stupid she'd been to think that, to let herself hope.

In the end, Mónica hadn't known what she wanted.

Or perhaps it was worse than that: she knew exactly what she wanted and it involved children, a ring on her finger, a man she could bring home to Papá.

"He wants to marry me" was all the detail she gave, over the phone, about the new man in her life.

Paz read between the lines: her lover didn't want a life of hiding, a life chained to a university dropout who smelled like sealskins and could never be presented to her family. Could never make a family with her. The gold in the ring, the approval of Papá, more important than love.

Flaca tried to comfort her. "For some women, that's the truth of their desire. What they want more than anything. To have babies, a man. To be a wife. You've just got to accept that."

"I can't accept it," Paz said.

"Think of it this way." Flaca handed Paz the *mate* gourd; they were on the Rambla, perched on the low wall, and the river stretched out long and flat before them, blue today, no ripple to be seen. "Someone's got to keep humanity going, right?"

"What for?"

"Oh, come on, Paz. Lighten up."

"Maybe cantoras should start having babies."

"Bah!"

"You said lighten up."

"Touché."

"It's just all so stupid—a white veil to pretend you're pure, a man to slather his surname over yours." Paz handed the gourd back to Flaca, watched her fill it again. "Then she can act like the noble one, the married one, who did things right, when really she's living a lie."

"How do you know it's a lie for her?"

Paz looked at Flaca, steadily. "You know exactly how."

Flaca laughed and drank from the *mate*. "You Don Juana, you."

"She'd been with men before, you know. She said it was better with me than with any of them."

"They all say that."

"I've noticed."

They both laughed.

Paz turned serious. "Do you think they mean it?"

Flaca handed Paz the *mate* gourd, full again, then lit a cigarette and took a long drag before answering. "Most of them. Yes."

"And the others?"

"The others say that to all their lovers."

"Well, Mónica wasn't one of those."

"I believe you."

Paz reached for Flaca's pack and lit a cigarette of her own. These women getting the best sex of their lives and still running back to men. What were the men doing? What did they have that she didn't? A cock, sure, but given the track record, what else? Veils. Rings. Sperm for making babies. Was that all? Is that all, Mónica?

Flaca seemed to be reading her thoughts. She had the *mate* again, poured hot water into the leaves. "It's the power," she said gently. "They want the power to be safe, and accepted. To have lives free of shame."

"And men give them that."

"Exactly."

And we can't. We don't have those things ourselves so we can't give them. "Sometimes I think it would be different," Paz whispered, "without *El Proceso.*" It was the Process, after all, that had blanketed the whole nation with fear, so that, for some women, the cost of living true could seem unbearable.

"Maybe. I don't know." Flaca didn't look around her, and there was no one nearby, but her body had gone tense and she seemed to be calculating every word. "The silence was here before, wasn't it?"

"I wouldn't know."

"Right. I forget how young you were, before—it."

It. The coup.

"Some things were different, but others weren't at all."

Paz drank down the *mate,* then watched Flaca drink hers, took another turn. They sat and watched the river kiss the shore.

"Damn Mónica, anyway," Flaca said. "There will be other women."

And on this, as on so many other counts, Flaca was right.

*

Romina felt the wind in her hair as the cart rode over the sand dunes. Malena was at her side, Flaca close behind her with her girlfriend Cristi. They were coming into Polonio to celebrate the growing warmth of spring; it was mid-October and the sky brimmed with a clear blue heat. Paz was already at the house, having made some preparations, they'd meet her there.

Malena. Open warmth. An ease between them, beyond words. Their bodies were not touching but they were close now to the place where they could hold hands, drop the masks, be connected without pretending otherwise. It had become more difficult over the years, this constant lie. Even though it was normal for sisters or cousins to occasionally walk arm in arm, and some cantoras, she knew, took advantage of this to touch their lovers in public, Romina didn't dare, afraid that her body would betray them with its secret speech, its touching that was not a sister's touching, how do you make your body lie? Romina chafed at this more than Malena, perhaps because she craved Malena's touch as a steadying force, an anchor. Hand to elbow, shoulder to head, feet on lap, thighs side by side on a sofa and she was home. It was not lust exactly, not most of the time, and, in fact, this private touch rarely led, these days, to sex, preoccupied as Romina was with organizing, the state of the country, the long slow political overthrow to which she'd devoted her soul. It was something gentler than lust, and more essential: a connection so instinctive it almost seemed an extension of herself. And she needed it. The harder she worked, the more she needed this woman who received her with a patient ear and steady hands, rarely asking anything in return, as if loving Romina, supporting Romina, were her own best sustenance. It was kind of her. Malena was so kind. It was a gift too large to ever repay, and Romina was grateful for it, though sometimes she feared that no matter what she did, she'd never be grateful enough. And at other times, worse, gratitude failed her, and she found herself irritated, sick of being the selfish one, the one with needs, the one to decide everything because Malena never had an opinion about what to have for dinner or whether to walk east or west along the river, *either way,* Malena would say, *I don't mind, no problem, whatever you want,* and sometimes Romina wanted to scream *can you just choose for once? do I always have to be the one? are you alive or what?* and then she promptly filled with shame. To have a woman who was such a saint, who gave everything for you, and not be grateful—what was her problem? *Why do you give me so much?* Romina once asked her, and Malena smiled and said *because I want to.* And so Romina accepted, again, this way of Malena's, this giving, which was her own way of expressing love, or of spurring the resistance, perhaps, by helping sustain one of its leaders. Which motive was more powerful? Resistance, or love? Malena never said, and Romina did not ask, and as the years passed, their way of being came to feel inevitable, at least most of the time, as natural as the bond between soil and tree, one low and still, the other reaching for the sky.

And what full years they had been. The resistance was gathering strength. Opposition to the regime was still a whisper, but it was a strong whisper, collective, insistent, a gathering hum like that of waves. It had been the plebiscite, two years ago now, that had changed everything—that first vote of the people, for which she'd organized communications for the Frente Amplio, all of them secret as the party was still illegal. The people had done it. They had voted NO. NO to the regime's new constitution, NO to their grab for more power, NO to their cocky attempt to make themselves look credible to others around the world. And not just that, the vote had come in strong, with 57 percent voting NO. For weeks afterward, she'd walked the streets in love with half the people she passed—even more than half!—for their bravery and willingness to put their lives at risk by voting against those who had the power to crush them or at least who claimed to have it, for what was power, what was crushing, who were those faceless men at the top of that grim thing known as a government? She wasn't the only one who felt this way. The nation was emboldened. After that November 1980 vote, over half of the population had heard itself speak and finally knew that it wasn't alone. The opposition had been silent for so long—if you didn't want to disappear, didn't want to be tortured, you shut up about the government, *punto*—and this form of speech, this vote, was the first trembling melody to enter that public silence, like a bird at dawn. People greeted each other more on the street. The grocer had begun looking at her as he weighed her tomatoes, inflecting his *quite a nice day, turns out, no?* with a momentary sparkle in his eyes. Clandestine meetings grew in size. And there were the *caceroleos*. Her cell had helped start them, spread the word. Once a month, at 8:00 p.m. exactly, people began banging their pots in kitchens across Montevideo. At first her parents heard the clamor but did not join in or say a word about it, though Mamá's expression became distant and inscrutable until the neighborhood finally went quiet. But as the *caceroleos* grew louder, a beat strong enough to shake the earth, even her own mother had joined in, so that now they stood together at the open kitchen window and banged their pots and pans together; on more than one occasion Mamá had broken wooden spoons against metal, and then kept on banging, Romina picking up the flung half of the spoon and using it to make more noise, because a broken spoon can also shout, oh yes it can. Sometimes Mamá wept as she banged, but she never spoke. Papá disappeared into the bedroom before the protest began, not joining, but not obstructing, either. Romina looked forward to those evenings now, to standing with her mother as they sent percussive wails into the night.

The government, for its part, had responded to the vote as if to a slap. She'd braced herself for assaults on the people, a bout of arrests, a crackdown, but it seemed that the men in the Presidential Palace were in chaos, too busy fending off international pressure and scrambling for the next move. Arrests dried up. The prisons were full, the secret detention centers exhausting to run, perhaps, Romina thought, trying not to wonder about the Only Three and where they were, what this lack of fresh meat meant for their prospects, were they out of work now, out of naked women to rape, forced to turn their weapons on their wives, their daughters? She thought too often of their daughters, prayed that they had none. Wished that she could free herself from thinking about them at all, that she could stop scanning buses and corner cafés for their faces—panicking all the while that she'd have no way of ever being sure, having caught very little of their faces and memory being a traitor to the mind—and wished that she could stop dreaming about them as shadows swooping over her, heavy, airless, suffocating, she'd wake up in a sweat but she never spoke of it, because she was one of the women who'd suffered the least, there had only been three and only for two nights, one night with one, one night with three, two nights instead of hundreds, a paltry arithmetic of pain, and so who was she to tell it when her experience was a speck compared to what other women had suffered, were suffering still? It was nothing, a speck in your eye, this Only Three. Shut up, Romina, get over yourself. The dreams were an embarrassment. The only person she told was Malena, who held her, rocked her, listened but gave her the kindness of saying nothing.

Meanwhile, the new laxness of the government had meant that she could teach. She was classified as a B citizen, which made working at a public school impossible, but she'd managed to find a position at a private school. She taught history to eleven- and twelve-year-olds, in just the careful dry and lying way the regime wanted her to. It was painful to distort history, but she told herself that this false surface would let her do her real work later on, in the night—the work that would give these children the kind of country where they could hope for a decent future. *This is for you, too,* she'd shout at them silently as she started her dull accounts of Uruguay's bleached perfection. Her students glazed over, took robotic notes, stared out the window or defiantly at her. Her silent shout did not reach them, and just as well. She had her paycheck and her secret work. Almost enough to assuage her conscience for the lies she fed her students.

She poured herself into the resistance. They were gaining traction. On some days, she thought she wouldn't live much longer, that each day she wasn't rounded up was a miracle. On other days, she thought she glimpsed her nation's freedom around the corner just one big collective push away. There was another election coming now, in November 1982—next month already!—for political parties to choose their own internal leaders, a massive step, given that political parties had been forbidden to operate for so many years after the coup—and she dared hope it might push things further open, though, with all the fierce factions on the left, it could splinter and shatter them too. Either way, she was determined to keep on pushing, determined to continue on.

She had also come to know Felipe again, in slow patient visits to the Penal de Libertad. Her father still didn't go, but she and her mother traded off visiting days. She came to see, through subtle signals, that he was well. That the visits fueled him. One day, though, he said, out of nowhere, "You're not married yet?"

She gripped the leg of the table, out of view. Why ask a question when you already know the answer? "No."

"Any contenders?"

"No."

"Romina. I'm sure you'll find someone."

"I'm fine the way I am."

He went grave, then. "Our parents need grandkids, *hermana,* and"—he gestured around him with his eyes—"I can't provide them. I need you to be the one."

She bit her tongue.

"Think about it. Our last name might never get passed down."

The man was in prison, had suffered what she never would, so be nice, she thought, but it tumbled out anyway. "If my babies wouldn't have the right name anyway, what does it matter?"

"What's wrong with you? I never said that. I'm just saying, our poor parents, try to make them happy."

"I do everything I can to make them happy."

He stared off at the bare, cracked wall for a while before responding. "You owe them this."

His harsh tone surprised her. He wasn't giving in. She stared at him, and he stared back, and for a moment they weren't prisoner and visitor but big brother and little sister, he explaining to her how the world worked, she folding his underwear and socks while he explained, she clearing his plate from the dinner table as he drifted off to relax or study or watch television while she scrubbed and wiped and cleaned. "It's my life," she said, then immediately drowned in a flood of guilt for saying it. She was the one on the outside, the one who had a life, while he—the pain on his face conveyed that he was thinking the same thing.

He put his palms up, a man under attack. "Calm down. I wasn't—"

"Time's up," said the guard.

On the bus ride home, she burned with rage and shame, a hot tangle that could not be undone. That night, she knocked on Malena's door unannounced, and they stayed together all night for the first time, at a cheap hotel, where they clung to each other in a bare anonymous room that belonged to neither of them, with a passion that made Romina forget for a few bright moments about belonging, the need to belong at all.

"Move in with me," Malena whispered into her hair at dawn. "We could get a little apartment. Between the two of us, now that you're teaching, we could manage."

"I can't. You know I can't."

"You can. We can. I can't stand the thought of you waking alone."

She wished she could say yes. She did. But it was bad enough that she'd stayed out for the night without asking her parents for permission, not even leaving a note or daring to call for fear that they would talk her out of this fistful of freedom. They must be worried. No matter that enforcement of night patrols had loosened up, these days: her parents worried. Pogroms were too close in her mother's past for her to feel safe with a daughter out in a city like this one, which had swallowed each of her children at different times and never given one of them back. How could she abandon her parents? Daughters didn't move out until they had husbands. She would never have a husband. *Try to make them happy.* She was failing them. They needed her. She was all they had left, with Felipe gone. Her mother's sadness was a river that she swam through each day, tending to its currents as though she could give them shape, rather than the other way around. It was murky in there, thick with life-forms, some foreign, some shudderingly familiar. No, she could not leave. She could never be like Malena, who had rented a little room in an old couple's home, who had cut ties with her own parents, something that never ceased to amaze Romina, as well as bewilder her, since Malena had yet to share the details of their estrangement. There had been conflict. They had not seen eye to eye. Well! What cantora had parents with whom she could see eye to eye? How could that be a reason to break with your own parents? There had to be more to it, more hollows in the telling. She longed to know the whole topography, but Malena always changed the subject, deftly, like the stroke of a honey-coated knife.

Malena. Honey-coated Malena. Romina adjusted herself on the horse-drawn cart so that they were facing the same direction as the cart turned onto the beach, the Polonio lighthouse and scattered huts at last in sight. She couldn't go live with her, for reasons Malena refused to understand, and for all the harmony between them this had now become a recurring argument, just beneath the surface, a fault line that awoke at the slightest touch, made all the more painful by the fact that Romina was arguing against her own desires. Of course she'd like to come home each night to a private sphere that she— that they—could fill with their real selves. An almost obscene luxury. What would they do with so much honest space? They had sex less often now than they did early on, but whenever they did, the gentle power of it always poured back in, remembering the way, like water in the thrall of gravity. Their sex together was oceanic, embracing, open, never forced. Malena waited for signals from Romina before ever initiating, even if the signals vanished for weeks. Which they sometimes did. She never knew exactly why; it wasn't necessarily when the Only Three pushed into her dreams, or when she felt the most frightened of the future. There was no pattern. Erratic tides. They left, then rose again, impelled by forces Romina could not explain. Only later, as their bodies merged, would she feel Malena's own hunger under the surface, waiting, quiet, like a creature unsuited to the hunt. It was enough and a relief to Romina. It seemed, at times, that this was the only way the world would be remade as the heroes had dreamed: one woman holds another woman, and she in turn lifts the world.

*

They arrived at La Proa and found Paz smoking a cigarette in the doorway, waiting for them, in a bathing suit and men's shorts. She'd gotten brazen that way, Paz, wearing whatever she wanted while she was in Polonio. Delight lit up her face at the sight of them.

"How was the ride up?" she asked.

"Long." Flaca gave her a kiss, then went inside to put her pack down. "This is Cristi."

Paz smiled. "Cristi, hello. Welcome to the Prow."

Cristi smiled, looking relieved at the warm reception. She had a birdlike beauty, and seemed sweet, though also nervous in her own skin—or perhaps that was because it was her first time gathering with *that kind* of women, beyond just two, and there was no manual of what to expect.

"How was your first day?" Flaca lit two cigarettes and handed one to Cristi. "What have you been doing?"

"I fixed another crack in the roof," Paz said.

"Excellent."

Romina and Malena came in, and soon the group was boisterous, laughing and all talking at once, and soon they were putting on their bathing suits to head down to the water.

The ocean received them greedily, stroking their skin with pale tongues.

Flaca and Cristi swam out to the rocks—her classic move, Paz thought, remembering the first time. How stunned she'd been to hear her and La Venus out there, making love. How it had changed her inside, closed the door on normalcy and opened the way for the life she had now. How young she'd been then; how lucky to stumble into this place, into such company, like that girl Alice finding a different land beyond the rabbit hole. Without that twist of fortune, who knew where she'd be? At the university, perhaps. Still living with her mother? Engaged to some boy? It strained the mind to think of it. Romina and Malena, meanwhile, floated and bobbed side by side, close enough to be touching underwater, though whether or not they were, it was impossible to say. The couples were being couples. She was alone. She would not think of Mónica. Damn herself for thinking of Mónica. Water. Salty depth. Vast and wet surrounding, hold me, take me, *see* me, she thought, strangely as the ocean had no eyes—or did it have millions?—and she felt in the lush waves that the ocean did.

That night, they made a feast under the stars.

They fell into a comforting rhythm, one chopping, one peeling, one cleaning the fish, one stoking the fire, preparing their meal the way, Paz thought, other families must do on their summer holidays. A warm sensation swept over her. Safety, or satiety, or connection, or some raw mix of these things. As a child, she'd heard other kids talking about their family vacations on the coast, in one of the many beachfront apartments or cottages that sprawled all the way up to the Brazilian border, from shabby to gleaming, and it seemed that everyone went to the coast in the summer: even before the dictatorship had hurled people off to exile, Montevideo had been a ghost town from Christmas to Carnaval. But Paz had never had a big family with whom to have such rhythms. It was always just her and her mother, and they usually just took the bus down to the urban beach in Pocitos and that was it. When they had taken summer vacations, before the coup, it had been just the two of them, at her cousin's borrowed house, or the two of them plus a boyfriend of the moment to whom Mamá gave all of her attention, nothing like this, the simple joy of cooking together, of feeling the sun and salt on your skin and people by your side who want you there, food under your hands and an eager belly, the animal pleasures of the tribe.

That night, around the fire, they talked about their lives, like old times, going deeper than they could in the city. Paz told stories of her adventures with vendors and cart drivers, escapades that made her friends laugh. Flaca told them about her mother, who'd become ill, though no one knew with what, and had taken to her bed. Flaca now oversaw all the housekeeping, and also took care of her mother and ran the butcher shop. Her father helped, of course, but he was also tired. Sometimes, when Flaca woke in the night to tend to her mother, she sat up long after her mother had gone back to sleep, holding her hand, staring into the darkness.

"I'm sorry," Malena said. "Truly, Flaca. Your mother is a wonderful person."

Flaca smiled at her across the fire and wondered for an instant whether Malena was thinking of her own mother, to whom she didn't speak, for reasons that had never truly been explained. Did it hurt her, to hear of other mothers? She searched Malena's face for pain but found no trace. It embarrassed her to speak of her mother in front of Malena, the way a glutton might be ashamed to feast before a starving peasant. And yet, if Malena ever felt a sting when the subject arose, she never showed it. She was kindness. She was solace. She comforted her friends through breakups, tended to her lover after long days of hard work, answered La Venus's letters from Brazil with more patience than anyone else. All that listening to others, and yet she barely talked about her life beyond Romina. Did she still have a life beyond Romina? Did she want to have one, or was swimming in her lover's currents more than enough? And what was that writhing thing beneath her layers of calm? Sadness? Self-hatred? Grief? A sense of defeat from forever ago? Perhaps some blend of all those things, or something else Flaca couldn't guess at, could only feel pulsing deep inside Malena and never see or reach because Malena didn't want her to, she bristled if you tried, tensed like a hurt street dog and clammed up and pushed you away. It exasperated Flaca sometimes. It was the kind of exasperation you can only feel with a sister, with someone you wholly love. She turned to Romina. "Tell me, *chica,* how goes the revolution?"

"Not so bad."

"You mean that?"

"Yes." Romina leaned her head back to face the stars. What a relief to be able to talk about it here. The soldiers were off in their lighthouse barracks, minding their own business, or minding someone's business but not hers. The sound of the ocean, *sssshhhh, ssssshhhhh,* was working magic on her body, opening her back up deep inside. "I think these elections might really help us on the way."

"You're involved with that?" Cristi asked, not hiding her awe.

"Romina," Flaca said, sweeping the air with her hand, "is involved with everything."

The fire sparked and hummed.

"I admire you," Cristi said.

Romina shrugged. "It's what I have to do."

"I've heard there's controversy," Cristi went on. "About how to vote."

"Me too," said Flaca. "What should we do?"

Romina stared into the fire, and launched into her best explanation. It was longer and more convoluted than she meant it to be. There was nothing simple about the situation: the military junta had decided to allow political parties to hold their own internal elections, selecting leaders, though whether those leaders would have any power or were merely symbolic, a circus for the public, remained to be seen. And only the two old parties could participate. The Blancos and the Colorados. The leftist Frente Amplio, a new third party, was still illegal, along with all the other minor factions on the left. They were not allowed to hold a vote, or to exist. As a result, the left was fiercely divided. What to do? Support the antidictatorship leaders of a moderate party because they were legally allowed to run, and because this gave them a small chance of one day toppling the regime? Or submit blank ballots in protest of the Frente Amplio's exclusion, holding to their values and flexing the muscle of the true left?

Debates pushed deep into the night, in their meetings in the backs of abandoned laundromats, in airless basements, in shoemakers' cluttered workshops. The meetings exhausted and riled her. There were former Tupamaros, leftist politicians, socialists, Communists, all working together at levels that had been impossible before the coup. They'd always fought with each other, but now they were the Frente Amplio, the Broad Front, a coalition putting aside their differences so as to win, so as to hold the slightest hope of overcoming the great beast before them. They either worked together, or were lost. It amazed her, often, that these people could all gather in a room. Coalition didn't always work. It crashed, soared, collapsed again. And now, this party election was the greatest test the united Frente had faced. It threatened to tear them apart.

She herself swayed between arguments: as she listened to appeals from both sides, she at times was in favor of the blank ballots—Frente Amplio or nothing, push for revolution, hold to our values and don't let those monsters set the terms—and at other times she supported backing a Blanco candidate, backing *any* candidate willing to stand up against the regime that had stolen their democracy, any candidate that had a chance of winning and a chance of saving them from the worst possible future, a future of eternal military rule.

Look at Paraguay, one man said, Stroessner's iron grip for twenty-eight years and counting, can we really afford to gamble with this chance to end the nightmare? and she thought, yes, it's what we must do.

Then another man cut in: but if we betray our Frente principles, our vision, we've lost everything. And she was pulled in by his words.

Haven't we lost everything already?

Back and forth, swinging, swimming.

Frente leaders even chimed in, in letters smuggled out of the prisons where they were held. Their words circulated underground and stoked the fires. One night, Romina heard a letter read aloud that laid out the case for voting for a viable candidate, and she finally landed on one side. It was not betrayal; it was strategy. It was their best hope and therefore the right thing to do. Not everyone agreed with this. The factions kept fighting. Romina's role was often intermediary; where conversations broke down and tensions rose, she facilitated, made peace, sought the common ground. It often wore her out, but she did it anyway, because she could. She could see all sides, negotiate, calm frayed nerves and fragile egos. She was, she realized, less of a purist than a pragmatist: she cared less about Communism than about ending the nightmare, less about the words of the dead (Marx, Guevara) than the needs of the living. She was one of the ones who'd been spared arrest, and this was what she could do with her guilt at having suffered so little when her brother and thousands of others had suffered without end.

"So that's how you're going to vote?" Paz said, prodding at the embers with a stick. "For the Blanco candidate?"

"For the Blanco. He has the best chance of beating the supporters of the regime—that's all that matters."

"That's what I'll do, then," Paz said. It was her first time voting, and the thought elated and frightened her at the same time.

"Me too," said Flaca.

The whiskey flask went around.

"So what will we do," Flaca said, "if it really works?"

"What do you mean?"

"I mean, if eventually, one day, we return to democracy? A president, a parliament—all of that? Will the censored newspapers return? The exiles? Will the prisoners be freed?"

Paz thought of all the books her mother had burned, which could never be returned, though for a moment she pictured them rising from the grill out on the patio, shaking off flames with their paper wings.

"Those are the questions," Romina said.

"The questions that what?"

"That we can't answer."

"We can only hope, I suppose," Flaca said.

"We'll get the prisoners freed," Malena said. "They'll have to be freed. Why would a new government want to hold on to them? And exiles will come back. They already long to come home—you can see that clearly in the letters and essays Romina smuggles underground."

"*We* smuggle," Romina said. "You help me smuggle them."

Malena shrugged, but she seemed pleased.

"But will this still be home for them?" Paz said. "For the exiles?"

"Of course it will," Cristi said brightly. She was slightly younger than Flaca, in her early twenties, a cook in her parents' restaurant. This was her first relationship with a woman, she'd told them earlier, with the cheerfulness and pride of a gardener pointing out her first batch of successful tomatoes.

"I'm not so sure," Romina said. "Their letters don't sound as homesick as they used to. Maybe they've made new homes."

"It can't be the same," said Flaca. "They'll never be as at home in Spain, in Mexico, France, Sweden, Australia, or wherever as they can be in Uruguay."

"Are we at home in Uruguay?"

The women looked at Romina in silence for a few beats as the ocean poured its liquid music all around them.

"I am," Flaca said.

"More than anywhere else," said Paz.

"I'm not." Romina picked up the flask, which had idled by her side.

"I am," said Cristi, though she sounded uncertain.

"I don't know what that is, home," said Malena.

Romina passed the whiskey back around the circle without drinking. Malena's drink, she saw, was long and deep. She never used to drink so much, but now it seemed that she was the first to bring the bottle out, and the one to drain it and reach for the next one. Romina fought back the impulse to stop her, to slow her down. Why did it bother her? Was it a need for control? *Relax*, Malena had said to her the only time she'd brought it up. Maybe she should.

"Maybe La Venus will come back," Paz said. "I miss her."

They were silent for a while.

Flaca swigged whiskey and wiped her mouth with the back of her sleeve. "So do I."

Her friends stared at her.

"You?" Romina said.

"Yes," Flaca said. "Me." She tried not to notice the way Cristi stiffened beside her. Spry, delightful Cristi, a woman like a spring breeze. Cristi knew that La Venus was a past lover, though not that she'd been the second woman to break Flaca's heart. Those were words Flaca had never said aloud. She'd never admit them to anyone. "Can't I miss a friend?"

"Let's sing a song," Paz said, and as their voices rose she dared imagine La Venus with them, her rich soprano rising into the sound of them, the circle complete again, at last.

*

The voting strategy paid off. The next month enough leftists rallied behind the antiregime candidate that he won his party's support, in a landslide, beating out opponents who were the generals' puppets. It was only a primary, and for a general election that might never actually happen, but still, the people had thumbed their noses at the government again. Romina felt euphoric for days, as if the streets had turned to clouds and she were walking through the sky, a sky that vaulted high above her sordid country, where things were light, were possible. And five days after the vote, she received a surprise. She was home frying milanesas for dinner, Mamá mashing potatoes beside her, when the phone rang. She picked up on the second ring.

"Hello?"

"Romina."

She waited, reflexively. People who didn't announce themselves could be dangerous.

"It's me."

It took her another beat to understand. "Venus?"

"Who else?"

Romina's breath caught in her throat. La Venus never called from Brazil, except on Romina's birthday. International phone calls were exorbitantly expensive as well as intensely surveilled. "The call sounds so crisp—"

"That's because I'm here."

"Where, here?"

"In Montevideo."

"What!"

"I just got back. It was sudden."

The word *sudden* made Romina's spine go tense. Brazil, after all, was a dictatorship too. "You're—all right?"

"Yes. I think so. I mean—if you mean—I'm fine."

In the pause that followed, Romina heard her mother down the hall, stacking plates in the cupboard, *clink, clink.*

"I'll explain when I can. How are you?"

"Fine. I mean. You know."

"I do. Or maybe I don't. I've thought about you all so much."

"We all figured you were having the time of your life in Rio."

Silence.

"Where are you now?"

"At my mother's house."

Not with Ariella, then. She wondered what had happened, and waited for more, but it didn't come. She didn't press. "We missed you."

"I'm dying to go to Polonio."

"We're going next week."

"Ah!"

"Yes, for New Year's."

"'We'? Who's 'we'?"

"All of us. Me, Malena, Paz, Flaca." And likely a couple of girlfriends, she thought, though she held back on this, as she was never sure until the last minute who Paz or Flaca would bring.

La Venus sighed. "I suppose Flaca won't want me there."

"Don't be so sure. You should talk to her."

"You think so?" The hope was raw and naked in La Venus's voice.

"Absolutely, I do. A lot's changed since you left, you know."

"I don't doubt it. All right. I'll give it a try." Pause. "Romina?"

"Yes?"

"You and Malena—are you still—"

"Singing?" Romina could hear that Mamá was still clinking, though less frequently, perhaps straining to hear scattered clues to her daughter's life. She kept her voice neutral. "Oh yes."

La Venus's raucous laughter filled her ear. "Well, thank goodness you make her sing. What's a life without music?"

*

A week later, they were back inside the Prow, the five of them together again, with two girlfriends in tow: Flaca had brought Cristi, and Paz a new girl called Yolanda. The sleeping blankets rose high and rich, the kitchen had been built up with a counter and shelves jutting from the walls to hold cups, grains, spices. The walls clamored with hangings, little paintings, and seashells, each a treasure with sentimental value, no doubt, a story inside each object to which La Venus was not privy, and she felt a stab of sadness at all the life she'd missed. Still, it was the same hut, the same room, and the same women. Her family. Her people. More so than she'd understood. She'd braced herself for awkwardness with Flaca, but as soon as they saw each other at the Montevideo bus station there was, to their mutual surprise, only joy, like that of sisters who'd grown up so close that squabbles were easily forgotten. They'd laughed and passed the *mate* on the long bus ride from the city. She'd already been asked several times about Brazil, but had insisted on saving the long version until they were all together at the Prow, when there was time and space and freedom, when the air could open for them all. And now they were here, the air lay open. The last time they'd all been in this room at the same time, she realized, Paz had been dragged out by soldiers. Three years ago now. Their presence in this room again, the five of them, the original five who'd found this place and made it theirs, seemed at that instant to have the power to restore them, to undo the violence of that night like knots in a half-made tapestry, in which they were each a strand, threading relentlessly through time, railing against the limits of the loom, making themselves stronger every time they found a way to interweave with each other. A five-colored tapestry. She didn't believe in God anymore, didn't believe in her country, and wasn't even sure she believed in the fundamental goodness of human souls, but she could believe in this, the shimmering power they generated collectively by being awake and together in this room.

"We should get beds one of these days," Paz said, glancing shyly at Yolanda, fearing her disappointment at the cramped quarters, though she'd tried to prepare her beforehand.

"Beds!" Flaca said. "What are we, queens?"

"I think it's perfect," Yolanda said slowly, gazing at Paz in a manner that made La Venus, watching, look away with a flush on her cheeks. Paz was grown up now, a woman, able to inspire that kind of look. Yolanda had seemed so reserved, demure even, on the bus ride up the coast, that Venus could not have seen this coming. But that's how it was, she remembered. Things were clamped down tight here, more so than in Brazil, where cities were much larger and lust a more ordinary thing to see on a woman's face. All the hiding and push-it-down of Montevideo meant that once you got out to a place like this, a place beyond your imagining, beyond the chains of everyday life, the pushed-down could burst upward with volcanic strength. Hiding either extinguished lust or made it burn all the more fiercely when it survived.

In the afternoon, the women scattered for a delicious swim and a trip to El Lobo's for greetings and supplies. El Lobo was warm as ever, his grandchildren shockingly tall: the girls were in their early teens now, while Javier, at ten, was a lanky and pensive boy who loved to read. Paz had taken to lending him books from the city, and she brought him a stack now to exchange for the ones she'd left with him before, while his mother, Alicia, insisted on preparing them her famous seaweed buñuelos to take back to the Prow, though they didn't make it back warm because Paz and Yolanda took a long detour to hide among the rocks and lose themselves in each other's bodies on the way home.

Later, that night, once they'd all gathered in the kitchen to slice and season and kindle in preparation for dinner and the *mate* gourd had started its lazy round, Flaca said, "All right, Venus, *chica*. You wanted to wait until we were all together, here we are."

"That's right," Romina said. "We're waiting for your story."

"But why me? We all have stories."

"You've been gone. We've got to catch up with your life."

"I've got to catch up with you, too, all of you."

"You will, you will."

La Venus took a deep breath, cut into the flesh of a potato, and began. It had been good at first, she told them, life in Rio, in their high-rise apartment overlooking Copacabana, that breathtaking beach, longer and larger than she'd known a beach could be, always pocked with people lying in the sun, building sand castles, swimming, drumming, selling young coconuts from which to drink. She often watched them for hours from the balcony, playing with Mario, keeping the house tidy for Ariella's return. Ariella was often gone from morning until well into the night, rehearsing, meeting with her fellow artists, performing. The nights were bright and alive. Music poured in from all directions, from drums and radios and samba singers on the streets, but also from the growl of cars and clop of horses pulling carts, the shouting and fighting and laughing of passing groups.

She tried to tell her friends of the city's beauty, its shocking mountains, rising steep and green against the sky, pressed close against the crowded streets so that it felt as if all human life were just a strip of noise between two giants, ocean and mountain, blue and green. The statue of Christ the Redeemer loomed over it all from a distant height, arms open as if to embrace even the most sordid corners of the world. And yes, there was a dictatorship there too, but it didn't press down on her in the same way, perhaps because the country's size let you be more anonymous, or perhaps because they were wealthy foreigners and floated above the terror, like human clouds. She feared, though she did not say it aloud, that she'd never be able to transmit the city to them in words, that even a photograph could never capture the spirit of the place and what it was to be inside of it, part of it, all that towering, all that vivid color, all that full-throated sound. She'd never be able to fully speak it. She carried so much clamor inside. And what to do with it? How to be? Why did life put so much inside a woman and then keep her confined to smallness? But she couldn't very well say that. Her life didn't look small to her friends, did it, when she'd just lived in a thrilling foreign city and been able to return, when they'd all been trapped here in their small broken country, when droves of exiles were locked out of home. So instead she said that the city was beautiful, and that she'd loved spending time with Mario in the apartment and taking him down to the beach while Ariella rehearsed, and that at first there had been babysitters who'd watched the boy while La Venus and Ariella went out to parties, performances, plays. Bohemian gatherings in candlelit salons. Refined soirees overlooking Ipanema Beach. They'd walk in together, dressed impeccably, and cause a sensation. *I bet you did,* her friends murmured appreciatively, no trace of envy, and the sense of them *with* her, journeying back through those nights, loosened something inside her. She stopped chopping and let Malena take over, sat down on one of their homemade stools, let Flaca light her a cigarette. She took a breath and went on.

That early period didn't last. Soon Ariella was leaving her side at those parties and laughing and talking in tight knots of people, her adoring fans. More than once she saw them kiss her, on the mouth, on the neck. Back at home, they fought. You left me, she said to Ariella, to all those prowling old men, they wouldn't leave me alone and where were you? Relax, said Ariella, you're not my jailer. I don't like being at parties alone, La Venus said, surrounded by a language I only half-understand. Then don't come, said Ariella, and after that she went out alone, or in the company of others, friends she'd made through the fellowship and her musical group, she was a star here after all, while Venus was nothing but a hanger-on with great tits and a titillating name. That's how it felt at times. Ariella took other lovers. She didn't announce it, but she didn't hide it either. There were musicians, a dancer with the ballet, the wife of a German diplomat. *You're not my jailer* was her standard line. She was here in Rio to be herself, to create, to shine. La Venus was here to be her Muse, her helper, her lover when desired—and the sex was still terrific, which only made things more complicated, she said now, putting out her cigarette and lighting another—and most important to be her nanny for Mario, who rarely saw his mother and had gotten used to not having her attention even when they were in the same room. Instead, he cleaved to La Venus. He turned five, turned six. They spent most of their waking hours together, cooking, playing, cuddling, telling stories that began in a high-rise Rio apartment and ended in unicorn cities or on distant planets where everybody flew. He did not go to school. She was his school. She taught him how to read, how to count beans and papayas and subtract them away. He came into her bed at night, when Ariella was out, and fell asleep twined around her body. She'd blended into him; their destinies seemed melted into one. You'll be here forever, Venu? he'd ask, and she'd say, yes, yes, I am your Venu, I am here. Every hug or shared laugh felt like a flag planted in the ground, *we belong to each other.* And for this reason, when Ariella's fellowship was extended for two more years, La Venus screamed inside against the thought of staying but she also knew she could not leave.

But then.

"Then what?" Romina said, gently, when La Venus did not go on. Dinner was almost ready, the plates were out, but no one moved to serve anything until the story had had its time. Instead, they'd each gone still, perched on stools, leaning in the doorway, cross-legged on the sleeping blankets, imagining Rio.

"Then her mother came," La Venus said. "Ariella's mother. She appeared unannounced. I'd heard Ariella becoming more and more exasperated on the phone with her, but I really didn't know much about her mother except that she's rich and bought Ariella that house in El Prado, and also that she knew about Ariella and me, what we were, and didn't like it."

Her friends nodded. Of course she didn't like it, what mother did?

"I opened the door and she barged right in, without even saying hello. Where's Mario? was all she said. Who are you? I asked, and when she said she was Ariella's mother the bitterness in her voice made me afraid. I pointed at the kitchen, where Mario was drawing at the table. I'd just bought him fresh colored pencils, he was so excited."

La Venus began to cry. She tried to collect herself, but only cried harder. Twilight had vanished as she'd told her story, and the lighthouse of Cabo Polonio swished its pale beam through the window of their hut. Someone had lit candles, she hadn't noticed. Someone was kneeling beside her now, enfolding her in arms, who was it? Malena. Sweet Malena, holder of pain. She let herself sink into her embrace.

"You don't have to go on," Romina said gently.

"She took him," La Venus said. "She took my boy. She grabbed his hand and said it was time to go. Go where? he asked, looking confused—he recognized her from photos but it had been two years since he'd seen her. She said, somewhere wonderful. With ice cream. I tried to stop her, I said she had to wait for Ariella, I grabbed Mario's other hand and insisted he wait for me to call Mamá. His grandmother gave me the most horrible look, I don't think I've ever seen a more horrible look on any human face, not even on the faces of soldiers." She flashed, then, on the faces of soldiers in this very room, the night Paz was taken. From her friends' expressions, she guessed they were thinking of it too. But she would hold to her comparison. That woman's look was worse.

"I dialed Ariella's number at the university, but of course she wasn't there. Who knows where she was, what she was doing and with whom. Mario was crying now, he said, you're hurting my hand, and I didn't want to hurt him but I couldn't let him go, but then his grandmother looked at me over his head and said, You pervert, this is no place for a child. What's a pervert? Mario asked through his tears. He was always full of questions and I always tried to answer them, so he'd know, so he'd learn. He looked up at me, trusting me to answer. And then I couldn't. I just couldn't anymore. I let him go. She didn't even pack him a bag. She just said, tell Ariella I'm at the Hotel Paraíso, and then they were gone. I called the university again and left an urgent message for Ariella, then sat by the phone. She called three hours later, and when I told her she was furious at me for letting Mario go. What was I supposed to do? I said. She's his grandmother. I'm his nothing. And it hurt me to say it because he was my everything. By the time Ariella came home, she'd called her mother at the Hotel Paraíso and they'd had a long fight on the phone. Her mother was demanding Mario's passport and signed parental permission for him to travel. She'd had enough, she was going to save her grandchild, take him back to Uruguay and raise him herself. And Ariella agreed. She told me to pack a bag of Mario's things, to take to the hotel. You do it, I said. You pack it. We fought. She left with the bag and the passport and when she came back home I wouldn't speak to her. Four days later I was on a plane back to Uruguay. I felt brokenhearted, not for Ariella but for Mario. As if my heart and lungs had been ripped from my body." She paused. There was more, the part she couldn't yet say aloud, about what she'd taken from Ariella just before she vanished without warning, what she'd stolen across the border into Uruguay, and then, too, there was the way it felt the second her plane touched the ground in Montevideo, the surprising lurch of relief to be home. Home. Despite the military junta and their stupid prisons and decrees, this was her country and she loved it, needed it, even. Uruguay would be in her always. "Even so," she said, "I was glad to be back. I'd missed Uruguay. I missed all of you. I missed Polonio."

Malena was still beside her, holding her hand, and she squeezed it with a startling force. "And now you're here."

"Yes." La Venus smiled. "I'm here. And ready to eat."

*

New Year's Eve arrived, and they spent the afternoon swimming in the ocean and lying out in the sun. The water surrounded them, each wave sloshing forward with its own wet, singular song, offering the pull of undertow and a brief respite from gravity.

Romina looked up from the waves and gazed out over the beach. Always, its desolation, the bare long stretch of it, provoked a deep sense of comfort. To be so far from the living was a solace. There were the rocks where she'd seen soldiers when they'd first arrived to take the lighthouse—such squadrons they used to send, back then! Now it was a meager encampment, who knew how many, two, maybe three, bored soldiers who ended up playing cards and getting drunk with the fishermen. She never spoke to them and didn't know their names, but knew their faces. You should always know your enemy's face. She saw two figures climbing up over the rocks, onto the beach. She tensed. But they were not the soldiers, nor were they fishermen or their wives, any locals she'd seen. They were two women, she realized. They were holding hands—sisters, maybe? She let a wave pass around her, hovered in the water, and watched.

Perhaps she was going crazy, but their body language did not seem like that of sisters.

Malena swam up to her, put her cheek to Romina's shoulder, followed her gaze. Her head jerked up. "Oh! That woman!"

"Which one?"

"The taller one. Do you know who that is?"

"Who?"

"Mariana Righi!"

"The singer? From Argentina?"

"Yes—don't stare. I swear it's her. She doesn't live in Argentina now, she fled to Spain."

"You're sure it's her?"

Malena stole glances. "It has to be."

"What would she be doing all the way out here?"

"What are you two whispering about?" It was Flaca, wading up to them, Cristi and La Venus close behind. It was all of them now, all except Paz and Yolanda, who must have stolen off for time alone at the Prow, or maybe in the dunes. The newer the couple, Flaca thought, the more urgent the stealing of private time.

"Those women. Malena says the tall one is Mariana Righi."

"Really?" Cristi did not hide the excitement in her voice. "I love her!"

"It can't be," Flaca said. "I heard she's in exile, in Europe somewhere."

"Spain," La Venus said. "That's her. I know her face. It's Mariana."

The two women on the beach leaned close to each other. Their foreheads touched, and they stayed that way, hands interlocked, faces communing.

"*A la mierda,*" La Venus said. "She's a cantora." She drew out the word *cantora,* her meaning clear.

"It can't be—"

"It is, it is, don't you have eyes in your—"

"Will you stop staring? It's obvious they came here for privacy."

"It's not her."

"It's *her.*"

The two women became aware of the figures in the water, with a strange suddenness, as if they'd just shaken off a spell. They waved. The women in the water waved back. Romina tried to think of what to say, gathered the courage to call out to them, but then the women had turned around and started walking back toward the path up from the beach.

"Mariana Righi," Flaca said slowly, savoring each syllable. "Who would have known."

"That she'd find Polonio?"

"That she'd be one of *us*."

"Sometimes," Romina said, "it seems like we're everywhere—"

"—and yet nowhere at the same time," Malena said.

"Yes. That's exactly what I was thinking."

"How many of our ancestors were like this too?" said La Venus. The two women were gone now, out of sight, but she could not tear her eyes from where she'd seen them. "Or would have been, if given the chance?"

"I wasn't given the chance." Flaca came up behind Cristi and wrapped her arms around her. "I took it."

"Mmmmm," said Cristi.

"That's not what I mean," La Venus said.

"But it's what *I* mean. What I want to know is how many of our fore-mothers got to *chucu-chucu* with each other. Actually did it." Flaca tickled Cristi and delighted in the way she squirmed against her, under the water, where nobody could see. "Took matters into their own hands."

"Ha! So to speak," said Romina.

"If they did, we'll never know," Malena said.

"No," La Venus said thoughtfully. "I suppose we won't."

"All that *chucu-chucu,* lost in history," said Romina, with an exaggerated, tragic flair.

"Rewrite the history books for us," said Flaca, stroking Cristi's belly in that way she could never tire of, such a miraculous belly, smooth and full of hunger like an eddy that could pull you deep into its whorl. "You're the brilliant historian."

"I am neither of those things," Romina said. "I'm a schoolteacher. I teach propaganda to bored children."

She was a demon, this Cristi, she'd guided Flaca's hand down to the rim of her bikini bottom, under it. Time to swim away. "Well, Ro, if not you, then who?"

*

A few weeks later, they would learn that they'd been right: the woman they'd spied was, in fact, Mariana Righi—and they hadn't been the only ones to see her. A newspaper in Spain published a grainy photograph of Mariana Righi on a remote Uruguayan beach, kissing a woman. The friends would always wonder about the mysterious photographer who'd sold the picture and blown Mariana's cover, their prime suspect being Benito of the Rusty Anchor, who possessed the only known camera in Polonio, though he would deny this charge vehemently for the rest of his life. As the scandal spread, articles in Spain and South America referred to the beach in question, this Cabo Polonio, as a "perverts' beach," a "land of Sapphic urges," a "paradise for *tortilleras, maricones,* and *invertidos* of all kinds."

The words were meant as insults. But the following summer, in late 1983, there would be new visitors, also castoffs. Cantoras. *Maricones.* Seeking the promised land of perversions. And so the change began. They were Argentineans, at first, fresh from the end of their own dictatorship, flush with possibilities, and the five friends who'd been there from the start would drink *mate* with them, share their fire, share stories under the stars. That first summer, there would not yet be many. Just a handful, really. Scraps of humanity, castoffs—the thrown out, the spurned, the invisible, the mocked, the hiding and hidden, the don't come-back-to-this-house-you-faggots—gathered at the world's edge.

Huddled together for warmth. Unfurling their fires. Unfurling what they'd buried since the dawn of their lives.

Not many, but enough to be changed by the seeing.

By the together.

By the glow and burn.

*

Before that, before any of that, six hours after seeing Mariana Righi or a woman who looked just like Mariana Righi on the beach, the women of the Prow had a feast and then rang in the New Year, drunk with hopes for a better future. They were in such a good mood that they even cheered for the fireworks from the lighthouse, even though they'd been set off by soldiers' hands, because what the hell, pretty lights are one thing, soldiers are another, no one would be saved by staying grumpy about a gorgeous sky, so why not revel in the show.

"*¡Opa!*"

"*¡Opa!*"

"Now that's a firework."

"My God, it's 'eighty-three. The century sounds so old!"

"It's an octogenarian. It needs a cane."

"My great-grandmother is ninety-six, and she doesn't use a cane!"

"Well then, it's a spry old century."

"Seriously. We're headed toward freedom—"

"Let's not get ahead of ourselves. We're a far cry from that."

"Things have started. The chink in the dam."

"Chink the dam!"

"Bash the dam!"

"Break the dam!"

"Seriously, *queridas,* I can't help it, I feel hope."

"Me too. Maybe because I just got back, but the country's changed since I left for Brazil."

"Really, Venus? What do you see?"

"I don't know. More buoyancy. Like people aren't drowning in quite as much despair."

"They're drowning in only medium-size despair?"

"Maybe. A medium-to-large river of despair."

"Instead of a Río-de-la-Plata-size river of despair?"

"Exactly."

"I'll take it."

"Better than nothing!"

"People still live in fear. Our prisoners aren't free."

"Oh, Romina."

"What? I'm just saying—"

"I know, I know, I just want to have a moment to feel what's possible."

"Ha!" La Venus leaned toward Flaca. She wanted to keep the mood bright and aloft. "You'd certainly feel that if I showed you what's in my bag!"

"Why? What's in your bag?"

"Something I smuggled in from Brazil."

"What?"

"Wouldn't you like to know?"

"Oh, come on, now you're torturing us."

"Guess."

"Drugs."

"Diamonds."

"Pirate maps."

"Guess again."

"Magic powders from the Umbanda priests."

"That would be good. This is better."

"You're killing us."

"Now you have to show us."

"I can't."

"Why not?"

"I'm not drunk enough."

Roars of protest.

"I mean it, I want to show you but it's too much."

"Too much, how?"

"Oh for God's sake, can't you see she won't tell us without more whiskey? Open another bottle and pour her a glass!"

"Here we go. Like this. A tall one."

"More!"

"More!"

"*Chicas, chicas—*"

"Don't you *chicas, chicas* us, Venus, you said you had to be more drunk, we're helping you."

"We're counting on you to set the tone for 1983!"

"Oh God."

"Well done. Another swig."

"You can do it."

"All right, *chicas*. All *right*!"

"Are you drunk enough yet?"

"Give me a second." La Venus looked around. She was very drunk. The room swelled, swam with candle flames and open faces, so many points of light, as if the world were burning brightly in this room, as if the world were composed of nothing but fires sparked in the faces of the living, as if nothing else could light the void or keep you warm. She wished the instant could last forever. "Yes. I'm ready."

She walked to her bag with the solemnity of a priestess guarding some ancient temple. She pulled out a bundle, unwrapped it. Inside lay a chaos of slim black straps and a red object, long and cylindrical like a piece of tubing, only it didn't seem hollow and had a flared base on one end, a rounded tip on the other.

"What is it?" Romina asked in wonder, though Flaca, holding her breath and furiously aware of Cristi's body beside her, guessed exactly what it was.

"You wear it," La Venus said. "To—" She raised her eyebrows, gestured.

"How—oh."

"Oh!"

"No."

"Ay ay ay . . ."

The women leaned closer, staring.

"Can I touch it?"

"Of course." La Venus laughed, emboldened now. "Don't worry, it's clean."

They touched it, gingerly at first, then with more confidence.

"Where did you get this?"

"Ariella bought it. In the Rio shops. You can get anything in Rio de Janeiro."

"I bet it's the only one in Uruguay."

"Probably."

"The first ever!"

"Perhaps."

"History is being made here, ladies."

"Who wore it? You or her?"

"We both did. Depending on our mood."

This produced a fascinated silence. Never had they spoken so frankly with each other about what they did, about what two women together could do.

"Mostly," La Venus added, "depending on her mood."

"Did she know you were taking it?"

"No. I took it from the drawer. I decided I had the right."

"I can't believe you got it through customs. You could have been arrested."

"I know. I hid the straps with my belts and wrapped the—thing— in a couple of blouses."

"Didn't they check your suitcase?"

"They did. It was a soldier, at the Montevideo airport."

"Did he find it?"

"Yes."

"Did he touch it?"

"Yes."

Cristi, who was holding the red part, dropped it to the ground and stared in horror.

"I've washed it since," La Venus reassured her.

"So what did you say?"

"I—I told him it was a potato masher."

"A potato. Masher."

"He bought that?"

"He seemed to."

"Potato masher!"

Roars of laughter.

"Mash my potatoes!"

"Mash them well!"

"Get that puree going!"

"I wish I had one of those," Paz said.

"I wish you had one of those, too," Yolanda said.

An uproar. Yolanda hid her face behind a curtain of hair. Paz felt herself flush but could not stop smiling like an idiot.

"I was thinking," La Venus said, "that I could—well—you know—share. Lend it out."

"You would do that?" Flaca said, trying hard to sound casual.

"Why not? We're family, aren't we? Just, you know, wash it before you give it back."

"Fair enough!"

"I don't think I'd ever want to use such a thing," said Romina.

Malena said, gently, "And you don't ever have to."

Romina looked at her with love and gratitude, at this woman of hers, who gave so much, who loved so much, I've been too impatient, haven't I, where would I be without her. "In any case, let it be known that we don't need one of those contraptions to mash potatoes."

"Oh, sure," Flaca said. "This is Uruguay. We're a resourceful people. Potato-mashing experts."

"It's a Uruguayan specialty," Yolanda said.

Paz beamed at Yolanda; her first night at the Prow, and she'd gotten right into the flow.

"It's not about *needing* it," La Venus said. "It's just one more fun thing for your—er, for your kitchen."

"But how the hell does it work?" Cristi asked.

"You just—put it on." La Venus picked up the straps, began to untangle them. "Who wants to try?" She looked at Flaca.

But Flaca, staring at the contraption hanging from her friend's hands, knew she could not try it on in front of all her friends, that just the sight of it made her skin burn and the pit of her body ache in a manner she'd never felt before; she didn't know what it meant or what would happen when she closed the distance between it and her; she longed to know, but the knowing would have to be private, in the dark, alone, the only way to meet buried parts of your own self.

La Venus looked at Paz, who flushed and shook her head, then at Romina and Malena, who sat holding hands in a united front of *no,* at Cristi, Yolanda.

"You do it," Cristi said. "Show us, Venus. Please."

La Venus complied. She took her dress off—there was no other way, the skirts would bunch. She was still wearing her bikini from their swim that afternoon. She turned her back to the women and pulled the straps up, clipped, pulled, fastened, pleased that she remembered the way, even now. Ariella slashed through her memory, on the bed naked, impatient—no, Ariella, get away from here, this is not your house, this is not your toy. It's mine now. Ours.

She turned around.

Her friends stared up at her in awe, at their friend, their Venus, standing with her open arms and glorious breasts and hard red cock at attention—the Venus of Uruguay, Paz thought wildly, the Venus of Polonio. A sight like no other in the history of the nation. An altar should be built, right here in their hut, to commemorate the place, the night, the apparition.

La Venus cupped her palms upward, dramatically, as if calling powers from the sky. The lighthouse beam slid through the window and washed her with soft, brief light.

"Happy New Year," she said.

7

Open Gates

FLACA HAD ALWAYS THOUGHT that the end of the dictator-ship would bring relief, even joy, that when the news came—if it ever came—the sky would open and sing blue. But it did not. It hung gray and exhausted outside her window. It was November, late spring, no sign of the summer to come. She was in the kitchen washing dishes as her father sat with a book open before him on the kitchen table, though he wasn't reading it as the radio announcer's voice sidled between them, measured, trying to contain its excitement about the results of the vote: Sanguinetti, the Colorado Party candidate, had won the first presidential election since the establishment of military rule, and would take his oath of office in March 1985, as Uruguay's next president, for a new era of democracy.

Democracy. That word. She hadn't heard it on the radio since her teenage years. The sound of it pierced through the fog of numbness. She wanted the man to say it again and again, wanted to hear it loud and slow, loud and fast, always loud, wreathed in the crackle of public airwaves.

Stubborn grease on the pot in her hands. She had been scrubbing but now found it hard to move. Out of the corner of her eye, she saw that her father was not moving either. The election result was not a surprise. With all the protests in the past year, the workers' strike, all the talks between regime generals and political candidates, this result had seemed to be on its way. What surprised her was the sorrow. How it poured in, flooding. Sorrow a sea filling the kitchen, submerging her, submerging the counter and her father and the knives and the dish rack, so that she stood under its waters, breathing not air, but sorrow. That the Process had swallowed the whole of her adult life so far, the past eleven years, and that now, at twenty-eight, she would never know how much of who she was had been deformed by dictatorship, like a plant twisting its shape to find light. That so much had been lost or broken. And for what.

That her mother had not lived to see the end of it. That she'd died in the middle of the story, in a nightmare that looked like forever.

But it wasn't forever. She tried to force herself up out of pain. The nightmare was ending, or at least shifting. Loosening its hold. Yes, those monsters were leaving the country a mess, with an economic crisis and endless human rights violations, families torn apart by exile, but at least they were giving up the reins. Mamá, can you see, can you hear?—it was not forever—

She turned to her father. Tears clung to his face. Their eyes met and she wondered whether he was thinking of her mother, too.

She put water on the stove for *mate,* and began preparing leaves in the gourd. Her hands trembled. Her father was still silent under the news announcer's chatter. So much silence. So much unspoken. Perhaps if there had not been so much silence in the country, there would have been less silence in her own life. In this house. Perhaps the plant of her would have risen taller and shown itself more fully in the sunshine. Perhaps not. It was too late to go back.

But not too late to go forward.

She drank the first *mate,* then filled the gourd again, and placed it in front of her father. She sat down.

"She would have been happy today."

He nodded. Tears fell freely down his cheeks. It was the second time she'd ever seen him cry; his wife's death had been the first. He brought the *mate* to his lips, drank. "It's a good day," he said. "A long time coming."

She thought of her friends in the Prow, chanting *break the dam!*

break the dam! and for a single absurd instant she imagined that their chants had worked, that they'd cast a spell, had some small part in the breaking. "Papá, I have something to tell you."

He passed the *mate* gourd back to her, his hand grazing hers. "Then tell me."

"I'm never going to marry."

He glanced at her. She couldn't read his expression. He looked down at his book, fingering its pages. "Of course you aren't."

"What do you mean?"

"I mean that—" He closed the book, opened it again. He turned the radio down so that the announcer's voice faded to the background. "That I know."

"Know—what?"

"About you. And your friends."

Breath trapped in her lungs. She looked up, into his eyes. It was all there. Had it been there before? How had she not seen it? Her last serious girlfriend, Cristi, had encouraged her to tell her parents, *if any of us have a family where it's possible, it's you,* but then Cristi was a bold spirit who'd surprised them all by moving out to Polonio after breaking up with Flaca and opening a restaurant there for the gently growing tide of tourists. Cristi was a rare creature. Flaca missed her. "How do you know?"

"Flaca. Please. You're my daughter." And then he smiled. His teeth had grown a greenish yellow, and two were missing now. He was aging rapidly, but his warmth had not abated, he was still the man who'd cleaved meat sunup to sundown to feed his family, who'd given everything for them and would have given more without a thought.

He knew.

Had her mother known?

If she'd done this when Mamá was still alive—

She thought of asking about Mamá, but couldn't form the words. Instead, the child rose up in her, the little girl who'd watched him rake the embers in the grill as if he were the King of Fire, wide-eyed, absorbing lessons that usually went only to sons, and before she could stop herself she said, "And what do you think of it?"

An aching silence fell across the table. *Until,* said the radio announcer, as if from a distant place, then blurred speech from which words sparked intermittently into meaning, *tabulation* and *transition* and *foreign powers.*

"What do I think?" He took the *mate* from her again, but did not yet drink. "I think that you, Flaca, are my daughter. And I think you know how to love."

Flaca blinked fiercely to hold the tears back but when she saw that her father was weeping again she lost the fight.

Her father turned the radio back up, and they sat together in the gray light of spring as a stranger's voice wove cautious optimism into the air around them.

*

That night, at one a.m., Paz went out for a walk, and at first every centimeter of her skin prickled in protest, it had been so long, the curfews had begun when she was a child and been followed by the years of patrols, and now here she was, twenty-three years old, walking at night and defying a regime that had announced its own death. The streets were quiet. She saw no soldiers, no police, not a soul. Dimly she remembered that when she was very small, people would come to the stoops with their *mate* and thermoses, talk, laugh, greet their neighbors as they passed through the hot night. It had been another country then and she had been a different creature. And now? She stared at the strips of light between window frames and closed curtains, the heavy wooden doors carved with the ornate décor of a long gone era, the scant trees, the apartment buildings rising dully toward the sky. Now, what kind of creature was she? What kind of creature would the country become? Uruguay like a snake shedding its skin. She walked and walked and no one came to stop her. A few years ago she'd have long been stopped by soldiers, and even a month ago she would not have risked it. But now the night air cracked open for her, parted and let her through. The cold slapped her face awake. It was November; any moment now the nights would warm and soften.

Then, summer. And at the end of summer, a new president and an end to the nightmare, if it could be true, if the radio could be believed. And then—? What would her life be like? She'd never planned for anything but survival. She reached the river but couldn't bear to stop, didn't know what would happen if she let herself sit, so instead she walked on along its edge, looking out at the black water, thinking that the river seemed to feel the same way she did: ravenous for the world.

As she headed home, she wondered who would be awake when she arrived. It continued to amaze her that her childhood house belonged to her. Ten months ago, Paz's mother had married a wealthy Argentinean and moved to Buenos Aires, where her new husband had gotten a job at a foreign company expanding its operations now that democracy was back, a high-paying job, fancy man, good for him, good for Mamá, who'd always wanted to get away, and Paz had convinced her—not without effort—to let her, Paz, have the house. Not as a gift. Her mother had still insisted on a sale, though she'd lowered the price for her daughter and made absolutely sure her daughter knew how much of a deal she was getting. Paz had used up all her savings from years of smuggling sealskins up the coast, all the building of her illicit business that had now slowed to a crawl because even rich ladies were pinching their pennies these days, sealskin coats were a luxury and the economy had gone to shit, that's what happens when you let a bunch of bloodthirsty generals drive your country into a ditch, but so it goes, no matter, Paz had managed and was managing still with odd jobs of every and any kind, painting houses, construction, repairing the neighbors' pipes in exchange for a platter of freshly fried milanesas, everything mattered, everything counted, and now she had her dream come true: a house in the city to share with friends. A cantora's house. A house for invertidas and invertidos. She had moved back into her childhood room, and persuaded La Venus and Malena to share the room that had been Mamá's. It wasn't at all hard to persuade them; La Venus had been desperate to get out of her mother's house but couldn't afford much on the receptionist's job she'd gotten, while Malena had welcomed the chance to move out of her rented room with the old couple. Paz offered them less expensive rent than they would get anywhere else, and, more important, the privilege of being true to yourself at home. Malena and La Venus made a schedule of when they had the bedroom, and when they had the sofa, and Malena could have Romina over on her nights, while La Venus could have this or that girlfriend over when her turn came. Even now, Paz got shocks of pleasure from seeing friends in the living room where she'd grown up, reading in the rocking chair, having a snack at the table, curled up on the sofa to sleep, as if they belonged there, as if the house had always been theirs.

With the flush of excitement of her new house, and the regime's enforcement waning, Paz began to throw parties. She still kept the music on the quiet side, but she let people pile into the tiny living room, as many as cared to come, and care to come they did. It was remarkable how hidden people found each other. Once you'd been lovers with people, you knew what they were, and they knew that you knew and they brought their new lovers with them and so the web of secret threads wove on. Women and more women, and a few men who either liked men or didn't mind women liking women, or who liked men or women or both but most important wanted to dress as women when the front door was closed and freedom opened its throat. Slowly, they—Paz, the women, and the few men—shed their Street Selves as the nights wore on, becoming people that the streets never saw. Flaca stayed all night, at these parties, and kept a nest of blankets in the basement. Romina stayed too, though less often, caught up as she was in the hard endless work of resistance—which, on this night, was clearly paying off—and when she did stay, she and Malena often retreated to the bedroom early, whether to sleep or talk or make love it was impossible to say. They never took Red, as they'd come to call La Venus's contraband from Brazil. In the year and a half since Red had arrived, Romina and Malena never wavered in not wanting a part in it. They left the friendly bickering to the rest of them—Paz, Flaca, and La Venus—and bicker they did, counting the days until their turn, haranguing when one woman exceeded hers, couldn't she stop, did she think she was the only one who'd found the gates of heaven? There were many ways through the gates of heaven. Red was only one of them. Its own glory. An exotic one, rare and precious like a spice from a faraway continent in the era before steamships. Paz had been shocked to discover that, when she wore it, she could climax right inside a woman, like a man. Or how she imagined it was for a man. She couldn't know for certain, had never seen a man do it, and even if she had she wouldn't know it from the inside. Red became part of her, fused to her body, a conduit for all its heat and pleasure. Was this normal? Did that happen to La Venus, to Flaca? Or was she the only woman on earth who could pour into a woman that way? She didn't ask, she couldn't ask, she lacked the words. Twice, Paz had had an ex-lover come back and ask to borrow Red. Both times she'd laughed. No. No! She'd almost shouted it. She could make new friends, keep old lovers as friends, but Red belonged only to the original circle, her tribe, her family, the women of the Prow, and they were five and would be five forever (or so she thought).

Paz reached her front door and stepped through. La Venus was in the living room, wide awake, surrounded by paintings in various stages of creation, brush in hand. That was the thing about living with La Venus: it was life at the center of a crucible. Who would have guessed that La Venus had had this in her, this explosion of color and vision? I've always had it in me, she'd told Paz, it's just that no one thought to look. I married an artist, ran off to Brazil with an artist, always somebody else's Muse. Was I drawn to artists because they mirrored something inside of me, something I couldn't dare to claim as my own? Well, to hell with all that, I don't want to be the Muse, not for a man and not for a woman, I want to be the artist and to find a thousand Muses hidden in the wrinkles of the world. What are the wrinkles of the world? Paz had asked, baffled, and La Venus had laughed and knocked back whiskey and that was the end of that. She couldn't stop painting. She'd started on canvas but soon realized she couldn't afford the material. So she'd gathered scraps from construction sites, which wasn't hard, as all she had to do was show up in a low-cut blouse and smile and the laborers fell over themselves to give her sawed-off chunks of wood, bits of pipe, used sandpaper, even a couple of hammers that she'd covered in exquisitely detailed vines. Mostly, though, she painted women—on planks and sheet metal, on wood and empty wine bottles: naked women with stars pouring from their hands, naked women at the market with baskets on their arms, naked women holding eggplants and tomatoes in delight, naked women dancing and eating and riding bicycles down city streets. She painted and painted with a joyful fever that eclipsed all other pleasures; she painted when newly infatuated with a lover, painted when the new lover was gone, painted before and after and night and day. Women fell for her like dominoes but it seemed to Paz that none of them stood a chance at La Venus's heart, as it now belonged to painting. She was ignited. She was happy. Even under the regime, she'd managed to be happy. Her favorite book, now, was a used paperback she'd found at the street market at Tristán Narvaja: a translation of *To the Lighthouse* by Virginia Woolf, who was British, and dead now, La Venus said, we were never alive at the same time and yet she saw right into me, this book is my Bible and Lily Briscoe the only Jesus I need.

"Hello there, wanderer," La Venus said without looking up from her project, a plank of wood that was beginning to hold an ocean.

"I thought you'd be sleeping."

"Why the hell would I sleep?"

"There's work tomorrow."

La Venus rolled her eyes. "There's work right here."

"Of course there is. I meant the other kind of work, the boring kind."

La Venus finally looked up from her painting. "I can't believe it's happening."

"Me neither."

"I'm scared to let myself believe and have it taken away again. Anything could happen. March is still a long time away."

"You think they'd stop the inauguration after all that?"

"Who knows?"

"Maybe you don't want to believe because it sounds too good to be true."

"Maybe." She cocked her head. "The real question is, what changes for us?"

"I don't know." Paz lit two cigarettes, passed one to La Venus. That was the question, wasn't it? The end of the dictatorship was a kind of death, not the sad kind, but one that could make you feel unmoored, because your life has been tied to the thing that's died whether you wanted it to be or not. If it hadn't been for the dictatorship, she'd probably have a university degree, the way she'd always thought she would. But then again, if it hadn't been for the dictatorship, she would not have met La Venus or the rest of them, would not be sitting here smoking, at peace in a house from which she'd once run away. "It all makes me feel restless. Like I want to do something. Build something."

"Build what?"

"I don't know."

La Venus took a drag of her cigarette and didn't take her eyes off Paz. Listening.

"I keep thinking about those people we met at Polonio this year. Who'd been thrown out of their homes, called faggots, *marimachos*. People like us. Just trying to live. So we're going to have a democracy— if we're lucky, if all goes well. Are people like us still going to get punished just for being? What good is democracy if we still can't breathe?"

"So what do we do?"

"I don't know. We make space for each other. We don't wait for anyone else to do it. We need a new kind of place. Where people like us can be together. Like the Prow, but in the city."

"Like this house."

"Sort of. Bigger. I had a crazy thought."

"Tell me."

"You'll laugh."

"I won't. I promise. Seriously, Paz, there is no art without crazy thoughts."

"I want to open a bar."

"A bar?"

Paz nodded. "For people like us. Like the visitors to Polonio told us about, in Buenos Aires, in Madrid, that one in New York they'd read about, what was it called, Wall of Stone?"

"I don't remember."

"Well, there's never been one in Uruguay, not that we know of. We need that."

"But would anyone go?"

"Why not? I would. Our friends would. And now, with democracy back, even if they do arrest anyone, there won't be political prisons to throw us in forever. A few days in jail, even a few months, is different from a lifetime." Her own few days in jail shot through her mind, how close she'd come to spending years behind bars. She'd been luckier than so many.

"There's still the fear, though," La Venus said. "Of being exposed to your boss, to your family. That's not going away. If you're found out, you can get fired, then you starve."

"Sure. But my bar won't expose people. It'll do the opposite."

"Which is?"

"Protect them."

La Venus seemed to consider this. Then she smiled. "I see your vision."

"Good," Paz said, "because I'll need your help."

"Don't be an idiot."

"You mean you won't?"

"I mean you always have it."

*

March 1985. President Sanguinetti was sworn in without a coup, without a fuss, and, as promised, he passed an amnesty law: most of the political prisoners would be released.

Romina shook outside the gates of the Penal de Libertad. The trembling shamed her but she couldn't stop. A revolutionary stands strong before the gates of power, defiant, and on a day like this, she trembles? Weren't the gates opening, hadn't they won? But the crowd around her did not feel triumphant, only stubborn in its presence on the sidewalk and fanning out to fill the street. Stubbornness. Longing. Ache. And silence. She stood among hundreds who only wanted their loved ones back and would stand in the cool dawn air as silent as mice if that's what it took to receive them. The regime turned us into a nation of mice, she thought. They pressed together in front of the gate that led to the inner courtyard of that wretched place she never saw without the urge to spit at it and perhaps now, one day, she would. Her mother on her left, her father on her right, Malena just behind her. It annoyed her that Malena stood behind and not directly with them, but what was there to do? It was a family moment, wasn't it, and Malena was, in her parents' reality, just a friend, not part of this, not part of them. Not the way a husband would be, and Romina had failed to have one of those. Still, Malena had insisted on joining them, even if it meant standing behind her like a second thought. Romina was glad she'd come. Her warmth a balm at the nape of her neck.

The double doors swung open and a stir rose in the crowd. Jostling. Murmurs. Names called out, *Joaquín, Tomás, Alberto,* as if names were magnets that could pull men to your side. But how many Albertos were there in the prison? And wouldn't the guards announce who was coming out? Surely there would be a line, papers, some sort of procedure? But there was not. Perhaps it had already taken place inside. No way to know, the guards said nothing, the inner courtyard was filling with prisoners now or rather ex-prisoners and if they couldn't find their families, who cared, not the guards, they could have let the crowd into the inner courtyard, couldn't they? but no, the sons of bitches had to leave the citizenry outside on the street as if to say *we still call the shots around here at least today and don't forget it and if that means you stand in the street where a car could run you down that's not our problem,* though the truth was that no driver in his right mind would drive down this street on this morning, cars did not own it, the people did, spilled in a flood as unquestionable as time, and there were voices now that signaled that they'd seen who they were looking for through the outer gates, *Tomás* became *Tomás! Tomás!* and then dissolved to weeping, Mamá started saying *Felipe, Felipe,* tentatively at first, Romina tried to join her but her throat was so dry she could not speak, she ached, and then the outer gates opened and the crowd outside collapsed onto the crowd inside and to keep from being pushed apart she grasped her mother's hand and her father's hand—where was Malena? no one took her hand, they lost her in the chaos—and in a chain they pushed forward and forward for what seemed like hours until her brother rose out of the blur of bodies and dissolved in their embrace.

The first night was a celebration. Mamá had cooked for three days and prepared a feast of all Felipe's favorite foods: milanesas, chorizo, spinach buñuelos, mountains of spaghetti, canelones, alfajores, chocolate cake frosted with dulce de leche, pebetes, the foods of a little boy's birthday party, enough to feed him for the twelve years he'd been gone. He didn't eat much, but he smiled and cried, mostly at the same time. Uncles and aunts and cousins came to greet him, and Malena came too and didn't seem angry at having been pulled away in the crowd, to Romina's great relief as she carried platters and poured Coca-Cola and tried to smile.

After a week, though, Felipe fell quiet. There was no plan. He was thirty-three years old, and had not finished the university, had never held a job, couldn't sleep a single night without nightmares, what was he to do with his life?

It was a question for all of them: for all the recently released prisoners, the thousands who'd spent the bad years inside. Like ghosts hurled back into the realm of the living. Where before Romina had poured her energy into the struggle for elections, she turned her focus now on gathering the stories of former political prisoners, against the tide, really, because unlike Argentina, where a truth commission had been created to uncover the truth of disappearances, to give atrocities voice and space, here in Uruguay democracy had come with a promise of impunity for perpetrators. It was rumored that the generals had insisted on this before handing over power. *Promise you won't do anything to us and you can have your country back.* And so, military officers could not be tried for the worst crimes committed during the dictatorship, when those actions had, after all, been part of their jobs, and so shut up about the torture, the electric machines, the rapes, the cages without trial, the abuse and starvation, the disappearances, the pain of broken people now released back into the world, you wanted them back, didn't you? Here they are, it's over like you wanted, off with you. Once again, the leaders on the left were divided. Democracy was fragile, and some thought it better to go along with forgetting, only look forward, at what's ahead, leave the terrible past behind, where it can't hurt us anymore. But to Romina, and to others, the past was coming with them whether they wanted it to or not. How could they silence those who'd suffered most? Granted, many of the former prisoners preferred not to talk. Felipe was one of them. He just shook his head when she tried to broach the past, wouldn't meet her eyes. But there were those who wanted to tell their stories, who only in telling their stories could find their way back to the outside, and these were the people Romina went to see, whose stories she gathered and gathered even when they shattered her, even when she wanted to scream that she couldn't take another minute and it couldn't really be that they came for you *again,* that they did that and also *that,* and she came home each night exhausted, shaking, raw as if her skin had been peeled off, as if the world had shattered into so many pieces that you could no longer walk without shredding the soles of your feet. With Malena now living in a house where she could openly be herself, Romina slept over there more and more often, despite her parents' obvious discomfort at her sleeping anywhere other than at home, as grown women do not sleep at other grown women's homes, not even spinsters, though they stopped short of asking too many questions as if they might accidentally brush against information they did not want to touch.

Romina wept in Malena's arms.

"There's so much pain," she said one night. "We'll never clean it all up, we're going to drown in it forever."

"Maybe," Malena said. "Maybe not. There's always been pain."

"Not like this."

"Not exactly like this. But what about the Nazis?"

"I mean here, in Uruguay," Romina said. "We've never had it here."

"The Nazis are nearer to us than people think."

"What do you mean?"

"I mean I met one once."

"You mean—a sympathizer?"

"No. I mean a Nazi."

Romina sat up. "Where?"

Malena tensed, hesitated. "Nearby."

She waited for Malena to say more, but nothing came.

Later, for years, for decades, until the final days of her life, Romina would regret not probing further, waiting longer, listening as gently and as widely as she could. Instead, she felt a flash of annoyance at her lover, who was not Jewish, bringing up Nazis as a way to dismiss Uruguayan pain. "Look, in any case, you don't have to tell *me* how bad the Nazis were. What I'm saying is that people are broken, thousands of them, and everybody wants to sweep it under the rug."

"I'm not one of those people," Malena said, tightly.

"I didn't say you! Don't be so defensive!"

"I'm not—never mind." Malena turned to the wall. "I'm sorry. I'm stupid. I should have just listened with my mouth shut like I usually do."

"What is that supposed to mean?"

"Nothing."

Romina reached out a hand and touched Malena's back. "Let's not fight. I can't take it."

Outside their darkened room, laughter spiked and receded, La Venus and Paz telling stories or flirting with a girl, carrying on as if there were still joy to be stolen in the world.

"I know," Malena said.

*

The basement transformed, brick by brick. It was the right kind of setting, low-ceilinged, windowless, impossible to see into from the outside, like a dungeon, and yet it had a front wall that faced the street, just high enough for a low door to be set in, a door for duendes, a door for cantoras and *trolos,* for invertidos, a door, Paz said triumphantly, for us. She had very little money to build this bar, so she did as much as she could with her own hands. She stripped back plaster. Dug out dirt from the basement. Dug out the crawl space that had once hidden subversives, including Puma, a cave that now became exposed to the light. Years had passed and the air molecules in there would be different ones entirely, and yet Paz stood for a moment, excavating that space, and inhaled as deeply as she could, as if to draw in particles of the past. Then she moved on. So much to dig and scrape and cut and plaster. It was dank down there, but there was space enough to carve out a long room. It took over a year and all her friends' help to dig the space out, wire the electricity, route water for a rudimentary bathroom in the back, plaster the walls, tile the floors, and install a door in the front wall, for which she built steps out of scavenged bricks and mortar so that when you entered from the street you immediately descended, head ducked, into a small alternate world.

By then she'd been back to Cabo Polonio and learned more, from the new Argentinean friends, about the bar up north in New York where *putos* and *maricas* had fought back against the police who harassed them, long ago in 1969, when she herself was eight years old. A bar named Stonewall. Wall of Stone. It had become famous in North America because of that riot, during which, the *argentino* said as they glided through water, the sissies and cross-dressers and outcasts had thrown stones at the police, and after that they started changing. Changing how? she asked, bobbing in the ocean waves. By being loud. Paz thought hard about this. She and her friends were not loud, not unless they knew that they were completely alone. Fighting back against the police in Uruguay, in '69 and especially a few years later, once the democratic government fell, could mean the end of wholeness, the end of safety. Even now, to be exposed meant the end of your life as you'd built it. And so she'd said, we can't be loud here, not like that. But, the *argentino* said, it's not like it was safe for them either, you know. People like us are never safe, not even in a place like New York, the heart of empire. Safe is never given. Safe is what you make with your own hands.

She named the bar La Piedrita. Little Stone.

There was no sign, of course, and no doorbell. You had to know about it, and to knock with the rhythm of an old nursery rhyme, *arroz—con—le—che,* before someone sized you up through the peephole and let you through.

She left three of the four stone walls exposed. She built in jutting shelves, as she'd done in their hut, and these she filled with pebbles and shells gathered in El Polonio—this was essential, as La Piedrita was in many ways an extension of the Prow, a carrying of that haven into a single underground room in the city. El Lobo, excited to help Paz create her own business, gave her sea lion and seal bones that had been stripped of flesh by the Atlantic and by time, and these La Venus painted with fanciful patterns and mounted in elaborate shapes on the wall. Hip bones splayed like butterfly wings. Ribs radiated from a central sun. Paz also found treasures for the walls at the stalls of the Tristán Narvaja street fair: spoons and glasses, aging postcards, curious pictures of wild animals, even yellowed books that had mysteriously survived the purges to seek rebirth on new shelves. This was her bar and there would be books in every corner, stacked and stashed like pirate treasure. There were more used goods than ever at Tristán Narvaja, perhaps because people were less afraid now of exposing what they'd had, but also because the economy was in shambles and as exiles returned to a city with no jobs, more people looked around their houses each day with eyes for what could bring home a few pesos. Once, in a stack of old records, she found a photograph of Rosa Vidal, a famous Uruguayan singer from the Old Guard of the tango, now living out her old age somewhere in Ciudad Vieja, who, in her time, had been known for performing in men's clothing, which was common knowledge though Paz had never seen a photo of her in that state, until now: there she was, in a man's suit, hat cocked to the side, leaning against a wall with a swagger of a smile. Paz could not breathe. She stared at the picture for a long time as the bustle of shoppers crushed around her. She bought the photo and made a frame for it herself, out of salvaged wood, and hung it on the back wall, behind the rudimentary bar where she'd preside, she thought, the way El Lobo did at his own counter in Polonio: with an old ship captain's calm.

And so she did.

She opened in February 1986, at the height of summer, as Carnaval filled the city with song, glitter, drums, lit nights. It started with her friends and their girlfriends and ex-girlfriends, plus the ex-girlfriends' new girlfriends, and a few *montevideanos* they met out at Polonio who'd been excited to hear the news of this place. Small scattered groups. Some nights were boisterous, some vacant. No matter. People came when they came. Paz put on music and women danced with women, men with men. If they shouted for tangos, she played tangos. Brazilian samba, Sandra Mihanovich, the more-beloved-than-ever Mariana Righi, the new sounds of Madonna and Michael Jackson: she complied. After the first couple of months, she built a platform along one wall that could, on some nights, act as a stage, and over time performers began to volunteer themselves: men dressed as women, women dressed as men, singing the old songs and some new, because, here at La Piedrita, you could do what you wanted: a man could wear a candombe dancer's glittering bra and plumed skirt and dance to shake the heavens, and a woman could don a fedora and sing the old tangos of Rosa Vidal, of Azucena Maizani, those singers who in the 1920s and '30s had so exuberantly invaded the terrain of men.

La Venus became known for her rendering of "El Terrible," wearing all her regular feminine clothes and an old man's hat that lived behind the sofa (which lurked in the corner by the bathroom and was always devoid of light and partially hidden by a curtain tacked to the ceiling, ostensibly to keep the bathroom out of view, but actually because Paz knew how rare privacy was for invertidos, she herself had had sex in public bathrooms and if she didn't provide a sofa her customers might never get the chance to pee; the sofa was always occupied by bodies pressed together and everyone respected the unspoken code of averting gazes while waiting for the toilet, it was a tattered thing, that sofa, stained, worn, a sacred space) and as she sang La Venus slanted that hat over her eyes in a manner that struck lust and awe into the heart of every woman in the room.

Money didn't come easily to La Piedrita. Nobody had much of it. And yet people came, even if they had to make a single drink last for hours to stay, or simply order nothing and sit in a dim corner at a table built out of repurposed crates to watch reality turn inside out for the night. It didn't matter how much or how little people paid. Paz was determined to keep things afloat, to hold on for as long as she could. She worked at the bar four nights a week, with La Venus covering two other nights, and Flaca one. Flaca, of course, didn't need the money, the butcher shop provided for her and her father, but she couldn't bear to be left out of an enterprise like this one. She thrived there. Her shift at La Piedrita was a welcome respite from the hard work of her days, which she spent running the butcher shop and keeping house and caring for her father, who had had a heart attack and needed the additional support, and though this was exhausting, Flaca told Paz, it was also beautiful to spend evenings at home with him, talking in ways they hadn't for years, catching up, It's really something, Paz, he's not just accepted me but my girlfriend, too, these days Virginia sleeps over and he doesn't say a peep, in fact he treats her like a daughter-in-law or even like a daughter, he begs her to read her poems to him, they laugh together like thieves in the night, and it's the strangest feeling, utterly foreign, I don't even know what to call it; wholeness, perhaps, or solidity, I don't know, I feel like an asshole even talking about it since I know most of us won't ever have it, but I can be honest with you, can't I, when my sisters bring the grandkids on Sundays we're all a big family and the happiness is fierce, concentrated, as if we're making up for years of lost time.

One night, in the middle of 1986, as winter pummeled the streets with icy winds that pushed customers into La Piedrita for the warmth of whiskey and a smiling face, as groups huddled around the tables and the windowless room thickened with breath and human heat, Paz caught herself looking up at the door as another woman, a stranger, walked in down the steps. *Is it her, is it—?* The thought shocked her. That it would spring up so fast and fierce in her own mind. The woman was not her, not the one she'd been waiting for, or bracing for, or both, without knowing. Puma. Puma like a twisted piece of driftwood that could wash up on her shore. Puma, whom nobody but Paz understood. Would she ever come to a place like this? Would she find it, want to see? Would they recognize each other? Would there still be a spark? Would she remember this very basement and understand that it was the same place where—? Puma. Paz ached to know what had become of her. Whether she'd been imprisoned, escaped to exile, survived the Process years or no, and, if she'd fled abroad, whether she'd decided to come home or to stay in her new, transplanted life, as many exiles were doing, because it wasn't so simple to return. Back then, when Puma hid in the basement, in 1974, there was no place remotely like La Piedrita, nowhere for her to see herself, find herself, or even safely show her face. Was she still the sort of woman who would seek out a place like this? It wasn't clear she'd ever been such a woman; it wasn't clear what kind of woman she'd been. She'd been the woman in the basement. Paz could see it better now: how broken she'd been, how hungry. She, Paz, was twenty-five years old now, older than Puma had been back then. She'd been a bold guerrilla, Puma, but she'd also been a terrified girl of twenty or so. Tortured and fleeing for her life. Had she poured that terror into loving Paz? Had she done something she'd later recall with horror or shame? Perhaps. Impossible to know. The stranger who'd just walked into La Piedrita reached the bottom of the steps and now stood underground, in the light of dim lamps, taking in the surroundings. She was not Puma but she was here, alive, needing a smile or a cigarette or a friend. Paz waited for her to look over so she could meet her gaze in greeting, thinking, what I can't give to Puma I will give to the Pumas of the world.

"Have you heard?" Romina said. "Ariella's back in Uruguay."

La Venus didn't look up from her painting, but her hand tensed around her brush. "I hadn't heard, no."

"She has a concert next month."

La Venus stabbed the tip of her brush into red paint. Mixed. Hard, too hard. It was not the thought of Ariella that stung, but the thought of Mario. How tall he'd be now. She imagined him with his face leaner, his eyes the same. She couldn't peel an orange without thinking of him, the delight on his face when the peel came away a perfect snake. She had never stopped hurting at the thought of him across town at his grandmother's house, one long bus ride away, yet out of reach. "Good for her."

"You don't mean that," Flaca said, pouring the *mate*.

"Do I have to?"

"No. You certainly don't."

They were in the living room of Paz's house, which, in truth, they all treated like their own home. It was a Sunday night, at eleven o'clock, almost time to open the bar. It was Flaca's turn to work, and she was enjoying one last round of *mate* before heading downstairs. They were all together: Romina, Malena, Paz, Flaca, La Venus, and Virginia, Flaca's girlfriend, in a languorous mood after having enjoyed a *parrilla* in the little patio in the back, where, as they all knew by now, Paz and her mother had once upon a time burned books, in another world, in another life. Dirty dishes towered in the sink. The house still smelled of smoke and roasted flesh. They were warm from wine and company, loathe to disperse.

"Are you coming down tonight, Venus?" Flaca asked.

"I don't know. The painting calls me."

"So does the dance floor," said Paz. "We always sell more drinks when you dance."

"Venus, goddess of the night," Flaca sang.

La Venus smiled. "We'll see." She knew that, when she danced downstairs, she became the center of the room if not the universe, and often it thrilled her. But it also tired her. For what she wanted was to paint. To be the one who looked, and not always the looked at, a role that came too easily to her, unbidden. People lavished their stares on her. She had to protect her power to look, to create, to be the shaper and not only the shaped. For a long time, she'd only painted for herself, hanging things around the house and downstairs at La Piedrita. The galleries downtown had no use for a woman who painted naked women, so she wasn't taken seriously until, in recent months, she'd started offering the galleries landscapes inspired by Polonio—ocean, shoreline, the lighthouse rocks—painted on urban castoff items such as bricks, planks of wood, battered kitchen pots. She meant it as a statement on the longing for nature in urban life, or maybe on the way your mind could carry oceans inside it no matter where you were. Either way, it didn't hurt that the objects were cheaper than canvas and easy to find. This series had just had an opening at a tiny gallery in Ciudad Vieja, the only one she knew of that was owned by a woman, Doña Erminia, the rich widow of a famous painter. The installation made almost no money, of course—the economy was so bad that no one had the money to buy art—but it had been well received, with good reviews in two of the smaller newspapers that had reopened with democracy's return.

"Well," Virginia said, "I, for one, want to see what you paint."

"Well, thank you, Virginia." La Venus beamed. "And what about you? Any new poems?"

Virginia shook her head. "Nothing that's ready to share."

"Oh, come on," said Paz. "Please. Your poems are beautiful."

Virginia turned and met Paz's eyes. "And how long has it been since *you've* read us a poem?"

"That's different."

"How?"

Paz shook her head. She wrote, sometimes, but it was scraps—her love of books never quite translated into writing of words of her own. She'd come to believe that her creative work, her truest art, was held in three things: her nights with lovers, the hut on the beach, and the bar in the basement, all of them perversions according to the world. But she couldn't speak this. It would become laughable the second she did. "I'm not a real poet."

"Oh, come on!"

"I mean, you're *named* for a poet!"

"So?"

They stared at each other, Virginia and Paz. It was a brief shared gaze, not longer than a single breath, but Romina saw it, and so did Flaca, who held her breath until Paz looked away, at the *mate* gourd in her hands. Never once had Paz stolen a girlfriend from Flaca. They were deep and loyal friends, nothing to fear. And yet. That look. As if they already shared a secret common tongue. Poetry. Maybe the spark was nothing more than that. Flaca was no fancy reader, she'd never even gotten through *Don Quixote,* not even when it was assigned at school. Virginia, on the other hand, was well read, a self-taught scholar of Latin American literature, named for Virginia Brindis de Salas, who, she'd told Flaca, was the first black woman to publish a volume of poems in the history of Uruguay and possibly in all of South America. Her parents had read Brindis de Salas's verses to her along with nursery rhymes, dreaming, for her, a life that transcended the cramped poverty of the *conventillo* they lived in until the dictatorship government forced them out without warning, displacing their whole community in one fell swoop to the periphery of the city, where she lived until, a year ago, they finally returned to their old neighborhood of Barrio Sur, *though most of us,* Virginia had said, *have not returned, they scattered us from our neighborhood without a reason, just to break our community, just to get rid of black people, and even now, tell me who's talking about our displacement in the news, or in City Hall?* She was as politically passionate as Romina, volunteering with a black community newspaper, *Voz Negra,* that had revived after the dictatorship ended, and that frequently published her articles and poems. She also lit candles to Iemanjá, the African goddess of the ocean, and knew all the traditional drum rhythms of candombe by heart, could tap them

out against her chest or thigh with perfect precision; and when the
neighborhood drums came to beating life, thirty strong, sixty strong,
she danced as if the sound had been deep in her bones since before
Uruguay, before ships, before time. Flaca found Virginia's writings to
be brilliant, intimidating. Here was a woman who cleaned houses for
a living and whose mind burned as fiercely as the sun. They'd met at
the street fair of Tristán Narvaja, selecting zucchini from a grocer's
stall, and had conveyed all the essentials through the linger of hands
on green vegetable flesh. They'd been together now for almost two
years, longer than Flaca had ever spent in a relationship, and she knew
that Virginia had the power to become the third woman to break her
heart.

"So," Paz said, "some people write, the rest of us just scribble."

"You don't really believe that," Virginia said.

Paz shrugged, trying not to smile.

"We need all sorts of scribbles, not just poems," Romina said,
thinking of the enormous number of articles and communiqués she'd
penned in recent months on behalf of the rights of exiles, of former
political prisoners, of those battling against the impunity of perpetrators. The work continued, essential, unending, unpaid, thankless. She
wrote opinion pieces for party leaders, men whose names graced the
bylines on pieces she'd written. Doing what was best for the movement. Who wanted to read an opinion credited to her name? Sometimes, now, she attended meetings with Felipe, as he started emerging
from his shell. It was good to see him doing better, and a relief, too,
that her parents now had him to focus on, to shower with their wor-
ries and attention, so that there was less scrutiny on her. She reached
out for Malena's hand, but when she clasped it, Malena did not clasp
back. The limp fingers alarmed her. Malena had been remote lately, in
and out of foul moods, drinking more heavily than ever. They bick-
ered more often. *You don't control me,* Malena had said to her the last
time they fought about the drinking. And maybe she was right. Maybe
she should back off and give Malena more space. And more attention.
She should devote more time to her—though just the thought of this
exhausted Romina, a weight piled up on so many other weights.

"On that note," La Venus said, "I have news. There's a Paraguayan painter who's been invited by the Ministry of Education and Culture, and remember Doña Erminia, the owner of the gallery that showed my work?"

"How could we forget Doña Erminia?" said Flaca. "I've never seen so many plumes on a lady's hat."

"Well, she's hosting an evening reception for the *paraguaya*. And I want you all to come meet her. Her name is Diana Cañeza and I'd bet you a thousand pesos she's one of us."

"One of *us*?"

"No!"

"You can't be serious."

"How can you know?"

"I've seen two of her paintings—"

"Let me guess: she paints like she's licking pussy?"

"Let her finish!"

"Thank you, as I was saying: she doesn't have a husband. And the way she paints women's bodies—there's something luxurious about it. I don't know how to put it."

"You want her. You saw her paintings and you want her!"

"I didn't say that."

"Ha, as if you have to."

"The thing is, Venus, you say everybody's a cantora."

"Probably because she could make any woman want to sing!"

"Ha—"

"Now, that's not fair," La Venus said. "Not *everybody*. For example, I've never said it about Doña Erminia."

"Now, *that* would be interesting!"

"Oh god, I don't want to think about that."

"Why not? We're all going to be old one day. Don't you want someone to love your naked wrinkled body and—"

"*Ay,* that's enough!"

"No, it's not, I want to hear exactly what happens to her naked wrinkled body."

"So do I."

"It should be whatever the old lady wants."

"Do her bidding, that's what I always say."

"No one here doubts that about you, Flaca."

"Well, as for me, when *I'm* old and wrinkled, I'm going to have plenty of *chucu-chucu.*"

"How can you be so sure?"

"We have to believe in ourselves!"

"Maybe by then we'll be able to kiss in broad daylight without fearing for our lives."

"Ha! You must be drunk!"

"I haven't had a drop."

"So, what, we'll be having orgasms in the plaza too?"

"Apparently."

"The last thing I want is the men of Montevideo watching me do the deed."

"I'm with you. I'd rather be a criminal pervert forever."

"A criminal pervert octogenarian?"

"Why not? That's more than our foremothers could have dreamed."

"*¡Epa!*"

*

The reception for Diana Cañeza was an elegant affair, in Doña Erminia's gallery downtown. Flaca searched the crowd for the mysterious Paraguayan. The paintings were voluptuous, large canvases full of warm colors, some of them stylized images of animals bursting from cosmic, life-giving stars, others realistic portraits of women drinking coffee, lying naked in a boat on a river, looking out of a window at a brick wall. The women were haunting, and Flaca could see why La Venus had been captivated by this artist; they seemed to share an obsession with their female subjects, with trying to bring their inner worlds to life on canvas. Or maybe she was just projecting. She knew nothing about art. It was a sacrifice to come to this reception; why did appreciating art have to involve wearing a dress? She felt costumed, false, even though the dress she wore was deeply plain, the same one she'd worn to the opera with La Venus that disastrous night years ago. Her one dress. Given to her by her sister from her arsenal of dresses. She chafed at the feeling of no cloth between her legs—the things I do for art, she thought, though in truth she was doing it for her friend.

And to see the mysterious Paraguayan. If La Venus tried to flirt with her, and the flirting was returned, she wanted to be there for the show, didn't want to miss a thing.

But it was Romina who saw the Paraguayan first.

She hadn't been looking for her. Hadn't been looking for her life to change.

She'd been standing in a corner with Malena, each of them lost in her own thoughts, Malena taking deep sips of her cocktail, Romina's mind roaming to the campaign speech she was writing for a mayoral candidate, a man with excellent leftist politics and an outsize self-regard. She had to get his voice just right to hide his arrogance, to help him connect with the people. The room was noisy, too crowded; maybe they'd leave soon. She didn't want to meet this painter, even though the paintings took her breath away, perhaps *because* they took her breath away; she was tired of brilliant people and their egos. She'd been teaching all day and still had her unpaid work, the unfinished speech, waiting for her at home. She wanted nothing more than to get those pages done and go to bed.

And then she saw her.

Diana, the painter. Smiling at a man who was expounding to her about God knew what. As if she could feel attention on her from across the room, she turned and looked directly at Romina.

Romina could not breathe.

The world collapsed into this moment, the meeting of this woman's eyes. This woman with a gaze that took in everything. Calm yet utterly solid. She was older than Romina, in her late thirties perhaps, in a green dress, commanding in a manner that belied her size, a small woman with an enormous presence and lush black hair loose around her shoulders that made Romina think of the rainforests of neighboring countries that she'd heard about but never seen, full of wild things, hidden labyrinths, damp relentless life.

She thought, with a panic, that the painter might come over and speak to her—and then what would she say? what would she do? But she did not come. Romina decided not to leave the gathering after all, and for the next hour, she was keenly aware of Diana's movements, where she was and who ringed her, as if a thread stretched between them, a spider's thread, glimmering and inexhaustibly strong.

By the time La Venus found her in the crowd to introduce her to the guest of honor, it felt almost as if they were sharing a secret, that they were past introductions, that the category of strangers was for them a kind of farce.

Flaca saw it.

She saw their first shared gaze and also saw Romina crossing the room with La Venus, it couldn't be, it wasn't possible, she was not watching a disaster begin in slow motion while Malena trailed behind her lover, smiling because she saw nothing, nothing at all.

*

Two days later, they met in secret, on the Rambla. Romina had looked for Doña Erminia's number in the phone book, as she knew Diana was staying there. Diana had not sounded surprised to hear from her. The call was brief, just enough to set a time and place. It left Romina shaking. What was she doing? She didn't know. Since the reception, she'd spent every waking minute in a fever, lit from within. She had not felt this way in years. It had never been this way with Malena. Even in the beginning, Malena had been a solace and a salve, a warm nest of a woman, while this was something else. Combustible. She hadn't felt this way since Flaca—an almost laughable thought, since she'd no more feel that way about Flaca now than about her own brother. But back then, it had been pure heat. Long ago in the early days. Before the Only Three. Before the coup. Before the world had shuttered. She'd thought that aspect of her had fallen forever into ash. Hadn't known embers of sharper lust were glowing underground, for all these years, biding their time.

They both arrived at the river's edge exactly on time.

"Do you drink *mate*?" Romina held up the gourd and thermos. It was an awkward greeting but she couldn't think of anything else to say.

"What do you think? I'm Paraguayan, of course I drink *mate*."

"I'm so glad—"

"*Mate* comes from the Guaraní people, you know."

Romina flushed. "I do know."

"My ancestors, they were the first."

She started to apologize, but then she saw the smile on Diana's face. She poured, and handed Diana the gourd. Diana studied her intently as she took it. Their fingertips brushed and Romina felt it like an electric pulse.

They began to walk slowly along the shore.

Diana took her time drinking, then handed back the gourd. "You never drink *tereré*?"

"What's that?"

"*Mate*, but made cold, with ice."

"No. Never. *Mate* is always hot for us, even in summer."

"In Paraguay, the heat becomes so intense, you would long for tereré."

Romina thought of heat, of Diana in the intense heat, slick with sweat. "I'd like to try it sometime."

"I could make it for you."

Romina waited for her to add *before I go* but she did not.

They walked in silence along the Rambla.

Diana was the first to break the silence. "How strange, the Río de la Plata."

"Why?"

"It does not look like a river. It is so wide."

"It's an estuary, really, but not the ocean."

"I have never seen the ocean."

The gentle deliberation of her words. You had to go quiet inside to make space for each one of them to land in you. Spanish was not her only language; at home, as a child, she'd spoken Guaraní. Romina wondered which language Diana thought in, or whether her thoughts lived in the space between languages, like a river that belongs to neither shore.

"I—we—my friends and I have a little house, a one-room house on a beach up the coast, on the Atlantic. We've been going there for years."

"What is the beach called?"

"Cabo Polonio."

"Cabo. Polonio." Each syllable savored. "I would like to see that place."

What did she mean? Was she flirting? It was impossible to tell. The signals were so different. Romina had only been with two women: young bold Flaca, and Malena. This was another universe entirely. A woman who was neither brazen nor pliant. A self-possessed woman who seemed to know herself so deeply that her sphere of knowing extended to you, who you were, what you wanted, what you didn't know you held inside. A woman from a vastly different country, from a world of rich rainforests, bleak poverty, melodious Guaraní.

"What other places would you like to see?"

Diana stopped walking and turned to look at her. The river lay behind her, flung open, stabbed with light. Romina thought that her eyes had no need of anything in this world that was not Diana. "What do you wish to show me?"

"Everything."

They stared at each other for long enough to dispel all the veils, dispel all doubt, and it amazed Romina that it could be so simple, so direct, that the path into the forbidden was in fact wide open right in front of you and that stepping onto it could be a kind of rightness, a vitality more powerful than fear.

"Then do."

*

It was only after they checked into a room that Romina realized she'd been to this hotel before, years ago, before the coup, as an eighteen-year-old seeking privacy with Flaca. Now here she was again, suspended in her own desire as if desire didn't live inside you at all but instead it was you who lived inside your desire, as if a woman's wanting could be oceanic, vast enough to be swum, to be submerged in. Dimly, she recalled a way of thinking in which it was wrong to be here with a woman who was not Malena, but that way of thinking seemed old, decrepit, entirely unclasped from reality, and its signal was drowned out by Diana's passion, which unfurled with an intensity that took Romina by surprise. She surrendered. She dissolved. She was everywhere and nowhere, naked and relentlessly alive.

Afterward, they lay in a slash of light that stole through the closed blinds.

"You could stay," she said. "Here, in Uruguay."

Diana was silent for a long time. "Is it possible?"

"I don't know. We could find out. I have contacts who've helped exiles return from abroad. Maybe they could help you as well." She hesitated. "Would you want to live here?"

Diana looked at her for a long time, a stretch of time in which Romina lost herself and found herself again. "You have no dictatorship. You are back in the light. While we, we have suffered under Stroessner for over thirty years and how do we know what else awaits us?" She stroked Romina's arm. "And yet, my family is in Paraguay. My mother, my brothers and sisters, my nieces and nephews. And I know what my oldest brother would say: he'd accuse me of abandoning our land for a nation that tried to destroy us."

"What?"

"The war."

World War Two? Romina thought. But it couldn't be. The Korean War? Uruguay had sold wool to the United States for soldiers' uniforms, but what did that have to do with Paraguay?

"The war of the Triple Alliance. It is very much alive for us. We have never healed."

You mean the Paraguayan War, Romina thought, and then she was bathed in shame. She taught this war to her students, of course, but as distant history, a war that ended over a century ago, in 1870, Uruguay had joined forces with Argentina and Brazil to invade Paraguay, and yes, there was devastation, the history books acknowledged this with generalized sentences, but still. That it would be very much alive. That Uruguay would still be seen through its prism. Paraguay was a much poorer country than Uruguay; did the people of Paraguay blame the war for this? And if so, were they right?

"Of course, he's a conservative one, my brother. Always over the top."

"Ah."

"And then, there is you."

Romina held her breath.

"Delicious you."

"I am delicious?"

"Yes." Her tone had lifted now. "But fruit does not stay sweet forever."

"I'm going to rot?"

"No. That is not what I mean. You might tire of me. And then? I have left my country, my family, and so?"

"I could never tire of you."

"You have a woman now."

She looked away, embarrassed. "Yes."

"You've tired of her."

"That's different. It was never like this, with her." She stroked Diana's thigh. "We started together a long time ago, I was young and in pain, more so than I knew. I was only taken for three nights—" Her throat closed up.

Diana looked at her for a long while. "Nights, years. It does not matter. They can break us in an instant." She put her hand on Romina. "But you survived."

Her phrasing was so careful, delicate in its simplicity, as if the indigenous Guaraní language flowed under the surface of all her words, all her thoughts. Hers was a different Spanish, a living Spanish of earth and river and ancient bones. It soothed Romina, and dazzled her, all at the same time, like a river the first time it surrounds you. "My brother was tortured for months. Imprisoned for twelve years. Everybody else suffered more than me."

"Suffering has no measure. There are no scales to weigh it. There is only sorrow after sorrow."

It was the first time anyone had done this for her pain, removed it from comparison, given it scope and space. Romina felt a burning ache inside her and thought she might dissolve into tears, but instead there was something else, a rising up, a verdant stalk of possibility. She saw her future anew, as a series of potential paths, and only one of those paths seemed lit by happiness. "Stay with me," she said very quietly. "Please. Forever."

*

She told Malena in the plaza on her lunch break, where they sometimes met for empanadas while Romina was on summer break from teaching. It was how they'd first met, eating empanadas in the plaza, how many years ago was it, ten, almost ten, though it seemed much longer, more than a lifetime ago. The sun was bright, the bench bereft of shade. She didn't look Malena in the eyes.

When she was done, Malena stared at the pigeons and said nothing for a long time.

When she finally spoke, it was the last thing Romina had expected to hear.

"You never asked me what I did for the Prow."

"What? What are you talking about?"

"The extra money I brought in, so we could buy the house. Remember? Where do you think it came from?"

Romina felt thrown by the sudden swerve into the past. She'd expected tears, hurt, perhaps pleas or shouting, but this she had not prepared for. "I have no idea, but listen—"

"No, *you* listen. You don't have any idea, because you never asked in all these years." Malena's face was shut tight, and she'd drawn back, a hunted animal, primed to attack or flee. "You've never wanted to know me."

This is Malena, Romina told herself, not a stranger, what on earth is she talking about—and yet nausea rose up in her, a kind of vertigo, and to steady herself she gripped the seat of the bench with both hands. "That's not fair."

Malena made a sharp, barking sound. "Fair!"

"Please don't shout."

"Stay away from me," Malena said, and she strode off before Romina could think how to answer.

*

"No. Romina, no," Flaca said, too loudly, forgetting for a moment that she'd called Romina from the butcher shop and a customer could walk in at any moment.

"What else am I supposed to do?"

"Stand by our friend, that's what you could do."

"I'm trying to. That's why I told her."

"You don't know how fragile she's been."

"You don't have to tell *me* she's fragile. I know, believe me."

"And you don't give a shit?"

"Flaca! What was I supposed to do?"

"Not fuck another woman?" Flaca said, regretting the words as soon as they'd left her mouth. She couldn't push Romina away, not if she wanted to be the bridge between her friends and help put things right again. She, Paz, and La Venus were all worried about Malena. She stayed locked in her room, even on the nights when it was La Venus's turn to use it—and this was deeply unlike her, to disregard an agreement she'd made with a friend—and she only emerged to go to work or to the bathroom. She'd stopped bathing, stopped eating, only drank. Whiskey bottles multiplied on the floor. It had to stop, but Flaca didn't know what to do.

"How dare you? How many times have you cheated on a woman? And taken forever to come clean!"

"We're not talking about me. And it's not the same."

"Of course it's not—you get your own special rules."

"Calm down, Ro—"

"You've never been with anyone as long as I've been with Malena, so what do you know?"

"I don't cheat anymore."

"Who cares? You've done it before, and I haven't."

"Fine. But this is different."

"Because?"

"You're everything to her. And she's really struggling."

"So what am I supposed to do? Deny my truth? Hurt myself to keep from hurting her?"

"No, but—I don't know." Flaca stared at the glass cases full of meat, red and tidy piles, cut by her own expert hands. Her head throbbed. Romina's news tore at something deep inside her, the circle of friends that was, aside from this cluttered little shop, her most important life work. They were each other's refuge. Each other's everything. It seemed a deep betrayal—not the sex, but this abandoning of Malena in a time of need, Malena, who was theirs, who was part of the pact they'd made years ago, around a fire, under the lighthouse beam. "We've always put our friendships first. Before anything else. We're each other's family, remember?"

"Malena would be the first to tell you that we don't owe our families our lives. Not even our blood families. She's always said that family doesn't own us, we get to be free."

She had to try another approach. She made her voice as gentle as she could. Romina didn't know, after all; she hadn't seen Malena in this state. It had to be explained to her somehow. "Ro, *querida,* listen—"

"No, wait, Pilota, you listen."

On hearing *Pilota,* her old nickname from the early days, Flaca's voice caught in her throat.

"What's the point of living the way we have all these years, breaking everything, the rules, our parents' hearts, our place in society, like it's all so much crockery, only to slouch back now into some old idea of duty? Of how horrible it is to be a home-wrecker, or betray a marriage, or some bullshit like that? I don't even have a marriage! There was never a contract to sign." Romina took an audible, gulping breath and barreled on. "You used to call marriage contracts a duping of women, designed to keep them down. Remember that? You said all kinds of shit about how only women like us could be free. Yes, I know you were drunk as a sailor when you said it, but you still said it, Flaca. So if not even women like us can follow our hearts, if even cantoras have to chain themselves down, and if even people who've spent their whole lives sacrificing everything for the resistance can't have a fucking taste of happiness when it finally comes their way, then what the hell kind of planet is this?"

A pause.

Flaca's turn. Her mind raced. There were infinite possible responses to Romina's words, enough to overload her mind. "I'm not asking you to be chained," she finally said. "I'm just asking you to be Malena's friend."

"I tried to be her friend."

"Keep trying. Please. You're the one who knows her best, the one with the best chance of reaching her."

"Ha! Give me a break. She's refusing to talk to me."

"That's because you're still with the Paraguayan."

"Fuck you, Flaca."

"Please calm down—"

"You're such a hypocrite."

"I know, I know, I'm a big slut. But Malena is family. And she needs us to stand with her—she needs—" What did she need? How to say it? What would pull Malena out of this hole? They'd been trying, she and Paz and La Venus, but nothing broke through.

"I need to stand with *me,* Flaca. Don't I ever have that right?"

"Of course you do, it's just—"

"Then don't ask me to give up Diana, ever again."

In the tense silence that followed, Flaca saw that the fight had been futile all along.

*

Two weeks later—once Romina had begun working on Diana's paper-work and making plans to find them an apartment, because she was finally doing it, finally moving out of her parents' house, to be with her new love—Paz called to say, in a shaking voice, that Malena was gone. She had disappeared from their house, leaving most but not all of her clothes and books, her bed made as neatly as ever, and nobody, not her boss, not her friends, not her neighbors, had any idea where she was.

8

Broken Water

IN HER LAST DAYS IN MONTEVIDEO, Malena couldn't stop thinking of herself at fourteen—how she split in two, what split her, the wholeness before that—so ferociously that it seemed as if time itself had collapsed and dropped her into its rubble. Fourteen. A fiery girl, Malena on fire, that's what she'd been at first, caught up in the spectacular illusion that the world lay open before her. So long ago now. Centuries ago, or so it felt. It was a lie that time healed all wounds. A vicious lie. Some cuts never seal right, and the best you can do is layer things over them—noise, days, love like a false skin—and turn your attention anywhere and everywhere else.

She'd tried to escape it all these years. The pain, but also the brightness before it, which was even more cutting because it gave measure to the loss.

How possible the world had felt. How clear. Fourteen, and before that, since the beginning of memory. At four years old she'd run on the beach and the wind had loved her hair; at eight, she'd sat on a park bench eating an ice cream cone and feeling alive in the most delicious animal way, marveling at the pigeons and the way she could kick her legs while the statue of some fancy man could not: he was large and male and important, everything she wasn't, but she was the one who was alive and she would kick and kick because of it. At eleven she'd been shaken to tears by a sad book whose title she no longer recalled, only that there was a sick girl in it with big dreams and a tragic future. For days, she wept, remembering the book, and after that her own dreams came into focus: she'd become a doctor one day and discover the cure for cancer. Why not? She was good at math and ravenous for life. Her parents always seemed a bit afraid of her, of her wildness, which did not fit into their strict ideas of how a girl should be, but they approved of her goal of becoming a doctor, as long as she also became a goodwife. So she was happy, she was normal, she was whole.

The first sign of trouble came when she was twelve.

She was in church, bored by the sermon, staring at a painting of the Virgin during the Annunciation. Her family was more devout than others; her mother took her children to Mass every Sunday and taught them from an early age to pray. To love the Virgin and be humble before her. The Virgin was pure. She was holy. And yet, gazing at this painting, Malena thought that the Virgin was also beautiful, flushed with ardor that was presumably for God, who, she'd just learned, was going to put his seed inside her body. Her hands were crossed over her breasts, her eyes half-closed in pleasure as the angel Gabriel told her his news. Malena wanted to be the angel Gabriel, the one to cause this heat in the Virgin's cheeks, the rapture on her face. Dimly, she understood that this was not the right way to love the Virgin, but it was too late. At night she dreamed of growing wings and flying to the Virgin's home to tell her of the seed that would be entering her, to watch her slow surrender to the entering.

Then, at fourteen, Malena met Belén.

She was a year older than Malena, fifteen, though so shy that it felt the other way around. She lived three doors down. One day, Malena had stolen a glance at Belén and found her staring too. It had grown slowly, the hum between them, at the delicious pace of honey spreading across a rugged table. The first kiss had been hurried and electric, in Belén's bedroom with the door open and her parents watching television a few meters away. The second time was in Malena's living room. Open heat. As natural as singing to the trees. As impossible as trees who sing back. It was obvious that these were things you were not supposed to do, and yet they felt so right that Malena did not question, did not stop, any more than she would stop herself from breathing. Belén's skin was full of songs, Malena made music against it with her fingers, and it all should have been perfectly safe because it was cards night and her mother always stayed out late when playing canasta at her sister's house, the house of Tía Carlota, and her father was working late, her brother studying at the university, so the house was theirs, or so they thought, the world should not have ended that night, her mother should not have come home unexpectedly to see her daughter topless with her hand up the neighbor girl's skirt. Later, Malena's brother would explain to her that Tía Carlota had sent her guests home soon after they arrived because her daughter Angelita had had the bad manners to show symptoms of coming down with the flu, that is to say, she'd vomited right into the bowl of green olives. For this reason Malena's mother had come home early, enjoying a leisurely walk through the streets after dark. It was 1965 and there was nothing suspicious, then, about walking after dark, or about congregating in a group of five or more to enjoy a game of cards. You could just walk, back then, or gather and play, and no one even thought to see these freedoms as precious things, possible to lose. Malena's mother, on that evening walk, had not yet heard of Tupamaro guerrillas, nor had she heard of girls who put their hands up the skirts of other girls; one of these forms of innocence was broken when she burst in on her daughter in the living room. Years later, as a thirty-five-year-old woman attempting to escape the life she'd built, Malena would look back on that night and wonder fiercely what would have happened if her cousin Angelita had not vomited into the olive bowl and thereby set in motion a subtle yet violent shift in destiny. Would she, Malena, have continued as the curious, expansive girl she was before? Would she have kept meeting secretly with Belén, long enough to feel the treasure between her legs without that thin cotton that barred and thrilled her fingers at the same time? Would she have become a doctor? Would she have been happy? Had there ever been a chance for her of such a thing?

Her mother in the doorway. Sharp intake of breath. A gasp as if fighting not to drown. *No,* Malena thought, and then, wildly, *you're not here.* She pulled her hand away from Belén, and Belén shrank from her, a double retreat, but it was all too late.

"I have to go home," Belén said, reaching for her coat as if for a life raft, head down in shame, and when Mamá said nothing Belén rushed past her and was gone.

Her mother didn't speak to her that night, and woke her the next morning for school with a tight face. Malena might have thought it had all been a dream, if not for her mother's brusque movements as she made *mate* and toast, and her father's refusal to meet her eye. He also knew. She kept her eyes down on her toast. Her stomach in knots.

"Why is everyone so quiet?" her brother asked. And then, leaning toward her conspiratorially, "For goodness' sake, Malena, what did you do?"

His joking words fell flat at the center of the table.

At school that day, she couldn't concentrate. Couldn't eat. Belén was not in class. What would she say to her parents that night, if given the chance to speak?

The chance came after dinner, washing dishes, Mamá's back to her. "How could you? How could you do something so—disgusting?"

Her hands trembled. "I'm sorry," she said, flooding with shame, not for what she'd done, but for this lie, a betrayal of Belén and of the butterfly thing they'd fleetingly become.

"This is not how we raised you."

Pray for us sinners went the Hail Mary, which her mother sometimes murmured as she stirred tomato sauce or breaded meat for milanesas.

"You promise me that you'll never do anything like that again."

Malena froze. Her mouth would not move to form those words. Stubborn mouth, rebelling against the mind, insisting on shapes of its own.

Her mother turned to look her in the eyes for the first time that day.

Malena tried to hold her gaze. That look. The deepest revulsion. She hadn't known her mother was capable of such a face. She hung her head and stared at the floor tiles.

"Malena." Her mother's voice was shaking. "You have to promise."

"Look what you're doing to your mother." Her father, from the doorway, how long had he been standing there? "She's trying to give you one last chance."

A crack in the floor tile. Hair-thin, right in front of her feet. She'd never seen it before. She traced it with her eyes. Silent crack. Silent Malena. One last chance for what? One last chance, or what?

Her mother started to cry.

"I told you, Raquel," her father said. His stout body seemed tense, like a wire, like an arrow in a bow. "Sin has taken hold in her, it's no use." His voice, too, was unfamiliar. "Come on, let's go to bed."

He left.

Her mother followed.

Two nights later, Malena and her mother boarded a boat to Buenos Aires.

Her mother didn't say anything about why they were crossing the river, or for how long, and Malena didn't dare ask. They rode across the Río de la Plata all night, and Malena didn't sleep, nor did her mother, who kept her eyes closed, but Malena knew her mother so well, the way her chest and eyelids settled heavily when she slept, the deepsea rhythm of it, and knew this was a different kind of closing. Pretended sleep. The boat cut the black water, drank the starlight. Malena had no jacket, no hat. *I'm cold,* she thought of saying to her mother, into her ear, shaking her arm, but she didn't dare. After the way her mother had looked at her in the kitchen, she would rather brave the bite of night air.

Once in Buenos Aires, they took a taxi through the city, and she watched the proud streets blur by through the window. It seemed a grand city, majestic and sprawling, an unlikely place to seek atonement. Maybe her mother was visiting that old high school friend who'd come to live here with her diplomat husband. Maybe she wanted to do some shopping at the boutiques that everyone knew had more to offer than anything in Uruguay, fashions fresh from Paris, something to distract her from the horrible pain of having a disgusting daughter, but then why would she bring that disgusting daughter along? To keep her from getting into trouble? As a way of forgetting? Wipe the canvas, begin again, nothing happened here. Maybe.

The taxi pulled up in front of a nondescript building on a tree-lined street. Only later would Malena realize that she hadn't caught the name of the street, or the name of the neighborhood, had no idea where she was in the maze of the city, and how can you plot escape when you don't even know where you are? Everything was large in this city, startling. Larger than anything in Uruguay. She'd thought she knew big cities, having grown up in the capital of her country, but Buenos Aires made Montevideo look miniature, almost toylike. They entered the building and a clean, polite nurse led them down the hall to an office. Malena followed, thinking, why a nurse? Her mother was sick? And hadn't told her? In that case she'd burdened her ailing mother with more problems. Shame burned her. She'd be a better daughter, she would find a way to help.

"In here," the nurse said brusquely, looking right at Malena.

Malena entered and put her suitcase down. Her arm ached from carrying it.

"Sit there until the doctor comes."

Malena did as she was told. Just as her weight arrived in the chair she heard the office door shut behind her and a key turn outside in the lock. She was alone in the room. And trapped. Her mother had not come in with her. Why not? Mamá, where are you?

*

She knew what she was going to do, and knew, even, that it wasn't Romina and the *paraguaya*'s fault, not really, it was all more complicated than that, much more complicated than anybody wanted to know. Including herself. She was tired of hearing her own mind. She took a room in a drab hotel at the outskirts of the city so she could put her suitcase down and find a bar. She walked. It didn't take long to find one. She ordered a whiskey and cupped her hands around it in a posture of prayer. A liquid rosary, she thought as she drank. What would the nuns from the Convent of la Purísima have to say about that?

Everyone else had been lifted by democracy, allowed somehow to expand the edges of their lives. Political prisoners were free. Exiles were returning. Journalists exercising their right to harangue. La Venus had picked up her paintbrush, Flaca's father loved her as she was, Paz had opened a bar for cantoras and *maricones,* one fucking miracle after another, and now this, Romina in love, everybody finding room to breathe. Everyone but her. The world pressed down on her unbearably. It had surprised her, at first, that the more the dictatorship faded into the distance, the more bleak she felt inside, when the rest of Uruguay seemed to be swimming in the opposite direction. As if she were dragged by currents only she could feel. When the battle had been everywhere, the bleakness around them all, she'd at least been able to connect with others in the stream. Carrying Romina had given her meaning, a way through the world. Romina had needed her, and this need had made Malena matter, given her a corner of the world to tend. It was more than that, too. They had merged souls, or so she'd thought. She, at least, had surrendered her soul to the merging. Loving Romina had completed her, given her refuge, streaked her days with blessing. She had been home inside Romina's arms. Romina and the Prow: the only two homes she'd ever known. With all that gone, she'd lost her anchor, and there was no replacement; nobody wanted to carry Malena the way she'd carried others, nobody wanted to see what she'd seen, she was useless, exhausted, a burden on the world, every day a fight against drowning.

A man sat down beside her, bought her a drink. Yes, she thought. Enough thinking. Try to be normal, isn't this what a normal slut would do? He was middle-aged, hunched over from years of office work, and didn't seem unkind. Sadness beamed from him. Also longing. If she were a normal woman, would she want him back? Could pretending to want him make her normal?

They didn't talk much.

It was all so easy.

She let him walk her to her room. He seemed kind enough, but as he thrust his way toward climax, she saw that the question she was asking her body could only have one answer. The disgust she felt for him was slight, and tinged with pity, but the disgust she felt for herself was so intense it took her breath away. The man sped up, mistaking her reaction for arousal. She should have known better. Than to think. That she could not be. What she was. Tomorrow, she thought. Tomorrow she would get on the bus and head northeast.

The man collapsed against her in a sweaty heap and stroked her shoulder with a tenderness or gratitude that made her ache with sorrow.

*

Her name was taken. Stripped away. *You'll have your name back,* Dr. Vaernet said, *when you're ready to be discharged.*

I'm not sick, she said, still thinking that her mother would burst in any moment and somehow explain the mistake, even though, by then, she'd already been held down by three nurses to be injected with she didn't know what, even though she was restrained, now, by belts on a bed in a bare white room.

You are.

I don't feel sick.

His eyes were a cold blue. He had a thick accent she couldn't place. *That, child, is exactly the problem.*

Call my mother. Please.

That's enough, Fourteen ninety-one.

That was her name now. 1491. The patients wore their numbers on the insides of their forearms, written in permanent marker that the nurses refreshed each morning along with breakfast and medications. It was hot in the clinic, despite the season, because the windows were tightly sealed and the air was thick, so the patients all wore short sleeves that left their numbers exposed. She didn't see the other patients for the first few days, which she spent restrained in her room, but she heard their shuffling footsteps in the hall. Later, she'd see that they were mostly male, one young woman. Speaking between patients was forbidden. Her mind was a thick fog, so that it became more and more difficult to hold on to time, to think of her mother, to formulate sentences that could insist on release, to remember the reasons for kicking and struggling against her restraints. The world blurred. The nurses called her 1491, and she wanted her name back, wanted her name to fill her ears, chanted it to herself quietly in the night, Malena, Malena, but not during the day as when she said it with nurses in the room they slapped her and said, 1491. Time melted, so she didn't know whether it was on her third or fifth or thirteenth day that she was wheeled to the Room for the first time. The Room had gray walls and black machines. The light was dim. Two doctors stood in the shadows, the one from the first day and a younger one, both with the same cold blue eyes. Her mind was a slow beast, she couldn't understand, why were they attaching wires to her forehead, armpits, the meeting of her legs? Why were they reaching up her gown as if into a bag of potatoes? Fingers that attached the wires and lingered there, slithered against her where nobody had touched her except herself when she wiped, the younger doctor's clammy hand. She could not close her legs, they had been tied apart. The shocks began. Time shattered. Rubble of it everywhere. She tried to scream. Something over her mouth. Survive it. Shards of yourself, grasp them. Live through the instant. Now this one. This one. Seconds too long, minutes unthinkable. Finally it pauses and the voice comes. *You will answer our questions. We are here to fix you.* Her mouth is back. She says *call my mother call my father.* The man's voice says *your parents asked us to do this, it's their will* and laughs a little before saying *a little more.* She says *No* says *no no no* but the wall swallows her voice and the pain takes her skin and shreds it into pieces.

Later, she would learn that the worst part of electroshocks was the way they burrowed into your flesh and stayed there, ready to spike without warning hours later when you were alone in your room, in the middle of dinner, in the middle of sleep. Electricity, intruder. Stowaway in the hurt ship of her flesh.

Later she would see many things.

She must be changed.

She was plagued by aberration.

It must be expunged from her.

The doctors, they knew how to do that.

They had methods. Machines. Surgeries they spoke of sometimes in triumphant tones.

Her mother had brought her here. Her father had sent her. It was their will.

She had to be broken.

She had been so wrong, the way she was, that she needed to be broken.

She struggled to rise over these thoughts toward another place, the one she'd known before, in which she could be alive, in which she had a name.

But she couldn't reach it. She was in too many pieces and before she could gather them they flung apart again.

She had been left here.

There was nowhere else to be.

She tried screaming.

She tried begging.

She tried praying to a God in whom she could not believe, a God who must surely hate her to have flung her so far away from what He saw as good; prayed to nothing; prayed to the void yawning around her.

She tried submission, made herself as pliant as the surface of a lake. An outer calm that would stay with her for many years to come.

A psychologist came to her room twice a day. Asked her a list of questions, about her impure thoughts, when they had started, how often, what they entailed. She never knew what she was answering. What her voice would do next.

The doctors had the same last name. Father and son. The son was already beginning to go bald. He came into her room at night without his clipboard. You have to learn how to be a woman, he said, though very quietly, as if he didn't want anyone outside her room to hear, and then he put his hand under her hospital gown and touched her in places that had been electroshocked and places that had not, and then he took her hand and wrapped it around his sex and moved it back and forth until he finished on her nightgown, which stuck to her after he was gone.

You wet yourself in the night, the nurses said in the morning, disgusted. And she had no reply.

But one of them, one morning, stood looking at the stain for a long time. She had moonlike eyes in a gentle face, and when she looked up at Malena her expression was sadder than anything Malena had ever seen.

The following night, the nurse with the moonlike eyes appeared in her room. "Fourteen ninety-one. Are you awake?"

She nodded, afraid to speak.

"Are you—all right?"

She shrugged. It was not a full answer but it seemed dangerous to say more.

The nurse sighed. Her voice went quiet, secret. "To be honest, you don't seem like a bad girl."

The rough covers made her legs itch but she didn't dare scratch.

"That older girl, she must have pressured you. I heard your story. Poor thing."

She couldn't breathe. There had been a girl. Her name. Her name. Belén. A wisp of brown hair in the darkness. Ache.

"Listen. I've got something to tell you. You're on the surgery list. For the brain procedure, the lobotomy."

Brain procedure. Not a good. Think, damnit. Not a good thing.

"Your parents can't help you, they haven't been told. Dr. Vaernet is eager to try it out on a female, you see"—she broke off—"but you're too young, don't you think, who knows, you might be able to change on your own, with the right guidance, but not if at night—" She paused. Took out a pack of cigarettes, fumbled to light one. "Anyway. I can't let it happen, can I?"

She couldn't see the nurse's face. Her silhouette a plush darkness in the bare room. She had to think. Shouted at her own mind to wake up. Awake. This could be a trap, a complicated ruse set in motion by the doctors: see which patient agrees to rebellion, then report to us. A spy. But if it wasn't? If this nurse, who was also a young woman who lived somewhere in Buenos Aires and was also, try to see it, a human being—if this nurse sincerely wanted to help? Cigarette smoke filled the room, the scent of the outside world, and she opened her mouth to gulp in what she could.

"Honestly," the nurse went on, "he just wants to keep on doing surgeries. He doesn't even know whether it'll work. It's all experiments to him, the way it was on those poor people in the camps—" She clamped a hand over her mouth. "I'm talking too much. Did you know about that? About the concentration camps?"

She shook her head, though the gesture was shrouded by the dark. Horror beginning to creep through her.

"Of course you didn't, why would you know?" She took another drag, blew out smoke. Her hand shook. "Dr. Vaernet was a Nazi. Is a Nazi. He worked for the concentration camps in Europe, operating on homosexuals—they let him do whatever he wanted—let him—" She stared at the wall as if it hid the missing words behind it.

Her limbs. She could not feel her limbs. Body cold against the bed. Her mind went lucid and she understood two things: first, she was in a worse place than she'd known; second, the longer this nurse's visit went on, the less chance that the young Dr. Vaernet would come tonight. Keep talking, she thought. Go on, go on, even if into a nightmare.

"Then after the war, he was going to be tried for war crimes but he got away and came here, and so, those bastards at the Ministry of Health what do they do? Send him back? No, why do that when you can give a monster money to keep hacking people up?" The nurse was weeping now. "They don't know I'm half Jewish. I shouldn't be telling you. My mother—her family—she escaped as a girl but they—"

Malena had never seen an adult cry like this. Sobbing and ferociously restrained, all at once.

"I didn't know, I swear I didn't, when I took this job. Only later did I suspect. So I went through his papers and—oh, child, I'm sorry. We've got to get you out of here before—" She broke off again.

She turned her face up to the nurse. One word she'd said hung in the air like a rope. *Out.* She pushed herself to speak. "What do I have to do?"

*

The bus ride northeast to the town of Treinta y Tres was green and open, fields and low hills dotted with occasional huts. Malena had never been to Treinta y Tres, and didn't plan to stay for long. She wanted to see Belén. Thirty-six-year-old Belén. She didn't know what she'd do if she succeeded. She wasn't even sure whether Belén was still there. It had been about a year ago, soon after the democracy began, that Malena had run into a childhood classmate at the grocery store and had learned, in the course of their brief chat (Malena always tried to keep such conversations brief so as to avoid too much probing), that Belén was now married to a hotel manager in Treinta y Tres. Malena had stored that information in a deep recess of her mind. But it surged up without warning, sometimes, pushing her toward her third or fourth drink of the night. What was Belén like now? The last time Malena had seen her, she'd been running out of the front door in shame. And in that moment, that Belén-running moment, Malena had still been whole, not lost, not yet split in two, still the seed of a future woman that she, Malena, would now never become. A woman who'd never set foot in Buenos Aires, though perhaps she might visit for the theater or the architecture, the cafés, the bright lights of Avenida Corrientes, the bookshops that never closed, the city's famous pleasures. A woman who only knew of electricity as a source of light (and yes, that woman-she-could-have-been would still see electricity become a source of horror in her country, but even that was different from the clinic because government torture, at least, would one day be known by the masses, people like Romina would gather testimonies, survivors would be held in reverence, stories would be told and

decried, and this telling, this decrying, would give the horrors room
in the fabric of the world). The woman Malena could never become
would have finished school and gone right to college. Become a doctor. Fulfilled the whole-girl dreams. Lost-girl dreams. Where was she,
now, the lost girl? The one who'd touched Belén's thighs with a pure
joy? She wanted to find her. Wanted to search for her in the face of
this older, married Belén.

Treinta y Tres was a plain, sleepy town. She'd thought she'd have
to do some detective work, but there was only one hotel, which, she
learned, was on the main plaza. She walked there, carrying her single
suitcase, working up a sweat. There was no trouble with booking a
room. That night, she sat in the plaza, where she was thankful that
none of the locals tried to talk to her, so she could stare in peace at the
statue at the center, which depicted the thirty-three men for which the
town was named, who'd bravely fought for Uruguay's independence.
Revolutionary heroes. Their faces frozen into expressions of bravery
and pride. Only five of them in the statue, to represent the thirty-three,
because, she thought, the country they'd fought for was still poor and
could not afford a bigger statue. Five, for Uruguay, was not so bad. The
sculpture sang of action frozen in time, arms raised in every direction.
Though the men were all the same dull greenish color, she could tell
that one of them was black from the form of his nose and the tight
curl of his hair, and she could hear what Virginia would say, *we've been
written out of all the histories,* which made Malena think of her old living room and Flaca with her arm around Virginia and Paz passing the
mate gourd around and La Venus painting and clucking her tongue at
the unwriting of histories and the pain of it stabbed Malena, that she
was gone from them now, from the only real family she'd ever known,
and they probably hadn't even noticed, had they, she washed away the
question with a long swig from the whiskey bottle in her hands.

She didn't see Belén that night in the plaza, nor in the hotel halls
the next morning or the morning after that. Finally, on the third day,
she said casually to the man at the front desk, as she renewed her room
for another night, "And, are you the manager?"

"No, *señora*."

It irked her, this *señora*, made her feel old and worn. When had she stopped being *señorita*? "May I speak to him?"

The man looked worried.

"Just to give him my compliments."

"Ah, of course. As it happens, he's away on business."

"I see."

"I can give him the message."

"Thank you."

"They'll be back the day after tomorrow."

"They?"

"He traveled with his family."

"Of course." His family. So she wasn't here either. "How nice, that he has a family. Do they live nearby?"

"Right in this building, *señora*."

"Isn't that lovely."

Two days more in Treinta y Tres, and there was no anonymity in this little town but no one asked her what she was doing there and for how long, even though she now knew every crease on the faces of the waiters in the hotel restaurant and the bartender down the block and corner store clerk who now rang up her grappa bottles with an easy smile, and she could guess what they thought of the sad thirty-something-old woman who was not a *señorita* and who didn't smile because, for fuck's sake, she didn't have to, and she also knew every crease now on the faces of the five frozen revolutionary heroes in the plaza of Treinta y Tres.

On the appointed evening, she sat in the shabby little lobby with a book in her lap, pretending to read. The poems of Sor Juana Inés de la Cruz. The book had been a gift from Paz, and for this reason she couldn't bear to focus on it. The black letters were simply a place for her eye to land. She waited. She turned a page. Sor Juana had been a nun, in Mexico, centuries ago. A verse of love to a woman. What did that mean? What was she saying? What did this Sor Juana know about women and love? Absurd question, she didn't know a thing, she was dead. Dead people know nothing. Dead people rest. Finally the door opened and a family entered. The man in front, a woman and three children behind. The woman was plump, stern-faced behind heavy makeup, exhausted from the journey or whatever life had thrown at her, overseeing the children like a sea captain bent on squashing any mutiny. She looked steely and capable, like so many matrons found throughout Uruguay, her unhappiness only visible in the tightness of her jaw and the blankness of her eyes.

The children were bickering breezily about something. The mother swatted one of them, raised her gaze, and saw Malena. Their eyes met.

It was not her.

It was a woman called Belén but there was nothing left in those eyes of the fifteen-year-old girl she'd been.

Malena went cold inside, then hot. What was she doing here?

The woman stared at Malena, as if trying to complete a puzzle whose pieces had flung to the winds.

"Mamá! She won't stop!"

The woman turned to her daughter, and in that moment Malena slammed her book closed and escaped the lobby before the woman could approach, because the hunger to speak to her had vanished now, replaced by the need to escape.

She reached her room and closed the door, heart thumping in her chest.

She crumpled to the floor without turning on the light.

The carpet smelled of mold and rain and artificial lemons.

Almost a relief. To know that it was done. No escape left from the tunnel, just the passage through.

Still she lay there in the dark for a long time. Through loss of time. Through a long dark melting of time. Half-waiting to see if a knock might arrive at the door, a question from the past, but nothing came. Grappa. The bottle on the nightstand. She crawled toward it, sat up, drank. Tomorrow she would go. She longed to go. She was done with everything and everyone.

And yet, that night, at four in the morning, she found herself picking up the phone and calling Flaca, dialing numbers as familiar as her own name.

*

The plan was as simple as it was dangerous. The following night, at 2:30 a.m., Adela—for that was the name of the renegade nurse—would unlock 1491's bedroom door and leave it shut. Fourteen ninety-one would wait at least half an hour, then slip down the hall past the dozing guard, through another door that Adela would secretly leave unlocked, and out into the night, where Adela would meet her two blocks down. From there, she didn't know what would happen. She couldn't think beyond the night. Her whole future collapsed into the coming hours of darkness and a vision of two doors. Two waiting doors.

She lay awake, not daring to doze and miss her cue. It wasn't hard to stay awake. The challenge was not to succumb to the fog. The younger Dr. Vaernet did not come. No way to know why some nights no and some nights yes. She filled her mind with the two doors, and thoughts of a brain cut beyond repair. Before and after. Click. The unlocking. Soft steps, moving away. Had anyone else heard? Electric bolt through her limbs, through the core of her. So much electricity had run through her by now that she could generate her own. It rose without her calling it. Shock. Shock. Silence in the hall. Safe for now. Half an hour, wait. She had no watch, there were no clocks, how would she know? Time had melted in this place, gone sticky. Viscous time. Try to think. Try to count. A minute. Another? What if she waited too long? What if Adela gave up and left their agreed-upon corner, abandoning her in this maze of a city with nothing but a drab hospital gown to her name? She sat up in bed. *Go.* To the door and down the hall on feet she willed to float.

The night nurse was in fact asleep—she brimmed with thanks—and she poured slowly down the stairs, aching to run, holding back into silence. She reached the doorknob, which chilled her hand and turned smoothly and *push!* she was out on the street. Bare feet on pavement. Night air a sweet whip. Never had she been so happy to be cold. Two blocks sped by as if her legs were jaws, opening and closing, ravenous.

Adela was at the corner, huddled in a coat and scarf. She draped a coat around her, gave her a pair of shoes that were too big but still a relief, and interlocked arms with Malena. "Let's go."

They walked in silence for a long time. The streets were quiet at this hour; it was a sleepy neighborhood, residential, with majestic trees and little corner groceries, bakeries, and butcher shops interspersed among the apartment buildings and ornate houses. All these people, sleeping and dreaming just a short walk from the nightmare. They couldn't know—and if they did, would they care? She began to flag. Electricity, call it back. Shout it through the body. Wake up.

"What's your name?" Adela said.

A sting of fear as the name poured back into her tongue. "Malena."

"Malena." They walked on. "I can't take you home with me. You understand."

"Yes," she said, though she understood nothing, not even her own breath.

"If they find you there—I'd lose my job, and, worse, you'd get dragged back."

Their steps rang out. A car growled by.

"You have to leave Buenos Aires."

"Of course," Malena said, though she hadn't thought that far ahead. Out, she was out—it was all she'd been able to see.

They turned onto a wider street: cars, cafés, music spilling out to the sidewalks. Adela flagged a taxi and pulled Malena in with her. They drove to the port, where it was still dark. The ferry station was closed. A sign said it wouldn't open until 6:00 a.m.

"Your boat is at six twenty-five," Adela said. She handed Malena the bag she'd been carrying, a ticket, and a wad of bills. "It's not much," she said apologetically, "but it's all I could do. You'll be dwarfed by my clothes, I'm afraid. But you'll be all right—you'll be home soon."

Malena stared down at the bills, ashamed, flooded with alarm. Home. Where was that place? If she went to her parents' house, would they send her back to the clinic? She saw her mother's face, that night in the kitchen, bathed in disgust. Heard the voice again, *Your parents asked. Their will.*

Adela gave Malena her ID card, stolen from the clinic files.

"You won't mind if I leave you here?" She glanced around her. "We can't be seen together."

She looked so panicked that it suddenly occurred to Malena that the nurse might change her mind, drag her back to the clinic, report her. As long as she was on this shore and Adela knew where to find her, she was not safe. "Of course. I'll be fine."

Adela nodded, then opened her mouth, as if compelled to speak. But then she turned and walked away without another word.

The ferry terminal opened and the boarding began and even then Malena kept seeing Adela running her way, shouting madly, or police officers in angry hordes, or the two Drs. Vaernet with lab coats rising around them like pale wings—but none of that happened. She set foot on the ship. From a sign on the wall she learned that it was a Wednesday, and that over four months had passed. The unhitching from the dock set off tremors in her belly. Water folded around her, black and sleek as the night sky. She watched it from the window until sleep rose up and mauled her from within.

She woke to the sound of chatter around her, from her fellow travelers. It was evening; the trip was almost over.

As soon as she saw her city—or, rather, the city that had once been hers—the thought arrowed into her chest: she had nowhere to go. The port teemed with people. A few women stood along the edge of the dock, scanning the disembarking men for possible work. *Mujeres de la calle,* she thought. Women of the street. That was how she'd heard them spoken of. They stood tired and erect in the growing darkness. She shouldn't be staring, they could glance over at any moment, she should avert her eyes, but before she did a thought tore across her mind.

You could become one of them.

It was a way to live, wasn't it?

A place to go.

Dr. Vaernet the younger's hand, forever closing in.

She hurried past them, averting her eyes.

She walked and walked that night, through all the city, thinking of calling her parents, afraid to call, afraid to be sent back. She had only two goals: to stay alive, and to stay free of the Drs. Vaernet. If she went home she could not meet the second goal. Which meant she could not meet either one. She walked her city, Montevideo, avoiding the eyes of strangers. She was a fourteen-year-old girl alone. Show me, she shouted in silence at the city. Show me there's a shred of space for me somewhere.

The only building that spoke back to her was a church. Its doors opened just before dawn. Look, it said. Look at my doors, how tall and wide they are, when so many doors are closed.

She went inside, crossed herself with holy water as she'd learned to do, and sat down in a back pew. Her legs were tired and she welcomed the rest. But she also felt tense with fear. House of God. And she with so much shame and so many sins she could not speak.

But where else?

There was a convent in the back of the church. She'd seen it from the street, the small cluster of nuns through the window, like the cluster of women at the port only turned inside out. She would lie to them. She stared up at the crucifix over the altar, at Christ's painted blood, as she formed her plan. She would tell them she'd been pressured into prostitution and had run away from the room where she'd been left with her first man. She would be vague and weepy about what had and had not happened in that room. She would be sinful and suffering, stained and innocent, all at the same time. She would tell them she was sixteen, a little older, and that she'd always felt a boundless love for God. That last lie was a slippery one, shot through with a new horror, for hadn't the Nazis embraced Christianity? Hadn't there been a crucifix on the wall of her room in the clinic, and even in the Room with the machines? But she would have to find a way to make the lie believable. To infuse the word *God* with enough passion for the nuns to take her in. She leaned forward in the pew and stared at the red slash on Christ's torso. When she said the word *God* she would replace it in her mind. She would tack another word beneath it like the lining sewn beneath the surface of a dress. Every time she said *God*—or *Christ* or *Holy Spirit*—she would secretly, in her own private code, be saying the word *forgetting*. *Oh, Forgetting, hear our prayer.*

*

Flaca answered with a thick, groggy voice. "Hello?"

"You used to be up at this hour."

"What? Who is this?"

The hotel room swirled. She'd opened another bottle of grappa. Another swig. "You don't know me?"

"Malena? Malena." Rustling. Audible breath. "Where are you? We've all been looking for—"

"I'm not in Montevideo."

"Then where?"

In Treinta y Tres, which is sleepy and boring but also a sweeter place than you'd imagine, and I'm spending the night in the same building as my first love but, ha-ha, it's not what you think. "Outside."

"We're all worried about you."

"Oh, really?" She was shamed by the bitterness in her own voice. "Romina's crying all day?"

"She's worried too, Malena—of course she is. We all are. Please. Come home."

She gripped the phone cord. "I can't."

"Are you in trouble?"

She wanted to laugh. What did that mean, trouble? Where did trouble begin and end? "Would you care?"

"¡*Chica!* Of course I would!"

Malena waited. Raw inside. Suddenly she imagined Flaca bursting through the hotel room door, shouting *that's it, you're coming with me,* and carrying her in her arms all the way back to Montevideo. Whether that was a dread or a wish, she couldn't tell. Her eyes stung. She blinked.

"Malenita, have you been drinking?"

"Fuck you, Flaca. Like you don't drink."

"Not like that."

"Who cares?"

"Malena, please. Tell me where you are."

Malena crouched against the wall, a cornered cat. "None of your damn business."

"It *is* my business."

"Why?"

"Because I love you, Malena."

"Bullshit."

"Come home."

But there was no home to come back to and it had been a terrible idea to call. Flaca was sobbing into the phone now, saying something through her tears, but she was somewhere far away from where Malena was and even further from where she was going, and there were no words or Uruguayan highways that would ever close the distance. "Goodbye, Flaca," she said with her finger on the cradle, and as soon as the words were out of her mouth she pressed down to hang up. When she let go, the dial tone blared at her. She listened to it for a long time.

*

The nuns were good to her, and after two years at the convent life began to occasionally feel bearable, but in the end she could not bring herself to make the vows. There were too many lies layered over lies, and she knew that her God was not the same as theirs. They loved the Virgin, and so did she, but her own love of the Virgin was now shot through with fear, tangled in danger, not enough to carry her through a lifetime of wearing the veil. The nuns helped her find her way beyond the convent, recommending her for her first job in the secular world, helping manage the books at a local cemetery that held handwritten registries of the dead. Malena had tidy, elegant handwriting, and she did well in the dusty back office where she could spend hours at a time in silence. The pay was not very much, but the groundskeeper let her sleep in the back room of the office until she saved enough to rent a room. He took pity on her because he believed what the nuns had told him, that she was an orphan rescued from the streets, and, in fact, this was not exactly true but not entirely a lie. Her parents were alive but she could not go back to them. She'd called home just a few times over the years. The first time was two months after fleeing the clinic, which was as soon as she dared. She'd had to wait until after all the nuns were asleep to sneak down the hall to the Mother Superior's office, and had dialed with trembling hands. Her mother picked up. Her mother stayed up much later than the nuns, and she sounded normal, awake. *It's me,* she'd whispered into the phone, and her mother had hesitated, as if wondering who *me* could be.

Where the hell are you, her mother had hissed.

Somewhere safe.

You don't know what you've cost us. In money, in shame.

I'm sorry.

Come home.

The pull inside to comply, to see her childhood home again, to melt into her mother's arms. *Will you promise not to send me back there?*

How dare you?

I can't go back, Mamá. I can't!

The doctor didn't finish his treatment. He says you're a terribly hard case.

You still speak to him?

Of course. He's your doctor.

He's a Nazi.

That's enough! Malena!

Where's Papá?

Out. And then, *you don't know how you've made us suffer.* Her voice rising with pain.

Malena hung up quickly. She stayed in the darkness of the Mother Superior's office until she could breathe normally again and sneak back to her cell.

*

The bus route from Treinta y Tres to Polonio was complicated, requiring an overnight stop in the coastal town of Rocha, where she spent the evening in a café writing a long letter that she left with the hotel concierge the next morning, to go out with the day's mail. Once she arrived at the Polonio bus stop, she waited again for a horse cart to take her over the sand dunes, as she didn't have it in her to hike to her destination and in any case there was no reason to pinch pesos anymore. She walked to the Prow and paused outside, but didn't enter. If she entered she might lose her resolve.

The Prow stood dwarfed by the gathering twilight.

A shack at the edge of the world.

Ocean enfolding it on all sides.

Still shabby, and still beautiful.

A perfect home.

So many pricks of happiness over the years, like tiny points of light.

But still, when she looked at the Prow, she also remembered what she'd done for it. How they hadn't had enough pesos between the five of them, and she'd promised to take care of it. And gone down to the docks. It hadn't been as hard as she'd thought it would be, though she made less than she'd hoped and the work was more laborious than she'd imagined. Still she went through with it, every time. The other women of the docks glared at her for invading their turf but didn't chase her away. She didn't go more than once a week because she couldn't bear to, it took her all week to feel her skin as her own again. And she tried to dissemble herself, hide, so that no one would ever connect the woman down at the docks with the Malena of her ordinary life. She had so many hidden layers now, the girl from the clinic, the girl who escaped, the girl who joined the convent to avoid the docks and because she had nowhere else to go, the woman who returned to the docks so she could scrape out a place for herself in the world with her bare fingernails, and not just for herself, but for her friends. A place to love. A place for love. For years, she'd feared being recognized, found out as a *puta*. In a small country, that was always a danger. The men you'd put inside your mouth roamed the same streets as you did. She'd been lucky, though, except for that one awful day in the café with her Polonio friends, when the man had put his hand on her shoulder and said she looked familiar. She'd recognized him too. She hadn't gone with him; he'd wanted a lower price than she was willing to accept, and he'd groped her brutally and left in a huff. When he recognized her in front of her friends she felt the keenest panic, followed by equally sharp relief at seeing that they suspected nothing.

She'd always wanted them to suspect nothing.

Oh, Forgetting, hear our prayer.

Perhaps she'd done it all wrong, this living, but it was too late now. She was tired and had nothing left. She turned her back on the Prow and walked toward the rocks. Night had fallen but there was enough moon to see the way. Her last victory had been to get here. To not end her story in Treinta y Tres, in Rocha, in a drab hotel room. She had almost done it; but the pull of Polonio had been strong. She'd thought of this so many times, over the years, looking out at the water and picturing it swallowing her whole. Had walked these very rocks so many times, imagined the leap, taken its measure.

Which was why she now arrived at the right place with startling speed. The lighthouse loomed at her back but no one was there, no one could see her, she was alone. She was high on a jagged outcropping, and waves crashed roughly below. They seemed otherworldly in the moonlight, rising ferociously, over and over, colliding against the rocks. Without shame. Without tiring. Without cease. Water could break and split from itself and in moments return to wholeness.

Or rip away and never return.

She couldn't linger. Couldn't change her mind.

In the last moment before she jumped, she saw her mother's face twisted into a scowl of disgust (and her father, behind her mother, staring past Malena as though she were not there, as though she didn't exist, had never existed) and she saw Romina too, blank-eyed, indifferent, the faces blurring into each other as one united truth, a thesis confirmed, this is this, this is not that, will never be. Spring, release, away from all that, into the ocean, the living ocean, the great blue arms of the only one she knew would never hate her, and she'd been planning for so long that she had no right to be surprised at the willing coil of her knees, the forward leap, her legs obedient and ready. Still, the air shocked her as she hung aloft, suspended so gracefully that it seemed for an instant that she'd been freed from the rules of gravity, that she wouldn't fall after all, that the sumptuous night would hold her in its embrace forever, and in that instant the urge to live rebelled in her chest and hammered criminally at her heart right as she began to fall, eyes wide open, wide enough to see infinity in each second as black night slowly collapsed all around her.

*

The body was discovered the following evening by Javier, the teenage grandson of El Lobo, as he snuck a cigarette among the rocks. The identification of the body was not difficult, thanks to the wallet in the pocket of her jeans. Paz was the first to receive the news, as their shared address was on the identification card, and though she did not have Malena's parents' phone number, she knew their first names and was able to find them in the phone book and convey this information to the police. To Paz's relief, they did not insist that she be the one to make the call. She learned, from the officer in Castillos, that the death had been deemed either an accident or a suicide. "Though who can trust the Castillos police," Paz had said through choked sobs, and everyone remembered her time in that tiny jail under the same rural jurisdiction. She called the police station again the following day and was shocked to learn that Malena's parents had declined to have her body brought to Montevideo for burial, that they weren't even paying for a headstone.

"But that's not possible," Paz said. "She has to come home, I'll pay for her transport if I have to."

"You can't do that, señorita."

For a fleeting moment Paz thought how strange it would be if she'd met this man before as his prisoner, or perhaps how ordinary, since there could only be so many officers in Castillos and where else would they go? Focus. Stay calm. "And why not?"

"Because you're not family. Only close relatives can authorize transport."

Paz went to Castillos to argue her case, speak to superiors, and try to bring Malena home. It was no use. She was nothing more than a housemate and a friend. La Venus and Flaca were with her, and La Venus tried her classic strategy of showing cleavage and lowering her voice to a purr, but even this failed to secure anything except a discount on a headstone in the local churchyard, which at least was better than the unmarked grave to which Malena would otherwise have been consigned. They attended the burial together, the three of them, along with the priest and a few of the good people of El Polonio: Benito, Cristi, El Lobo, Alicia, Óscar, Javier, Ester, and Lili. Malena's parents never came, nor did her brother, who lived somewhere abroad, Sweden, or Switzerland perhaps, no one could remember exactly. It was Romina's absence that cut Flaca the most. The night before the burial, she'd called Romina from the dingy little inn that passed for a hotel in Castillos, and begged her one last time to come.

"We were her family, Ro. We were all she had."

"I know. I know."

"And don't you care?"

"How can you ask that?" Romina sounded strangled, though it could also be a bad connection. "Of course I do. But what if her parents come?"

"They won't. They want nothing to do with this."

"But we don't know for certain. And we wouldn't be welcome."

"Who cares about—"

"And anyway, I don't need to go, that's just a body in that box, it's not Malena anymore."

"Just a body? A body you loved."

Romina was weeping now, but quietly, fighting to stifle the sound. "I know."

"How can you be so cruel?"

"Please stop."

"Me?"

"Yes, I can't bear it, Flaca."

"You're glad she's gone."

The line went silent. Flaca thought she felt Romina on the other end, gathering her rage into a weapon. But instead, she began to wail. It was the most terrible sound she'd ever heard. She wanted to comfort Romina, though she also for an instant had the deranged thought that, if Romina suffered, Malena might come back. She sat frozen with the receiver against her ear. Waiting for Romina's wailing to subside. Waiting for the ache to stop. "Please come," she whispered.

"How dare you," Romina said, just before a dial tone swallowed her away.

For the second time in their lives, Flaca and Romina did not speak for a year.

*

Three weeks after the burial, Malena's letter arrived: a missive penned by the dead, defying the river of time. It had crawled through the postal system from Rocha to Paz's house, which was also La Venus's house and La Piedrita's house and even Malena's house before she disappeared. The envelope named Paz as the recipient, but the letter inside opened, simply, with one word.

Friends—

Part Three

2013

9

Glowing Magical Creature

IT WAS THE TWENTY-SIXTH ANNIVERSARY of Malena's death, though Flaca wasn't sure any of the others would remember and that wasn't why they were heading out to Polonio, why the dunes sped past her now in all their splendor, the same dunes as always, the dunes of today, made unique each moment by the unrepeatable ripples of the wind. This was a celebration, so best not to mention Malena at all.

It was still strange to her, this riding into Polonio in a double-decker commercial jeep, packed tight between tourists eager to see the brightly painted bohemian restaurants and hostels, take pictures of themselves with the lighthouse in the background, buy necklaces beaded with local shells and peace pendants manufactured in China. Polonio was a tourist destination now, named in Brazilian and Argentinean guidebooks as a jewel not to be missed, as a gay and bohemian refuge, as well as a sea lion refuge, a confluence of language that made Flaca feel like part of a species subjected to protective measures and gawking. Also, Playa Sur had grown in appeal among luxury vacationers, with white stucco cottages sprouting up along the rocks, featuring private generators and whalebone sculptures and diaphanous curtains, behind which, presumably, the wealthy pursued the erotic delights of paradise. Nothing like La Proa, which remained as stubbornly shabby as ever, though La Venus's mural of sea creatures entangled in what resembled love had given the front wall its own bright character as well. Despite its humble appearance, La Proa now fetched high rents for them in the summer months when they weren't using the place themselves, an income for which they were all grateful, times being what they were.

La Venus sat beside her, taking photos of the passing landscape, as if she were one more tourist who'd never seen this place before, though in fact she was working on a photographic installation on the dunes. Flaca thought it was impossible to capture the dunes on camera, not the slightest aspect of their essence or power. But she was not the artist—perhaps, she thought, precisely because of thoughts like these. Artists don't give up on trying to render things just because rendering them is impossible. Romina sat across from her, hair wild in the wind. She smiled at Flaca, who smiled back, wondering whether she too was remembering past crossings of this landscape, or whether the present or future had her more in thrall. Romina was pressed close to Diana, and everyone was pressed close here, even strangers, as the jeep was crowded, but still their bodies seemed to hum together, harbor and ship, ship and harbor. Holding hands for all to see. Newlyweds. Flaca still couldn't believe it and strained to wrap her mind around the thought. Romina and Diana, married. Two women married. Each idea uniquely insane, plucked from the edge of possibility. She tried to imagine telling herself of this, the self who first kissed Romina in the bathroom of a nightclub, when they were teenagers deep in that mode that people now called *el armario,* the closet. Forty years ago now. She would not have believed it for a second. Yet here they were, fresh from the Civil Registry, one of the first couples to take advantage of the new law. Wife and wife. Romina had seemed nonchalant about it, perhaps because, through her professional life, she'd seen the change coming for a long time. Why shouldn't the two of them make vows, sign their names in a legal book, get the blessing of a functionary of the state, if they planned to be together forever?

Death and marriage. Marriage and death. Twenty-six years ago today—they wouldn't remember that, of course, and why should they? She would not remind them. She was happy for Romina and Diana. She celebrated their marriage with as much joy and stupefaction as everybody else. And yet, she hadn't been able to shake the feeling that there was someone missing from the mass of people crushed into the city registrar, a hole in the shape of Malena, who should have been there to weep with rage or jealousy or sadness or maybe shudder the way everyone else did at the marvel of light slanting on two brides, in Uruguay, as they reached for each other's hands.

*

Flaca and La Venus lived together now in the small house where Flaca had grown up, above the butcher shop. After her father died, she had lived alone for a few years, but once she turned fifty loneliness rose around her like a subtle tide, and she was relieved when La Venus asked to move in. She took over what used to be Flaca's parents' bedroom, the biggest one in the modest house, and just as well, as she needed every inch of space and crammed it with canvases in various stages of creation, along with found objects she was painting, as she'd continued doing that for the joy of it, even though she could now more easily afford canvases thanks to her job teaching painting at a high school and the decent stream of gallery shows and commissions that came her way.

One recent evening, a few weeks before this trip to Polonio, they'd opened a bottle of wine and marveled at their strange fortunes.

"Look at us, single in our old age—"

"Speak for yourself—I'm not old."

La Venus raised an eyebrow. "Ha. As I was saying. Single, as we begin to have, oh, just a few wrinkles on our impeccable faces."

"That's more like it. You still turn heads wherever you go, Venus, you know that."

"Do I?"

"You're being coy."

La Venus smiled seductively. "It's one of my superpowers."

"Don't I know it." Flaca poured more wine into both of their glasses. "What's really funny is that I used to dream of growing old with you."

"No kidding?"

"No kidding. Before you left me for a glamorous diva who whisked you off to Brazil."

"What glamorous diva? I recall nothing of this."

"If your memory's gone, then you *are* getting old."

They laughed. And La Venus thought, then, not of Ariella but of Mario, the boy she'd loved, the child returned into her life a beautiful man. He'd reached out to her ten years ago. When he told her his name on the phone in that deep adult voice of his, the room had melted around her, become liquid and bright. They agreed to meet for coffee. She changed her outfit six times before leaving the house, finally settling on a modest dress, no risks taken. At the café, they took a table together awkwardly, stealing glances at each other as they waited for their coffee. He was twenty-seven years old, the same age she'd been when she first went to Polonio and started dismantling her married life—*a phoenix age,* she thought, *at least for me*—and he was crushingly handsome, yet the little-boy face was right there under the surface of his features, open, tender. It flooded back to her, a love so intense she could have ripped a building apart with her bare hands.

The coffee arrived. She stirred in sugar, waited. Tried to breathe.

"I didn't think you'd come," he finally said.

"Why not?"

He shrugged, eyes on his coffee. "I didn't think you'd want to see me."

She couldn't imagine it. He was the one, after all, who'd been raised by a grandmother who surely taught him to hate her, or to forget her, or both. She sipped her coffee to steady herself. "I thought you wouldn't remember me," she said, almost adding, *I think of you all the time.*

"What?" He looked genuinely confused. It was his eyes that hadn't changed at all, that still held three-year-old Mario, six-year-old Mario, all the Marios inside them. "You were like a mother to me."

She couldn't breathe.

"I think of you all the time."

Her words. Her own swallowed words.

"My abuela—I can't forgive what she did to you. It's horrible, what she said."

"So you remember."

"Of course. I remember everything. I didn't make sense of it until I was much older. It was a confusing time, leaving Brazil. And after that, living with my grandmother—well. She wasn't kind."

He looked up at La Venus, expectantly, but she held her tongue. He didn't need to hear venom for the woman who raised him.

"I can see you're not surprised," he said. And he laughed. He had none of the arrogance of the rest of his family. He seemed warm, bookish, like a socially awkward yet bighearted librarian, not quite ready for the thorny world. "Anyway. I can't believe we're really here."

"How did you find me?"

"I've been following your career for years. Your work is beautiful, I love it." He looked sheepish. "I've even bought a painting."

She longed to know which painting. One thing at a time. "But you didn't try to call me."

"Not yet. I was a coward."

They crushed into her mind, the myriad things she longed to say, she couldn't parse them. She placed her hand on his. He studied their joined hands in silence for some time.

"So can we stay in touch?" he said quietly.

"Of course."

"I'd like you to meet my daughter."

Air trapped in her lungs. A daughter? How had time sped like this, so that Mario was the father and not the child? "How old is she?"

"Two. Her name is Paula."

"I want to meet her," she said, and then, before she could stop herself, "I love her already," and in the weeks and months and years that followed those words were over and over proven true.

Now, ten years later, sitting in the kitchen, she watched Flaca light another cigarette. She'd tried to quit several times over the years. La Venus, who missed cigarettes dearly but was determined to hold her ground, watched the smoke curl languorously between them.

"I suppose we *are* old," she said. "When we first met, I thought sixty-three was ancient." Just last month, Paula had said *Abuela, when I'm old like you* as if it were the most normal thing in the world, and La Venus had wanted to laugh from the shock of it, of *old* but also of that name that even now made her body sing, *Abuela.* "But here I am, and I still feel like my same self."

"Except for your knees?"

La Venus spread her arms in a gesture of surrender.

"The thing is, my fantasy of growing old together was a little different."

"Oh?"

"It was *chucu-chucu* every day."

"Sounds nice."

"Does it?" Flaca looked at La Venus. It was true that she was still striking, a vixen turned elegant, and of course La Venus knew it, carefully applying lipstick and styling her hair. Every once in a while, the question of what could happen between them shot through Flaca's mind, but then it quickly disappeared into the ether. They'd come too far now. It would be like having sex with a sister. "I don't know. With this sore hip, I'm not sure I could take the excitement."

"Oh, come on! What about that Teresita?"

Flaca smiled. She couldn't help it. She'd run into Teresita at the Feria de Tristán Narvaja a few weeks ago. Teresita, the second woman she'd ever had sex with, after Romina, right after the coup. Back then, Teresita had been a restless young housewife, trapped in her apartment and her fears of expanding repression, and it had frightened her, the thing between them, she confessed right there between the open-air market stalls crammed with zucchini and old antiques and the cheap clothes from China that were putting local craftsmen out of business, you were terrifying to me, Flaca, I wanted so much to have children and a normal life, and I wasn't in my right mind—*no one was,* Flaca interjected, and Teresita gestured her agreement and barreled on—but I never forgot you. Not for a single day. They stared at each other in silence as the sun bore down on them. Flaca thought of the young Teresita, her limber thighs and acrobatic passion. Colors brightened in the cluttered stalls. They talked on. Teresita had four children, and five grandchildren. She'd been divorced for a decade now. It was never a good marriage, she said calmly, as if assessing spoiled vegetables in a time of plenty. You look good, she added. Flaca thanked her. I mean really good. Slowly this time, and Flaca took a closer look at the plump grandmother before her, the way her gray hair quaked insistently in the light.

They'd made a plan to meet again a few days later, in the Plaza de los Bomberos. Teresita had brought the *mate*. They'd stayed, talking, until twilight fell and Teresita had to go to her grandchildren; she'd promised to watch them while their parents went out to a movie.

"Nothing's happened between us," Flaca said to La Venus as she put out her cigarette. "Who knows what it is."

"Oh, come on, Flaca. She wants you, and why wouldn't she? You make her feel young."

Flaca thought of Teresita as she'd first known her, lithe and tentative, then fierce and hungry in the dark. How much they'd all changed, their bodies gliding relentlessly on the currents of time.

"And you make her feel hot."

"We'll see."

"Just give me warning if you decide to kick me out, all right?"

"What! Venus, don't be ridiculous. You're family, and this is your home."

La Venus studied a crack in the wall tiles. Flaca couldn't decipher her face.

The word *family* coiled between and around them like some translucent dragon, a glowing magical creature of their own making.

*

Romina leaned into Diana as the jeep carried them forward, forward, through the dunes toward the distant thumb of land that was her second home. Flaca and La Venus sat across from her, lost in their own thoughts. It wasn't easy, in any case, to talk over the roar of this vehicle that clattered across the sand full of tourists. She and Diana weren't trying to talk, though for the first time she could remember, they were holding hands on the ride, making no attempt to hide their bond. It was astonishing that Diana had not yet released her hand. When it came to visibility in public places, Diana was even more fearful than Romina. But there they were, hands still clasped, fingers twined and speaking to each other, exhilaration twined with fear. Diminishing fear. They had just married and this was their honeymoon and she'd be damned if she would let go of her bride's hand to placate any of her fellow passengers, the families, the hippies, the Brazilians or Argentineans or Montevideans, they could come to Polonio if they wanted but they could not steal her day.

Not that anyone seemed to mind. They were two old women holding hands, and so? Who cared about the hands of old women?

They'd been together for twenty-six years now. And yet, they were also newlyweds. At once a forever couple and a fresh one. She was still amazed that it had happened, the ceremony at City Hall, the room where her own parents had gotten married seventy years before, now bursting with people. Diana, of course, had none of her Paraguayan family there, and would tell them in due time, perhaps, when she was ready. Already some of her siblings—the evangelical converts among them—saw her as a defector to Uruguay, land of leftists and sinners and perverts, and she only talked to them on trips back to Paraguay. She didn't go back for them, but for her mother, whom she loved without bounds, and with whom she only spoke in Guaraní, a language that cascaded from her mouth on phone calls home like a clear, wild stream. Romina loved to hear it, and had tried to learn words from Diana, who was a patient teacher and never teased Romina about her trouble holding on to those new, supple words that slipped through the fingers of her mind. The only sure words were *I love you*. They poured from Romina's mouth, always rising, never enough. *Rohayhú. Rohayhú etereí.*

All of Romina's family came to the wedding: Felipe and his wife and children, now young adults in their own right, and Romina's mother and father, ninety and ninety-one years old, leaning on their grandchildren's arms and walking slowly toward their daughter, who was finally, and in a manner they never would have dreamed of, a bride. They had embraced Diana a long time ago. In the aftermath of Malena's death, Romina had come to see secrecy as a kind of poison that eats people's lives from the inside, all the more so when it festers into shame. Still, it took some years for her to tell her family. She'd started with hints dropped here and there, about Diana, hints her parents had let sit untouched like lures in the water, spiked with hooks, not to be bitten. When she finally told them outright, they were almost relieved, and her mother even chided her for the years of secrecy. Why? she said. Romina had tried to explain, about duty, not letting them down, but her mother had shrugged and said, *your grandmother didn't survive everything she did for you to live in hiding*. It took days for Romina to recover from the shock. It gradually occurred to her that her mother had had years of suspicion in which to quietly grow used to the idea, to formulate a way of absorbing it. Felipe took it the hardest. He did not approve. He'd had his suspicions. He hoped she wouldn't be one of those women who tries to distract the political movement from serious issues with, well, things like this. Things like what? she'd asked, unyielding. Faggotry, he'd said. Things were tense between them after that for years, though for their parents' sake they both tried to stay civil at family gatherings. It was only after she ran for Senate, and won, that he reached out to her again. Suddenly he was proud of his sister, a victorious party leader. They formed a fragile truce. And now here he was, with his family in tow, his children who, as young people in their twenties, found their father's attitudes backward and embarrassing and bragged about their aunt's marriage on networks online that they navigated with a baffling ease. Romina was glad Felipe had come, even if, during the ceremony, he looked as if he'd just stumbled into a jungle full of beasts he could not name. Romina's mother, meanwhile, wept with joy. Cameras flashed, some of them belonging to friends, others to journalists covering the wedding of this congresswoman who'd voted for gay marriage, helped the law pass, and then publicly declared her intention to marry, it was a new time for Uruguay, the leftist Frente Amplio ran the nation, from the Presidency to Congress to the capital's City Hall, and here they were, one of the first gay couples to marry legally in Uruguay, the articles would say, inevitably adding, with Uruguay being the third country in America to legalize gay marriage, after Canada and Argentina, and before the United States. The leftist papers would say it proudly, the conservative papers grudgingly. And their photographs would be in the papers. All the more reason to get out of the city. After the ceremony, they'd had a simple lunch at home, with family and friends crushed into the apartment, with nowhere to sit and a buoyant feeling in the air, and that night, as Romina was clearing dishes and secretly hoping the last guests would leave so she could finish packing for Polonio, the phone rang. It was President Mujica, calling to congratulate her on her marriage. The call was brief, warm, and jovial, as things usually were with El Pepe. A man who'd been imprisoned throughout the dictatorship, survived torture, and attempted as a young Tupamaro to overthrow the government, did not become the head of that same government without a healthy sense of humor.

The next morning, Romina woke beside Diana and watched her sleep for a while, a miracle. This woman who had blended lives with her. Who asked her every morning to share her dreams. *You,* Romina always wanted to say, and sometimes did. *You are my dream.* Or she might say *I dreamed a beautiful Paraguayan let me kiss her breasts. Oh, am I supposed to be jealous? No,* Romina would answer, *flattered.* And Diana would protest, *dreams are powerful, amor, you're not taking this seriously,* but the swatting away of hands was playful and often turned into something else. Afterward, the dreams poured out, and Romina was always shocked by Diana's uncanny insights.

"Good morning," Diana said, without opening her eyes.

"Good morning, *esposa*."

"*¡Esposas!* Such a strange word. Meaning wives, but also handcuffs."

"I know. It's the patriarchy."

"Have we joined it now? The patriarchy?"

"It certainly doesn't feel that way to me."

"Me either." Diana's eyes were wide open now.

There was so much to do, to get ready, to reach the station on time for the bus to Polonio. The older Romina got, the longer everything seemed to take, and at fifty-eight years old she knew it was unwise to linger in bed instead of starting to prepare. And yet, she longed to stay where she was, to savor Diana's skin beneath her fingers, to hold this moment deep inside herself. Why on earth had she planned a group honeymoon?

But she knew why.

Diana relaxed into the pleasure of Romina's touch, and Romina thought, oh hell, we'll be late, so be it, and then Diana said, "You're thinking of her."

"What?"

"Aren't you?"

"How can you tell?"

"I know you, *querida*."

"I'm sorry."

"Do not be. How can I be jealous of the dead?" She said it playfully, but when she saw the expression on Romina's face, she added, "You'll always love her. And you should. That's part of why I want you, what I treasure about you: that you can't get a woman out of you once she's found her way in."

Romina squeezed Diana's hand as she thought of this now, many hours later, as the jeep pulled onto the Playa de las Calaveras and Polonio came into distant view. The sight still took her breath away. She could die happy in this moment. She thought this, sometimes, when beauty struck her from within, that if this was the last of it she'd have no reason to complain. Death hovered close now, every waking hour, despite her good health, a presence that had no need to seduce you in order to slide between your sheets. A presence that grazed your flesh like a promise, the only one that would definitely be kept. Coming fast or coming slow, it was coming for her, as it did for everyone, whether you ran from it or hurled yourself in its direction as Malena had done, as she had failed to stop Malena from doing. The sand and waves roared past her fast, faster, already they were turning onto the cape itself and then they were approaching the center of Polonio, the cross-roads that now had the warmth and bustle of a town plaza. The jeep came to a halt. Tourists began to spill from their seats, gazing around them at the stalls full of seashell jewelry, the brightly colored signs, the restaurants boasting fish empanadas and beer, the beach and ocean and lighthouse beyond. The travelers' expressions seemed satisfied, as if to say, *yes, indeed, it's paradise.* But as Romina descended from the top deck, holding carefully on to the ladder, she thought of the first time she'd brought Diana here, just the two of them, soon after they became a couple. Those had been heady days, Diana's first time seeing the ocean, their first time entering the waves together, a quiet unleashing for them both. On that trip, they'd learned that Benito, the *náufrago,* the shipwreck survivor, had died of a heart attack, and his son had taken over running the Rusty Anchor.

"Imagine that life," Romina had said. "Living in a place because your father was a náufrago."

"But, my love," Diana had asked, fingers in her lover's hair, "aren't we all children of náufragos?"

*

Paz received them at the door of La Proa, book in one hand, kitchen knife in the other.

"Where's Virginia?" La Venus asked.

"Down in the water. I told her I'd meet her later, I wanted to welcome you all."

"Brrr! A swim?" Flaca grimaced. "In October?"

"It's warm for October."

"Climate change," Romina said, kissing Paz in greeting.

"There she goes," said Paz, grinning. "Even on her honeymoon, she can't stop worrying about the world."

"*Fighting* for the world," Romina said.

"How romantic," said Paz.

"That it is," said Diana, and all the women laughed together.

"I can't wait to swim," said La Venus. "Cold or no. Shall we all go?"

Soon they were walking toward the beach, avoiding the village center, still full of tourists from the recently arrived jeep, taking pictures and fingering merchandise and eating fish empanadas. There was no way, Paz thought, that any one of them could ever love this place as she did, that they could even see it clearly, but then again, she too had once been an outsider here, flung in from somewhere else. Whenever her mind grumbled for too long about the hippie boys with their blond dreadlocks and guitars and designer windbreakers or the Brazilian businessmen looking down their noses at the hippies, she thought of El Lobo, heard his voice, *come back and I'll tell you the story.* El Lobo was gone now. Polonio was still sleepy when he died. Now his grandson, Javier, ran a hostel behind the store and the beds were full throughout the summer.

They reached the shore, blue everywhere, flung open majestically before them. The waves were cold but Paz welcomed their bite as she waded in. Flaca was yelping and protesting the cold, Romina threatening to splash her, Diana gliding in to the neck. Paz had seen this before. Malena submerging her body, the first to surrender—that very first time—and there it was, the pain, the always pain. *Malena, the water is cold today, I'm heading in deeper, cold, do you see, Malena?* If she stayed near her friends they might read her thoughts, and that didn't seem right. This was a honeymoon. She looked for Virginia, and when she saw her out on the rocks she swam toward her.

"How are the brides?"

"Happy," Paz said. "Glowing."

"As they were yesterday," Virginia said. "It was such a beautiful ceremony."

"I still can't believe it," Paz said. When a group of gay rights activists had started meeting at La Piedrita, she'd thought to herself, gay rights? what rights? Marriage had seemed preposterous, an imported idea that had started in the first world but had nothing to do with Uruguay, where gay couples didn't even tell their coworkers or their families what they were. These younger people spent much more time on the Internet than Paz did, and knew a great deal about what was true for people like them in other parts of the world and therefore was possible. She'd gladly helped them, offered them the space in which to organize, at first touched by their earnestness and soon amazed by their collective power, at the tenacity with which they fought for their dream, unhampered by memories of what it took to survive the Process, which, of course, they'd never had to do. "A gay wedding—it still sounds strange."

"I know."

"Like some bizarre experiment. Frankenstein's monster."

"Ha! Don't let the brides hear you say that!"

Virginia threw her head back as she laughed. Paz swam closer, kissed her neck.

"Mmmm, they could be watching."

"So?"

"You're the worst," Virginia said, biting Paz's ear.

The waves enfolded them, held them up, and it amazed Paz that no matter how much her body changed—she was fifty-two years old, larger, heavier, rounder in some places and flattened in others, yet steady in a new way, as if time had rooted her in the soil of truth—the ocean's body was as fresh as ever, and as ancient as ever, knowing just how to surround her. Wrap her perfectly. Press her with the gentlest force. Press her and her lover together, in a rich embrace. She could hear her friends' voices in the distance, yelping from the cold, arguing cheerfully about how long they'd be able to stand it. "Are you sad that we're not marrying, too?"

"Not sad, no."

"But you want to? Because you know I would."

"You've made that clear."

"All right."

Virginia was silent for a while. "Paz," she finally said, "you're mine. We're bound to each other. And the thing that binds us together is holy. No matter what."

Paz ached inside. Three years now they'd been together and she never tired of the way Virginia said the word *holy*. After Flaca and Virginia broke up, years ago, they'd fallen out of touch, and Paz hadn't seen her for almost twenty years. Then they'd run into each other on Playa Ramírez, at the annual festival of Iemanjá, where thousands of Montevideans thronged to make offerings to the Yoruba goddess of the sea. Candles shone in pits dug into the sand, bright with prayers. White flowers sprouted and swayed in the waves. Watermelons rolled out into the water, sticky with molasses and hope. Little boats struck out laden with offerings, pushed forward by believers dressed in white. Song erupted along the shore. Priestesses offered cleansings to strangers who lined up for their turns, while vendors hawked popcorn, candles, and prayer cards embossed with a picture of Iemanjá rising from the water, stars spilling from her hands. Paz had gone to watch the lights set out on the water and to hear the chants of devotees, whose faith she found moving even though she didn't share it. She spied Virginia in a long white dress and head wrap, sitting at the edge of a hole in which she'd lit candles with her friends. They talked. They kept talking. Paz knew immediately that she wanted to stay at the edge of that hole as long as Virginia would let her, and this turned out to be a long time. Weeks later, as they lay naked together, Virginia told her what Iemanjá meant to her, *sacred and female and black, no separation, all vast like the ocean, all holy and all one. Like the energy we just generated together, which also belongs to the gods.* And Paz had thought of the Polonio ocean, how vast it was, unknowable. How the first time she saw it, at sixteen, had been her first time feeling free. Ocean as church, she thought. Woman's body as church. She had so much to say to Virginia, then, but only said it with her hands.

"You," she said now, holding Virginia close inside the body of the ocean. "You are what's holy."

"I don't need the piece of paper," Virginia said into her ear.

"Well, if you want it." Though Paz herself didn't want it. She wanted only the word *holy* spoken in this woman's voice, and the woman herself, enfolded in waters that reached to the horizon and beyond.

*

That night, they held a wedding feast: Flaca grilled chorizos, lamb, fish, eggplant, bell peppers, and sweet potatoes, while the others prepared the salad, rice, and sangria. La Venus had made alfajores the day before, back in the city, and brought these out as dessert. As they ate, the lighthouse beam swooped over them, *swish—swish,* as it had done for so many years.

"Is it just me," Flaca said, "or have the tourists gotten even ruder this time?"

"I know. Polonio's changed so much."

"They think they own the beach."

"In other ways, though, it hasn't changed at all. The ocean is the same."

"Remember when we had the beach to ourselves?"

"Remember when we could stay out on the beach all afternoon because there was no hole in the ozone?"

"Now we'll be lucky if the ozone hole is our only environmental problem," Romina said, though she too chafed at the restriction of having to go inside and avoid the sun's rays between noon and 5:00 p.m. every afternoon. The UV ray warnings had started as a three-hour block, and had now expanded to five. Gone were the unfettered rhythms of the old days, when you sunned yourself and swam whenever you liked. "Sea levels are rising everywhere. All of Polonio could be swallowed up one day."

"Do you think our house could end up underwater?" asked Paz. "It'll be like those shipwrecks that are out there right now, on the ocean floor. Can you imagine future generations diving under to find our things? Calling them treasures?"

"I'm scared to imagine those future generations," said Romina, thinking of the debate in the Senate about what to do about climate change, the helplessness of a tiny nation whipped by harsh new weather patterns sparked in another hemisphere. *They caused the problem,* some of her fellow senators said, *they should pay to fix it,* a line of reasoning that would leave them ideologically pure but ripe for disaster. Her dreams were haunted by violent floods and worsening storms.

"Our house won't ever be underwater," Flaca scoffed. "It's too high up."

"The whole of Cabo is vulnerable."

"I can't accept that."

"It'll happen whether or not you accept it. That's the thing about climate change."

"Oh God, *chicas,*" La Venus said, "can we please not talk about this? Enough doomsday. This is supposed to be a happy occasion!"

"All right then, no dreary talk of the future."

"I think the future is promising," said La Venus. "I mean, look at this: you two are *married.*"

"Hear, hear!" said Paz. "Now, that's more like it."

"If only our young selves could see it," La Venus said. "Do you ever think about what would happen if you could collapse time and talk to your past self?"

"Only when I'm very high," said Paz.

"I'm serious! The past versions of us could be here in this very room, listening."

"I'm sure they are," Virginia said.

"They wouldn't believe it," Flaca said, "about the marriage. Not ever."

"I'd tell them about it just to see their faces," said La Venus.

"Cantoras in shock."

"Back when we were cantoras," Flaca said. "When we didn't have the other words. Now we have all these words and nobody's a cantora anymore."

"That's true," Paz said, thinking of the young activists in La Piedrita, with their *gay* and *lesbiana* and *bisexual* and *queer* and amusement at learning the word *cantora* from her, as if it were a curiosity, a brooch from your great-aunt's drawer that you'd never wear yourself. "But isn't it better to have more words? Not to have to speak in code about ourselves?"

"Of course it's good. Of course it's better. It's just—" Flaca strained to think. "I don't know. Don't you ever feel like you're disappearing?"

"We're not the ones who disappeared," Romina said. And then she said, "Malena."

Silence spread through the Prow.

"Tonight she's been gone," Romina said, looking right at Flaca, "for twenty-six years."

Flaca struggled for what seemed like hours to find her voice. "You remembered."

"You thought I wouldn't?"

Flaca couldn't speak.

"I always remember the date." Romina stared at the rustic wall. "It destroyed me, you know, not to go to her funeral."

"I know," Flaca said quickly, though she hadn't known. In all this time, they'd never spoken of it directly. Her entire body felt raw, as if stripped of skin. "I understand."

"You sure?"

"Yes," Flaca said, though all she could be sure of was that the past couldn't be rewritten, that reassurance was a kindness she could give.

In the silence that followed, the lighthouse beam came to wash them with such stealth and persistence that it almost seemed as if light could be made sound.

Diana was holding Romina now, behind her, rubbing her back.

Watching them, Flaca thought of the early years, how long it had taken to forgive Diana for what she'd catalyzed, how long it had taken to see her formidable heart. Diana had never blamed her for the rancor, kept the door to friendship open until Flaca was finally ready to walk through. Had the situation been reversed, she doubted that she'd have been capable of the same.

La Venus broke the silence. "Remember the first time? When we were just starting to become *us*—how she swam out farther than anyone?"

"She was like that. Quiet but it always seemed that she saw further than the rest of us."

"Further into things."

"Exactly."

"And yet there was so much she never told us."

"That's the part that kills me," La Venus said. "That she didn't speak, that she didn't trust us."

"Maybe it wasn't that she didn't trust," Paz said, "but that she just couldn't do it. If we'd known—" But Paz stopped, thinking of the letter, where everything had come out, all the horrors, all the secrets, the clinic and the docks, the Nazis and Belén, the hiding and the longing and the pain, all of it in a jumbled roar that arrived too late. The most important word, the first one, still waking Paz in the night like a spear: *Friends—*

"How could we have known?" Romina said very quietly. "I've asked myself this too. I failed her more than anyone else. I was the one right next to her. I kept trying to help her by suggesting she reach out to her parents. I'm so ashamed of that now. I didn't imagine, I couldn't know. But look, I never meant to kill her. You have to believe me, Flaca."

"I do," said Flaca. The room had tipped and spun, she felt a fear of falling even though she was sitting on the ground.

"I can't go back and change what happened," Romina said. She leaned against Diana, a steady anchor. "I can't spend my life staring down the gun barrel of the past."

"No," La Venus said, "You can't."

"I blamed myself too, for years," Paz said. "I was living with her. I tried to reach her. But I don't think you killed her, Ro, nor me. I think silence killed her."

"Yes," Diana said. It was the first time she'd spoken since the subject had arisen, and her voice rang clear. "That is the way of silence."

"What do you mean?" La Venus said, gently, knowing that there was more beneath the surface. With Diana, there always was.

"That the silence of dictatorship, the silence of the closet, as we call it now—all of that is layered and layered like blankets that muffle you until you cannot breathe. For many people it is too much. In Paraguay we have seen it. And so, here, none of you should carry the blame."

Flaca wrestled with these words. She had the terrible thought, the new thought, that all these years she'd still clung to blaming Romina, deep down, and that this had been a shield from blaming herself. She, La Pilota, forger of the group, should have saved Malena. She'd been the last one to speak to her and she'd run that phone call through her mind for twenty-six years, seeking the hole through which her friend had slipped away. But to heap that on Romina. Romina her heart. Romina her first love, with whom she'd remapped the world.

"And yet," Virginia said, "the story doesn't have to be over. She is on the other side, but she is still with us."

"I go to the rocks behind the lighthouse sometimes," Paz said, "and try to talk to her."

"You do?" said Flaca. "To Malena?"

"Yes. Who knows whether she hears me, but it helps." It had been Virginia who'd initially suggested this. She spoke to her ancestors all the time, as was normal in her spiritual tradition; Paz had felt silly doing it at first, but it soon became enough of a comfort that she'd kept going without fretting over whether she believed in it or not.

"I haven't gone down there," Flaca said, "not since—" And then she couldn't speak.

La Venus put her arms around Flaca, wiped her tears and snot with her sleeve.

"You know what I think?" Virginia said. "I think we should go to the rocks. Together."

"What?" said Flaca.

"When?" said La Venus.

"Tonight," said Virginia. "Right now. To remember her—our own kind of ceremony."

"But this is Romina and Diana's night," Flaca said. "This is supposed to be their honeymoon. It seems wrong."

Romina felt for Diana's hand before responding. "Actually, it feels right to me. We have this triumph, but not without losses."

"Not everyone survives the tunnels," Virginia said.

"Yes," Romina said, startled at phrasing she'd never heard before but that required no explanation. "Exactly."

"So?" said La Venus. "Shall we go?"

Flaca looked around, at La Venus and Paz, who nodded; at Virginia, whom she would always love (three ex-lovers of hers in this room and she loved all of them, they were life, blood, sapphires in the crown of her accumulated years); and then at Romina and finally at Diana. "You're all right with it?"

Diana smiled. "What is love," she said, "if it can't hold all the channels of the spirit?"

*

It was windy on the rocks, but not cold, and they pulled their jackets tight around them more for comfort than for warmth. There was no one else nearby. They weren't sure what they were going to do, and stood uncertainly at first. Paz looked out at the ocean and thought of Iemanjá, fruit and flowers, all the offerings they had not brought. She clasped Virginia's hand. Romina leaned close to Diana, and La Venus had an arm around Flaca, who dug her hands into her jacket pockets and fidgeted with the lint she found there. Rocks. They were just rocks. The same as always. Somewhere here had been the last step, the leap, and yet it was a normal place, just like any other, there had been no phantom waiting for her, they should just go.

And then Paz said Malena's name. So did La Venus. So did Virginia. So did Romina, Flaca, Diana. The sound of her name became a chant, a meandering melody, unscripted, sung into the wind. Stories arose, retellings, memories, wishes, confessions, praise. They did not rush. They ebbed and flowed. Their voices overlapped, there was no plan, no rule, no such thing as interruption. Together they made a tapestry of sound that had never been heard before and would never be heard again. When it subsided, when they were finally done, they lingered for a while and listened to the ocean, pulsing its own rhythm against the rocks.

On their way back, they took a circuitous path to avoid the village center, where music pounded and laughter flowed because the night was just getting started. The lush strains of a bandoneón rose from Cristi's restaurant; she must have tango dancers performing, a strategy that never failed to win her customers. She was doing good business with the tourists, that Cristi. On another night, they'd go visit, and she'd surely welcome them with a bark of delight and wine on the house for the brides. For now, though, they all knew, without saying a word, that they wanted to be together, to stay quiet, to lie close to each other in the dark. There was only the barest sliver of moon. The ramshackle beauty of the Prow would not be visible, but it would be with them. It would hold them, they thought, as they took the long way home.

Acknowledgments

For the existence of this book, I owe thanks to many.

Deep gratitude to my formidable and visionary agent, Victoria Sanders, and her extraordinary team, including Bernadette Baker-Baughman, Jessica Spivey, and Allison Leshowitz. Your tenacity, skill, and faith in me are a wonder. I'm also extremely thankful to the team at Knopf, including Carole Baron, editor extraordinaire, who has journeyed with me through five books now, all of them made better by her tireless craft, brilliant eye, and downright good humor; Sonny Mehta, for continuing to believe in and support my work; Genevieve Nierman, for her dedication and incisive contributions; and all the wonderful people who work miracles behind the scenes at Knopf, Vintage, and the international publishers who've been kind enough to give my books a home.

In Uruguay, I'm immensely grateful to many people who shared stories, time, thoughts, joy, and hospitality as I gathered the material that inspired this book. I have been listening to stories of Cabo Polonio's cultural history for eighteen years. It was Gabi Renzi who first took me there, in 2001, when I was a young queer woman from the diaspora seeking my own connection to Uruguay. I have since come to see, over and over, that Gabi is one of the most generous people to walk the earth, and that her insights and knowledge are unparalleled.

Acknowledgments

Leticia Mora Cano and La Figu have also been incredibly giving over the years, of their time, thoughts, stories, homemade milanesas, and remarkable memories. Zara Cañiza shared insights, vision, her home, her time, her transcendent artistry, and her singular perspective. These women are not just sources to me: they are friends, inspirations, my heart. This book would not exist without them, and my gratitude is boundless.

Research for this novel took various forms, from long nights of *mate* and starlit conversation to poring over stacks of books. I owe a debt to both the Biblioteca Nacional de Uruguay and the UC Berkeley Library for their invaluable collections. Though the works I consulted are too extensive to list here, I do wish to extend particular thanks to Juan Antonio Varese, whose scholarship on the Rocha Coast has been essential; Tomás Olivera Chirimini, fearless preserver of Afro-Uruguayan history and heritage; Silvia Scarlatto, biographer for El Zorro of Cabo Polonio; the many survivors of the Uruguayan dictatorship who have bravely given testimony; and Peter Tatchell, for his crucial role in exposing the crimes of Carl Vaernet, both at Nazi concentration camps and in his later years in Argentina.

Sincere, profound thanks to those who offered key feedback on my manuscript, much-needed encouragement, or other forms of generosity that helped shape the book, including Marcelo de León, Chip Livingston, Raquel Lubartowski Nogara, Achy Obejas, Aya de León, Reyna Grande, Jacqueline Woodson, and Sarah Demarest. You are each magnificent. And also to San Francisco State University, for the Presidential Award that gave me precious time in which to finish this book, and to all my marvelous colleagues and students on campus, who kindly provide me with a continuous stream of learning and inspiration.

The gratitude I owe my wife, Pamela Harris, has no measure. I won't try to contain it in a sentence. Our children, Rafael and Luciana, transform what is possible and expand our world; therefore, without them, this book would not be. My family held me through thick and thin as I worked on this novel. I can still hear my mother-in-law,

Margo Edwards, sending me out to my writing studio with the cheerful words, "Break a pencil!" Thank you. Also, to my extended family, particularly in Uruguay and Argentina, where the hospitality, love, and patience with my seemingly bizarre lines of inquiry have been immeasurable—thank you.

In telling stories that are largely absent from formal histories or from the great noise of mainstream culture, I never forget that there are thousands if not millions of people whose names we may never learn, whose names are lost in time, who made our contemporary lives possible through acts of extraordinary courage. Their stories have all too often gone unrecorded, but I am here today, and able to speak, because of them. And, finally, to anyone reading this who's struggled through a chrysalis to become her or his or their authentic self: I see you, I thank you, I'm glad you're here, this book is yours as well.

THE GODS OF TANGO

Arriving in Buenos Aires in 1913, with only a suitcase and her father's cherished violin to her name, seventeen-year-old Leda is shocked to find that the husband she has travelled across an ocean to reach is dead. Unable to return home, alone, and on the brink of destitution, she finds herself seduced by the tango, the dance that underscores every aspect of life in her new city. Knowing that she can never play in public as a woman, Leda disguises herself as a young man to join a troupe of musicians. In the illicit, scandalous world of brothels and cabarets, the line between Leda and her disguise begins to blur, and forbidden longings that she has long kept suppressed are realized for the first time. Powerfully sensual, *The Gods of Tango* is an erotically charged story of music, passion, and the quest for an authentic life against the odds.

Fiction

RADICAL HOPE
Letters of Love and Dissent in Dangerous Times

Radical Hope is a collection of letters—to ancestors, to children five generations from now, to strangers in grocery lines, to any and all who feel weary and discouraged—written by award-winning novelists, poets, political thinkers, and activists. Provocative and inspiring, *Radical Hope* offers readers a kaleidoscopic view of the love and courage needed to navigate this time of upheaval, uncertainty, and fear, in view of the U.S. presidential election.

Politics/Essays

THE INVISIBLE MOUNTAIN

On the first day of the year 1900, a small town deep in the Uruguayan countryside gathers to witness a miracle—the mysterious reappearance Pajarita, a lost infant who will grow up to begin a lineage of fiercely independent women. Her daughter, Eva, a stubborn beauty intent on becoming a poet, overcomes a shattering betrayal to embark on a most unconventional path. Eva's daughter, Salomé, awakens to both her sensuality and political convictions amid the violent turmoil of the late 1960s. *The Invisible Mountain* is a stunning exploration of the search for love and a poignant celebration of the fierce connection between mothers and daughters.

Fiction

PERLA

Growing up as a privileged only child in Buenos Aires, Perla Correa learned early on not to discuss the profession of her naval officer father in a country still reeling from the abuses of a deposed military dictatorship. But when an uninvited visitor appears in Perla's home, this encounter sets her on a journey that will force her to confront the unease she has suppressed all her life—and to make a wrenching decision about who she is, and who she will become.

Fiction

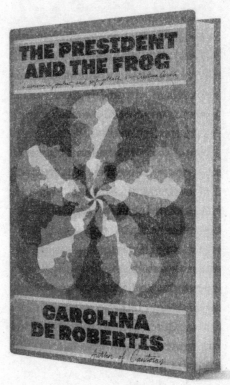